THE LADY AND HER MISSION

THE LADY OF BOHEMIA, BOOK 5

SARA R. TURNQUIST

MOUNTAIN
SUMMIT PRESS

If you would like to stay up-to-date on this and all other series from Sara:

https://saraturnquist.com/list

*To my husband, who supports me and has helped
make my writing dreams come true.*

THE KINGDOM OF BOHEMIA DURING THE HUSSITE WARS

PROLOGUE

It is the year 1424, nine years after the martyrdom of Jan Hus for his outspoken challenges to practices of the Catholic Church. This tragic loss sparked his followers to rise up against the powers over them, thrusting off Holy Roman Emperor Sigismund's tight grip. It has been a long, hard-fought conflict, with the Royalist Catholics leading two anti-Hussite crusades into Bohemia, only to be beaten back.

Despite their shared goals, there is now in-fighting in Czech lands, creating even more challenges. An offer of the Bohemian crown to Poland was met with interest. Prince Korybut of Lithuania has journeyed to Bohemia in answer to lead the rabble. Yet whether all will embrace his leadership has yet to be known. The longer the Hussite Wars continue, the more fractured the Czech people become.

They have thus far been held together somewhat by rallying behind General Jan Zizka, who championed their military efforts. However, even as the Third Anti-Hussite Crusade has been thwarted, it came at great cost—the great general lost his vision completely to an errant arrow. In the weeks that followed, he has also fallen ill.

In the years that have passed since these friends—Pavel, Zdenek,

Radek, Stepan, and Lukas—hunted together in the woods of Hradek Kralove without much care in the world, ignorant of the years of war they would face, the battles waged without and within have separated and severed their friendships in ways that none expected. But their trials are only beginning.

Baron Pavel Krejik, *en route* to offer his sword to the Hussite cause, has been captured by Ulrich of Rosenberg, the man who murdered his father. His wife, Karin, had been ignorant to this fact, anxiously awaiting her husband's safe return from battle. Until someone from her past arrives to tell her that Pavel was taken prisoner. Although, to what end, still remains a mystery.

Patricie of Hradek Kralove and Lord Stepan Dvorak, having found one another under dire circumstances, journeyed back to Hussite-controlled Bohemia. They have professed their love for each other. But just as their paths converged toward matrimony, Stepan left for a mission of great import. Patricie awaits his return, and also her sister's. Only time will tell if she and Stepan will actually become one in truth.

Patricie's sister, Eva, and her husband, Lord Zdenek Ambroz, continue to make a way for themselves in the world, but do not have the one thing they want most—a child. Lady Karin gifted Eva a guard to protect her as she searches for her sister. Additionally, she picked up something along the way. How will Patricie react when they are reunited? Zdenek, having parted from his wife for the sake of supporting his friend, Pavel, has been captured alongside the others. What will become of him?

Meanwhile, their friend, Lord Radek Miklas, has found his own happily-ever-after with Duke Novak's daughter, Lady Hana. Though safe for now and enjoying wedded bliss, they seek where their place in the conflict lies. With Radek's uncertainty about the Hussite movement and Hana's passionate defense of them, what will they decide?

Another of the friend group from the days before the conflict in their homeland, Lord Lukas Vitek is still wasting away in a dungeon.

He had been coerced years before into taking part in a plot to end Lady Karin's life. And now he awaits news of his imprisonment term in the light of recent events. He is prepared to languish for his crime, but his family holds out hope that one of their appeals will be heard.

And now, the continuation...and finale...

CHAPTER I
KARIN & PAVEL

Pavel Krejik scanned the forest surrounding him. He had managed to keep himself awake through the night. The gaze of the knight stationed to watch him hovered, heavy and constant. Would there be respite? The camp had proved to be more heavily guarded and provisioned than he would have guessed. Especially for a man in retreat. What, after all, did Ulrich of Rosenberg want? Why had he taken Pavel prisoner?

Would these next hours be Pavel's last? He well knew how little regard Ulrich had for life as the monster had snuffed out those of Pavel's men. Even Zdenek. That thought was almost too painful to attend. So, Pavel pushed it away. It couldn't be so. Though he had watched Zdenek fall. And Ulrich would not have left anyone alive to report back.

Now Pavel was here, alone, facing this foe with his unknown, but no doubt nefarious, intentions.

Of what value could Pavel possibly be to the man? Why, then, had he been kept alive?

His head bobbed low, but he jerked upright. He refused to lose hold on consciousness. He would not. For, should an opportunity present itself, he must be ready.

"If you will not sleep, perhaps we might continue."

The deep voice grated on Pavel's every nerve. He cringed and met Ulrich's gaze. "What is it to you?"

"I cannot have you bedraggled...and unfit for travel. My men are far too taxed with your care as it is."

"Pity." Pavel looked to the ground. How could the man think Pavel had a care for those guarding him? In fact, he watched for a weak spot in the line of guards taking turns.

"Come now, Lork Krejik, it is not so bad. If I thought you would accept my hospitality, I might offer you better accommodations. For what there is to be had, at least." He waved a hand about the treed area around him.

Pavel fought a sneer, for he did not wish the man to be able to read his every thought. "What is it you want?"

He had asked this question a number of times in the last however many days. Each time to no avail, but he could still hope...

"All in good time, Baron. All in good time. There is, however, a bit of a loose end."

Pavel jerked his regard toward the man, but kept his lips sealed.

Ulrich waved a hand, and one of his mercenaries dragged another man into the light.

Pavel recognized the colors that the Krejik knights bore. It was one of the knights from his castle. Did this mean Ulrich had somehow penetrated the walls and worked harm upon his family? Pavel pulled against his bindings.

"There now, Lord Krejik, no need to upset yourself."

Pavel narrowed his gaze and glared at the beast of a man, barely able to choke out the words. "What did you do?"

Ulrich chuckled.

The guard released Pavel's man and he fell to the ground in a heap, clearly having suffered much at the hands of these mercenaries who were no better than common brigands.

"'Tis no matter." Ulrich gritted his teeth. "I will have my due."

What could he mean by that? *His* due? Had Pavel or the Krejik family somehow wronged him? Is that what brought the man's ire against him now? And against his father in the year past? Had the man seen to it that Pavel's...that his son had met with a swift end?

And what of Karin?

Pavel couldn't bear it. He leaned against the oak that had become his prison, his breaths coming fast and hard.

Ulrich smirked then unsheathed his sword and put a swift end to the already wounded knight.

Pavel wanted to balk at the barbarism, but he was far too stricken after fear over the possible fate of his family. The death of the men with him had been difficult to watch, this made just one more tally mark against the hulk of a man before him.

"Nothing? Not so much as a grimace for your knight?"

Pavel would not give him the satisfaction.

"*Hm*...perhaps you have more mettle about you than I thought."

Pavel clamped his teeth together as he met the man's steely gaze. He would not betray his emotions, would not plead for his life, would not even allow that he died inside at the thought of what Ulrich had done or may yet do to his beloved wife and child.

"So be it." Ulrich spun and looked toward the wretched guard. "Wake me if he utters a word."

The mercenary nodded and settled eyes, devoid of emotion, on Pavel. "Aye, my lord."

Pavel shifted farther away, as much as he could. And worked to shove his pain, his heartbreak, and his fear far within himself. Or he might as well give up right now.

Karin gaped as she watched the man standing in front of her. It couldn't be! How was Tomas here? Alive? It didn't make sense. None of it.

If this was truly the man to whom she was once betrothed, she could no longer know what was real and what was imagination. He had died. Quite certainly.

Perhaps he was some sort of apparition, only a trick of her mind. And, if not, where had he been all this time? All those days and nights that she had mourned him, missed him, grieved for him? Where had he gone? And why?

Sir Marek walked toward the space between her and the man claiming to be Sir Tomas. "My lady, I will see that this man is questioned. Thoroughly."

Karin held up a hand, halting the captain of the castle guard. "No."

Her voice trembled. Indeed, everything about her shook. She stepped closer to the man, who appeared older than his years. Had life been so cruel to him? Still, she was pulled, as if a moth to a flame.

"No, my lady!" Sir Marek moved to intervene, stepping directly into her path.

Karin waved him off, wishing she had the words to explain, and hoping her eyes said enough.

He removed himself but did not take his hand off the hilt of his sword. His muscles clenched as if poised to leap into action, prepared to protect his lady.

That was all the thought Karin could spare for the faithful knight. For everything in her was fixed on the interloper.

"How is this possible?" she muttered as she took another step. "You...died." Her voice caught on the last word.

"Yes, I did..." Tomas's voice was quiet. Almost too quiet. "Enough for a hundred lifetimes." There was something eerie about the way he spoke those words.

Karin closed the gap between them, reaching forth to test the mirage.

Sir Marek made a sound, but Karin again ignored him and pressed fingertips to the side of Tomas's face.

Tomas remained as still as stone, but his skin held warmth. Could it be?

"Is it you?" Her whispered words were harsh, her heart untrusting.

"Very much so." Tomas looked downward, shuttering his eyes and denying her what may lay in them.

Sir Marek grumbled and shifted, his movements jerking Karin from her reverie.

Only then did she realize that she still traced the side of Tomas's features. It was highly improper for her to be touching this man—who was not her husband—in such a way. How could she have lost herself even for a moment? She dropped her hand to her side.

What would Pavel think? Would he understand?

Pavel!

Hadn't Tomas claimed he bore news of her husband? What was it he had said?

Karen's eyes filled, and a tear slipped down her cheek. For Tomas or for Pavel? Even she was not certain.

Swallowing her trepidation, and a great many other things, she looked into his eyes. "You came to warn me of something? You said you bear news of my husband?"

Tomas stepped back, shaking his head. Was he, too, entranced by the moment? "Yes." The word, and his voice, were firm.

"How...how did you come to know this?" Though many questions swirled in her head, she gave voice to the most immediate.

"That...is a long story, Lady Karin."

Whether or not she wished to hear it, she must.

"Please," she said as she moved across the room toward the front of the Great Hall, keeping her back to Tomas.

She couldn't let him see how his sudden appearance affected her. Not any more than she already had.

"Come sit with Sir Marek and me. We would very much like to hear your tale."

She closed her eyes and thanked heaven for her return to sanity. All answers would come...in time.

"Baroness," another voice came from the direction of the corridor.

What now?

A man barreled into the Great Hall, one of her guards trailing.

"My lord, you must be announced," came the insistent plea of the guard.

"I will not be delayed."

The voice was familiar. A chill traveled up her spine.

As the figure came more into the light, her breath caught. And then yet another man she had not anticipated to ever again cross paths with stepped forward–Stepan Dvorak.

CHAPTER 2
PATRICIE & STEPAN

Patricie strolled down the street of the small village. She'd heard word that Eva sought her and had been directed here. She could hardly hold herself back from the fray that awaited the provisions promised with the coming contingency. At any moment, she would be reunited with her sister. It had been too long since she'd laid eyes upon her precious Eva...and much had happened in that time.

Stepan had chosen her, had saved her...and had decided to join the Hussite effort.

Though what that might look like, she wasn't certain. What would his life be now that he was a nobleman without an inheritance, disowned by his powerful father?

It mattered not. They had each other.

That is, she'd thought that was the case...until he left on his errand of great import...or so he said.

Movement at the edge of the village caught her attention. Yes—two horses bearing riders drew near. It must be them!

Patricie ran a hand over her plaited hair and could not help the tremor of excitement filling her limbs. How did one contain such excitement in their body?

How she wished Stepan would be with her to receive her sister. The two most important people in her life...and yet his place beside her was empty.

Soon enough, the outlines became figures.

Patricie could hold back no longer, she rushed forward, ignoring any sense of propriety.

"Patricie," Eva called out.

As Patricie neared the large animals, Eva dismounted and gathered her taller, but younger sister to herself.

"I was so worried I'd never see you again." Eva's harsh whisper and thick words told that she spoke from the depths of her heart.

Patricie blinked, as if that would stop her tears from coming. "I know."

Eva leaned back but did not release her hold. "You look well enough. But I am quite certain you have a tale to tell."

Patricie nodded, wiping at her face.

"And I want to hear everything. Each and every detail."

Was there a bit of hesitation about Eva? As if she would continue with a statement that negated her words?

"I have set up a room for you and Sir Zdenek at the inn." Patricie waved a hand in the direction of the modest structure. "I do not doubt you are much in need of rest."

Eva moved toward the man still mounted and nodded. "Aye...as if I haven't slept in days."

The man atop the horse offered a quick smile in her direction. And Patricie noted two things—one, the man was decidedly not Zdenek, and two, he bore a strange bundle in his arms, though he held it rather awkwardly.

"What is this?" Patricie's curiosity got the better of her, as did her inability to mind her own speech. Where was her sister's husband? Beyond that, it wasn't like her sister to take in a stray dog. Is that what she had done? "And where is Sir Zdenek?"

Eva bit at her bottom lip and held out her arms toward the man who dropped down from the saddle. "He has gone to join the Hussites...with Lord Krejik. But Lady Karin gave me leave when word had reached us of your disappearance. I was...delayed finding you. And then I found something important I had to attend to."

The knight, Patricie could only guess by his bearing and clothing, passed the wriggling mass to Eva.

Her sister held it more adeptly as she moved toward Patricie once more. "I want you to meet someone."

Patricie held her breath. Was it a child? It couldn't be from Eva's womb. They hadn't been apart long enough. How then...

As Eva neared, she pulled back the top fold of the blanket to reveal a young child's face.

The small one's curious gaze took in everything, flitting here and there, not truly resting on anything.

"Did you...?" Patricie managed.

Eva's eyes softened as they gazed at the small features. "The boy was left at the church in Prague. He needed someone to look after him." Eva glanced back to her sister. "So, when my path crossed through the city and the nuns spoke to me of it, I agreed."

"You...what?" Patricie needed to choose an emotion, but it was difficult with so many swirling within. She glanced at the knight, who simply moved off with the horses.

"Meet Michal." Eva adjusted her hold so Patricie might see the child better.

Patricie pushed past a stunned silence that had enveloped her and reached forth to touch the child's hand. As the small boy turned, Patricie got a full view of his features.

She had to catch herself.

He had a mark on the right side of his head—the mark of the devil.

Nothing could have prepared Stepan for what he found when he entered the Great Hall of the castle upon Pavel's lands. Lady Karin stood in the middle of the room, while a knight quickly moved into Stepan's path. But that was not what disturbed him so. It was the other man looking longingly after the lady...the wife of Stepan's one-time closest friend.

It brought to mind the sting of the betrayal he'd felt when she'd walked away from him those years ago. Would she cuckhold Pavel in his own demesne? A flare of anger swept through Stepan, so strongly that he was unable to keep it from his features.

Karin's eyes widened and her mouth gaped. Surely, she had not expected to be discovered...least of all by him.

"Sir, you are not to approach the baroness." The older knight threatened in word and body as he drew his sword and maintained a firm stance.

Was Stepan truly the one to worry with here? What of the lady of the castle cavorting with a man not her husband? He sensed that pointing this out would not help him.

Stepan craned his neck and glanced around the knight, but the man matched him move for move, blocking his efforts.

"What do you seek here?" the man spat out. "By my life and honor, you shall not aggress upon Baroness Krejikova."

The other man, standing farther back, stepped closer to Karin...as if preparing to defend her as well. The cad!

"I seek an audience with the lady. Although I see that she already entertains one." Stepan ground out the words, making no attempt to disguise his disgust.

The knight lifted his sword. "I will not have you speak thusly of the lady of this castle."

Karin peered around the human barrier, setting a hand to the upper arm of the vile man, pressing him to the side. "Stepan?"

He grimaced. "You would address me so informally?" Did her sins know no bounds?

She made a coughing sound as she moved closer. "What are you doing here, Lord Dvorak? I was quite certain—and determined—that I would never lay eyes upon you again. As were you, if I recall." Her eyes glistened, as if warring emotions threatened to spill over.

"As I wished it to be. But I come for the sake of your *husband*," he pressed out through still clenched teeth. "Though I see much in need is he for eyes upon his property and his wife." Shooting a glance at the man still behind Karin, Stepan lowered his brows.

Karin glanced between the stranger and Stepan. "Is that what you think? That I would...betray my husband?"

Stepan settled into his stance. "Do you deny it?"

She tossed another look at the man beside her. "I do."

Stepan grimaced. "You would dare."

"I don't answer to you." Karin's voice was even and yet harsh. She turned to leave, taking long strides in the direction of the stairs. Was she as cowardly as she appeared?

The man who had trespassed also watched her walk off. But soon after set his gaze upon Stepan, making his own move in that direction. Would he threaten Stepan so?

Karin whirled. "You cannot possibly imagine that there are things you don't understand, can you?"

This was not how he had imagined this would go. It wasn't as if he had anticipated a warm reception, but that didn't mean he expected hostility. Though he hadn't foreseen catching Karin in such a compromising situation.

"Then perhaps," Stepan called after her. "You can *explain* it to me."

She set a hard gaze on him, an eyebrow piqued. Did she consider his challenge?

The knight that had blocked him took another step toward him. "Perhaps it is best you take your leave."

"I will do no such thing." Stepan stood his ground despite the threat the man's sword made. Would Karin allow this knight to visit harm upon Stepan simply to cover her own sin?

Karin folded her arms over her chest. "As I will not have you spreading falsehoods about my innocence, I may just well explain how you are wrong."

Now there was that fire he knew, the spirit that moved just beneath a serene, carefully controlled surface.

He guarded his expression. It was best not to give away his thoughts on the matter.

"This man is but a childhood friend. That is all."

Stepan scoffed.

"*And* he bears news of my husband."

News of Pavel? Had something happened? Stepan squared his shoulders and glared at the man with new eyes. "What is this?"

The unkempt man's own muscles tensed beneath a calm exterior, though his control was not as tightly held. There were cracks about his steely expression. Due to feelings he possessed for Karin? "For the sake of the lady's fine reputation, I will tell you," the man fairly growled.

Karin was by her companion's side in a moment, a hand upon his arm. "No. He does not need to know. He does not *deserve* to know."

"But I will have satisfaction in this," Stepan said, his words edged with contained rage. How much longer must he play this game?

The older knight turned to Karin. "Shall I remove this annoyance?"

She held up a hand. "No. I will not have him spreading lies about that which he does not understand."

Stepan held his breath as she drew in air and pressed it out. But he held his tongue better than he did his patience.

She looked to the other man and bit at her lip before turning to Stepan. Would she lose her hold on her weaker feelings? It seemed as if she might.

"Baron Krejik is in danger," the man beside her said, facing Stepan.

"Tomas..." Karin's tone held a rebuke.

"Danger? What say you?" Stepan stepped forward, forgetting

about the knight's sword. The edge of the blade pressed against his chest in the next moment. His heart tightened at the news.

Pavel? In danger? It couldn't be.

Surely, his former friend—and one-time opponent—was capable enough to defend his person.

"You will maintain your distance," the older knight grumbled.

Karin's eyes misted, but all vestiges of harshness had abandoned her features. "There is much that is not known...and more that I would not tell you."

Stepan wanted to shove the sword to the side, but he knew such would be a foolish gesture. The tension in the man's blade told of a strength remarkable for his years. A strength that would not yield.

"And now, I bid you...leave me be." Karin turned yet again.

"Karin," Stepan called out, unthinking of his address.

She spun, strain about the lines of her face.

"Baroness Krejikova," he amended, shooting a glance at the knight and the man she'd called Tomas. "I have come to repent of my sins. And to seek absolution."

Her brows furrowed as if she did not believe him.

"I have." He strained against the weapon at his sternum. "If you would but grant me a few moments, I shall prove it is true."

There, a glimmer of hope appeared in her eyes. If it held true, she would give him the time he requested. He knew it.

The man, Tomas, spoke low to her at a level Stepan could not discern.

Karin shook her head and exchanged further words.

The man stepped to the side, glaring at Stepan over his shoulder, but only for a moment.

Karin moved forward. "Release him, Sir Marek."

The knight did not relent.

"I do not believe he means me any harm." Karin held her ground and spoke with authority.

Sir Marek hesitated then dropped his weapon but a few inches. "My lady, I must insist you—"

"*I* will insist, sir knight, that you bring Lord Dvorak to the solar." She glanced about the room at the servants coming and going, preparing the hall for the noon meal. "There are many ears about. More than I would care to have entertain such sensitive news."

Sir Marek's mouth twisted as if he fought his own better judgement. But at last he spoke, "Yes, my lady."

Karin whirled again and led the small contingency to the stairs.

Stepan didn't know what would come of this exchange, but he was determined he would know the whole of it.

Just then the door to the Great Hall flew open.

Karin spun in the direction of the sound as Sir Marek stepped between her and the potential threat.

A guard entered, rushing to the pair. "Sir Marek, Baroness!"

She stepped around Sir Marek, who resisted moving. "What is it?"

"A scout has found a massacre. In the wood. And a man who is barely alive!"

CHAPTER 3
ANICKA & LUKAS

Lukas stared at the stark gray walls. They had become almost black over the years. Not that it mattered—it was a wall, all the same. And it had been Lukas's only companion for quite some time. He'd lost track of just how long he had been confined. Certainly, long enough to have become addled. Still, he refused to give in. There had to be hope. Had to be. It was the only thing that allowed him to retain some semblance of sanity.

The clinking of keys against each other alerted him that one of the guards drew near. For what purpose? Did the man come to harass Lukas again? How he tired of these games. But it did bring some variety into his miserable life.

As the guard approached, he said, "Someone wishes to see you."

That surprised. He had not had a visitor in some time. What could this mean? Who had come? And why was he being permitted a visit? Though he knew better than to pose any of these questions to this man. The guards only followed orders. They had little power when it came to such matters.

Lukas rose as the guard slid a key into the lock and turned it. But he did not step closer to the barrier. He dared not. Even in this place, there were rules and accepted practices...and things one did not do.

The man scoffed as he moved to the side only slightly. Would that permit Lukas to pass out of the cell?

Either way, what did it matter? Lukas had long since ceased caring about these things, such as asserting himself and demanding better treatment. His will had been bent. But had it been broken? That remained to be seen.

He gathered himself and stepped out of the cell, brushing a bit too closely to the guard. This particular guard could be belligerent if given any reason to be harsh. Pulling in a breath, Lukas waited for the repercussions of his actions to be visited upon his person.

Yet they were not. Had the guard sensed that Lukas no longer had a care? Or did he finally tire of taunting?

Lukas still paused to give the man leeway to step in front and lead him.

"You know the way." The gruff voice sounded impatient. As if they had been through this many times.

Lukas took a long moment to consider it before complying. Though he did worry a delay would be punished, the greater likelihood was that any perceived assertion would be.

The guard jerked his head in the direction of the stairs farther down the narrow passageway. "You need an engraved invitation?"

Lukas shook his head and moved onward. Still, he remained leery the man may inflict some form of pain. Though, as the seconds ticked by, the more confident he became that the overbearing guard would not trespass.

As Lukas neared the top of the stairs, more light filtered into the darkness. The starkness of it made him blink, urging him to turn back. But he did little more than flinch, attempting to keep any evidence of it from his body. He must never show any sign of weakness...nor give any indication that there were vulnerable places the guards had yet to exploit.

"Move," the man demanded.

Perhaps Lukas's pause had been longer than he'd thought. He moved out of the dungeon and into the corridor.

More guards awaited him. One nodded to the guard escorting Lukas from the bowels of the castle and he was then flanked on either side, with an additional knight in the lead. These were not men he had seen before. Were these guards better situated than those who had seen to his confinement?

Without a word, the leader moved toward what Lukas could only guess was the Great Hall. Was that their destination? He had not seen this much of the castle as of yet. But he halted all wishful thinking. He'd girded his hopes too often for his own sanity to remain secure. They likely brought him here to issue another pronouncement upon his sentence. Perhaps his most recent appeal—rather the ones his family insisted on petitioning—had been denied. Just as they all were.

Wasn't he beyond caring? Hadn't he resigned himself to this life? He prayed he had not. For once he gave up hope, all was truly lost.

It wasn't as if he didn't deserve every bit of this punishment. He had committed the crime he was accused of. He'd been a part of the attempt on Lady Karin Bornekova...now Krejikova. He had let the Viscountess sway his better judgment, taking advantage of his devotion to his family—another vulnerability. One that he feared he retained. Not that he could do anything to either protect or support them. It had become quite the opposite. *They* were taking care of him. As much as they were able.

The corridor indeed gave way to the Great Hall. Servants bustled about preparing for the evening meal. Many tossed glances in his direction. Did they know who he was? Did they know what he had done?

He told himself their looks and stares were more due to the guards surrounding him. But as they skittered out of the room as quickly as possible, he could not convince himself it was so.

"Good day, Lord Vitek." A larger man stood at a table near the hearth. Was this a man of authority? He dressed as a member of the nobility, but his manner gave hints that he was less refined.

Lukas faced him and gave a slight bow.

"You may not know me. But I am Count Joseph Hudek." The man seemed rather bored with the whole affair. Still, he paused as if Lukas were supposed to respond. But he knew not how.

After shrugging, he continued, "I have received word about your appeal to the council."

Lukas's eyes widened. He had not been given leave to testify on his own behalf. This could not mean good things. Clenching his teeth, he awaited whatever may come.

The man waved a hand as if this were but a nuisance, not the words Lukas had prayed over for the last several years. The final say on his future.

"You have been pardoned."

Anicka turned the page over and pressed her hand to the words. Settling into her favorite chair offered her some reprieve from an aching neck. Perhaps she leaned over too much. But as the chair squeaked on its joints, she frowned. This was her place of solace, though that did not mean she was invisible. And if Mother should happen upon her...

She didn't want to think about that.

Closing her eyes, she breathed out, trying to relax her shoulders. There was no reason to believe anyone knew where she was. Though she was daft to think so. Everyone knew she spent every free moment in the library. And that's what she feared.

But the last she knew, Mother had slipped below stairs to attend to something in the kitchens. Then she intended to oversee the preparations of the hall for the evening meal.

Anicka shook off her lingering trepidation and scanned the written lines upon the parchment. Then she picked up her quill and

set it to the blank space to forward the world created for her characters. Should she put the heroine in peril yet again? What benefit was
a story without trouble for those involved? That was real, and raw,
and interesting. Not like her life—dull, and boring, and mundane.

Though as long as she might have these times to escape into her
imagination, all would be well. This was where she truly longed to
be anyway.

Poring over her words, the work of her own hands, she continued
to write. Before long, she had filled the page with the next happenings—another meeting, by happenstance of course, of her dashing
knight and the fair maiden. He was everything a brave, caring suitor
should be. And the lady...needed saving.

"What is this?" a voice rang out from over her shoulder.

She didn't need to turn to know it was Mother.

Anicka tucked the papers to her chest, but it was too late.

Mother grimaced. She had seen.

"Are you wasting your time with this nonsense again?" Mother
reached for the pieces of parchment, but Anicka jumped up and
stepped back before she took hold of them.

"It is nothing. I only while away the time." She wanted to reason
with Mother, but of what use were her pleas?

Stepping to her daughter, Mother held out a hand, her face a
mask of anger. "Give them to me."

Anicka shrank back, crushing the writings to herself. And shook
her head.

"Hand them over, Anicka." Her mother's insistent words were
hard. There was no hint of compassion about them.

What could Anicka do but comply? Still, she hesitated.

Mother's nostrils flared and her eyes lit. "I will not have you
wasting time better spent on developing useful skills." The woman
jabbed a finger toward the papers. "Now give them to me."

Anicka frowned. "I do try to work at my sewing and music. But I
tire of it."

"Yet you find the energy for this."

How could Anicka expect her mother to understand? It was hopeless.

Still, she opened her mouth once more.

Mother snatched at the papers, tearing several from Anicka's grip. "You will not defy me."

With regret, Anicka loosened her hold and handed the remainder of her work over. "If you would let me read it to you, you might find it diverting." This was but a blind attempt, one that made Anicka's heart thump harder. She had never read any of her writings to anyone. Nor could she imagine doing so. To share her heart, her very soul with another. Especially someone who could never understand her work...or her.

"I am not interested in your flights of fancy." Mother glared at her. "And you must learn that this is a fruitless endeavor."

Would Mother take them and lock them away? Could Anicka plead enough to get them back?

Mother crossed the room and, without ceremony, threw the precious papers into the fire.

"No," Anicka cried, rushing forward.

Mother blocked the way to the flames. As if there were ever any hope to retrieve them. "Anicka," the woman warned. "You *will* hear me."

Staring as her story slowly turned to ash, Anicka fought an overwhelming sadness. Letting Mother see that would only make things worse.

"You spend too much time with your head in a fantasy and not enough on making yourself into a worthy bride. Do you wish to be alone forever, depending on the good graces of your father to survive?"

Anicka wanted to lower her gaze but could not tear her eyes from the precious words that were vanishing. "No, Mother." Her voice hitched. Her emotions threatened to press moisture from her eyes. She could fight it. She *had* to fight it.

"Then I suggest you mind your domestic skills and quit 'whiling away your time.' Your future will be more secure if you can make yourself a tempting offer for a fine lord." With that, Mother tossed another glance at the fire.

Nothing remained of the pages—of Anicka's heart—but soot and ash.

"Come, then, let us tend to the Great Hall."

Anicka drew in a shaky breath, a slight sniffle accompanying her attempt.

Mother's eyes were sharp as they jerked to Anicka's face. "What?"

"Yes, Mother." Anicka dragged herself from the hearth and took up step behind her mother.

But she wondered if she would, in fact, be successful in garnering a good marriage should she even try. It wasn't as if she hadn't. Perhaps if she had a prospect, she wouldn't be so drawn to her stories. Perhaps.

It mattered not. Her mother would never give her such freedom. Her worth was in what manner of marriage she could make. And without hopes of a husband who might give her such leave...or even hopes of a husband at all, she was left with naught but to obey.

No matter how it rent her heart in two.

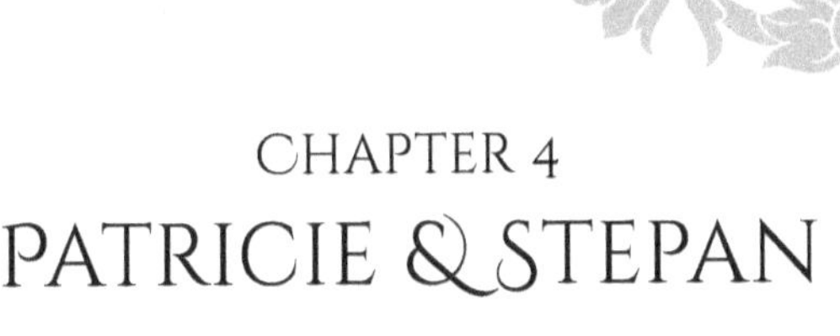

CHAPTER 4
PATRICIE & STEPAN

Stepan followed Karin into the solar. He wished he could gain more space from the grousing knight at her side. Sir Marek did not remove his glare from Stepan, except to eye the other man among their company. What had happened before Stepan arrived? For the knight didn't appear to trust Sir Tomas any more than he trusted Stepan. Sir Marek was a good man, noble in his duty and diligent in his charge to protect his lady.

And what of the injured man? And the murdered knights? When would they address them? Karin had insisted the village healer be summoned. That she would tend the survivor soon enough.

As Karin settled into a seat behind the desk, she motioned to Sir Marek. "Please close the door."

What was there to be shared? Did it require such privacy?

Sir Marek obeyed, leaving her side only long enough to do as she bade.

Stepan's impatience became a living thing within him, pressing upward until the words came unfiltered. "What is the meaning of this?" He glanced between Karin and Sir Tomas. "Where is Pavel?"

Karin looked to Sir Tomas as if he should answer. Did the man have such familiarity? Did he now speak for her?

That did not ease the boiling within Stepan. He opened his mouth once more. "I will not stand by and watch this. But I will know what has happened to Lord Krejik." Of this, he was determined.

Sir Marek rejoined Karin and eyed Stepan, his hand once more falling to the hilt of his sword.

Karin's brow furrowed. "You *will* calm yourself, sir knight."

She continued to order *him* about? What madness was this?

But as he drew in a breath to speak farther, Sir Tomas stepped closer to him, his stance firm and his hands balled into fists. As if he wished to take physical action.

That, Stepan would not stand for. A man who acted every bit the part of the adulterer would not tutor him on what should be. As Stepan seethed, his chest puffed, and he gripped his own sword hilt.

"Stop it," Karin cried as she whirled toward them. "For the love of all that's holy, stop it."

Stepan halted but did not dare remove his hand from his weapon.

"Lord Dvorak, you will stand down." Sir Marek's threat was evident in the gruffness of his voice. "Or you will be removed."

That, he did not wish for. He had to know what had become of his friend. Settling back into his heels, Stepan stretched his sword arm, allowing the weapon to fall from his grip. And as he glanced back at his opponent, he noted that Sir Tomas had done likewise.

"If you two are finished posturing," Karin said as she set eyes on each of them before her attention fell to Sir Tomas. "I would hear the whole of it."

Did this Sir Tomas, then, hold the answers he sought? Had the man seen to it that Pavel was detained? Or otherwise incapacitated? To what end?

Sir Marek grunted.

Stepan realized he had tightened his shoulders again and his hand wandered closer to his sword. What madness was this?

He lifted his hand and forced it to fall to his side.

Sir Marek nodded and relaxed his stance as well.

Karin let out a breath and fell into a nearby chair. Only then did Stepan note how worn she seemed and how fragile she presented. She had used every bit of ire she could summon to keep his head leveled. He regretted his actions...or did he? For if she had cuckholded his friend or intended to do so...

Sir Tomas shifted his footing and watched Karin.

She leaned back and her gaze landed on Sir Tomas, her eyes intense. "Now, tell me what you know."

He looked to Stepan as if to ensure he had the lady's approval to speak before him. Who did this man think he was?

Stepan was tempted to assert himself and insist he remain but held back. Such would not likely bode well. Karin allowing him to stay was a gift. He'd best not trespass upon her goodwill.

"Proceed." The green in Karin's eyes sparked.

Sir Tomas nodded. "As I said before, Pavel has been captured..."

Stepan's heart thudded. "Captured?" The word was out before he could stop it.

Karin eyed him then turned back to Sir Tomas. She, too, seemed to barely restrain emotions lying beneath a thin veneer. Though he wagered that while his was anger, hers was perhaps a far more tender emotion.

"Baron Krejik is at the mercy of Ulrich of Rosenberg." Sir Tomas fairly tossed his statement on the table.

Karin gasped and her hand pressed to her chest. But she gathered herself rather quickly. "How...how do you know this?"

Again, Sir Tomas's gaze flitted to Stepan. It was evident the man didn't trust him...and Stepan was thankful that Karin did. Or at least seemed to. Else why would she allow him to remain?

A growling sound emitted from deep in Sir Marek's throat. And the man bristled.

"Tomas," Karin's words softened as she stood once more. She stepped around the table and nearer the man whose title she eschewed for something too familiar.

It made Stepan rather uncomfortable. But he held his breath in hopes Sir Tomas would reveal the whole of it.

Karin stopped just short of the man. "I beg you. Tell me what has happened to my husband."

Perhaps Stepan had been too hasty in his judgment. For Karin did appear every bit as disturbed as he. Even more so. All may not be as it seemed. Perhaps.

Sir Tomas cleared his throat and glared briefly at Stepan. "I...was among Ulrich's men."

Karin's eyes widened. "You? You gave aid to the man who saw my husband's sire killed?" Her voice gained strength, though her affect told that she was torn.

Sir Marek unsheathed his sword.

Karin stopped him with a wave of her hand. "I know that cannot be. Not you, Tomas."

She spoke with a tenderness that should be reserved for her husband. It irritated Stepan. Though he still held himself at bay, hoping to gain more details.

"There is more to say, but I cannot. Not here."

Sir Tomas would refuse to divulge the very reasons they should not assume him the enemy?

Sir Marek stiffened, his shoulders tight.

Stepan ground his teeth.

Karin only watched the villainous Sir Tomas. It became clear that she held back a sheen of tears.

"If he cannot prove himself friend and not foe," Sir Marek interjected. "Then I shall see him set in the dungeons." He stepped forward.

Karin turned, pleading with Sir Marek. "No."

The knight was none too pleased by her statement.

"If I may but have a few moments to speak with you...alone...I will share what more I can." Sir Tomas's gaze hardened.

Never. That must never happen. Could any reasonable person trust these two alone? What with the way the man looked at her?

Karin hesitated. Then there *was* some amount of judgment and prudence about her.

"I think it best you speak now." Stepan was surprised at the animosity betrayed in his tone.

"Leave us." Karin did not look away from Sir Tomas.

"My lady," Sir Marek was quick to say, "You cannot mean that—"

"*Leave.* Us." Her words were hard and determined.

Sir Marek did not move. Neither did Stepan, nor did he intend to.

"I have been charged with your safety," Sir Marek stated forthwith.

Karin turned her gaze to Sir Marek. "Believe me, sir knight, I have nothing to fear from this man."

Sir Marek did not appear to believe her. Not in the least.

"I do not think it fitting for you to entertain this man for any purpose without benefit of an audience." Stepan hoped his words would speak some sense to her.

Her eyes flashed once more, only this time they did so as they set upon Stepan. "*I* will decide what is fitting." Then she turned toward Sir Marek. "You may remain in the corridor on the chance I require assistance."

Then she clenched her jaw. To show strength in her words? Or to keep emotion from spilling out?

Sir Marek did not move for several moments, then he acquiesced and faced Stepan. "I will see you out, Lord Dvorak."

Stepan opened his mouth, prepared to protest, but a leveled glare from Sir Marek bade him think better of it.

And so, with reluctant steps, he did as requested, and shuffled into the hall with a measure of reluctance. But no farther than the space just beyond the door. He would not.

Patricie looked about the immediate area. Who else might have seen the child's mark?

To her relief, she found that those few about them appeared caught up in their own reunions. Gripping her sister's arm, Patricie steered Eva farther from the mingling crowd...and the many eyes that may turn on them.

Eva resisted lightly, and her voice radiated frustration and concern. "What is it?"

Patricie continued tugging her sister without a word. After pulling Eva an appropriate distance for privacy, she halted, turned, and hissed. "Can you not see?"

Eva jerked her chin upward for a moment, then looked at the child who grabbed for her hair. "See what?"

Would Eva make this more difficult? Playact as if she didn't know? Patricie blew out a breath. She didn't want to draw undue attention, but she reached for Michal all the same, setting fingers on the tender skin. "This mark. How can you pretend it is not so?"

Eva tucked him closer and lightly bounced the boy as she pressed a kiss to his forehead.

The small child giggled, then squirmed.

"What of it?" Eva's voice hardened. "Does it offend?"

Patricie jerked back and set hands to her hips. "It is not me you should worry about."

Eva's lips pinched.

And Patricie regretted her words.

They stood in silence for several long moments.

After a while, Eva spoke into the awkwardness. "And...what do you think? Are you afraid of this innocent child?"

Patricie crossed her arms, would that shield her from Eva's assumptions. "You know that is not the case."

Eva avoided Patricie's eyes, instead settling her gaze on the boy. "Then what is it you fear? The opinions of others?"

Patricie loosened the grip of her arms around herself. "It is more. You know what people will say. You can even guess what they might do."

Eva's chin jerked, and the hardened edge of her gaze landed on her sister. "I care not what others think. This babe is alone in the world. He needs me." She pressed another kiss to the lighter colored curls.

"That may be…" Patricie didn't know quite how to finish that sentence. She allowed her own gaze to fall to the child.

He waved his arms, full of life. And the way he huddled closer to Eva. Was he so attached? Already?

Patricie softened her gaze. "I just…worry about you."

Moisture collected in Eva's eyes. "I know. But I need you to stand with me."

Patricie frowned. Of course she would always be by her sister's side. No matter the fact that it wouldn't make any difference. The superstitions of the many would not yield to Patricie's thoughts on the matter. Of what use was her support in this?

The guard appeared at Eva's elbow. "I wondered where you had gotten off to. Remember, Lady, I am charged with your protection until we return." He glanced between the sisters, a look of concern covering his features.

Eva looked to her sister. "We were just…discussing some things."

The man continued to look at the pair. "Oh?"

Could this guard guess what Patricie had brought Eva aside to speak about? How could he not? What were his thoughts? Was he prepared to battle harsh words and impossibly strong-headed people? For the sake of a child not of his master's blood? Would Zdenek? What would he think?

Patricie had reason to doubt. Would her sister, in the end, have to choose between her husband and Michal? For there was no doubt of her sister's fierce loyalty to both.

The guard nodded and stepped away. "I'll be just here should you need assistance."

Patricie's heart warmed to see her sister so well-tended even in Zdenek's stead. But an ache filled her at the reminder that she was herself without her beloved. Where had Stepan gone? How did he fare in his quest? She wasn't certain when he would return for her. Or if he ever would.

Things between them had become strained after he'd become well enough to walk and make his way about on his own. Perhaps such was only her imagination. Or was she truly worth so little to him? The uncertainty nagged at her. It didn't help that he delayed their plans to marry.

"Patricie?"

She shook her head and looked to Eva. "What?"

"I asked if you wish to join us for a meal." Eva's brow scrunched.

"Oh." Patricie paused, considering that for a moment. She would either be with Eva and Michal or avoid any connection with them. Was she so uneasy about the babe's mark? She had never thought of herself as one who gave credence to such notions. But here she was, doubting herself.

"Patricie?" The hurt was evident in Eva's eyes, and the lines of her face deepened. There was more to her question than simply a prompting for an answer. She wanted to know if Patricie would, in fact, stand with her.

Taking in a deep breath, Patricie extended a hand to her sister. "Of course. Let us get you two something to eat."

Eva's features softened to permit a smile. She grabbed onto Patricie's hand and fell into step with her sister as they moved toward the inn.

CHAPTER 5
KARIN & PAVEL

Karin stared at Tomas across the solar and gripped the table to keep her place. What information did he have that necessitated she be alone with him when he shared it? Were there things that would be difficult for him to share? Perhaps harder for her to hear?

She blew out a breath, and the tension of the last several moments with it. "What do you know?"

Tomas watched her. It seemed as if he might see straight to her heart.

She prayed that the pounding of it within her chest was singularly for Pavel's safety. Though she could not deny that Tomas's appearance, while startling, had stirred feelings long believed buried.

"Tell me," she beseeched, wishing to no longer give weight to those imaginings.

"Aye." He stepped to the table; now it remained the only thing separating them.

And she prayed he would allow it to continue to do so. For the previous moments had proven her apt to forget herself.

Pavel. She reminded her wayward thoughts. Her beloved Pavel... had been captured and was likely injured and suffering. She must find a way to reach him and bring him home. Without delay.

"'Tis not so simple," Tomas said, his voice calmer than she would have expected.

"No?" Her breath caught at the way his eyes delved into hers. Was he likewise riveted by memories of what was? Of what could never again be?

"There is much to tell." His tone was flat as if in defiance of the emotion in his gaze.

"I do not think I can reasonably keep my husband's man at bay for more than a few moments. Nor do I wish to." The last piece she added for her own reassurance.

He lifted an eyebrow. "Forgive me," he said after a few heavier breaths. Then cleared his throat. "I did not expect..." The words trailed.

She wanted to ask him to finish, but it was not necessary. She knew what plagued him. All too well. "Tell me what you know of my *husband.*" Yes, perhaps this assertion would place a needed wedge between them. Between what had been and what was no longer. For that was the reality. She had married someone else. And she *loved* her husband...very much.

Tomas looked to the floor as if there were something among the rushes to assuage him. "Much has happened since last we were...in each other's company."

She bit at the inside of her lip, willing away the mental images of that last exchange.

"I...have been to the ends of myself and back again."

Her heart fluttered as if it wished to move, in sympathy, toward him. What had he endured? How could she remain so uncaring after what befell him these last years? Yet she must. While she wished desperately to know his story, this was a time to focus...and to take action.

He drew in a long breath and continued. "Through circumstances best left unsaid, I found myself in the charge of Ulrich of Rosenberg."

Had that man tortured Tomas? Had her…friend…been at that monster's mercy all this time? If so, she might assume he was only whole in body. For sooth, his mind and soul could not have remained thusly intact.

She allowed but a crack in her exterior. Less permitted really, and more it seeped through, unbidden. "I…cannot imagine what you must have suffered at that man's hands."

Tomas's brow furrowed. "I was not his prisoner. I was in his service."

Her eyes widened. That couldn't be true! Not Tomas. She took a step back, wishing she had not so easily dismissed her protection. If those horrid words were so, something had greatly changed him. Or had she not ever known him? Perhaps he had become something more twisted than her heart could fathom.

She halted her whirling thoughts and pinned her mind. Tomas was no villain. And she had nothing to fear from him.

"I see in your eyes…" He paused, the weight of it nearly stealing Karin's breath. "It is the very reason I have carried this heavy weight of guilt upon my shoulders."

Karin flattened her lips, praying she had regained control of her mask. Could she no longer fit it so well it would not slip? Then again, she had never had cause to use it in Tomas's presence. That was then…and this was now.

"By the time I did find relief from my sentence, the conflict for Bohemia had commenced."

So he had joined the ranks of Ulrich to gather information for the cause?

"I…did things I'm not proud of. Things that will haunt me until the day I am released from this life."

Though he maintained his hard exterior, she knew him too well. And she saw the pain and regret that flickered in his eyes.

She wanted to speak into his hurt, to assure him that she understood what a horrendous position he had been put in, surely forced into. But did she?

"When we...when Ulrich ambushed Baron Krejik, I could not..." He drew in a shaky breath. "I had to help. Somehow."

Karin nodded. But she wondered all the same if he had misspoken. How deeply had he burrowed into Ulrich's ranks?

She shook her head. It mattered not. Tomas was here before her. And he would help her get her husband back. "Let me gather some of the castle knights. Sir Marek should hear this, be a party to plans we make for Lord Krejik's rescue." Karin stepped around the table and moved toward the door.

Tomas called after her, "He will have to be well with only the details I am willing to provide."

Confusion swept over Karin and she stilled.

Would Tomas protect his own interest that he might rejoin Ulrich? Surely not.

But it nagged at her, an itch that must be scratched...if he were able to escape and come to her now, what had kept him loyal to Ulrich all this time?

She couldn't permit her thoughts to venture there. No, it couldn't be so. "You will not tell all? For sake of our rescue?"

"Our?" Tomas's voice cut through the space. And he stepped to her. "You cannot mean that you intend to join the well-trained knights you will surely send."

She squared her shoulders and gained what stiffness she could to her spine. "I assure you, I do."

Her words surprised them both. She had not the time to think on her involvement. But in that moment, she knew it was so. Though the Krejik knights—and certainly Sir Marek—would resist her on this, she would be among them in their efforts to free their lord. Of this, she was determined.

Tomas shook his head, curling his lips. "You cannot. It is not fitting. Nor will I risk you."

A flame lit in her belly, licking at the coolness she wished to press around her heart. "You have no say in what I will or will not do."

His stance remained as firm, his face impassive. "If you will insist upon such a foolhardy mission, I will not be party to it."

She narrowed her gaze. "What do you mean?"

"You will get nothing further from me. And I will not regret it. Not when it keeps you from following this misguided race into danger."

He would further risk her husband's life? He couldn't mean that. But as he settled into his stance, she knew it was so. They were, then, at an impasse.

"Sir Marek," she called.

The creaking of the door assured that he had heard...and entered.

"Yes, my lady?" Ever the dutiful caretaker of his lady.

"Take Sir Tomas to the dungeon." Her voice wavered, but she pushed the words out all the same.

Tomas's face remained stoic but, again, his eyes betrayed his true emotion. Her words had surprised him.

"My lady?" Sir Marek said from his position behind her.

She whirled on him, wanting to rid herself of Tomas's presence lest she betray her emotions the same as he had. "*Now.*"

Sir Marek nodded and stepped around her. Stopping only a couple of paces short of Tomas, he glowered at the man he had long since deemed an intruder. "Do you intend to resist?"

Karin forced her gaze to remain on the floor. She did not wish to see whatever exchange would happen between the two. As she closed her eyes, the clomp of boots told that they moved out of the solar and down the stairs.

Pavel awoke to another dawn. One that many of his knights did not get to experience. Because he had failed them. They had been slaughtered—there was no other word for it—by the man who now held him captive. And would do who knew what to Pavel...and his family.

Yet there was hope. For he did not truly believe that Ulrich had taken hold of Karin and Jaromir. There was reason enough to think that his family remained safe and well-guarded within the walls of the castle. Something deep within, something Pavel could not quite explain, told that Karin was well and whole.

And he must do everything he could to keep it so. Even if he must pay with his own life, he would not let this mad man get his hands on Karin. No matter what.

So, he watched. And waited.

He studied the movements of Ulrich's mercenaries. There had to be a break in their processes...had to be. And when he found it, he would exploit it.

As he considered these things, there arose a disturbance about the camp. Men moved here and there, as if with a purpose, no longer idly as they had been. What went on? Did they work to break camp?

The men charged with his watch kept a wary eye on those around them. And on him. He was tempted to engage them that he might glean some information. Anything might offer insight. Not that he wouldn't know soon enough.

For the hundredth time, he tested the tightness of his bindings. Both the rope that held him to the tree and that which bound his ankles. As before, there was not enough give to merit additional effort. Yet.

He must not give up hope. For just as the guards had their moments of vulnerability, so, too, they would be found lacking in his keeping—be that the bindings or the maintaining of their watch.

As the men moved about, he picked up snatches of conversation. Indeed, even the two that minded him talked in low tones amongst themselves.

Pavel strained to make out their words.

"I'll be glad to return. Even a thin mattress is preferable to this bedroll." The larger one grumbled.

"What of Ulrich's plans for the woman and child?"

"I overheard that someone has been planted within the castle —one of Ulrich's men." The first one tossed a look in Pavel's direction.

Pavel kept his features placid, hoping he betrayed no hint of emotion, keeping his focus intent on the ground. Perhaps these guards would think he but rested. Though within his chest, fear for Karin and his son swelled. One of Ulrich's men had found a way into the castle? A spy now lay in his family's midst, serving as a knight or soldier? And there was no way he might warn them. Or protect them. Not until he found an opening in the guards' vigilance. Mayhap he could trust Sir Marek to have ferreted out such a double-minded man.

"Poor sap indeed," the larger man groused.

The conversation halted abruptly as movement stirred not far away.

Pavel glanced in their direction, hoping they were sufficiently distracted.

One of Ulrich's bodyguards strode toward them. What news might this man bring?

It was for naught...the man stepped near enough the guards to speak with them quietly and not permit Pavel to overhear.

Pavel frowned. These men who were closer to Ulrich exercised more care. Though there was hope. The men charged with his guard were less so. There...the weakness.

"What are you looking at?" The larger guard had turned and spotted him watching.

Pavel did not avert his gaze, the urge to intimidate in any way he could claimed the better of him.

"You'd best mind yourself," the more trained knight muttered to the oversized lackey. "Don't give him any length of rope else you intend to hang him with it."

The guard frowned, thoroughly enough chastised. And irritated.

Indeed, the man became more frazzled the longer Pavel stared.

The knight moved off shortly thereafter, but the one guard continued to become more agitated.

"If you know what's best for you—"

The thinner, but still rather well-sized guard cut the first one off. "Don't pay him any mind."

As the larger man heated even more under Pavel's scrutiny, he pulled free of the other. And closed the gap between himself and Pavel.

Still, Pavel tested the man's limits—not with words, but with an intensity in his glare.

"Stop it, I say." The guard clearly lost hold of his control.

Pavel knew the man had reached the end of his tolerance and that he should turn away and avoid another beating. But the taste of victory, small as it was, drove him on.

Even as the guard's fists collided with Pavel's shoulder, he found reason to tuck hope near his heart. For he had discovered a weak link.

CHAPTER 6

ANICKA & LUKAS

Lukas heard the whispers. He knew the villagers' thoughts on his return quite well. Their lack of trust, of faith, of respect. Despite their meager attempts to shield their comments, he heard them. And, while he did not want to give them weight, his father's absence did not help matters.

While Lukas's mother had welcomed him with open arms, even if she had been a bit stilted in her affection, his father had thus far been unavailable. That could not mean good things. It never did.

It was difficult for Lukas. Knowing the lengths he had gone to just to ensure his family's continued good standing. And now they acted as though shamed by his presence. And why shouldn't they be? He regretted his choices, his actions, and the fact that he had to continue to live with such besmirching of his name.

The only respite he found was in these daily jaunts upon horseback. It offered a moment to get away from the judgments, the insinuations…and just be himself for a few moments. Even so, he could not escape his own self-recrimination or the demons that plagued him, thrusting his guilt at him. Perhaps he never would fully be at peace again.

No matter how serene the vistas of his home were. No matter how much he told himself he would find a way. Still, he suffered.

Slowing the animal upon approaching the stables, he dropped out of the saddle and handed off the reins to one of the stable hands. Thankfully, the younger man avoided making eye contact with him. Even as Lukas wondered if that should bother him so, he did not want to see judgment in the man's glare.

For certain, that's what he thought. It's what everyone thought. How could they not? It's what he thought.

He moved into the keep, determined to find quiet in his chamber. But a call from the opposite side of the room halted him.

"Lukas? Is that you?"

It sounded like Mother, but she was not visible among those that moved through the Great Hall. Still, he searched for her.

The slender figure emerged from the door to the kitchen. "Ah, it *is* you." She fairly glided across the space to intercept him.

"What do you require?" He tried to keep his response short. For he longed to be away from questioning stares and whispered comments.

"Your father would like to speak with you."

Her words could not have surprised him more. He had well enough decided that Father would avoid him until it wasn't possible any longer—something he hoped would not be soon coming. And yet, here they were.

Lukas scanned the room once more. "Father?"

"Yes." She slid a hand through the bend in his elbow and urged him toward the stairs. "He is in his solar and requested you be summoned as soon as you returned."

Lukas swallowed. He wasn't ready to see his father. It had been difficult enough to manage the disappointment of the townsfolk. How could he face his father's certain disdain?

There seemed to be little choice, however. For his mother directed him up the stairs. The landing where the solar lay drew closer. How would his father receive him?

The door was ajar, and Lukas became fully aware that this was his last chance to break away and avoid this. But his mother spoke out, making all within aware of their presence.

Movement told that the door opened wider, and Lukas looked up as the space within welcomed them. Would it be the only thing welcoming about the exchange?

His father sat at his desk, but he did not pore over the ledgers as expected, rather he was positioned with hands folded on the tabletop, watching. Unfortunately, his face was an unreadable mask.

"Close the door." Father's deep voice commanded the knight that stood just within the room.

The man obeyed, leaving Father, Mother, and Lukas alone.

Mother relinquished her hold on Lukas and moved to sit by the fire.

"Son," Father said, tipping his head. "It is…good you have come home."

Lukas nodded, unsure what to say. Unsure of where he stood. As always.

"I trust that your release and journey were well." Father leaned forward.

"Yes, I was quite pleased to return."

Father nodded and tossed a glance in Mother's direction.

"Lukas." His mother's voice was gentle. More so than it had been. What was coming? "Your father and I have invited the Count Vorisek to dine with us."

Lukas was not certain why they felt the need to inform him. Perhaps they had no desire to delve further into his imprisonment, then. "Very well."

"There is more." Mother tossed another glance at Father, who nodded again. "He will bring the countess and their daughter, Lady Anicka."

Lukas had a strong memory of the lovely dark-haired girl who had been a playmate on occasion. Count Vorisek was the closest noble family to their own lands. His father and the count had always had a good rapport. It was only fitting, then.

"I look forward to it." Whatever lay beneath the surface here, Lukas would do his best to keep his chin up and maintain as little a presence as possible.

"His *unmarried* daughter," Father interjected. There was a directness to Father's tone.

It wasn't difficult for Lukas to pick up what was being insinuated. "Father, I appreciate your desire to see me matched, but I am not certain that I—"

"But you will," Father said as he rose. "It has been decided, and that is that."

Lukas balked. Would his father force the young woman on him? And he on her? How could he consign a fair maiden to weather Lukas's situation alongside him? No, it would be best to endure it alone.

"Respectfully," Lukas started, "I must ask that I have more time before a marriage arrangement is made."

"It is done. The arrangement is made. It has been agreed upon by myself and her father." There was no hint of softening in the man's words. "And it is *for* your benefit it has been done."

Lukas's brow furrowed. "My benefit?"

"You cannot think to regain any sense of honor should you remain unmarried. This will show everyone that you are respectable and secure in your place. All the more when you provide an heir."

An heir? Father couldn't mean to thrust such an edict on him.

"And what of Lady Anicka? What if she does not wish to be connected with a...pardoned criminal?"

Father's glower settled on Lukas. "You cannot be so daft. She has reached the age at which she must make a good marriage...or risk the prospect of no marriage at all."

Lukas searched his memories. She was younger than him by a few years. But so was the case with maidens. Their usefulness in making a match did not extend far into their adulthood. He remembered Lady Anicka being of fine face and amusing disposition. A fine playmate. But a wife? He wasn't certain he would wish to take on any marriage prospect at this point. Much less a woman who could have other options. Better options.

"Her father and I have settled the matter. You will have the opportunity to become reacquainted with her. A gift. And the banns will be cried on the morrow."

The morrow? So soon?

Lukas opened his mouth to protest but knew it would fall on deaf ears.

Mother stood and moved toward him. "I beg you to see reason. See this for what it is—an opportunity to regain your standing. And have a hope for an honorable future."

Lukas nodded and looked to the floor. As much as his heart thundered and the very idea weighed an anchor in his stomach, he knew he would do what he must.

"Aye. I thank you." He looked to his father. "Both of you."

The older man's shoulders relaxed. Had he been tense? But there was an easing there that was apparent. "Then we shall resume our preparations?" Father looked to Mother, who smiled.

"Of course," the lady said, taking Lukas's arm once more and steering him toward the door.

Was that all this was? Father saw him but to order him to fall in line? Then he was so easily dismissed?

But what else could Lukas expect?

What else indeed?

Anicka held her breath as the door to the carriage was opened. Mother glared at her. But there was more than the typical disappointment in her stare. It was as if the woman wished to warn her. But why? She knew better than to not be on her best behavior.

Besides, Lukas was here. It would be so good to reconnect with the boy she had enjoyed playing with as a child. Perhaps that was what Mother's apprehension was rooted in—for she and Lukas could create quite a stir with the grand adventures they imagined and took up.

Father reached in to assist Mother's exit. As the woman abandoned the space, Anicka took the moment to breathe in deeply. Would her mother's scrutiny overshadow her reunion with her one time friend?

It was not important, she decided. There was precious little diversion about her days, she would not let anything steal her anticipation over this outing.

But as Father reached in after Anicka, she froze. What if Lukas had changed? What if he no longer cared to interact with her? Would this be one more lonely evening in her string of nothingness?

Father cleared his throat and pressed into the carriage a bit more.

Anicka smiled at him and set a hand into his. Then he tugged her forward and out into the open.

Lukas's parents stood waiting, and beside them, the boy she'd known, no longer a boy, but a man.

Anicka's breath caught again. Though she had always found Lukas handsome, the features he had grown into were ten-fold more becoming than when last she'd laid eyes on him.

He stood beside his father, nodding in greeting to Anicka's family.

"It is good to see you, old friend," the Baron Vitek said as he stepped forward and intercepted Anicka's father.

"I agree." The count took Baron Vitek's arm. "It has been too long. I am all too glad for the occasion which brings you to my home."

Was it Anicka's imagining, or was the baron's gaze darting in her direction intentional? Or did he only wish to determine how the young woman, older than she ought to be as she remained unmarried, appeared?

"And this...the Lady Anicka? How she has grown in beauty." The baron's words were kind, but the attention...all these eyes on her... disrupted her hard-fought stability.

In her loss of inner balance, she found she could not look to Lukas to see if he agreed.

"Ah, yes," Anicka's father muttered. Dismissive. What else could she expect? Would Father return the gesture and mention Lukas? Or was he so tarnished by his recent imprisonment in the count's eyes that such niceties would be omitted?

Anicka didn't have to wait long for the answer, for Baron Vitek drew Father toward the keep, their conversation no longer audible.

Another cold look shot in Anicka's direction. She felt it before she noted that it was so. Mother warned her against a loose tongue.

The older women stood watching their children. Anicka could not have been more uncomfortable if she had been on a platform in front of hundreds of people. Perhaps even that would be better.

Lukas's mother shot him a look as well. What was happening here? Would he need to be induced to be kind to her?

Anicka's heart fell. Mayhap, then, the years had undone what connection the two had shared.

Lukas stepped forward after some long moments of silence thickened the space between all present. And his blue eyes settled on her. It stole her words. "My lady, might I have the pleasure of escorting you within?"

He extended his arm, but it felt forced. What was she to do? She wanted no part of whatever game was afoot here. Though, if she did not play her part, surely her mother would punish her. And that she feared more than her trepidation.

Laying a hand upon his arm, she nodded, but any words she might wish to impart were caught in her throat.

His arm stiffened at the contact, but he offered nothing more than a gentle, slight smile. And the intensity of his gaze. How was it possible that for all his reservation, those eyes captivated her so?

"I thank you." She looked away, making a show of gripping the long skirt of her finest dress as she stepped forward.

Lukas steadied her perhaps more than he realized as he led her into the keep and toward the great hall.

She wished for conversation, words, anything that might banish this tension. But nothing would come, from either of them. Was Lukas so put out with her presence? True, she was not the young girl he had known...yet she was so, in all the ways that mattered at least. It was that very youthful spirit and innocence which incensed her mother so.

"It has been many years." Her voice was timid to her ears.

"Yes." His words were abrupt.

She feared he would speak nothing further and leave her in a lurch.

But he did press into the silence again. "The years have been... kind...to you, Lady Anicka."

That surprised her. A compliment? Was it founded in a sincere admiration? Or an attempt after propriety at its best?

Either way, she could not stop her wandering gaze which settled on his profile. Nor could she help that she was unable to look away.

A lack of forethought, for certain, and she knew it well when she stumbled over a skirt that she had not been prepared for before this day.

Lukas firmed his hold on her and added the extra support afforded by his other arm coming around to keep her upright. And for that moment, she saw concern in his eyes. But there, again, was more to it. Something deeper that sought...what?

A sharp intake of breath behind warned that Mother was there and saw Anicka's misstep.

She righted herself and urged Lukas to move forward again. Though she hoped it made little of her folly, she knew she would hear of it later this night.

Soon enough, the corridor opened into the great hall. And Anicka prayed all was forgotten as they took their seats. Lukas led her to the high table and settled her into a chair beside the one he took. Was this a hope to encourage further conversation between them? Or did their parents conspire to something more?

For certain, Lukas was more aware of any plot afoot than she. Was that what spurred his hesitation? Did her father seek a match made here? One that Lukas did not want? What would she wish for if such were revealed as the point of this night's exchange?

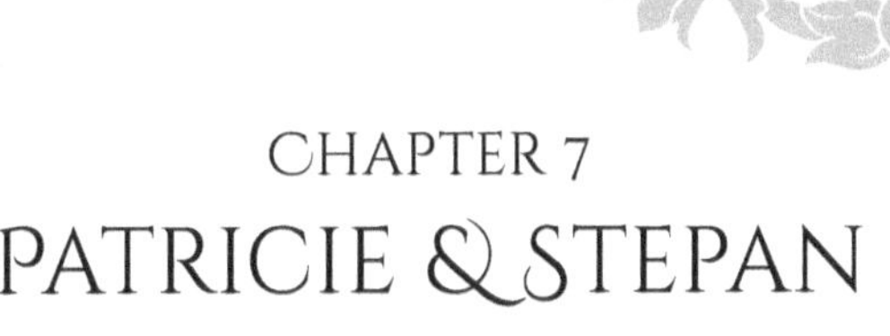

CHAPTER 7
PATRICIE & STEPAN

Patricie led Eva, Michal, and the loaned knight into the inn. The room was full of those imbibing and enjoying what she could identify as venison stew. It was a specialty of the tavern's keeper.

Relieved that no one stirred or minded them one bit, she pulled out a chair and invited Eva to join her. But she kept her gaze flitting about the room. Would others notice? Would they care?

Satisfied that everyone was otherwise engaged, she settled into the seat and smiled as the innkeeper stepped over.

"What can I do for you?"

Patricie looked up at the portly man with kind eyes. "I think we'd like some of that stew I hear so much about."

"That you shall—" His voice cut off.

Patricie's back straightened. What had caused him to still?

Eva leaned back, shifting the young child, who's head she had uncovered completely. Michal's mark was on display.

"Almighty," the man muttered.

Patricie shot Eva a look. Her sister was too brazen, inviting ridicule and disquiet.

Indeed, the man stood gaping at them.

As well, the din of voices quieted as the other patrons looked at what had bothered him so. This was what Patricie had hoped would not happen but knew would.

"I'll have no part of that in here." The man's voice was fearful but stern.

"You cannot mean that you are afraid of a small child," Eva challenged.

The guard set an arm to the table as he reached for his sword's hilt. As if to communicate she was under his protection.

Still, the keeper's voice was gruff, but his concern laced his words. "Aye, I can. Do you not see it, woman?"

"This child is innocent. What does it matter if he has a slight mar about his person?"

Patricie opened her mouth. Couldn't her sister see reason? They'd best move on. However, her words were cut off before they were formed.

"It is not welcome here." The innkeeper backed up. "Leave. Now."

A shiver ran down Patricie's spine. All the more as she noted the firm set features on the men surrounding them.

"I have no intention of letting superstition decide how I will conduct myself," Eva said, holding the child closer.

Patricie forced her way into the moment. "Can we not find somewhere less...conspicuous? Somewhere that—"

"Where? He needs sustenance the same as anyone." Eva glared at the patrons around them. "Would you deny an innocent child food? What next...shall you skitter away from a sickly cripple?"

As much as Patricie wished Eva's words were for those around her alone, her sister stared at her.

"Please," Patricie pled. "Let us have some consideration!"

The knight leaned in toward Eva. "Let's not stir things further. You have made your point."

Patricie looked to him. So, he did not feel the same as Eva. Why was her sister so personally affronted by the reaction? A reaction she very well should have expected.

The guard rose and cupped Eva's elbow.

Eva jerked free, shooting daggers at both the knight and Patricie.

"Listen to yer husband. We don't want trouble here." The innkeeper peered to his right and left, his anxiety visibly growing as others became more disrupted by the scene.

Eva shot to her feet, her jaw set. Would she declare that the knight was not her husband and open herself all the more? But when she spoke, she only said, "Very well. But I will not be run out of town by idiocy."

Patricie drew nearer her sister. "Do not make this worse." Why was Eva so bent on making this as difficult as possible?

Eva pierced Patricie with her glare. Accusing. What was Patricie supposed to do? Incite a battle?

The men at the table nearby started to rise.

The knight blocked Eva with his body. Would Eva have so little care for the man's wellbeing? Would she force him to defend her with life and limb?

"I beg you!" Patricie reached for Eva's arm. "Let us continue this discussion elsewhere."

Eva resisted, but as she scanned the room, she relented. Couldn't she see how impossible the situation had become? Patricie prayed so.

"Pardon our intrusion," Patricie said to the innkeeper. "We meant no harm."

The man's brow furrowed as he frowned. But he kept any thoughts to himself as the knight, placing himself between Eva, Patricie, and Michal and the men who were becoming more and more agitated. As the guard moved, he pressed the small group out the main door.

If they were not welcome in the inn any longer, where would they pass the night? It was unlikely any other establishment would permit them lodging. Would Patricie be shut out from the village altogether? Dare she trespass into such uncertainty?

With these thoughts swirling in her mind, she had nothing for her sister when she turned on her and said, "Where are we to bed down? Perhaps we can find food there."

Patricie closed her eyes so they would not betray her feelings. "We were to take rooms in that inn."

Eva frowned. Did she regret her actions? Her words?

That was not truly what Patricie wanted.

Eva shook her head. "It matters not. We will find a place in the camp."

Patricie didn't have the stomach to tell her they would be unlikely to find a place there either. Though she prayed they would.

Stepan watched as Tomas was led away. The man did not resist or struggle, but calmly kept in step with Sir Marek. It was strange... disconcerting even.

That left Stepan and Karin, as well a squire stood in the corner of the room. Thus, they were spared an inappropriate situation, but it remained difficult all the same. He and Karin had not been alone since he struck at her with his sword, determined to snuff out her life.

She glanced across the length of the room, her gaze colliding with his. Was she just as aware of this fact as he? It seemed so.

Tilting her chin downward, she shifted further such that the table was between them.

Stepan opened his mouth; but as he watched her, he thought differently of his entreaty. For she appeared moved quite nearly to tears.

"What goes?" He kept his voice gentle, bringing to mind how he had cared for her. And how, even now, he wished to lend aid.

Her regard lifted from the smoothed wooden surface to him. There was surprise in the green depths that met his gaze.

She looked away but did not sufficiently disguise how upset she had become.

Stepan dared take a step closer, thoughtful to keep the table between them while lowering his voice to keep his words from the squire. "You feel for the man."

She lifted an eyebrow and seamed her lips.

He was certain it would be only a moment before she banished him from her presence—this time permanently. For she'd not had the power to do so before, but here and now she did.

But when she spoke, it surprised as much as did the gentleness of her tone. "Aye."

And, as she swiped a hand across her face, likely to prevent the spilling of her emotion to betray her, he became all too aware of the glistening there. "I know we have a...rather sordid...history between us. But I assure you, I only wish to see my friend freed and returned to his wife."

She startled at that. "And I am simply to trust you? After..."

He did not—and could not—pull his gaze away as she fumed and faltered.

But with a sincerity that arrested him, he said, "I would pay penance a thousand times over for my actions that day." Flaring nostrils, he hoped the openness of his words and emotion would speak beyond his words. "For I regret them more deeply than I have ever regretted anything. You cannot know how I..." He was unable to finish. What cowardice was this?

Her eyes widened. "Still, I cannot abide making you my companion in this effort when I cannot reasonably think to turn my back on you."

His face fell, but he gritted his teeth against baring himself farther. Too much was at stake for him—indeed his very soul—should he fail to gain a place among her men. As much to protect her as to see his former friend restored. "You cannot think to attempt this."

Heat filled her eyes. "And just who are you to stop me?"

He held up hands that had been fisted at his side. "I speak out of turn, my lady. I only wish to ensure the safety of Baron Krejik. I would...give my life to that end."

She watched him as if seeking the untruth in his words. At length, he became more uncertain what she might discover there. Did she seek honestly? If so, she would know the veracity of his concern. And of his desire to aid.

After some moments, her shoulders hunched. "I am weary. Of so many things."

"Aye." Stepan knew her feelings well enough. For he, too, was quite nearly drained of any will to continue fighting. Almost.

"I discover Tomas is alive, only to find him perhaps the very enemy that thwarts my beloved's return home." She choked back a sob, but not soon enough.

It did not escape Stepan's notice that she once again eschewed the man's title. Such familiarity bred an unsettling in the pit of Stepan's stomach.

"If you would allow it, Lady Karin, I would wish to lead the effort."

"Lead?" The surprise in her statement was evident in her features as well. "Do not think, Lord Dvorak, that anyone will spearhead this venture but myself."

Now it was his turn to startle. "My lady, you cannot be in earnest!" Indeed, there was no sense in it. She was no warrior. He knew that most assuredly. She was but a delicate flower whose petals may have already become singed by what she had endured.

"I assure you, I neither ask your permission nor your tolerance."

He bit back the forthcoming response that raced to his tongue. But the ire that continued to overwhelm him at her suggestion would not quell.

His anger simmered, and he began to see reason again. As determined as she was, the only path to his atonement would be to convince her that their chances were better in concert. So, he steeled himself with some longer breaths.

"Of course, my lady." But how was he to proceed? Then it occurred to him.

While it was unseemly to offer his fealty to a woman who but wished for battle, his choices were few. And so, he bowed slightly, leaning toward her as he spoke as firmly as he could manage. "I vow, my lady, that you will have my sword and my allegiance. Henceforth."

Her eyes narrowed, and it first seemed she might refuse him.

But the steady fall of her chest with her every breath gave him reason to hope.

And though the moments passed so very slowly, he remained as he was...watching, waiting.

Then she nodded.

A knock on the solar door drew their attention in that direction.

Stepan rose quickly.

"Come in," Karin called. Would she be so brazen?

A small woman stepped within, wiping at her hands with a cloth. There was dried blood on it.

"What say you of the survivor?" Karin said, her voice quieter.

"I believe he will pull through. Though I stitched him, there may yet be infection looming. He is a fighter though."

"Did he wake?"

"Aye. And said his name is Ambroz?"

Zdenek? Stepan sucked in a breath. Had something indeed gone awry with Pavel's mission?

He looked at Karin, whose face had paled. "Take me to him."

CHAPTER 8
ANICKA & LUKAS

The meal could not have felt more tortured. Anicka spent the hour feeling every bit alone as she would were she dining at her father's table. Forgotten. Regretted.

Lukas would not give Anicka his regard for anything. Indeed, he appeared, for all purposes, uninterested in her or whatever game their parents played at. If they did desire a match here, would he not have the choice to refuse it? For certain, he had more autonomy about it than she.

It mattered not. She wasn't even sure that this occurred. She'd best not give herself to this idea until all was known.

As Baron Vitek pushed his trencher to the side and the meal concluded, another, even more awkward moment fell on her and Lukas. What was to happen now? But she could have guessed. The baron set a knowing look upon his son. Even as Lukas feigned ignorance, he bristled under it.

Should she rescue him? Would her efforts be thwarted and her hopes crushed should she try? But she knew he was only playing a part the same as she. Might he wish for such respite?

"Sir Lukas." She turned to face him.

He shifted toward her, an eyebrow piqued.

"I would very much like to see the gardens. Very rarely have I the pleasure of such fine gardens as there are at Vitek castle." Indeed, she did remember them to be quite remarkable.

Lukas watched her face as if to gauge her reaction. Did he wonder about her knowledge of any attempt to press them into a match?

Still, she prayed he would not deny her this opportunity to step away from the boring glares of their parents.

"Aye, my lady." Lukas pushed his chair backward and stood. Then he pulled her chair out and assisted her to her feet. "You shall be much satisfied with the progress my mother makes on the roses."

She felt the intensity of her mother's glare but did not yield to it. Instead, she risked pressing closer to Lukas, with a hope that it might shield her in some way.

But none challenged their movements or their intentions.

As they turned a corner, she could pull an adequate amount of breath into her lungs.

At last.

Lukas did not seem more at ease in the least, however. What bothered him so? Had she assumed correctly? A forced marriage underway—one he did not want?

They stepped into the briskness of the evening in the courtyard.

She halted for a moment, to once more catch her breath. A difficult thing with the tightness of the corset, pulling her body into proper form for this absurd dress.

"Are you well?" Lukas's eyes lit with concern again.

"Aye." She risked a smile. "I am only glad for a moment where I am not scrutinized." But was she truly free of such? Or would Lukas now look for any sign to put his parent's plans to the side?

"Are you certain?" The concern in his eyes did not weaken.

She realized she frowned. "Aye," she insisted. "I am only...weary. It has been a long day."

"Perhaps we should return? Or find you a place to recline?"

She set her free hand on his arm. "No." The word came out harsher than she'd intended. "That is, I do so wish to see your mother's roses."

He nodded, with some hesitation, before leading her farther among the foliage. "My mother has always enjoyed this place." His words were wistful.

"As have I." She spoke before considering if her words would be welcome. "That is, I...have fond memories of this place."

He chuckled. It was the first moment she felt at ease.

"If I remember correctly, your mother found us crawling about in the dirt."

Anicka's face heated. Indeed, her mother had been rather vexed by the state of Anicka's dress...and her lack of propriety. Naught had changed from that time for her. Had it for Lukas?

He shifted to look at her. "Was your dress saved?"

Anicka smiled and shook her head. "No, it was not."

The laughter emitted remained in his chest as a rumble. It was a pleasant sound.

Would it be so bad if they were joined in marriage? Provided he did not outright object. Did he fear her rejection? That she would not wish to be wed to a man once imprisoned?

She watched him. There had never been a moment she believed him guilty. She knew his heart. At least well enough to know that murder was not in him.

No matter what everyone whispered.

Her grip on him tightened.

He flinched.

She loosened her hold, but he set his hand atop hers again. "Do you tire, lady?"

How she hated that he maintained these formalities in the privacy of this moment. Had he ever called her by her title in the time they had been acquainted? She could not remember it being so.

They paused near a stone bench. It invited her, a chance to further their conversation with ease.

"Mayhap I am more in need of a moment's rest than I thought."

He nodded and stepped her to the bench. But as she settled upon its cool surface, he did not. Instead, he stood several paces away, looking into the night.

How was she to proceed? This was nonsense. And she would not have it.

"Lukas," she started.

He jerked toward her at her use of his Christian name without title.

"Have we not known each other long enough not to play at niceties?"

He dipped his head. "I suppose."

And here her problem always, she eschewed the proper for what her heart wanted. Always a challenge. One that her mother had berated her for more than once.

Although, her mother was not here now.

"Will you tell me what you know? Do our parents plot?"

His gaze sank into hers. And he nodded but did not come closer.

Her heart fell into her stomach it seemed. For it must be true that he had no wish for it. "And that displeases you?"

She was bold. But she had to speak it. Had to know.

"Do you wish yourself joined to a man such as I?"

"A man such as you?" She rose. "The boy who was my only friend? Someone who knows full well that my mother's only design and desire for me is to make a good marriage and nothing further." The truth hurt. But indeed, he knew it all.

He turned to face her. "And what of my crimes?"

She stepped closer. "You speak of your imprisonment? Do you think that I believe you capable of such? I know you are innocent."

He looked at the ground.

The desire to console her friend was great. She moved ever closer and set a hand to his arm, feeling the muscles ripple underneath. The awareness of his strength restrained brought a swell of warmth to her midsection.

"I know you are," she insisted, willing him to look at her.

"That is where you err," he said with an even deepness as he lifted his gaze to catch hers again. "I am every bit guilty."

She widened her eyes at his insistence, involuntarily backing away. "No. You cannot be. Not of…"

His features became hard. "Say it."

She shook her head. "I won't believe it."

"Regardless of your naivety, it is so. And your foolish blindness to the truth cannot change it. You would bind yourself to a murderer?"

He swept an icy glare over her once more and then walked away.

How could she think such? Where did this blind faith come from? A childhood spent as friends? Ludicrous.

Lukas needed to remove himself from her presence. Before he said something further that he would regret more deeply.

"Lukas," she called after him. What could she wish to say? How could she want anything more from him?

Yet even as he continued with determined steps that would create much needed distance, he sensed that she moved in his direction. Still, he refused to yield. Their parents may have plans here. Their thoughts perhaps to rescue him with her innocence. But he would not sacrifice her on the altar of his convenience.

"Lukas!" Her call became more desperate.

Must she insist on eschewing his title? It bred an intimacy that no longer existed.

"Pray, let me speak!"

She must be dim witted indeed. Regardless, he would not take advantage of her lack of foresight.

The whisper of slippered feet sounded much farther away than could be possible. For in the next moment, her hand grazed his shoulder.

He whirled, stepping back that he might not cause her to lose her footing. Still, she wavered at his sudden movement.

And though he should not, he reached out to steady her.

Widened eyes caught his before she gathered herself.

"What do you hope for here?" His tone was harsher than mayhap was necessary. But he must make her understand that there was little future for her to be found in pursuing him.

Then a thought occurred...what if it were not simply their parents forcing this? What if she had a hand here? He would not, could not allow it.

She drew back as if hurt by his curt response. Indeed, it was as he wished it. But then, not. His heart pulled at the injury displayed on her features.

"I...did not mean to offend." Her words were all but whispered as she drew in a shaky breath.

He looked off to the darkened sky. Offend? Is that what she thought? That he was but offended at her insinuation?

"That...is not what bothers."

Her wounded gaze did not repair in the least. Must he go on?

"This is not an arrangement that will be most suitable to you." His mouth tightened as if to cut off further explanation. Could he go on?

Her face perfectly portrayed her *naïveté*—smooth lines devoid of tension, mouth slightly parted as if wishing for words that may improve upon the situation.

"I...think you give much more credit than I am due." Her voice was soft as if pained.

By what?

"Do you not see what goes?" Her gaze finally caught his.

Indeed, there were emotions within he preferred not to delve into. It became all he could do to hold her regard in the face of her vulnerability.

"I...am beyond the age at which I can make a desirable match." Her voice wavered.

That couldn't be true. She was young enough to make a fine wife for a more noble man than he. Wasn't she? He allowed himself to see her. Really see her. And, though he found no flaw or fault in her affect, his memories of their younger years reminded that she was not as youthful as she appeared. Why had she not met with a finer pairing by now?

"My...mother is more concerned with wedding me than all else." Anicka looked away. "Perhaps more so than I care to truly consider."

Lukas swallowed. What could he say? Anicka had all but admitted that her prospects were few and that her mother cared little for her future. Would he wish his onetime playmate to be passed off to a man whose intentions may be less kind?

But dare he place her in such a position that she would be scorned alongside a husband of ill repute?

Or could a marriage to a lady of good standing offer him something he had dared not hope for? Redemption.

He watched her gaze move about the garden, seeking refuge everywhere but him. Was that a foretelling of a possible life together?

"I cannot let you bear what should be mine alone."

Her glazed blue eyes found his once more. "Can you not let me decide which path I would take? For, as you should be able to see, there are not many available to me."

"So, I am the lesser of the evils before you?"

She flinched at that. But he did not scoff at her for such. What would he do in her position?

Take the best offer available. And, in her mind, that was him. Though he knew better.

He stepped closer, drawing a warmth he did not expect from the space between them. As much as he wished to fill his being with the heat, he also fought the urge to step out of it. Did she sense it as well?

The curiosity in her gaze belied that she did.

He sucked in an uneven breath. This was nonsense. And he chided himself for it. "I do not wish to—"

"Please..." she said as her eyes misted. "Do not turn me away. You are my best hope for any kind of life."

How could she believe that? And how might he deny the one who looked to him with such longing? For *him* though? Or for what she thought might be her salvation?

He let out a long breath. It was decided. "I will marry you."

She cried out and threw herself into his arms.

He caught her, taken aback by her display.

"I will be a good wife. I swear it."

He tried not to think of how good her body felt pressed against his. Nor did he let himself dwell on the fact that she was but a lamb... and he, the slaughterer.

CHAPTER 9
KARIN & PAVEL

Karin thrust the door from Zdenek's sick room out of her way. What a day this had been. And what confusion it had wrought. How was it possible that mere hours ago, she had believed Tomas dead and gone. Now, this...

Zdenek held to life, but barely. The healer thought him capable to pull through, and Karin had prayed over him that it would be so.

But he had slept, caught in the slumber of the wounded. Hopefully, in order to recover.

And then Stepan...

What, in fact, did she feel? She reflected on the question perhaps best left unanswered and found she did not truly know. The wound of his betrayal was greater than any of the other emotions swirling about her, wrapping about her like a vise. Would she suffocate from the overwhelming turmoil in her heart?

She drew in a deep breath and stepped to the window.

No. This would not be permitted. Not these feelings, long dead and buried with Tomas's memory, not this tugging at her heart for how he may be treated in the dungeon, not even the distraction that Stepan's presence and words had offered. It was too much.

Pressing fingers to her forehead, she wished she could wipe away all memory of the morning. Indeed, of the reality of what was. For Pavel was in danger. And this was mayhap what her heart avoided facing. There was no ability within her to continue without him, should his life be snuffed out.

Movement in the hall beyond the solar pulled her from such thoughts. It would not do for her to betray weakness. No, the castle folk, the servants, even the knights needed to see her strong and resilient. Let them say what they may, but she would not give them cause to support any beliefs to the contrary.

Gurgling accompanied the whisper of slippered feet and she knew...someone brought Jaromir to her.

Pushing back from the window and the darkening sky beyond, she turned to greet her son.

It was the dowager baroness who stepped within as she lightly bounced the child.

"My lady." Karin moved to intercept her husband's mother. "What are you doing up and about?"

"Oh, fie!" the woman scolded. "I am quite well enough to move about the castle and entertain my grandson." Though she spoke to Karin, her regard was on Jaromir, her eyes full of light.

Yes, Jaromir had that effect. He could bolster anyone's mood.

Karin watched her mother-in-law move about the space, walking the small lad to the window and muttering sweet words about the lands that would one day be his.

It brought a smile to Karin's face. Yes, she, too, was subject to the babe's fancy. Her arms ached to hold her child, but something gave her pause.

Marketa shifted her hold on Jaromir and sat on a nearby chair.

For his part, he shoved a hand into his mouth and kept watching the woman whose attention was equally wrapped up in him.

They did make a pair.

"You seem distracted." Marketa's words were resolute, but gentle.

"I…" How could Karin tell her what had happened? What might she give away of her own thoughts and feelings if she tried? Might she even allude to a turning of her heart that she prayed was not there?

"I understand that a man now calls one of our dungeon cells his bed for the night." The older woman still did not look at Karin, but her words had thickened.

How could she know? Had one of the guards told of Karin's plight? What had been shared?

"Yes," Karin pressed forth, choosing her words carefully. "A man I knew from childhood came to speak with me."

"This I know."

Exactly how much, then, had she been made aware of? Karin must tread cautiously. "You seem to have ears and eyes enough."

The words were not harsh, but neither were they as tentative as she'd wished.

Marketa's eyes shifted to meet Karin's. They searched, questioning, seeking…what?

"I apologize, my lady." Karin let out a sigh. "It has been all so much. This man, I believed him dead many years ago."

Marketa nodded, but her expression didn't soften.

"He brought news of Pavel."

"As I have also been informed." There was a catch in Marketa's breath. For worry of her son? For concern after Karin's thoughts?

"Then you understand we must do what we can to gain that which Sir Tomas holds close."

Marketa nodded again. "Aye. And soon."

Karin licked her lips, fighting against the image of a Krejik knight questioning Tomas, using force to draw out the answers they so desperately needed.

"It may be best if Sir Marek take this on himself." Marketa's words were abrupt and devoid of feeling.

Karin looked in her direction, but the dowager baroness had refocused on the babe. "Perhaps…"

"It is not necessary, daughter, for you to expend your energy. Or sully yourself in attempting to gain what may be meant to trap you."

Karin grimaced. She had guessed as much. Tomas may play at some game, some plan to trick her. Ulrich would be wise to utilize Karin's long lost friend in such a way.

"Then we are agreed?" Marketa rose, bouncing the child once more.

Karin watched but could not make herself relent. Was this the best course? Or dare she give Tomas exactly what he asked for—an audience with her alone? It may be the only way to secure reliable information about Pavel.

"Aye? We are agreed?" Marketa stepped closer to Karin and settled her gaze on her daughter-in-law once more.

Karin wanted to nod, moved to nod, tried to make such a motion...to agree to keep her distance and let this play out as it would with Sir Marek at the helm. But she could not—neither leave Tomas to the knight's mercy, nor likewise distance herself.

Too much was uncertain. Too much was at stake.

"Karin?" Marketa's tone became more insistent.

"Pray, my lady, I cannot." Karin moved past Marketa and toward the door.

A sharp intake of breath preceded Marketa's shocked "Cannot?"

Karin continued. She didn't need to explain herself to Pavel's mother. After all, Karin was now baroness of these lands. And it was she who held the authority to make this decision.

"Or will not?" Marketa's words hit Karin's back as if a bolt.

Karin froze. Would her mother-in-law not see the best in her? Did she truly think so little of Karin and her marriage vows?

Turning her head slightly, Karin glanced back into the ever darkening room, where Marketa held a squirming Jaromir. Did he sense his mother's turmoil? Or that his father was at the mercy of a madman?

"What I do, I do for love..." Karin spun and let the heat in her chest flash in her gaze. "...of my husband." Her breath heaved for a moment more as she and Marketa stared each other down.

Only then did the dowager baroness's eyes soften. "I pray that is all, daughter."

Karin looked away and then nodded.

"And that you do not let your heart rule your head and defy your better judgment."

"Aye. I pray that as well." Then Karin whirled back to the door and, determination renewed, marched down the passageway.

To be led where one didn't want to go. Was anything more degrading for a warrior? Pavel settled back into the saddle, using bound hands to remain upright as the horse's movements jerked him up and down.

He had no control over the animal, surrounded by guards and mercenaries. Still, there had to be hope. This time, when they were on the move, was the most promising for him. One of the men watching him need only be distracted by something in the distance. A horse need only be spooked slightly to create an opportunity. Any of these, or a number of other vulnerabilities in the ranks, and Pavel would have his chance.

As it were, the guards maintained a close watch. For now. The time would come. Pavel need only trust and pray that it would be so.

The cluster of men on horseback moved through thickened forest to some destination unknown to Pavel. Did they journey out of Bohemia? To Ulrich's castle? To another safeguard? To the battlefront in hopes of thwarting the Czechs in exchange for Pavel?

He could not let himself be used as a pawn. Yet even more he could not allow his family to be harmed. It was imperative he claim his freedom.

His throat constricted at the thought of his wife or son in peril. And his muscles tightened with the desire to exercise their strength and ensure he returned to them. But he must hold himself in check. For these men would be remiss if not expecting him to try to escape. No, it was best they believe him weary and much more incapable than he was.

Glancing from side to side, he observed the two who had been charged with his watch. The one had eyelids that drooped. While the other fidgeted with the pommel of his saddle. Indeed, they tired. But many others surrounded him. Would this small opening give way to a chance to break away?

The day dragged as minutes in the saddle became hours. How much longer would they push on? It couldn't be more than an hour hence. For the horses required refreshment and the men, their opportunity to relieve themselves.

As if he himself had gauged it, men ahead called for all to move closer to a nearby stream. Might this be his chance?

The guard to his right moved closer, prodding Pavel's horse to obey and stay among the others.

Those in front, closest to the stream dismounted.

Pavel searched for sight of Ulrich.

There, among his bodyguards, as they moved away from their horses, letting others take charge of their refreshment.

Would the guards be more or less vigilant now? Ulrich was not there to criticize them, might they relax their watch?

It was not likely. Not with a prize such as they believed they had. What, in fact, did Ulrich intend to do with him? Did he think General Zizka would risk the whole of the Czech cause for one man? Ludicrous.

That was of little consequence to Pavel. As much as he had pledged himself to the Hussites, his heart beat for his family's well-being. And he prayed never would he have to choose one over the other.

Men milled about with their mounts at the stream's edge, taking turns moving off into denser places in the forest around them.

The larger of his guards dropped out of the saddle and came closer, gripping the horse's bit and urging it forward.

Pavel retained as much of a slump as he had been able to maintain since the previous evening—letting all think his wounds were more of a hindrance than they truly were.

But he scanned the area while keeping his head down. As scattered as the men were, and as lax as his guards may become, there was no way he might urge the horse into the forest and not be overtaken. That led him to examine the stream more closely. It was difficult to determine the depth of the moving water. Might he press the animal to cross? Would he get far? It was unlikely. Yet the current had strength. A dangerous strength. Bound as he was, it would almost certainly be suicide to allow it to carry him away from his imprisonment.

As more of the men loosened their hold on their guard, trusting the two who minded Pavel to do their job, he began to form a plan.

But he had to act fast.

The large guard neared. "What are you looking at?"

It was now. Or never.

Pavel thrust his foot, kicking against the man's chest with all that he had.

The man fell back against a horse that then reared up.

Pavel's mount leaned away, shifting its hooves as if it, too, might rear or buck. Gripping at the pommel was all that kept Pavel astride. Mayhem ensued with startled horses and guards rushing about. Pavel kicked at the horse, deciding he cared not where the animal would take him. But praying that the way would be clear.

Shouts surrounded him as his horse took flight. But his every thought was spent on remaining upright and in the saddle.

As the animal pushed into a gallop, speeding around trees, Pavel knew it was only a matter of time before he lost his firm grip.

Reaching for the horse's mane, he jerked to slow the animal. Would his only hope to stay ahead of those who no doubt pursued him lie in diversion?

Several seconds passed in which Pavel did not think he would be able to keep his seat. Then the horse halted. Without further thought, he threw himself to the ground.

The hard earth knocked the wind out of him, and he struggled to regain his breath. Ignoring the pain radiating from his side, he pushed up to his knees, then his feet.

Hoofbeats echoed in the distance. Along with the cries of warriors hungry for blood. His.

Pavel slammed his body into the horse, urging it to continue its race farther into the cover of the trees. And he prayed that would buy him a few more minutes.

Ducking, he rushed, stumbling as the intensity of the pain in his chest overtook him. But he recalled Karin's face and pushed on.

There was little chance all his pursuers would be fooled. He had to move faster than he ever had before.

Climbing a hillside, he topped it to find the trees opening and the great rush of the river below him.

He turned, considering his options. But crunching through the brush promised that his captors were almost upon him.

Looking down at the rock and rushing current that were his only hope, but also likely to be his grave, he spoke into the wind, "Father, don't let me die."

Then he plunged into the watery depths below.

CHAPTER 10
PATRICIE & STEPAN

Stepan crept down the steps into the darkness below. It was foul and filthy, but that did not deter. His coin purse was a bit lighter from having bribed the guard at the top, but it was no matter. He had to find answers. And pray Karin would never know he had skirted her authority to do just that.

He neared the base of the stairs. All was dark save a small lantern illuminating the outline of cells beyond. Were others housed here? It had not occurred to ask the guard plied with drink and coin. Though that would have been easy enough. He would just have to discover for himself.

Though Stepan made every effort to soften his footfalls, as he rounded the last corner, the man in question stood at the bars, awaiting the intruder to his imprisonment.

Stepan nearly startled at the sight but remembered why he had come. His friend, former perhaps, yet still a friend who had been his companion, was at risk. As were the wife and child left behind. Stepan would not let it be. If there was dirtying of one's hands to be done, let it be his.

"What do you seek?" Sir Tomas asked as Stepan stared openly at him.

Stepan scoffed. It was a useless question. They both knew why he had come.

"I tell you," Sir Tomas seethed. "You will have no satisfaction here. So, be gone." Then he turned his back on Stepan and walked to the opposite side of the cell and sat.

Would this man...this villain...dismiss him so summarily? It irked that there was little with which Stepan might intimidate him. Although...he allowed a small smile to part his mouth as he rubbed the key in his pocket. There would be time aplenty for that. Should it be merited.

"I am here for a conversation."

Sir Tomas sputtered. "Conversation? I doubt that. You intend to extract information. You know it and you know that I know it."

"Perhaps you might save us both the time and effort then...and just tell me." Stepan kept his voice as even and untouched by emotion as possible. But a smirk slid onto his features. "And I will be on my way."

"You think me a simpleton?" Sir Tomas pressed out. "As I stated, I must speak with Karin alone."

"Surely you do not think the whole of the Krejik knights so foolish. Why would any think you would not use the promise of information to get close to the lady and exact harm upon her?"

Tomas watched him, his stare cold. "I think you know otherwise."

Why would he say that? What could Stepan know about him? Did he mean to imply that Stepan had a care for Karin that went beyond the boundaries it should? In this, Sir Tomas erred. It may have been true at one time, but no longer. Stepan's feelings for Karin were only of a protective nature.

"It seems we are at an impasse." Stepan let his hands work into fists and permitted his muscles to tense, knowing the flickering of the gentle flame could not reveal all to the man behind the barrier.

"As it would seem, Sir Dvorak." Tomas's voice was deep. And eerily calm. It was unnerving.

More than the tone, his awareness of Stepan's family disturbed. But should it? This man had been under the command of one of the more notorious antagonists in the Bohemian lands. Surely, knowledge of anyone of importance would behoove him.

Either way, Stepan prayed his features had not betrayed his surprise.

"What say you, then?" Tomas challenged. It was equally unsettling.

"You give me no choice." Stepan set a hand to the hilt of his sword.

Tomas laughed. It did not lighten the air about them. It was menacing. Who was this man? If he had died, as Karin supposed, might this be a ghost?

Instead of disturbing him, Stepan let the man's reaction fuel the ire that threatened to overtake. He clenched teeth to the point his jaw ached. "I will not allow you to visit injury upon the lady. Or her husband."

"And what do you intend to do about it?"

Stepan slid the key out of his pocket and moved toward the lock on the cell.

"You would sully yourself? I do not think you have what it takes to steal life from a man."

Stepan paused, the memories of those he had struck down in battle all too present for him. Did their ghosts haunt him still? He shook his head to clear it. His mission here was simple. He had to have answers. The preservation of his soul demanded it.

The lock clicked. Stepan neither shifted his footing, nor moved his hand from his blade. This would end—here and now—one way or another. Which of them would be standing in the next moments? Which would still draw breath?

Gripping the metal, which was colder than it should be, Stepan swung the gate open ever so slowly. Deliberately staving off what must come. While he knew he had the determination to do what he must, he did not relish the thought...the possibility of taking another life. One more apparition to fill his nightmares.

Tomas's gaze narrowed as he spread his feet ever so slightly. Did he think Stepan would launch at him? Was that what he planned?

Stepan was not encouraged by his own lack of forethought. Was he so impulsive? Would that serve him here?

He let the scrape of the blade against its scabbard issue a threat. For there was not as much strength to his resolve as he had hoped.

"What do you do?" The harsh voice gave Stepan pause. As he shifted his regard to the narrow walkway beyond the cell, the anchor in his stomach sank.

"Karin," Stepan admonished. "Get away from here."

"I will not!" Her wide-eyed gaze followed his every move as she stepped even closer.

He could not allow her to do so. Jerking toward her position, he moved to halt her.

And there were arms about his person—a muscular forearm surrounded his neck as a fist slammed into his back.

He lost his air and his hold on his weapon.

"No!" Karin yelled as she pushed into the cell.

"Stay back," Stepan beseeched her, but his words were weak with little air to support them.

"Tomas, you cannot." Her words were pleading. Certain that Stepan was unable to help himself. Was he?

Bending forward, he attempted to create space between their bodies, but Tomas's hold was too firm. Stepan ended up pressing out more of his breath.

"Do you not see what this snake intended?" Tomas's deeper voice chilled Stepan even as his hot breath fell on Stepan's ear.

"I beg you, Tomas," Karin's eyes glistened in the dim light.

Stepan's anger roiled, his stomach now a thick mire of regret. How did this happen? Would his lack of ability to protect himself lead to Karin's demise as well? For what could stop Tomas once Stepan's life was snuffed out?

"Karin," Stepan forced out, intending to bid her run up the stairs, but all his air was gone. Tomas's arm prevented any more from entering his lungs.

Even as he struggled against Tomas's hold, he did so in vain. The man's grip was as a vise.

Instead of doing the sensible thing and fleeing, Karin stepped closer.

Stepan kicked back in hopes of weakening Tomas's stance, but it was not to be. Every attempt was thwarted and his feet never connected. His vision wavered. Dark spots further dampened his ability to see clearly.

Karin's hands were near his face. Would she attempt to wrest Tomas's hold away?

A feminine shout that was otherwise indiscernible preceded a release of the pressure on Stepan's neck.

He fell, slamming into the stone floor.

Then Karin was beside him, hovering over him. And her voice flitted about his awareness. As Stepan fought to return to himself, he focused on that—on her concern and compassion. Neither of which he deserved.

But, little by little, he strengthened his hold on consciousness and moved to rise into a sitting position. Hoping to soon be on his feet and able to defend Karin.

Firm hands pressed his shoulders. "Do not try to sit. You are not well."

"Be that as it may—" His voice was more scratched than he'd expected. And painful. "I will rise."

The point of a blade pressed into him, near his heart.

"You will do well to listen. Or I will fell you for certain."

That villain Tomas. How had he taken the weapon? And how would Stepan preserve his and Karin's lives against this foe?

"Tomas, 'tis not necessary," Karin admonished, her words sharp. "Let him go."

The press of the sword's edge released.

"Very well. But I will not tolerate his presence any longer."

Stepan wanted to balk at that...on what grounds did a prisoner speak such? But then, Tomas was as good as freed. Due to Stepan's negligence. And pride.

Grabbing for Karin, Stepan wished to put her behind him. As if he could do anything but delay any harm Tomas wished to visit upon her.

She resisted. "Stop."

Stepan turned to look at her, a question about him. What was she doing here? And what did she intend to do? Perhaps this wasn't as it seemed. Had she come for a liaison with Tomas? What went here?

Karin turned to Tomas. "Let him leave and I will speak with you."

"You cannot," Stepan choked out.

Karin leveled her gaze on him. "I will do as I please."

Beneath her words, he sensed a scolding. And a reminder that it was he who pledged his fealty to her, not the other way around. But how could he let it happen?

He thought to call for the guard, but he remembered the man had abandoned his post at Stepan's behest. And that had opened the way for Karin to come down here. Her life now assuredly forfeit. Unless...was this as it seemed? A meeting in secret?

"I will not let you betray your marriage vows," Stepan sputtered.

Karin's green eyes hardened. "You think I would betray my husband?"

Stepan looked between her and Tomas's even more strained expression.

"I would speak to that, but it is not your concern." Karin stepped back, no longer giving him her protection.

Stepan glared at Tomas, who brought the blade back between them.

"You will go and fetch the guard you dismissed." Karin's voice was icy.

"I will not leave you, my lady."

"Go."

The weapon once again upon Stepan, it bit into his arm, no doubt drawing blood.

What was he to do? He couldn't leave Karin with this man. Nor did he wish to sacrifice himself to stop the inevitable.

"Lord Krejik will know of this," Stepan seethed.

Karin's lips wavered. "I pray that is true."

"Now, go," Tomas ordered, pushing the tip of the blade farther.

Stepan scooted back and rose. "I will have no part of this."

"So be it." Karin stared at him. It was not a gentled gaze, plagued by emotion. But it, too, was as firm as stone.

He pulled himself out of the cell and reluctantly to the stairs. As he moved out of sight, he paused, leaning toward them to pick up their words.

After some moments, their voices were discernable, but only that. No words were decipherable. What had he wrought here? And might Tomas seize the opportunity to strike down Karin? Once again, Stepan had failed his friend.

The dream world was not as inviting as usual. For the chill about Patricie pervaded even that place that often offered solace. Not this night. She opened her eyes to find that they were, indeed, sleeping on the ground just in the forest line. Was this what safety was?

A presence hovered over her. Had someone come to challenge even that assumption?

She peered upward and saw the knight sent to protect her sister, the lines of his face strained.

"Eva?" Patricie shot up. Had something happened to her sister?

Where was she? Patricie glanced about in the moment it took the knight to answer.

"All is well. She took Michal to the stream." From seemingly nowhere, the man produced a portion from a loaf of bread. "Take it. It's not much, but it will satisfy."

She nodded and reached for it. Then it occurred. They must not have much to sustain them. Did the knight give her from his own stores?

Pausing, she wanted to ask these things, but he pressed it to her hand.

"Take it."

"But..." She could not finish the thought. It would insult him. So, she took the morsel and rose to a seated position. The bread proved to be nourishing, yet stale. This may be what remained in the knight's and Eva's packs. And she would not begrudge it.

The man looked toward the stream where Patricie could now hear the echoes of her sister soothing the small child.

"How is Michal today?"

"He has not slept well." There was no more to the guard's response. Just a matter-of-factness about him.

"I'm sorry." If the young one did not sleep well, that must mean that Eva, and perhaps the guard, would have lost rest as well. What little rest was available after bedding down here with no other options.

The man shrugged.

"What is your name, sir knight?"

He paused and looked over his shoulder. Did he resist becoming better acquainted? "Sir Antonin."

"It is good to meet you, Sir Antonin. I cannot thank you enough for what you did for my sister...and me." Suddenly, she felt self-conscious. Why?

He met her gaze. "I would do it again."

There was a tension building between them.

"As is my duty," he added.

She looked away. Pondering this thickness between them. "What will she do now? Where will you take her?" Patricie kept her words gentle. Worry for her sister flooded her being.

"She wishes to return to Hradek Kralove...to your father's home."

Patricie nodded. Indeed, they did not have many options.

"I am not certain my mistress would approve of Lady Eva being so near the fighting."

"What of you?" Patricie wondered out loud without thinking.

His regard fell on her.

Her face heated. "I apologize. It is not for me to concern myself."

He sighed. "I may try to convince her to return to Krejik lands. To my mistress, Lady Karin Krejikova. That may be where Lord Ambroz awaits."

Patricie's heart swelled for her sister. Eva's husband was a man who cared deeply for her and for God's will. What more could she ask for a much beloved sister?

"I hope—"

The knight halted Patricie with a motion of his hand. And then cocked his head. "We are no longer alone."

Patricie rose, dread filling her as even she discerned the crunch of grass beneath feet. She whirled, scanning the area. Where did it come from?

Then she spotted him—the priest—coming from the direction of the small village. What could he want? The question, though just in her head, chastised Patricie. She knew all too well what the man wanted. It had been her hope to avoid this...for naught.

The man approached with steady steps. Both he and a Hussite soldier at his side.

"Join your sister." The knight's hand moved to his sword hilt as if ensuring the weapon remained at the ready.

"No." Patricie surprised herself.

The guard jerked his head toward her. "Now."

"I will not let you fight this battle alone."

His gaze was hard on her, but he said nothing further.

"Patricie of Hradek Kralove," the priest called in greeting. "Sir knight."

"To what do we owe this pleasure of a visit?" Sir Antonin's voice had lightened, but it still held an edge.

The priest drew nearer. "Let us not mince words, nor insult each other with simple pleasantries."

Sir Antonin nodded. "Of course."

"I have...heard disturbing things." The priest stopped some paces away. Was he fearful of being deemed unclean by association? "About a child traveling with you."

The older man's gaze moved between Patricie and the guard, landing firmly on each.

Patricie wanted to shift under his inspection but found herself determined to not flinch.

"I am certain that what you have heard is from an overly-superstitious mind." Sir Antonin seemed almost dismissive of the man's concern.

"I truly hope so. But I must see for myself if what I have heard bears merit." The priest's eyebrows rose. Then lowered as his features became tight. "I would ask you what an unmarried woman is doing alone with an unattached man."

Patricie glanced at Sir Antonin, who settled a hard gaze on the priest. A very heated glare.

She stepped forward. "Father, it is nothing to worry with. My sister is nearby."

Sir Antonin drew in a quick breath. Did he fear for Eva? Had Patricie erred in her declaration?

The soldier with the priest moved his hand closer to his sword, but the priest pressed his hand down as if to quell the man's nervous reaction.

"What say you?" the man of the cloth shot back.

"I only mean to speak on my sister's behalf."

"There is no need for that." A sharp-edged voice spoke from behind.

Eva.

Patricie closed her eyes, wishing that her sister had stayed a fair distance away.

"Oh?" The priest did not seem amused by the intrusion. "I wish to see the child in full."

Eva held Michal close to her chest as he rested his head on her, asleep. "You will not come closer."

The priest smirked. "I do not believe you have authority over me, my child."

Eva bristled at those words, shifting the small one and causing him to wake.

Patricie stepped between her sister and the priest. "Believe me, I see no ailment in the child. No reason for alarm."

"What is this with these women?" the priest spat out as he looked at Sir Antonin. "They would speak for you and show such disrespect?"

The knight frowned. "I am not their lord."

Patricie again took a step forward.

The Hussite soldier unsheathed his blade and moved to protect the priest.

"I mean you no harm. None of us would think to move against your person," Patricie insisted.

Sir Antonin, pulling his own weapon, moved between the women and men again.

"Enough," the priest bellowed. "I will see the child!"

The two armed men squared off for a moment.

Patricie knew this would not go well for them should they stand their ground. She turned to Eva. "Please, bring the child closer."

Eva pressed Michal's face to her shoulder and appeared as if she would refuse. Indeed, she seemed to weigh her options. But she relented and came alongside Patricie.

With the priest looking on, Patricie helped Eva turn the small boy.

"Almighty," the priest exclaimed. "It is true!"

Sir Antonin tensed and tightened his grip on his sword.

"There is naught to fear," Patricie said. "He is but a boy. And will bring no harm on anyone."

"Can you not see he bears the mark of the devil?" The priest stepped back then. "This must be dealt with before it brings the devil upon us." The man's face reddened.

"We will do no such thing," Eva screeched. "He is my son!"

The priests eyes widened. "Do not speak so. It cannot be tolerated!"

"We do not ask that anyone 'tolerate' our presence." Sir Antonin's intervening words were surprisingly firm. "We only ask that we be allowed to leave."

Again, the priest turned a wide eyed look upon them. "You cannot be in earnest. This evil will follow you everywhere you go."

"That's a chance I am willing to take." Sir Antonin's tone was resolute.

The priest looked to Patricie. "And you, healer's apprentice. What of you?"

"I will not raise a hand to stop my sister and her family from finding solace."

"Then you, too, are unwelcome in this place."

Did he mean Tabor? Or the whole of Bohemia? Surely not everyone gave credence to such notions as this.

Patricie had not been prepared to leave Tabor. But her options had just run out.

CHAPTER II
ANICKA & LUKAS

Anicka stirred. Was it morning already? She reluctantly opened her eyes to peer at the sun peeking into the room. It was indeed day. Stretching, she relished the feeling of sleepy muscles coming to life, tingling, contracting, and relaxing.

Her thoughts ventured to the conversation she'd had with Lukas. He had seemed rather reluctant to agree, but he had. So, they would be wed. And soon enough. There would then be no escaping the match.

Still, it must be better than life with her mother. The woman had become rather intolerant...more so each day that passed with her daughter unmarried. Was Anicka such a burden?

She shook that thought away. There was nothing to be gained by dwelling on such thinking. It wouldn't be much longer anyway, and she would be out from under her mother's glowers and grumbles.

Forcing her body to relax into the mattress, Anicka let her eyelids slide closed. And focused on the air moving in and out of her nostrils. This was a new day. There would be many new things to face, but this was certain—it was her life. A life she would build with Lukas.

Lord, please let him grow to care. Even a little.

The door to her chambers slammed against the wall.

Anicka jerked upright, prepared to leap from the bed if necessary.

Her mother strode into the room.

"Mother, what has happened?" Was something amiss? Had something happened to Anicka's father?

The older woman's gaze cut to Anicka. "You are yet abed? Are you ill?"

"No, Mother." Anicka slid her legs out from under the coverlet. "I am well enough."

"Then why do you linger?" Mother stopped at the vanity table and waved in a couple of servants.

"I...was not aware that my presence was required." Confusion swirled about Anicka's thoughts. What was the meaning of all this? "I—"

Her mother cut her off with a wave of her hand. "Don't be absurd. It's your wedding day."

"My...wedding day?" This did nothing to ease Anicka's uncertainty. "I don't understand."

Mother's eyebrows rose as if Anicka were the one creating confusion. "Sir Lukas assured that you had consented to wed."

Anicka's face heated. "I...did. That is, I—"

"Then we must make haste." Mother turned her attention to the trunk being brought in, raising the lid and reaching in after the contents.

"I don't understand. What of the bans? They have not been cried. How can we—?"

"Don't be daft." Mother jerked her regard to Anicka. "You shall wed today."

It wasn't possible. The church might very well annul her marriage if the bans were not cried. Was Mother forgetting that?

Anicka opened her mouth to insist on something she might understand. But she swallowed her words. Mother refocused on the items being pulled out of the trunk, all but dismissing Anicka and her concerns.

"There." Mother ran a hand over Anicka's best dress—a blue gown with lace and ribbon trimmings. "Make sure this is made ready for the lady." Then her mother passed it off to a waiting servant.

Another lady's maid entered the chambers and set aright a tub. Then others brought in steaming water.

The room was quickly becoming overcrowded. It only increased Anicka's discomfort.

"Mother," Anicka insisted, her words sounded timid even to her ear. "I don't understand. Will I not return home to prepare for—"

Her mother's glare cut off her words. Then she stepped to where Anicka had remained near the bed. "Do not embarrass me with your dim wittedness. It will be today. That has been decided."

Anicka looked to the floor, unable to bear her mother's scrutiny any longer. "Yes, Mother."

"There, now." Mother moved away and back to where the servants pulled things from the trunk.

Only then did it occur to Anicka. This trunk had been packed before they left. Somehow it had traveled with them to Lord Vitek's castle. For this purpose.

Anicka chewed on the inside of her lip. It didn't make sense.

Was this an abrupt decision? Or had her parents arranged for this to be such? That she was not to return home again? As if they wished to rid themselves of her altogether.

A shiver shook her body though it was not cold in the room. But as it subsided, a tightness remained in her chest as her heart throbbed.

There was no escaping this reality—this was what her parents had intended all along.

A maidservant touched Anicka's arm. "My lady, your bath is ready."

Anicka looked in her mother's direction but did not resist as the servant led her toward the tub that had been sprinkled with oils and rose petals.

She was numbed, frozen by all that ensued about her. Even as the maidservant worked to remove her chemise.

Anicka could no longer avoid the truth—she had never been anything more than a burden to her mother. Perhaps that was true of her father as well. She was a problem to be simply dealt with...and then passed on to a husband.

A harrowing thought struck her, delaying the tears that welled. What if she was but a burden to Lukas? The only salvation was that she offered him a way out of being ostracized. Perhaps nothing more.

As she slid into the heated water, she wanted to slip under the surface and away from all the goings on around her. How would her heart survive this? How would she make it through this day?

Lukas watched the hall with an anchor in his stomach. What was he doing here? Was he rescuing Anicka with this marriage? Or was this a way out of his dejected status in the world? If so, how could he ask her to take that on?

The priest shifted nearby. Did the man understand what he and Anicka were about? Did he approve or did he simply do the bidding of Baron Vitek? Perhaps that was all.

Lukas let his gaze wander to where his father had settled. The man was rather aloof...had been for the last several interactions between them. Did the man regret his association with Lukas? Why wouldn't he? Lukas had shamed his whole family and opened them to ridicule.

And now he did that to Anicka.

As he moved his weight from his right foot to his left, he let his mind wander to what he remembered of Anicka. She had always been pleasing to look at. All the more so now. Her beauty had taken him by surprise last eve. Even in her sadness.

They had been good playmates. He found her to be considerate and caring. Was that why she had agreed to wed him? Because she was kindhearted?

He shook his head. Whatever the reason, she had been quite determined that it would be so. It was almost as if she needed him just as much as he needed her place in society to improve his.

The swish of skirts and slippers pulled him from his thoughts. She was coming.

And with gaze trained on the turn in the corridor, he waited with bated breath.

A tug of regret pulled at him, but he called up her words from yestereve.

"Please. Do not turn me away. You are my best hope for any kind of life."

That gave him determination. Yes, she needed him, too. They would be good for each other.

She appeared around the corner. Her hair shined and braided away from her face as if a crown. Her gown perfectly accented the smallness of her waist. Indeed, she seemed almost frail. Could he offer his strength?

He shook his head. Such nonsense.

Anicka moved toward him as if she floated. In his mind, it was as if she did.

Soon enough, she drew near, and her hand was set in his. A thickness filled the space between them as her fingers—cool to the touch—met his palm. Was she chilled? The room was rather warm.

He shrugged it off and turned her toward the priest, who wasted no time in beginning the ceremony.

Although the man spoke, Lukas could not pull his attention away from his bride.

Today, he smelled roses. His proximity to her caused the scent to fill his senses. It was intoxicating. He imagined running his hands through her hair as he had done only once before in their childhood. She should not have permitted it then, but she did not chastise him as a young man curious about the silken strands. Would her curls be as soft as they had been then?

His fingers itched to know.

And his face heated at that thought which was inappropriate. But then again, was it? They were to be wed. Here. Now. Though he had not imagined he would be so drawn to her.

The priest continued the words that filled every wedding ceremony he had ever attended. Words of love and fidelity. Good words. Solid truths.

But Lukas was attuned to his bride.

As he peered at her, he noticed her breath caught.

Did she feel some of what he did? Or could she read his thoughts? He prayed not.

Lukas tried to attend the words spoken by the man of God, but he could not keep his mind in check.

There it was again—her uneven breathing.

Something wasn't quite right about it.

Looking over at her, he noted that she did not seem to be watching the priest at all, rather her face turned to the floor, her affect somewhat dejected.

It gave him pause. Did she decide she didn't want this? But felt compelled to follow through?

He would not have that. No matter how she insisted last evening. He would not force her to join her life to his. Especially as he did not believe she deserved to be chained to his sin.

No matter what anyone else might think. He turned his attention fully to her.

The priest stumbled in his oration for a moment but continued.

But Lukas didn't care. He had to know what Anicka was thinking.

As he watched her, it became clearer that it wasn't her breathing at all. No, her breath hitched because she sniffled.

From a seasonal ailment? Or from tears? He wished he could see her face, but no matter how he willed her to, she would not look up.

His heart fell. He couldn't do this.

"Stop." The word tumbled from his lips. But it had not the strength it needed.

The priest again tripped over his words. And paused. Glancing in the direction of Baron Vitek, he raised the Holy Book and began again.

"Stop." This time, the word had more force.

Enough that Anicka's gaze jerked toward him. The skin around her eyes held some swelling to them. There had for certain been tears.

"What?" Her words were whispered, perhaps discernable only to his ears.

Lukas shifted his focus to the priest. "I won't do this."

CHAPTER 12
KARIN & PAVEL

The current pulled at Pavel, dragging him under. He fought but was helpless to break the surface for air. On and on it went, until he was certain his lungs would explode.

And the next thing he knew, the water thrust him upward. As he kicked to aid his ascent, he knew his opportunity had come. He sucked in as much air as was possible before being covered once more. The rope about his wrists prevented him from making meaningful strides to free himself from the rush of the river, but he refused to give up. There was more at stake here than him.

That brought up an image of Karin and Jaromir in his mind. He let himself dwell on Karin's eyes, trusting and concerned. They reflected his own desperation. But he put them from his mind and forced himself to focus on his predicament. Being distracted by his wife's face would not serve him.

He maneuvered his legs, trying to will all he had to find the surface again. And fight he did. Against the current, against the river, against the voice within that bade him relent. He would not.

The darkness reached snaky fingers into his consciousness. He was cold. So very cold. And battered. His side flared with pain from his earlier fall. Still, he pushed on.

Another gulp of air had him beseeching God for aid.

Then his body slammed into something hard and unforgiving. His body was once more fraught with pain, and he gripped for something of the solid wall he seemed to have found amongst the rapids.

As he pressed into it, his entire torso screaming at him to stop, he discovered he had hit a large rock. Was this God's answer? Another obstacle?

Yet, he had something to cling to. Though he did a quick assessment. The jagged edges of the boulder had sliced into his skin made more pliable from being immersed in the water. And he was certain he had a number of broken ribs.

But it might prove to be his salvation yet.

He moved his bound hands along the surface, jerking back when they rubbed against a particularly sharp, jutted out portion. How had it not been more smoothed by the river's constant press?

Nevertheless, he now had a deeper wound to care for.

Although...

He pushed down his trepidation and shoved the bindings against the jutted piece of rock. It might be just what he needed to free himself.

As he worked with hands numbed by the cold, he struggled. At least it prevented him from feeling every abrasion he was certain he visited upon himself. Still, he rubbed the bindings and his hands. The water rushing over the rock and his wrists had reddened.

He did not let up his fervor for the task...no matter how the pain enveloped his awareness. Though he be broken and injured, he must get to Karin. This was his chance. Perhaps his one chance.

His muscles ached from clinging to the boulder. But he ignored their screams for release.

After some more moments of visiting even further injury on his hands, the first piece of rope gave way. Then he worked his hands and wrists to widen the gap. His hands proved slick from the mixture of water and blood.

He wasn't altogether certain he had the strength to continue. Or, even if he freed his hands, would he be able to make it to the bank. But he pushed on.

Moments later and more cutting of the rope, and he was free.

He wanted to cry out with joy but stifled that urge. He was still in danger.

Leaning and clinging to the boulder, he tried to assess his situation as the water buffeted him. He was some distance from the river's edge. And the current would have no mercy on him. Though if he could rub life back into his hands, he might have a chance.

His body did not want to continue. Every fiber of his being needed rest. But he fought those instincts and considered what his chances truly were.

How far down river had the current carried him? Where were Ulrich's men? Did they have a sense about where he was?

Scanning the embankment to either side of him, he saw no hint that anyone lingered, watching. Perhaps...just perhaps...though he suffered at the river's mercy, might it prove his salvation?

He looked heavenward. *Father, grant me mercy. And help me.*

That was all the thought he could spare as his flesh seared and pained him, pulling him toward a welcoming, warm darkness.

Again, he fought back. This was too important, and his opportunity too small.

He gathered several full gulps of air. It had to be now. Whether he was prepared or not.

Shoving off the rock, he moved toward the land to the east, as it was closer to his position.

The river taunted and tore at him, preventing his progress. It was as if it laughed at him. But he was in no mood to give in. He would die fighting.

Pressing impossibly harder, he prayed he moved even a little bit toward the side. A couple of times, the water succeeded in jerking him under for what felt like minutes at a time.

And, finally, his feet hit the river bottom. He rose as much as he could, which was a pitiful effort. Not able to be fully upright, he bent his knees, and relished a lessening of the water's tug on his body.

He shouted and grunted as he used his feet and hands to pull him ever closer to the grassy shore. His watery foe was angry, intensely so. But he was confident he had won.

Then, long moments later, he fell upon the dirt and grass. The air rushed from him, and he sucked in the second chance that he had been gifted. Letting the fresh air fill him with hope.

He did not know how long he lay there...or if he indeed lost consciousness for a few seconds. But as he brought his mind around to the present, he knew that something wasn't right. Had he, in fact, not made it to safety? Did he succumb to the river? Was he in heaven? Dare he open his eyes and confirm it?

For his body ached but was mostly numbed still by the cold.

Though, as he tuned his ears to his surroundings, he knew.

He was not alone.

His head throbbed as he turned it to confirm what his every sense had already told: one of Ulrich's mercenaries stood over him, a look of sick satisfaction on his face.

The darkness around Karin and Tomas was thick. Almost as thick as the space between their bodies. Too much had happened. Too much was at stake. And here she was thinking back to the past, when she should set her mind on what needed to be done to secure her husband's freedom.

"At last, that meddling whelp is gone," Tomas grumbled.

What exactly had happened between the two men? Karin was uncertain. But she looked in the direction Stepan had walked. There was no sign of him, but she would be ignorant to think he did not linger just out of sight. As well, she was grateful for it. For she wasn't confident about Tomas...his intentions nor the veracity of his words.

"He is not wrong," she said, jerking her regard toward Tomas. "It is foolishness for me to be alone with you. Not only for my reputation, but for my safety."

Even in the dimness, a nearby torch gave Karin a view of Tomas's solemn features. And his eyes which deepened in that moment.

"Is that what you think? That I would visit harm upon you?" His words were so gentle and his affect so tortured, she regretted her words. But only for a moment. Then she drew her thoughts to the present. Her childhood friend he may be, but he had spent the last so many years being hardened by who knew what...the least of which was serving as one of Ulrich's men.

"I cannot pretend all is well between us. I wonder..." Her words trailed as she caught back emotion rising in her throat. She could not betray what she truly felt and how she struggled. It wasn't right.

"What, Karin?" It did not escape that he used her Christian name again. "What do you wonder?" His voice was barely above a whisper. And the tension between them was as if he drew near though neither moved.

"I wonder if I know you at all." She pressed a firmness into her words that she wasn't certain she felt.

Then he did step closer. "You know better." His voice deepened. What did he attempt here? Was he so swayed by past memories that he forgot himself? Or was he drawn into the moment she sensed passing between them.

Enough! She could not—and would not—allow this.

Karin moved a step back, turning to slip outside the cell and setting the bars as a barrier between their bodies.

He could follow. And for a moment, she feared he might, but he remained in the cell. Perhaps not all was lost of her friend.

"Please," she said before clearing her throat, hoping that would clear her mind as well. "Tell me what you know of my husband." She put an emphasis on that last word that was likely not necessary. But she did so all the same. Was it for his benefit only? Or also hers?

He looked to the ground, and she sucked in a breath at the reprieve. For he had not taken his eyes off hers for one second. Indeed, it was as if she could breathe fully for a moment.

Then the pierce of green was upon her again. And she could not disguise the sharp inhale.

"You have to understand. It is a thin line I walk here, tenuous at best." His tone was clearer, as if he set any effort to sway her to the side.

"Why did you come here then?" She drew hands over her arms, crossing in front of her chest. Did she appear more defiant than she felt? At least her arms added one more barrier to her heart. "What are your intentions?"

He stepped closer, clasping his fingers about the bars. "I was sent. By Ulrich."

Her heart stopped. So, he was an agent for that monster. Had she erred in her judgment here? "No."

His features were downcast, but an eyebrow piqued as he looked at her once more. "Do you doubt it?"

"I cannot believe you would be in league with that man."

His glance seemed to home in on the wall behind her. "There are...things I have endured that I refuse to visit upon your mind. Things that...can change a man."

She shivered. Would the same be true of Pavel? The war had already altered him. Was he, even then, being tortured? Karin shook the uninvited images from her thoughts.

"No," he said, sighing. "I do not wish to disturb you more than I must. It is not fitting a flower so delicate be made to entertain such dark things."

She squared her shoulders. "I am stronger than you give me credit for. I have seen my fair share of hardship in these last years. Least of all your—" She bit her lip to keep anything further from escaping.

"Least of all my death?"

Her eyes stung, though she must suppress her softer emotions. Now was time for strength. For boldness. So, she only nodded, not trusting her voice.

He reached through the bars and laid a hand on her forearm. "If I live a thousand lives, I will not stop regretting putting you through that."

She wanted to pull away but didn't wish him to know that he affected her in the least.

"Maybe...things would have been different for us."

She shook her head, partly to deny his claim, partly to hide the watering of her eyes. "Stop."

"Karin," he breathed.

She jerked her head to face him. "Tell me what you know." Her words were hard.

The faintest slip in his features proved her tone had fulfilled its purpose. He drew his hand back to his side. "Your husband was set upon by ambush. The others with him died by those swords loyal to Ulrich."

"And...Pavel? Is he...?" She couldn't make herself say it.

"He is alive. At least, he was seven days past when I was still in the camp."

"What—" She paused and drew in a shaky breath. "What does Ulrich intend to do with him?"

Tomas didn't so much as flinch. "He will use him as a pawn to get closer to General Zizka's men. Then, he will kill Lord Krejik."

The words were delivered with such a lack of emotion. Moreso than Karin would have thought possible. Had Ulrich destroyed what was good in her childhood friend? Was he but a shell of the man he once was?

She pushed those thoughts out of mind. Her husband was her mission. "Do you know where they are camped?"

"Yes and no."

"Do you play games now?"

"I know where the camp was, but Ulrich had plans to proceed while I came here and insured you..." He paused. "...and your son were neutralized."

Karin shook at the mention of Jaromir. How did the evil man know of her and Pavel's son? Was there anything the man didn't know about them? "Neutralize? What does that mean?"

He stared at her; his eyes reflected the light of the flickering torch. And nothing more.

A chill ran down her spine. Something unsettled her about Tomas's affect. She stepped closer to the cell door. It would be best if she secured him until she could determine which side he was truly on.

But he moved toward the door's opening as well.

She grabbed for the door a second before he thrust out an arm to stop her. Widening her eyes, her gaze flew to his face. What might she do if he intended to aggress upon her? She had no weapon. No protection.

"Remember what I said," he was quick to say. "I would never harm you."

Should she trust him? She tugged at the door, but he would not permit it to move.

His body shifted closer to her.

And she froze. Completely paralyzed by indecision and fear.

He slid his free hand to cup the side of her face. "Believe me, Karin." His words were soft, defying his actions. "I won't let anything happen to you."

She shivered despite her resolve to keep herself in check.

He leaned toward her.

Would he press his lips to hers? Or seize the moment to entrap her? Either way, she found herself unable to move. His eyes were once again on hers, calling to her. She remembered those same eyes drawing her in as a younger woman about to experience her first kiss.

She should push him away or pull back. But she didn't move.

"The dowager baroness sent me down here," a gruff voice announced.

Karin jerked away from Tomas, spinning to see Sir Marek but several paces away.

"I see that she was right to be concerned." Sir Marek stepped closer. "For something foul goes here."

CHAPTER 13
ANICKA & LUKAS

Lukas stared at the priest, resolute in his statement. He would not continue with this sham. With forcing an innocent to bear his burden.

A sharp intake of air beside him drew Lukas's attention to Anicka.

Her eyes rolled, and she went limp.

Lukas barely had time to react, but he did, gathering her into his arms. A wave of uneasiness filled him as he looked at her. How unwell was she?

Muttering to the side threatened to pull his thoughts from her, but he couldn't tear his gaze away. He tugged at her until he raised her enough to loop an arm under her knees and lift her.

What was he to do? He needed to get her settled somewhere safe. Somewhere that the healer might attend her.

Moving toward the back of the chapel, he was somewhat surprised he didn't meet with resistance. Where was her mother?

He didn't have a moment to appease his conscience, however. All his focus was on Anicka. Slipping from the chapel, he pressed on toward the nearby bedchambers.

As he pushed onward, a sigh and moan emitted from Anicka. Was she waking? He paused and heard the halting of footfalls behind him. Others followed, but he cared not who.

Shifting his attention back to Anicka, he watched as her eyelids fluttered open.

She shook her head and then gripped at the air.

"All is well," Lukas soothed, wishing he could calm her.

Her hands clung to the front of his doublet.

"What?" Her response was breathy. "Where am I? Wha—what happened?"

He pressed her closer. "There will be time for answering questions. For now, you need to be seen."

She shook her head and her hands became fists. "No. I assure you. I am well."

He did not think that was true.

Her gaze wandered to those behind. She flinched at what she encountered.

It disturbed Lukas so much he turned to see what might have bothered her so.

Her mother and maidservants were there, a scowl on the countess's face. Was she not concerned after her daughter?

Lukas pushed these thoughts to the side. He couldn't dwell on them right now.

His mother came alongside him, touching his shoulder. "Let's take her to the solar." Then, stepping in front of Lukas, she led the way.

"No," came a silent groan from Anicka. "Please," she whispered. "I do not want all of this melee. It is nothing."

He refused to look at her, though something about her tone pinched his heart. And his senses were overwhelmed with the scent of roses. From her hair perhaps? As well, the feel of her body securely in his arms warmed him.

She buried her face in his shoulder as she shook. Her breath on his neck was intoxicating. Almost too much so. It became difficult to concentrate on what he was doing. But he followed his mother until they reached the room that belonged to his parents.

Mother ushered him in, indicating the bed. But she blocked further intrigue, permitting only Anicka's mother to enter. Then she commanded a maidservant to get fresh water, and another to go for the healer.

Lukas lay Anicka on the bed, breathing in the scent of her fully. Had he meant to? Or was it just the exertion of having carried her that caused him to inhale so deeply?

Still, Anicka clung to him, preventing him from standing upright.

He pressed her hands as he disentangled them from himself.

She did release him in the next moment, slipping her hands from his.

Seeking her eyes, he looked to her face. Her features were drawn and her eyes pleading. Because she did not wish to have a fuss made over her? Or was there more?

"Thank you, Sir Lukas, for your assistance." Countess Vorisek stepped forward. "But I need to attend my daughter in private."

Anicka stiffened beside him. And even he resisted a shiver as the hairs on the back of his neck prickled. At best, this woman was forcing her daughter into an unwanted marriage. What else might be behind that?

"I will remain," he insisted.

Anicka looked away. What went on here? Could he unravel it? Did he wish to?

But he knew...he cared. More deeply than he intended to. And he had to know.

"Sir Lukas, surely you can see that would be most inappropriate." Countess Vorisek admonished him.

"We'll all remain," his mother said, as if to settle nerves in the room. It did not.

The countess bristled but did not speak further.

Tension filled the spaces between Lukas, his mother, and the countess, who had not made a single move to ensure her daughter's comfort or wellbeing. He was becoming all the more concerned at what that might indicate of Anicka's treatment.

The rush of skirts in the corridor gave Lukas reason to think the healer had come. And, as the older woman appeared in the doorway, he thanked God for her timing.

"What goes?" the woman asked as she moved toward the bed.

"The lady fainted," Lukas said.

"Fainted?" The healer hovered over Anicka. "Lady, are you uneasy? Can you breathe well?"

Anicka sucked in a breath as if to test that. "Aye."

"I will never understand the fascination with corsets which prevent one from catching air fully." The older woman looked in Anicka's eyes and pressed fingers to her neck and then to her wrist.

Lukas became aware that he was out of place. Even if he wasn't ordered out of the room, perhaps it would be best he go. He glanced at his mother and then the countess. She fairly fumed. It would not surprise if flames came from her nostrils, she seemed so enraged.

What did go here, indeed?

He looked to Anicka, who tried to assure the healer she was well. Just as she had him. As if she felt it wrong for others to be so concerned after her. Was that how she was treated?

"How is she?" he demanded, his tone more gruff than intended.

The healer turned toward him. "I think she is well. She does not seem ailed in any way. Perhaps rest is all that is required."

Lukas nodded. "As you finish your examination, I would like to speak with Lady Anicka." Then he looked to his mother and the countess. "In private."

"That is unseemly!" Countess Vorisek flared.

"Vladimira will remain," Mother said gently as she stepped toward the countess. "There is no need to worry."

Countess Vorisek looked to him and then to his mother. It would be an affront to contradict the lady of the castle. And, at first, it seemed she might do just that. But at length, she nodded and allowed herself to be led out of the room.

The healer caught his gaze, "I will stoke the fire and warm some water."

He would have responded, but his attention was on Anicka.

She moved to sit up, but he rushed forward. "There is no need for you to push yourself."

Looking at the floor, she said, "I do not wish to feel so...vulnerable when you say what you must." Her head tilted upward, and her gaze met his briefly before she turned away. As if she had reason to be ashamed.

Ashamed in *his* presence. That was odd. Was he not the sinner here? The one who attempted the unthinkable?

Still, he did not stop her as she rose to a sitting position and drew her arms about herself as if chilled.

"Vladimira will have that fire warming soon enough." He wished to reassure her. To make her comfort his highest duty. And the urge to touch her became almost irresistible. Would she pull back if he tried?

He laced his fingers together in front of himself. That was probably the best occupation for them.

"What...do you wish to speak with me about?" Her words were timid, her voice shaky.

He considered her for a moment.

She appeared so small, vulnerable even though sitting. She wouldn't meet his gaze again and that bothered.

A desire to protect her, to shield her rose within his gut. Did she desire such? From him?

He could no longer hold in the thing that plagued and he blurted, "Do you wish to be free of me?"

Anicka's ears rang with Lukas's question. What did he think? That she had a choice? That her life didn't hinge on his decision?

"I...don't understand," she managed, peering at him.

He pushed a hand through his hair. "I won't force you to marry me."

Then he didn't realize that her options were few. Limited. And he the best of them. How to tell him it was not he that forced her hand, but he was her best way out?

He moved to the window and all was silent for a few moments, but for the healer tending the fire.

"I *do* wish to marry you." Her words were quiet, even to her ears.

"Do you?" He whirled toward her. "Then why the tears?"

"What?"

"Why were you crying at our ceremony? If it was not for reluctance to marry, I cannot determine the source of your tears." His hands were fisted tightly to his sides.

She pushed out a breath. "It was not that."

He stared at her.

Would she ever be able to be honest with him? How would he react if he knew he were but the lesser of the evils before her? Maybe not even that. For she did care for him. Perhaps not for a love match, but enough to build a future upon.

Lukas turned back to whatever lay outside beyond the window.

Would she trust first? Be open first? But could she risk it? What if he knew and rejected her all the same? For certain, he would not wish to be bound to her as an escape route.

She cleared her throat. "It was...the timing of the wedding that surprised me. That is all. I have not changed my mind since yestereve. It is my intention and desire to be wed to you." There. Not altogether true, but no glaring falsehood either.

He shifted to look at her once more. "I will not force you," he repeated.

"I know that." She offered him a small smile. Where was the boy that had chased her in the meadows beyond these castle walls? Where was the young man who had sought to kiss her not too many years past? Was there anything left of his consideration for her? Had it ever been there? Or had she only been a means to an end?

Moving his weight to his other foot, he appeared to think on her words. And his eyes, bright and hopeful, met hers. "As I know you would sacrifice yourself for another."

The words caught her off-guard. He did remember their days as playmates. Enough to notice this chink in her armor. Was that not reason to hope?

She stood, wavering slightly.

He stepped forward.

Anicka held up a hand to stop him. She was not an invalid. Nor was she injured. She would not be treated as such.

When she steadied herself and looked up, she noticed that only an arm's length of distance separated their bodies.

She took a step and, in a bold move that defied how her heart pounded, she reached for his hands.

He slid them into hers.

"There is something of the young friendship here, then." She offered a smile, hoping it warmed him as much as his touch heated her. "And I think…it may be a fitting foundation for a marriage."

His eyebrows gathered. "Are you certain?" His words were tender, almost pained.

Her smile spread wider, warming even her as she reflected on their many years of acquaintance and friendship. "Yes."

He searched her features. What did he see? What he wanted to? Or did he see her?

Now that was too much to hope. For she was ever the hindrance, the burden…she was just transferring herself to be another's problem. Selfish, really. But she told herself that he needed her, too. It wasn't perfect, but it was something.

Lukas turned toward the healer that Anicka had all but forgotten was still in the room. "Is the lady able to be upright for mayhap an hour more?"

Anicka's heart raced.

Vladimira nodded, her hand over her heart. "Yes, my lord."

"Then let's get to the chapel." Then he smiled. "Perhaps the audience has dispersed, and we might marry without the press of so many eyes."

She gripped his hands tighter. "That sounds perfect."

He pulled one hand from hers and set the other on his elbow. Then, with a sparkle in his eyes, he led her out of the solar and up the stairs.

To her future. To *their* future. Whatever it may be.

CHAPTER 14
PATRICIE & STEPAN

Stepan could not help it. He was bothered. He was sore. He was bitter. And so, he brooded. What was in Karin's head? What was she thinking? Did she have any sense of propriety about her?

If Stepan didn't care so much for his friend Pavel, he would have been out of here as soon as dawn broke. But, as it was, he owed Pavel. And he doubted he would ever be free of the demons plaguing him if he didn't secure Pavel's forgiveness.

So, stay he would.

It didn't matter that his heart tugged at him to flee into the countryside. He set a saddle atop his mount. It would be so easy to do just that.

No, this was only a chance to get some space and clear his head. He needed to refocus his energy on what was truly important here. And try to see past Karin's actions.

A stable hand watched Stepan go through the motions of readying his horse for his ride. But Stepan ignored him. The man was eager to be helpful, most certainly, but Stepan could manage on his own. The last thing he wanted was the man crowding him.

As he tightened the straps for the last time, keeping his back to the intrusive onlooker, Stepan ached for the rush of the wind against his skin. He could not get in the saddle fast enough. Too much had happened. Too much he was injured by Karin's actions and his own suspicions regarding Tomas.

And too much he longed for Patricie. How was it that she had become so much a part of his daily thoughts and musings? As if she had become a part of *him*.

Had she?

He led his horse past the other stabled animals and into the open. Then he lifted himself into the saddle. And, without a look back, spurred the animal into motion.

A trot became a canter, but it wasn't enough. Pressing the destrier for more, the animal gave him a full gallop.

The wind bit at him, a hint of a chill about it. But he relished it. The sting reminded him he was alive and he felt. Dear Lord, how he felt. Everything—anxious for Pavel, conflicted over Karin's behavior, untrusting of Tomas and his motives, and longing for his Patricie.

He had tamped this desire down so he might focus on what demanded his attention—namely Tomas. And even Karin. But as he became one with the speed of the horse, the press of air pushed all of that behind him. And thoughts of Patricie remained.

As much as he wished to hold her and take comfort from her kind heart, he was glad he had instructed her to stay in Tabor. She would be too much of a distraction were she here. His thoughts were clouded enough with her so many miles away.

But he permitted himself to draw up imaginings of her face. Her smile. Her lips.

Almighty, he did miss her.

The horse's footing altered. How long had the animal been gifting him such speed? Perhaps it would be best to find a stream and refresh the destrier.

Stepan turned the horse into the forest line as he bade the animal slow.

The horse seemed prepared to do just that.

Moments later, Stepan dropped from the saddle and allowed the horse to drink his fill. Stepan scanned the area. All was as it should be—the trees engulfed and enclosed him and the horse, gifting them shelter from the wind and sun. For a moment, all was still but for the small movements of the animal.

Stepan closed his eyes and sucked in a deep breath. If only it could cleanse him as completely as it rid his lungs of all but fresh air. To every part. Could it?

He looked heavenward. Patricie had spoken to him often of her faith. But he did not share it. A friendship with God? It sounded preposterous. Even if he believed such a thing were possible, did he want that? His life had not been without trial. So much that he doubted he could put stock in a kind God.

Regardless, he did not dismiss the idea completely. It was obvious that God existed. But care for his creation individually? That was a bit far fetched.

Stepan's thoughts wandered to the previous evening as he had hid in the darkness of the dungeon, wishing he might hear Karin's words more clearly. For she and Tomas had spoken in hushed tones.

Then Sir Marek had come to the dungeon. For what reason, Stepan was uncertain. Did he know that Karin had ventured into the bowels of the castle? If so, how?

Still, Stepan could do naught but remain concealed as Sir Marek secured Tomas's cell and escorted Karin above stairs. Even as Stepan had wished to discover the extent of Karin and Tomas's connection, he had been grateful Sir Marek brought it to an end.

Rustling of leaves pulled Stepan from his thoughts. Was that the product of the strong breeze? Something was unsettled in Stepan. His senses were on alert. For what?

Did others bring their horses near for drink?

He surveyed the area and did not see anything to confirm such. But he couldn't shake the disquiet within himself. Someone was there, watching him. He would stake his life on it.

Readying his blade, he stilled to listen more acutely.

There...among the trees to the right...movement. Or perhaps it was merely a disruption of the color filling the branches. He stepped closer, homing his vision to discern more clearly.

Yes, someone moved about the trunks ahead. He knew it. What should be his plan? What viable plan might he have? If the man had a weapon, it would not be wise to approach. And Stepan was most certain that someone sneaking about in the forest had nothing valiant driving them.

And he would be a fool to think he had not been spotted.

"Who goes?" he called. It was his best option. So, they both knew the other had been spotted.

More movement. And a man, smaller that Stepan, shot out from the bushes and ran.

Stepan shifted into a run in pursuit. But he could not match the smaller man's speed. Soon enough, the man had evaded him completely. No. Not completely. He must still be about.

Finding himself at the edge of the tree line, Stepan crouched and looked around, straining his ears for better acuity.

The earth vibrated. Was that...hoofbeats?

Too late, he realized that man had secured Stepan's horse and was bearing down toward him, sword at the ready. The man swung and the blade grazed Stepan's arm as he jerked to the side. He spun in time to meet the next swing with his own weapon.

This was far from over.

Patricie longed for rest. For even just a moment. But Sir Antonin had been insistent, pushing them onward before dawn graced the edges of Patricie's awareness. But she complied. Because this was not about her. It was about keeping Eva and Michal safe.

The horses, likewise, seemed to be heavier of step than earlier in the day. Had they, too, worn out their muscles on this journey?

But as they crested a hill, she spotted it. Sitting on the horizon, in the distance, the newly erected walls of a castle.

Please let this be our destination. Our sanctuary.

Patricie hoped that the knight and Eva were not wrong about the Baron and Baroness of the castle welcoming them—even with the child's mark. Though, Eva assured her again and again that these were friends, and that they had provided Sir Antonin to guard Eva on her journey. She told also that they were not likely swayed by such nonsense as the devil marking an innocent.

As if anyone should be. Michal was a child. A *child*. And he was unfortunate enough to have been marked at birth. Nothing more. The earlier words of the priest stung as they reverberated in her mind. What was the world coming to?

Sir Antonin, in the lead, held up a hand to slow the small group. Perhaps it was time to refresh the horses.

Patricie hated to stop so close to their destination, but she again would yield to the knight's better judgment. He was likely more aware of the horses and their needs than she.

However, as they came to a stop, Sir Antonin remained as he was, still as death. Why?

He then cocked his head to one side and to the other. The inaction was maddening.

"What is it?" Patricie could not stop the question. Surely, she was reaching the end of her patience. Even more so than she had realized.

A jerk of his arm and his finger pressed his lips—a clear demand for silence.

For the next several moments, all Patricie could hear was the snorting of the horses, and the small sounds coming from Michal.

She held her breath. Maybe if she did so and counted to ten, she would calm herself. But as she reached seven, she heard something more in the distance. What was that?

The clanging of metal?

Sir Antonin turned. "Keep inside the tree line. And don't make a sound."

Then he took off. What was his intention? His plan? How was that sound signaling something more important than watching over Eva, Patricie, and the defenseless child?

As she watched, Sir Antonin moved toward the open field, but turned.

Soon enough, a horse tore through the trees, racing as if for its life. Or for the life of the man it bore.

The horse and rider passed by without offering them so much as a glance, leaving nothing in his wake but the echo of the hoofbeats.

How odd.

A whistle drew her focus back to the knight. He signaled for her and Eva to follow.

Looking to her sister, Patricie wanted to argue such action, but Eva simply spurred her horse onward. What was Patricie to do then, but go along?

As they neared, Sir Antonin called to them in a harsh whisper. "Stay behind me. And stay close."

Eva reined in after him and Patricie did so as well.

They moved closer to the forest line.

As they came to the opening, she heard rustling of grass and clothing and grunting. What was that? Rather...who was that?

Sir Antonin dismounted and drew his sword. He let the weapon precede him as he crept forward.

One second, he was on his guard, the next, he relaxed the tight stance and rushed ahead.

What went here?

Eva looked to Patricie. "Help me."

Patricie dropped from her horse and assisted Eva and Michal to the ground.

"We should stay here," Patricie murmured. "It might be dangerous."

Eva shook her head. "Sir Antonin would have said as much."

Patricie gripped Eva's arm.

Her sister shot her a harsh look. "If you wish to remain, you may do so. I intend to stay close. As directed."

There was more to it than that—Eva's curiosity clearly pulled at her. Even had Sir Antonin not asked them to remain close behind, the dark haired beauty would have pushed on. It was her nature.

Patricie's stomach flipped. The whole thing made her rather uneasy. But she swallowed and moved forward with Eva, not taking her hand from her sister's arm.

They stepped just beyond the trees to find Sir Antonin leaning over a man, who shifted even as the knight had restrained him. Or had he?

Sir Antonin called over his shoulder toward Patricie. "You are needed."

Whomever was injured had been well enough subdued by Sir Antonin by the looks of it. Still, Patricie's hands shook until she clasped them together. But after only a moment's hesitation, she stepped forward. If someone was hurt, she would do what she could. No matter what harm they might have intended this day.

Picking up her step, she fairly sprinted to Sir Antonin's side.

"What are *you* doing here?" an angry voice all but growled.

A voice she knew all too well.

Stepan.

As her gaze settled on his, she took in the distressed lines of his face. Was he upset with her? Was he not relieved—not even happy—to see her?

She pushed her disappointment and hurt to the side and fell to her knees, glancing over his person to determine his injury.

He bled from one of his upper arms. And he pressed a hand to his head. Had he sustained a blow to his head? Some other kind of wound?

She bit back a gasp at seeing the man she so cared for bleed. A quick examination of the cut on his arm proved it nothing worth concern. But the head...that may be another story.

He allowed her to tend him, but as she pushed his hand to the side for a better look at his injury, he seethed, "I told you to stay in Tabor."

Her heart dropped, but she pushed even that away. She had a job to do. And she would do it. "Be still."

He obeyed and bit at his lip as she moved closer to the red, swollen place on his head. "What happened here?"

"I was attacked. And...he got in a good thump on my head before taking off on *my* horse." Was he more upset about his animal than he cared for her wellbeing?

She turned to Sir Antonin. "Do we have any bandages? We need to stop the bleeding in his arm and perhaps wrap his head."

"Do not bother. I am well enough." Stepan tried to sit up as he glared at the knight. Only to press the back of his hand to his mouth. Did he fight to hold to his last meal?

She pressed his uninjured shoulder and chest. "Please, lie down. Let me tend you."

He looked up at her. "I didn't want you to come here."

"Not much I can do about that right now, is there?" She tried to keep her emotions out of her voice. Those she could deal with later. Not now. Not in front of Sir Antonin and...Eva—she who was already unsure about Stepan as a suitable match for her sister.

"Please, Lord Dvorak, be still." She placed a hand to his elbow, hoping the gesture would calm him.

It did not. He remained agitated and restless. "The man. Did he...?"

Sir Antonin spoke up. "He got away."

"No." Stepan grimaced.

"Who was he?" Sir Antonin pressed.

Patricie shot him a hard look. Now was not the time for questions. She needed to calm her patient. And that's what Stepan was at this moment—her patient. Nothing more and nothing less.

Sir Antonin's expression remained impassive, unfazed by Patricie's silent command.

"I believe...he was an enemy scout."

"A Royalist soldier?" The knight's eyes widened. "On Krejik lands?"

The green in Stepan's eyes darkened. "Worse. One of Ulrich's men."

CHAPTER 15
ANICKA & LUKAS

Married. Anicka sighed as she scanned the Great Hall, full of celebrating nobles. So...at last, she was *married*. Last night she had gone to bed, alone and uncertain. Today she became a wife...and would forever be bound to Lukas Vitek. As overwhelming as that was, she found herself more in wonderment about the future. Especially the next several hours and what they might bring.

She stole a glance at her husband of only a couple hours. Was he so changed from the boy...the young man she had known? What had happened to so alter him that would make him a criminal? There was nothing in her that was able to put thoughts of his crime and him in the same space.

He shifted his regard toward her.

She jerked back at the sudden glare in her direction. What was this?

His features betrayed his surprise...and something else. The downturn of his lips proved him injured by her reaction.

Was she scared of him? Her reaction had surprised her as well.

She pushed out a breath and leaned back into her chair, hoping she might communicate her apology with a gentle gaze. But as she turned back to him, he was no longer looking in her direction. Could she hope he would? Dare she reach out to him?

Her nerves wound into a ball in the pit of her stomach, and she was paralyzed. This would not do.

Yes, the wedding night lay ahead for her. And she had every right to be anxious. But this was more. His confession yestereve plagued her as it had not done before.

Was it possible he had raised a hand...or a weapon...to another?

She shook her head. Such was preposterous! He was a kind soul. A gentle man. Though his features were chiseled into a grim expression in that moment, and his eyes hard...she knew it was so. And she would continue to believe that. Her sanity depended on it.

For the alternative was that she had wed a man capable of great harm. And without the scruples to hold himself in check.

A mostly shrill laugh echoed in the room. Mother. This was indeed a rather joyous occasion for the older woman. For she had successfully rid herself of Anicka. Had she been so much for Mother to bear? It had never been her intention. That did not mean it wasn't so.

Her goblet was scooted closer to her hand. Looking in that direction, she held back her reaction. For Lukas once more had settled his gaze on her. And though there was a hint of guilt and hurt about him, his mouth tipped slightly in a small smile.

"For your nerves," he said low.

She reached a shaking hand for the vessel. Never one to overindulge in wine, she pondered the wisdom of his words. Yes. That might be exactly what she needed to calm her heart and mind.

Lifting it to her lips, she allowed the cool liquid to pour down her throat. And was surprised to find the burn much stronger. This was different than the watered-down wine she typically had. This was more...fire.

She set widened eyes on Lukas, but he had once more turned away.

Was he anxious, too, about what lay ahead? That seemed counter to everything she had heard of a husband's appetites and a wife's obligation to meet them. Perhaps that's all this was...a means to an end.

As much as her heart ached for more, she could not begrudge her new husband. For this marriage had done for her what she'd wanted—freed her from her mother's grasp.

Yes, she was certain she could be a dutiful wife. And mayhap find in it some freedom to do as she pleased outside of the solar. Perhaps.

She continued to drink for she found it soothed. More and more. And a pleasant warmth filled her core and spread to her limbs. Was this due to the drink? Or something else? Lukas's closeness?

A maidservant continued to fill her cup as often as Anicka imbibed from it. And soon enough, Anicka found her head swimming and her thoughts difficult to follow. What was this lovely sensation? For sooth, her stomach was no longer in knots.

An uproar came from the center of the high table.

Anicka's ears seemed muffled. She could not hear clearly enough to discern the words.

But Lukas looked to her, his gaze searching.

She stared at him. Goodness, he was handsome. It brought a smile to her face.

He frowned. Then stood with the others around him.

Where were they going? What went here?

Lukas leaned in. "Lady Anicka, it is time."

Time? For what? She swayed a bit as she stood.

His hands shot out to steady her. "My lady!" He looked to her goblet and frowned. Was he angry? Disappointed?

She couldn't bear to disappoint one more person. But try as she might, she couldn't seem to collect her senses.

He set an arm about her and leaned closer. "Lean on me."

She did so—a necessary thing. For she found her feet quite difficult to control. Would she be able to climb the stairs? As much as it should bother, she couldn't find it within herself to care. In fact, the realization of her slippery feet made her chuckle. And she slapped a hand to her mouth to stifle the sound.

Lukas's arms about her stiffened.

His very strong arms. Yes, he was a man of great strength. Probably muscles worked and honed in knighthood training. It was rather nice to be held by those arms.

The warmth in her stomach gave way to a slight twisting. What was wrong with her?

"I am not certain I am well," she moaned.

He paused and knocked on the door in front of them. Had they made it up the stairs then?

Her lady's maid opened the door. "Lady Anicka."

"Make certain she is prepared." Lukas's voice was neither tender, nor harsh. But as if he were bored with the whole affair.

Is that how this was? Did he find her tiresome?

She frowned and leaned forward as he released her.

The lady's maid clutched her as Anicka lost her footing.

Lukas grunted and closed the door.

What had she wrought here?

How could he have watched that happen? Lukas groaned as he loosened the ties of his tunic. Anicka had clearly been upset... nervous. All he had wanted was to offer some liquid courage. It never occurred to him that she would continue drinking until she had lost all her senses.

But that was what happened. And he was left to face it.

He looked to the bed and the priest moving beside it. What a horrid tradition...to have a man of the cloth and others present when the bride and groom were put to bed. It was all the more keenly felt this eve, knowing the state of his bride and her anxiety. Perhaps, at least, that had faded into her loss of clarity.

Lukas's parents chatted casually as if this practice were the most normal thing in the world. Did they think such?

His father caught his eye and looked away. Could Father not even manage to meet his gaze anymore? How vile was Lukas to the man? How deep did his disappointment go?

Lukas's gaze fell to the floor. He deserved every bit of it. And more.

Now, he had dragged Anicka into his shame. How had he allowed that to happen? Even with every trepidation he had felt.

But it was done. All that remained was the consummation. Though he was reluctant to move forward, knowing her state of mind. Or rather her lack of a state of mind.

Still, avoiding this next part was not done. It was only honorable to seal their vows this way. It was what was expected. Even by Anicka.

The door squeaked and he looked up. There she was, scantily clad in her chemise. For everyone to see. How was this not frowned upon?

The men in the room did not even try to hide the appreciation in their eyes.

Lukas fairly boiled at the looks thrown in her direction. Perhaps it was best she had imbibed so much. For she seemed oblivious to the leers thrown her way.

She didn't appear as confident as he'd expected either, though. Her shaking hands translated into shivers in her shoulders and arms. Was she cold? Or apprehensive? So small, so delicate. The desire to wrap her in his arms and shield her from these men—and her own fears—overwhelmed him. Yet the protective urge rushed through every part of him, taking hold of his heart.

It drew him to step to her and take her hands.

She kept her gaze on the floor, on his chest perhaps, but no higher.

He rubbed thumbs across the backs of her hands, ignoring the audience they should not have.

"My lady," he managed to whisper despite the thickness in his throat.

She peered up at him. And for all he could see, she was shamed. By her behavior moments before? Her lack of attire? Or her fear of what was to come?

"Out," he seethed the word.

Several gazes shot to him. He could feel the intensity of their curiosity.

Scanning the room, he spoke again. "Everyone. Out."

"But I must—" the priest started.

"Do as you must in the next two minutes." Lukas glared at the priest. "While everyone else leaves."

"This is not proper," the Countess muttered.

Lukas fixed a hard stare on her. "I don't care."

The Countess bristled under his scrutiny. "Well, I *never*..."

"Regardless, you will all take your leave." He let his glare wander over those who were perhaps surprised into inaction. "Now." The last word was almost growled.

Only then did he look to his wife again. She bit at her lip, her cheeks all the more reddened, and her eyelids pressed down.

He hadn't wanted to make this worse for her, but he could not allow them both to be a spectacle. Certainly not her. What had she done to earn such?

The bystanders looked to the Baron Vitek. Who shrugged and, taking his wife's arm, moved to the door and out of the room. Others trailed out behind him.

Only then could Lukas breathe again.

The priest murmured a few words over the bed and, with one more long look at Lukas, exited the room.

Lukas then directed his full attention to Anicka. He rubbed hands up and down her arms, hoping that might calm her shivering. It did not.

"It is all right. Everyone is gone," he soothed.

She continued to tremble.

"Lady," he said, tipping her chin up so that she would look at him. "I'm not going to hurt you."

She nodded. "I know."

"How..." He paused and cleared his throat. "How are you feeling?"

If possible, her face tinged brighter. "Better. I...am so sorry for drinking so much."

He set a hand to the side of her face. "Don't. It is my fault for encouraging you."

Her eyes widened as they settled once more on his. "You are too kind." The words were barely whispered.

"Lady..." He stopped himself and opted for her Christian name. "Anicka..."

Her eyebrows drew upward at his more intimate address.

"Nothing will happen here that you don't want."

Her brows furrowed. "But, we are expected to—"

"I don't care what is expected." His words were harsher than he'd intended.

She flinched.

He set his other hand to her face, now framing her features. "I'm not a monster."

She pulled in a ragged breath, and when she exhaled, much of the tension in her body went with the pent up air.

He smiled at that. It had been his true desire to ease her trepidations.

She set her hands to his forearms. "Do you...not wish to...?" Her sentence trailed and she seemed to lose her nerve.

He ran a thumb across her lips, silencing her. "Don't think that."

Her lips parted at his touch. They were quite irresistible. And he became all the more aware that they were underdressed for this contact. But he didn't care. Those pink lips pulled him in, drawing him irresistibly to her. As gently as he could, he slanted his mouth over hers.

She shivered.

He wrapped his arms about her. And though he intended to remain gentle, he deepened their contact.

She melted to him.

It was intoxicating.

Her body pressed to his; he trailed kisses over her face and to her neck.

She clung to him as if he were the only thing keeping her upright. It did little to dampen his ardor.

And as he encouraged her to move to the bed with him, he sensed resistance.

Pulling back, he looked into her eyes.

There was fear there. And resignation. Was that all this was to her?

She still gripped at the front of his tunic, but not due to a passion within her. Her knuckles were paled. She was afraid of him and what he might intend here. As if she were bound by nothing more than duty.

He loosed her fingers from his shirt and sat her upon the bed. The blood pumping through him drowned out most thought. But he held to a thread of control. And stepped back from her.

There was surprise in her eyes. As well as something else...something that pained him to see in her reaction to the space between them—hope. Did she hope that he would leave her be? Walk away?

He pushed out a breath and ran a hand through his hair as he tried to cool himself.

"Is something wrong?" Even the lilt of her voice held a hint of hope.

"No." His throat scratched as he pressed the word out. "No."

Confusion registered over her features. But she did not try to stop him as he moved across the room. "I am not...right." Her words were timid.

He looked back from his place near the hearth. It was his turn to be confused.

A tear slid down the side of her face.

Stepping back in her direction, he wanted to gather her to his chest once more. But that might make it impossible to walk away this night. So he stopped himself and, with great reluctance, turned his back to her.

Her sniffling threatened his resolve.

And it took every bit of strength in him to exit the room. But he did.

<h1 style="text-align:center">CHAPTER 16
KARIN & PAVEL</h1>

Karin sank into the warm water in the tub. How could she have let these things happen? Sir Marek—and probably her mother-in-law—were clearly suspicious of her affection for Tomas. As, truthfully, should they be.

She resurfaced, breaking through the level of the water to take in air once more. As she did, she wiped excess water from her face and rubbed her hair back.

And suddenly, she realized she was done. It had been enough—all the tarrying and currying favor. In short, there had been enough delay. She must mount a rescue for her husband. And she needed answers in order to do so.

But were those answers to come from Tomas? If he was even privy to such information, would he reveal it?

There was reason to doubt that.

Perhaps it would be best to leave him in the dungeon and take her chances with only the knights of the castle. That was certainly safest. But was it the wisest thing? If Tomas had knowledge of Ulrich's movements and his camp, why abandon hope of his aid? If he would help...that was.

A knock on her door was followed by a feminine voice echoing in the space—her lady's maid. How long had she been in the tub? Had the young woman sought her lady in worry?

"Come in," Karin called, settling herself amid the cooling water.

The girl rushed in and grabbed for a towel, her movements quick and decided. "My lady, a group of travelers are here to speak with you."

That was suspicious indeed.

"Travelers?" she queried. "I wasn't expecting anyone. Has Sir Marek been notified?"

"Of course, my lady." The woman stood by the large metal container, her movements hesitant and jerky. But she held up the towel in an offering to her lady. "It was Sir Marek who requested your presence."

Karin frowned.

As reluctant as the younger woman seemed to urge Karin out of her bath, she stood prepared, apparently, to do just that regardless.

Karin stood and the girl wrapped the cloth about her, gripping to her wet skin, but only slightly breaking the chill in the air.

The girl rubbed the towel at Karin's skin, but she waved her lady's maid away.

"Did he happen to say who had requested my presence?" Her irritation at being summoned thusly and at such an hour poured through her tone.

The girl flinched. "He did not."

Karin let out a sigh. It was not the girl's fault. Sir Marek would have to answer for that.

Stepping forward, she allowed the younger woman to dry her off and then to redress her to receive. The process took longer than usual...or so it seemed. Perhaps it was naught but her impatience tugging at her to make it seem so.

Before long, Karin strode down the corridor and to the stairs that would drop her into the Great Hall.

As she rounded the last corner, she peered over, while doing her best to maintain her composure. It was not necessary for all to know she was called from a bath, one that she had believed would be the last thing of the day. But as her gaze caught on Sir Marek, she also noted three figures—a man and two women. And one woman carried a bundle of sorts.

At the rustle of her skirts, all turned to face her.

Sir Marek stepped closer. "Sir Stepan came upon this group while scouting the area around the castle. He was wounded and is now being tended. But I thought you may have questions for them."

Karin looked closer upon those before her. These were not inter-lopers...or strangers. This was Sir Antonin, the knight she'd sent to protect Zdenek's Lady Eva, who was among the trio. And another woman she wasn't familiar with stood nearby.

But anyone companionable with Eva was welcome here.

There was a fatigue about Eva's eyes and a concern creasing lines in Sir Antonin's.

"My dear friend," Karin rushed the remaining distance to them. "You have come!"

Lady Eva spoke out then, her tone desperate. "I understand that my husband is here? Where? Is he well?"

As Karin neared, she noted that the bundle in Eva's arms wriggled.

Eva bounced the cloth covered lump and made a faint shushing sound. Almost like Karin did when her Jaromir was disrupted. Was this then...a child? But how?

Karin paused, looking between Eva and the blanketed figure and back. "What is this?" She kept her tone gentle as she slowed her rush to a soft footfall, curious about the young one and trying to guess at how this came to be.

Eva removed the cloth wrapped over the child. It was, indeed, a small, dark-haired boy. His chubby cheeks split with a small grin. His wide dark eyes shone that he was clearly intrigued by her.

"Hello there, little sir. And who might you be?"

"His name is Michal," Eva crooned. "And he is a very good boy."

She bounced him once more. "I came across him in Prague. And promised the nuns who found him that I would love him with my whole heart."

Eva's companion did not seem as thrilled as she was. Rather, she looked worn and weary.

Karin settled her gaze back on Eva's concerned eyes. "Lord Ambroz is here and well, resting above stairs and recovering."

"I would like to have a look at him." The other raven-haired woman stepped forward.

"Oh, pardon my thoughtlessness," Eva begged off. "This is my sister, Patricie. She is a gifted healer."

Karin offered her a smile. "It is wonderful to meet you. I think so very highly of your sister."

An uneasy smile graced Patricie's lips. What was that about?

Karin once more looked between the three and Michal. She turned to direct Sir Marek and his guards to move on. But she spun and found that he was just at her elbow.

"Sir Marek!" She attempted—perhaps in vain—to disguise her surprise. "These are welcomed guests in my home. You may move on with your men. Sir Antonin, I shall want a full report."

Sir Marek lingered still, waiting for some time before speaking low, "There is the other matter, my lady."

She waved him off. Speaking of Tomas right now was the last thing she wanted to do. The very last thing. "We shall discuss it on the morrow."

Sir Marek opened his mouth as if he would naysay her. But he closed it, bowed, and signaled most of the men about the contingency to fall into line with him.

Then she, Patricie, Eva, and Michal were alone, save a couple of guards and the maidservants making ready the space for the night-time occupants. And Sir Antonin, who stood near Patricie.

Finally, she could breathe easier. Redirecting her focus to Eva, she chanced pushing into the silence. "Is something amiss?"

Patricie's worn look sparked anew. "What do you think of his mark?" Her question was lightly delivered, but Eva still shot her an angered glare.

"What mark?" Karin peered closer at the child while Eva attempted to shield him, turning away from her.

Karin caught her shoulder. And then Eva's wide green eyes were on her.

"You have nothing to fear from me," Karin assured her.

Eva's tight muscles about her shoulders relaxed. And, another look pierced Patricie as Eva settled Michal in front of her again.

Karin watched with bated breath as Eva urged the hood, already askew, off the shadowed portion of Michal's face.

She was careful to school her features as the mark of birth was revealed. It was ill-placed, but not unsightly. "What is the matter with that? He is a fine, quite handsome son."

Eva's eyes glazed as she snuggled the boy closer.

Patricie met Karin's gaze. "We fear not all will see it so. There are...those...who believe it more...evidence of something wicked."

"Oh, how preposterous!" Karin offered an encouraging smile to Eva as she held out a hand to touch the thick curls about Michal's head. But she was not oblivious to what many believed about such markings. "You are safe here."

Eva looked to Patricie, who noted an errant tear. One that she hoped was borne of relief.

Karin allowed Michal to capture her finger. "Now, we must see to your comfort."

"That is not necessary," Eva protested. "I only wish to see my husband."

"Your comfort is important," Karin insisted. "I shall have water brought up for your ablutions. But I will take you first to see Lord Ambroz."

"*I* will do that," a voice from behind called.

Karin turned to confirm that it was her mother-in-law. She smiled at the older women, thankful for the moment.

"Allow me to take you to Lord Ambroz." The dowager baroness

indicated the stairs. "Then to your rooms. I am certain you are quite road weary."

"Indeed," Eva said, the word drawn out as if it just occurred to her that it was all right for her to admit as much.

Karin followed, but Marketa paused, giving her a pointed look.

"There are...other matters...for you to attend to, are there not, Lady Krejikova?" She stressed the title as if to remind Karin once more that she belonged to Pavel.

Karin frowned.

"I have encouraged Sir Marek to wait for you in the solar."

Karin wished to insist once more that the forthcoming conversation was not necessary to be had at this moment. But she held her tongue on the matter. "I do hate to trouble Lord Dvorak, but I would ask if he is able, that he might join myself and Sir Marek in the solar." If she was to go into the lion's den, she would not do so friendless. Was Stepan a friend, though? It had become difficult still to think on him that way.

Patricie glanced at her sister before settling her gaze on Karin. "My lady, Lord Dvorak's injuries may be—"

One of the side doors opened, distracting Karin and halting Patricie's words.

Stepan fairly stomped within the Great Hall and moved toward the stairs, a bandage had been wrapped about his head. It seemed as if he, too, were headed somewhere. Such as the solar? Had Marketa gathered a small army to face Karin down?

But it was Patricie's intake of breath that once more pulled her from her thoughts. She looked to the younger lady, who stared at Stepan.

He, too, seemed quite taken aback. What went here?

"You should be resting," Patricie protested.

Stepan quickly caught himself. "My lady..." he started.

Though from Patricie's attire, she doubted Eva's sister was nobility. Why, then, would he address her so?

"Lord Dvorak," the woman managed. "Your wound is not to be trifled with. You should not be up and about."

There was a strained tension between them.

"A wound?" Karin looked to him.

"It is nothing," Stepan waved a hand. Though his gaze settled on Patricie. And his glare was not kind.

Did he notice, as Karin did, that there was a discernable ease between the young lady and Sir Antonin? She wasn't as well acquainted with either Patricie or Sir Antonin, but she knew what it meant when a companionable rapport was between a man and a woman. Especially an unattached man and woman. But why would that disturb Stepan? What could be improper about such a fine match? They seemed well suited enough.

Karin stood, caught in a moment of indecision.

Patricie sniffled lightly.

Sir Antonin looked to her, perhaps intending to help her find her comfort.

But Karin had no time for that. She called out, "All questions will be attended to in time." Then, to Stepan, she insisted, "Lord Dvoark, to my solar. Now."

She whirled from Stepan, pressing through the small cluster on the stairs and marching toward the solar. Stepan had best follow forthwith. For he had better not wish to face her ire. It would be fierce.

Pavel dragged himself to consciousness. Reluctantly. With great fear at what he would find in the light of the morning. Indeed, when he opened his eyes, he discovered his vision quite blurry. The beating came back to him. How the mercenaries had taken great pleasure in thrashing him. But he had not caved to their words. Had not responded to their verbal attacks. And had resisted fighting back. They would not win.

Yet as the images took better clarity about him, his heart fell that it was not his wife's features that greeted him. But the cold hard earth. And Ulrich's guards.

"He's awake." One of the men hunkered over him.

Would they take this opportunity to kick him once more? Inflict some other sort of pain? What they didn't know is that no ache could be greater than that he felt for his wife and son.

"Tell the baron," the other man scoffed as he shifted his weight but did not move any farther away.

"Shall we bring him some water?" the first asked gruffly.

"Not until *he* has allowed it."

The voices quieted and the thud of footfalls on the earth carried one of the men away.

What was this? What would it become? How much longer would Ulrich keep him alive? And...for what purpose?

Clomping of boots on the hard ground foretold that the large Ulrich drew near. Then the footfalls paused.

"Thought to escape me, did you?" It was Ulrich's menacing tone.

Pavel did not respond. Did not even move. Just counted his tortured breaths in and out.

"Very well, then. Allow me to be the first to congratulate you."

On what? Being recaptured? The man had no sense of mercy.

"Not interested? I wager you will be when you hear that I have finally been rid of my enemy."

What did he speak of? Did he refer to General Zizka? The man had certainly had his fair share of clashes with Ulrich. Or was there another?

"Yes...I see you have guessed it."

Pavel had forgotten to control his reaction.

"It is so, young Lord Krejik. The old man is gone. Zizka..." The sneer in Ulrich's voice came through quite well enough. "And I pray he rots in his grave!"

Pavel turned away. He wished the larger man wouldn't see the wayward emotions that threatened to slip through.

The large man trudged forward and grabbed Pavel's hair, forcing his regard upward and into steely eyes. "It will not be soon enough."

Pavel gritted his teeth and seethed. "Take your comfort while you can."

"Ah, the little weasel shall speak?"

Pavel tried to pull free. It was useless. "The Hussite army will see to your end. We have right and truth on our side."

Ulrich clucked his tongue and shook his head.

An upward jerking brought Pavel to his knees.

Then came the dark voice he had become all too familiar with. "I predict quite the opposite. That one's death will create greater instability. And with the old lion gone for good, the jackals will feast!"

He laughed and shoved Pavel away. And with his arms bound, he could do nothing to stop his body as it slammed back to the earth.

Pavel bit at the inside of his mouth until he tasted blood. He would not relent, would not show how concerned he truly was.

"You do yourself credit, Baron Krejik. It is a pity you will not live to see what I will do to your wife and son."

Pavel jerked up onto his side before the full force of the pain that movement caused shot through him. "Cur!" He threw at Ulrich's back.

The man turned slowly. "Cur, am I? Now that...is a matter of perspective." His rough chuckle vibrated in Pavel's ears long after Ulrich had walked away.

Pavel had to do something. Somehow. He could not allow this evil man to take his wife and son. To do with them what his sick twisted mind could conjure up. A growl tore through him, rising from his very core. And he howled...a sound more akin to a beast than a man.

As he lost all strength, he collapsed once more. Hot tears of frustration and helplessness stung him. But they, too, could not rescue him.

His pleas for Zdenek's life, and those of his other men had fallen on deaf ears. So, too, would Pavel's protests and howling. He might rail against the inevitable, but he knew his life was forfeit.

If only he could keep Karin and Jaromir from the same fate. Or worse.

Did Ulrich have a spy in Pavel's castle? In the home his family found refuge in? Had *he* allowed a man with divided loyalties to swear fealty to him and so take his place among the guard?

Would that there was something he could do...anything. Yet, once again, he remembered that there was. Prayer.

But as he attempted to quiet his heart, he found that there was not a posture of submission to the Lord, only a thick, unyielding anger.

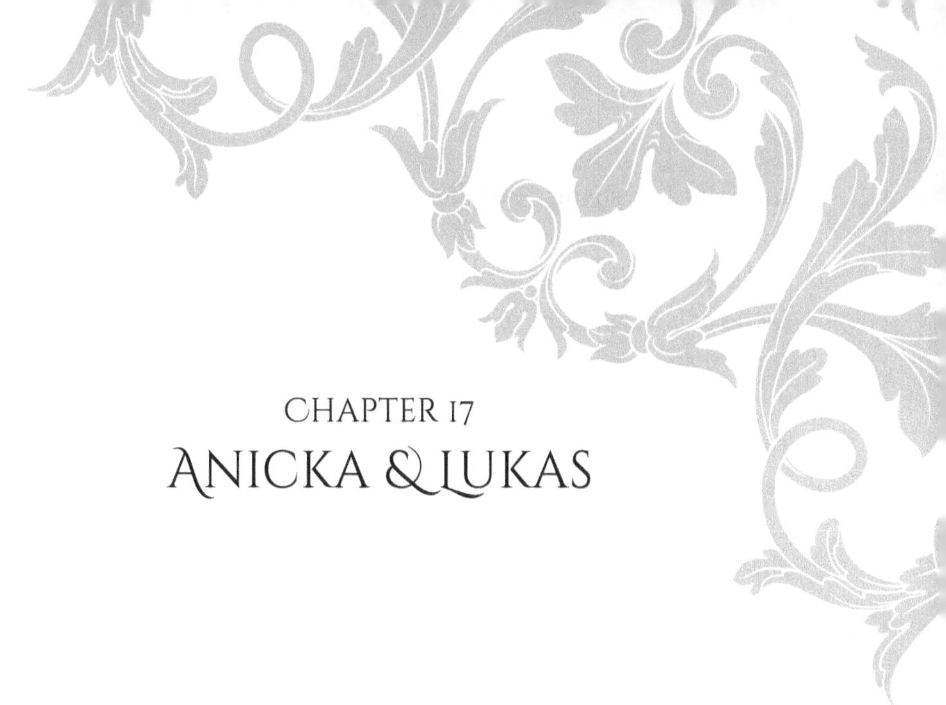

CHAPTER 17
ANICKA & LUKAS

Anicka tucked her cloak around herself, fighting against the frigid air. Alone in the carriage, she dared a glance out the window at her new husband upon horseback just outside. Protecting, guiding.

She watched the scenery shift as they moved upward in elevation. This stronghold that would be their home for a time was not so far from Lukas's father's castle. Yet the journey stretched on as she sat, lonely, within the confines of this moving box.

This wasn't how it should be, should it? She longed for his assurance that all was well. But this morning, he had simply handed her up into the carriage and moved off to his horse. No words. She wanted to believe his hand had lingered on hers, but that may only be wishful thinking.

Was she so abhorrent to him yestereve? That he would not take what was rightfully his...

Her face burned at the shame of it all. She was an unwanted bride.

Had she tricked him into this arrangement? That would only

intensify her shame. But she knew better. Their parents had had some ulterior motive in this.

Her mother's plan was not so difficult to uncover...she wanted to be rid of her headache of a daughter. Were Lukas's parents punishing him for something?

Though...Anicka should be happy. How often had she dwelt on tender thoughts of her childhood friend? Of a future with him that seemed out of reach?

The warmth that even now pooled within her had been the same that inspired many tales of love from her quill.

Yet, he had left the room without a word last night. Without a word...no explanation, no apologies. What had he truly thought of her lack of foresight in imbibing so much?

Even now, she longed for parchment to capture her thoughts, her emotions. For they beat greatly within her. Yet there was no way to do so. No implements, no opportunity. Would there ever be?

What would Lukas think of her writing stories? Would he ridicule her and forbid her to continue? That would break her heart, shattering what was left of her resolve. But could she truly stop the breathings of her heart?

Must she keep it secret? Write in the spaces that were afforded.

The carriage came to a halt. What went here?

She looked out the window to see Lukas approaching. Was all well? His expression appeared pained in some way.

He dismounted and took hold of the carriage door latch. "We have paused to see to your comfort."

That was wholly unnecessary.

"Do you need to..." He swallowed, clearly having difficulty. "Do you need a moment of privacy?"

Then she understood. He had stopped the group for her to relieve herself. The whole idea was comical to her.

Until she felt the tug of fullness about her abdomen.

"Yes," she said, looking down, avoiding his gaze. "That would be good."

The door swung wide, and he reached in to assist her down.

After she was solidly on the earth again, she chanced a glance at him. "How do you fare?"

His hold on her faltered. Had her question so surprised? They had been the best of friends once. She had known him better than anyone. And he, her.

"The way is well traveled. All is well." He offered her a small smile as he led her toward a collection of trees. Would he escort her to a private place for her needs? "And you? How goes the journey for you?"

"It is quite..." Should she put a brave face on and tell him what he wanted to hear? No, that was not who she wanted to be. Not with him. "It is boring."

His eyebrows arched.

"Not that it is dull. The view has been a wonderful companion. It is just..." How might she put it? "It has been lonely." She quieted her voice.

"Ah. My apologies for not thinking of that. I only wished for your comfort."

They had come to a place farther in the copse of trees that she had privacy. Yet she did not wish to end their engagement. "I am comfortable." Her face heated. "At least as much as I can be. Though..." Dare she ask? "I might wish for—"

"Do you not have a need for privacy?" he broke in.

Indeed, she did. "Yes." She looked around.

He grinned. "There looks to be a place just there." He pointed at a cropping of large stones and shrubs.

"Ah, yes." She released him and moved off, reluctantly. There had been the flavor of their friendship seeping into their exchange.

She did as was necessary and returned. To find him gone. Had he abandoned her? That did not seem right.

"Lukas?" She scanned the area.

"I am here." The voice came from behind some trees to the right.

She stepped in that direction.

"Do not, my lady," he said abruptly.

She halted.

"I am taking advantage of the privacy as well."

Then she understood. And that brought a burn to her face. Had she truly almost walked upon him in a compromised state?

In a matter of moments, he stepped through the brush and to her side. A smile about him.

"My apologies, my lord. I but..." Where were her words today?

"Do not worry yourself." His grin was infectious. "It is understandable."

She let a small smile touch her features as she looked down.

"Did you think...?" He paused as his smile fell. "Did you think I had left you?"

She turned away, but he caught her chin.

"Did you?"

She frowned. "I wondered..."

His tone became firmer. "Know this, Anicka, I will never leave you thusly. I am your husband. And I will be your protector. With my life if necessary."

Her lips parted as she marveled at the ferocity of his words. And found herself speechless.

"Let us return to the others," he said plainly.

It was clear he was upset with her. What had started as a hopeful chance to not be consigned to the carriage with the older nursemaid slipped through her fingers. Why could she not trust Lukas? She never would have doubted him those years past. But she did now.

As they approached the contingency of gathering knights and guards, she moved toward the carriage.

"Would you...?" Lukas started but paused. "Would you prefer to ride with me, my lady?"

She wouldn't have been more surprised were he to suggest he might turn into a pumpkin. "With you, my lord?"

He gave a sharp nod. And she saw it...his trepidation, his nervousness at her potential response.

But she was all too thrilled at the prospect. "Aye."

His lips split into a small grin that he quickly straightened out.

"My lord, would the lady not be more comfortable in the carriage?" The elder maidservant groused from the steps of the carriage where a knight attempted to hand her up.

Anicka opened her mouth to protest, but Lukas beat her to it.

"I think a reprieve upon horseback is in order." That was all he said. And all he needed to say for the older woman's mouth to turn downward in a huff as she stepped within the large box.

Good riddance to her, then. Anicka fought a smile at her thought. It was highly inappropriate.

Lukas led her to his horse and helped her up to the front of the saddle. Then he lifted himself atop the animal.

And their bodies were all too close.

A thrill of sensation swept through Anicka at the connection points of their bodies. Her senses swam as they had the night before. Would the excess drink be affecting her still today? That didn't seem likely.

Perhaps, then, this was something else, something new.

She hesitantly leaned back against her husband's chest and said, "Would you tell me of the castle that is to be our home?"

A rumbling in his chest vibrated through her, carrying heat as it went.

"You shall see for yourself soon enough."

His arms came around her to hold the reins. But she imagined they secured her, hemmed her in, protected her. And she could believe all was right in the world.

With a kick of his heels to the horse's flank, they were off.

The day had waned on before they approached the lesser castle on Vitek lands—the one his father was passing to him. If he believed his father, the larger castle would one day be his.

Should he prove himself capable with these smaller portions of lands.

Though Lukas imagined the knight that oversaw the lands now would be none too happy about being usurped by a criminal.

Enough of that! How would anyone else see him differently if he did not?

He did not miss the glances and whispers of the men at camp the night before. Each comment drove the spear of his fears deeper. To the point he may never dislodge it from his heart. He would forever be the baron's murdering son, scheming and reaching for favor that was not to be his.

The fact that it wasn't the truth didn't matter.

The fact that he was coerced didn't dull the sharpness.

The fact that he'd been given his freedom again only made him question the validity of the law.

And the fact that he shouldn't be given a fine wife ground painfully, grating salt into the fresh wound of his soul.

Still, he could do nothing about it. So, squaring his shoulders, he urged the horse onward.

A soft moan from Lady Anicka who was reposed in his arms reminded him she slept. At least she had slept.

Peering down, he saw as well as felt her shift against him, but her full weight leaned upon him. So, he doubted she had roused completely...if at all.

The rhythm of the horses changed as they climbed the last hill. And there, on the next rise, was Zamek Kopec, the place that would be their home for the coming years. Who knew how many?

This was the place he and Anicka would oversee and, Lord willing, have children. He tugged her closer. The feel of her against him had made him...think. About things he hadn't wanted to. About feelings he'd decided were not his due. But she had awakened feelings he believed safely buried.

He began laying dirt upon his heart's renderings, in fact, just as he had started distancing himself from the lady in his arms. He had not forgotten how they spent hours together as playmates in their younger years. Or how his perception of her had changed when her dresses made her more womanly figure visible. How she had hated the restriction of the stays and corset. But how they had fascinated him. At least...with the way it brought a greater awareness of their reaching the age to which they would be married off.

She had hated the very idea. And he had been loathed to hear it. The truth was, that he had hoped his family would turn a favorable eye toward her as his bride. And her family to him as a suitable match for her. Now, here they were. Yet their first eve as man and wife, she'd been so put out that she drank herself into a stupor.

He refused to force himself on her. Or make her uncomfortable in any way. Wasn't that why he had given himself to his knighthood training and studies of law so many years ago? To separate himself from the ache of not being as handsome to her as she was beautiful to him?

Yes, he must keep his feelings in check. For dare they escape, havoc they may well wreak. And once they were fully out, would he be able to rein them in?

"Baron Vitek," one of the knights nearby called out.

He turned, careful with his movements, and reluctant to be pulled from his more pleasant thoughts. "Yes?"

"The nursemaid is...insisting that your lady wife be returned to the carriage."

Lukas glanced back at the carriage and frowned. Who was this woman to give him instruction? "Tell her that Lady Anicka will ride with me until it is she who insists on returning to the carriage. Not her maidservant."

The look of discomfort that crossed the worn guard's face gave Lukas pause. Was the older maid so difficult? Would she not give way to his words?

It mattered not to him.

He turned his full attention to Zamek Kopec. And pressed the horse onward.

Mere moments later, thundering hoofbeats drew Lukas and his men to halt. What was that?

Then hordes of well-armed men crashed upon them from beyond the tree line.

Lukas had one thought—that he should have put Lady Anicka into the safer confines of the carriage. For he could do naught to aid his men with her on his horse. So, he leaned over her and spurred the horse into a full-out run, praying that his men would cover their escape.

CHAPTER 18
PATRICIE & STEPAN

Patricie longed to reach out to Stepan. To assure him—well, perhaps more herself—that all was well. He seemed so distant. So...dismissive...of her. But she was helpless as he moved up the stairs, following Lady Karin. Was this the woman he was once betrothed to? That thought did not settle well. Still, when Stepan struggled to keep his footing even on the steps, it was all Patricie could do to restrain herself from going to him.

"Patricie," Eva entreated her. Glancing in that direction, Patricie noted that the older baroness and Eva awaited Patricie's attention.

"Lady?" Sir Antonin sought her gaze.

She offered him a slight smile. "I am well."

Grasping her skirt so as not to trip, she allowed Sir Antonin to take her elbow and help her up the stairs after the elder Lady Krejikova.

"Shall I take you to your accommodations?" the dowager baroness asked as they reached the next level.

"I would implore you," Eva said as she jostled the child a bit, "to take me to my husband first."

The baroness stopped on the stairs and looked back, glancing at Michal and then to Eva. "Mayhap it would bode better for your sister to take the child and get him better acclimated to the castle.

It was not a suggestion, though it was spoken with a kind lilt.

Eva hesitated, as if she resisted the instruction.

In truth, she had clung to the child. Almost as if he were supplying her with a lifeline instead of the other way around. Patricie realized she had not yet held the child.

The need to be at her husband's side and her desire to maintain her hold on the young one warred within Eva. The battle was plainly written in the way her features scrunched.

Patricie took one more step to come beside her sister. "I will care for him well."

Eva's eyes were wide as they landed on Patricie.

"On my life, he will not be harmed," Patricie whispered.

Eva looked to Michal and pressed a kiss to his forehead.

The small boy stirred and let out a frustrated grunt.

Patricie held out waiting arms but realized she would have to help her sister. So, she hooked the boy under his arms and lifted.

There was a little resistance as Eva fought herself letting go.

"I will escort Lady Patricie to their chambers for the evening," Sir Antonin offered.

Baroness Krejikova nodded. "They are to be in the room next to Jaromir's."

The man nodded and laid his hand on Patricie's upper back, urging her forward.

Patricie allowed him to lead her away, but she did not miss Eva's longing look that followed them.

Michal squirmed, but Patricie maintained a proper hold on him as Sir Antonin led her down the corridor.

Her thoughts were on Stepan and what he might be feeling or not feeling for the beautiful Lady Karin. But she refused to let her mind wander at its own whim.

"Tell me," she said to Sir Antonin, "What is the state of Bohemia?"

"What?" The surprise in his voice was quite evident. As if that were the last thing he expected her to care about.

"Sir knight, I served as a healer in the Hussite camp. I am not immune to talk of war and death. I have been distant from any good source of information. But I know the guards and knights talk of it often. Please, tell me what you know."

He directed his gaze forward and swallowed. "Very well. But I fear my news may not be any more recent than yours."

She looked down. "I know of General Zizka's illness. How does he fare?"

Sir Antonin jerked toward her. "You have not heard?"

She halted, a foreboding chill sliding along her spine. "Heard what?"

Sir Antonin chewed at his lip. Did he try to decide what to share?

"Please, Sir Antonin, just tell me."

"General Zizka has passed on."

"What?" Patricie stopped. Her knees became weak, and she gripped Michal tighter, fearful she may lose her hold. But as her knees lacked proper support, she swayed.

Sir Antonin grabbed for her.

She swallowed and breathed. And steadied herself. Soon enough, she waved Sir Antonin off. But when she tried to speak, there was sorrow in her voice. "Passed on?"

"Yes." Sir Antonin seemed rather concerned. "I should not have told you."

Now standing on her own, she wiped at a tear. "No. I pressed you to tell me. And I'm glad you did."

His eyebrows lifted. He wasn't certain about that.

"Please, go on."

He studied her as if gauging what, if anything, to tell her.

"I can handle it. I was just...surprised."

He nodded. "We are almost to your chamber."

She was thankful for that with the squirming child in her arms. Would he enjoy moving more freely?

Sir Antonin indicated a nearby door.

"Is there another leader in place?" Patricie asked as she stepped into the vacant room. The sounds of another child could be heard through the door just to the right. That must be Jaromir. Was that the younger baroness's son?

Patricie took in the elegant bed, big enough for two, and the fine tapestries smoothing the harsh stone walls. The fire had been stoked in the hearth and two chairs by the fireplace beckoned. Perhaps she might set Michal on the fur clad floor there and sit for a rest.

But not before she gained more insight from Sir Antonin.

"I will leave you to settle in." He gave a slight bow.

"No!" The word shot out before she could stop it.

He lifted his head and caught her gaze. There was something there in his eyes she couldn't quite discern. And wasn't certain she was ready to.

"I just...I need to know the state of things in our lands. It has been difficult to not be in the midst of the camp."

His look was rather curious then—uncertainty and...maybe, respect. He cleared his throat. "There is gossip..."

"Gossip?" she prompted.

"Of more crusades coming against Czech lands. There is tension abounding about it. Many are tired of the fighting...and are losing sight of why we even started."

Patricie looked down. "I doubt the loss of General Zizka will help with that."

Sir Antonin shook his head. "If anything, that has increased the doubt. The loss of the general has left...a space. More than that. A dark pit. One that is uncertain and so very empty."

Patricie stepped to the hearth and set the squirming Michal down then offered him a piece of bread from her bag. "What do you think?"

She looked over her shoulder at him.

He was taken aback. By her inquiring after him? Was it not typical for others to care about his thoughts?

"I...would rather fight for bread than bishops." He indicated the child, gumming the crusty stuff.

Patricie directed her gaze back to Michal. "I will pray then."

She sensed that Sir Antonin came forward a step or two, but no further.

She continued, "I will pray that God will raise up a new leader. One that will reinstall a purpose in us all."

Silence swept the room. The only sound was the movements of the child.

"I will pray for that too, then." Sir Antonin's voice was soft.

It made Patricie want to look at him, but something told her that she should not.

In the moments that followed, the silence became thicker. And Michal became more visibly frustrated with his inability to eat the hard bread.

"I will leave you to tend your nephew."

That drew her regard. Nephew? She had not thought of Michal quite like that. But he was. If Eva and Zdenek were to raise Michal, he was her nephew for all that mattered to the world.

The question was...would she embrace that?

Her gaze settled on Sir Antonin.

He nodded and turned, stepping into the corridor and closing the door.

And leaving her alone with her thoughts.

Stepan moved up the stairs, trying his hardest not to think of how the knight had looked at Patricie. And had offered a hand in comfort. It vexed Stepan, to be sure, but was it for him to worry with right now? It was not. He needed to focus on his mission—getting Pavel home safely and keeping that devious, usurping Tomas away from Karin.

Indeed, he was in the dungeon still, so that boded well.

An ache in his head overwhelmed Stepan and he paused, pressing a hand to his forehead. Why must he be delayed by this minor injury?

As he was able, he shook his head to clear it and continued to the solar, entering several moments after Karin.

Sir Marek was there already.

As was...Sir Tomas.

He was still shackled, and he sat in a chair with guards to either side of him. But he was there. As he should not be.

Karin stepped to the lone desk in the room and whirled about. "We must ride out. Time is of the essence."

"What do you mean *we*?" Sir Marek prompted. It was not for clarification whether Karin would go. It was a hope that she would identify the remainder of her party.

"Sir Marek." Her voice gentled while staying firm. "I need you by my side."

Stepan tried not to squirm. There was no way he would permit her to leave him behind.

Sir Marek dipped his head.

"Lord Dvorak, you will be an asset as well," she said slowly.

Was that a reluctance in her voice? For he was a great asset. His determination to rescue Pavel notwithstanding, he must be along to prevent anything untoward. Not that she would take Sir Tomas along. That would be too great a risk.

She considered the men about her. "Sir Marek, I trust you to select forty of your best fighting men."

Forty? Did she think such a large contingency would be able to move with any stealth? That was absurd. Did she not trust Sir Marek and Stepan to keep her safe?

"And then divide them between our party and the guard to stay and defend the castle."

"Divide them, my lady?" Sir Marek appealed. Did he think they needed all those guards with them? Could he not see the logistical problem?

"Yes." Karin's eyes flashed. "I will not risk the castle and my people even for this venture."

Sir Marek bowed his head.

"Lord Ambroz will assume leadership of the castle in my stead."

That, at least, was a good plan. *If* Zdenek was able to do so.

Karin cast a glance in Sir Tomas's direction. Would she now make a pronouncement about him? That he should be punished unless he gave up the information required?

"And Sir Tomas," she said flatly, but her eyes spoke more… tenderly.

"My lady?" Stepan and Sir Marek said together.

She did not shift her gaze from the prisoner. "His knowledge will be invaluable."

"We would certainly be betrayed from within!" Stepan spared a glance at Sir Marek. Surely between them, they might speak some sense to her. But when Sir Marek looked to Stepan, he gave a slight shake of his head.

There was a knock at the door.

At last, Karin tore her gaze from Sir Tomas.

Stepan was less certain about what had gone between them. And what may transpire yet. But he was determined he would not permit it.

"Come," Karin called.

The dowager baroness slid into the room and resealed the door. "Pardon my lateness. I have settled the women and the child."

Karin's eyes widened. "I did not intend to imply that your presence was required. You may tend to your tasks."

"I will not." The elder woman's tone was hard. "This is my son." Her voice shook on the last word. "And I will see this through."

She could not mean that she would come along. Beyond the fact that Karin would slow them, the older baroness would delay them further. Far too much.

Karin's brow furrowed, creating lines on her pretty features.

Stepan looked away. He could not...would not think on her that way. His heart was otherwise engaged. And he wasn't certain he had ever truly loved Karin beyond a surface admiration of her lovely person.

"Baroness," Karin said, "You cannot mean—"

"I do not intend to be a member of the party. But best know that I intend to be a party to what I can be," Lady Marketa insisted.

Karin visibly relaxed. "We discussed that Sir Marek will post twenty of his best men to the castle and twenty to come alongside us."

"Us?" The dowager baroness was caught on that word.

"Yes, I intend to lead the effort." Karin firmed her jaw, clearly a challenge to her mother-in-law.

"But..." the baroness managed to get out. "You are a woman."

"That I am."

There was a fire in the dowager baroness's eyes. "You cannot think to lead these men."

"I believe that in France, the lady known as Joan of Arc is leading an army. Why can I not lead a rescue mission?"

The older woman sputtered. Then said, "This is not France."

Karin's mouth pinched.

Sir Marek stepped forward. "I will lead the party." Did he think that would diffuse the situation? It might appease the dowager baroness, but it would only inflame Karin. This, Stepan was certain of.

And indeed, she fumed. The reddening of her features betrayed it as well as anything else. "You...?"

Sir Marek moved closer, his hands raised slightly as he appealed. "Perhaps we can name me the lead. But only as if a figurehead. You can trust me. I will yield to your judgment and planning in every way."

She considered the man.

Stepan did not like this one bit, but she needed encouragement. This arrangement was the best anyone would make with Karin. Perhaps with Sir Marek named the lead of the party, he could overtake Karin's leadership should the situation call for it.

"It is a sound plan," he said, keeping his tone low. "We will give way to your every consideration. But we will not draw ire from the men with us who may not be as...understanding." Stepan felt his reasoning was well enough.

Karin eased a little. "Including my decision to bring Sir Tomas?"

It was a challenge. If Sir Marek led in more than just words, he would yield in this. But he was also the last hope that Karin's determination to take Sir Tomas would be thwarted.

What would Sir Marek do? What did Stepan wish him to do?

A silence fell upon the room. It was rather awkward.

"Aye." The single word was barely more than a mutter from Sir Marek. It was clear he did not like the corner he had been backed into. But he was helpless to make any other decision.

Though Stepan wasn't helpless. He would keep his eyes open as well as his ears. He would guard Karin—not just her life, but her propriety. Come what may.

"There is another matter." The dowager baroness stepped forward.

Karin lifted her eyes to her mother-in-law. "Yes, Lady Marketa?"

"With Zizka's death, there is much unrest. There are forces fighting under Prokop the Great and other commanders. Loyalties are shifting. There is much danger about."

Karin blinked. Did she, like Stepan, find surprise in the elder lady's grasp on the power struggles in Czech lands?

Sir Marek did not seem as astounded by it. With a neutral face, he gazed at the woman closer to his age. Was that so he wouldn't give away something? For his features seemed forced into their place.

Karin frowned. "Yes. We will have to be wary of anyone we encounter. Loyalties are divided and unclear."

Stepan blinked. Karin had matured in tamping down her fiery impulsiveness. Though a part of him was saddened by this observation. The better part of him was thankful. They would need level heads that overruled hearts on this journey. For no one could succeed if he—or she—were at the whim of their passions. Not now. Not ever.

CHAPTER 19
TOMAS

Tomas watched the interplay between those around him. The plan had worked. Lady Karin would leave the safe confines of the castle for the hope of rescuing her husband. Then she would be more vulnerable.

His heart stirred at the thought of what lay before them. Before him. What he had been charged to do. And what he must do.

The sin of his betrayal would singe him, marring his soul permanently. As if he weren't already destined for destruction.

He'd done too much, seen too much...

There was no hope for him.

At least, he would spend these next days in Karin's company. He had forgotten how beautiful she was. And how she moved his heart when he was in her presence. She was magical—not only lovely to the eyes, but her fiery and passionate drive made her fairly sparkle.

Truly she was a diamond among the rocks.

He'd always thought this. Even when he was fortunate enough to be her friend. Then, her intended.

Before Hus and his infectious teachings had changed everything.

Everything.

But any lingering attraction to Lady Karin, he would have to put aside if he was to do as he'd been instructed. He would have to bide his time...wait for the right moment. Again, he had no choice.

CHAPTER 20
KARIN & PAVEL

Lady Karin Krejikova looked out among the bailey as preparations were being made. Servants and guards moved about, making ready what she and the knights would need for the journey—horses, foodstuffs, tents and bedrolls, and the like. How long would their mission be? What would they find?

She couldn't dwell there for long. For she couldn't let herself think that they would search in vain. Oh, she was determined they would find her husband, but what condition would he be in...that was unknown.

"My lady..." A voice to her left requested her attention.

She turned to the familiar tone and found true, that Zdenek stood beside her. "You should be abed."

He gave her a scoffing look. "You have trusted me to keep the castle well and safe in your stead. I intend to do so. And not from a sick bed."

She glanced over him. He did seem much better. Though there were still colorations from bruises and healing slices upon his person, he did appear stronger. More capable.

"I must speak with you about Pav—"

"We have made ready the things needed. And we have assigned your guard that will stay and defend under your command." She had no desire to hear talk of the trouble they may face nor speak of the doubts within her being.

"I have seen them."

Of course he would have. He was a born leader. Though, with his jovial leaning, she had wondered at times whether that was the case. But in the last several years of hardship and war, the man had more than proved himself.

She turned away from the scurrying below and shifted toward him. "And the Lady Eva? Michal?"

There was an uncertainty crowding Zdenek's features. "They are well. Settled."

Karin jerked her head in a nod. "How has the boy taken to you?"

Zdenek's eyes widened ever so slightly. And there was a pause before he spoke. "He is a pleasant lad, ready to please."

"He is rather attached to your lady wife." Karin permitted a smile for thoughts of Eva and how protective she had been of the child—fierce, bold. Michal's mother in truth. At least in all the ways that mattered.

"Yes." He smiled a bit. "Eva is quite taken with him."

Then Karin understood. Zdenek had not a choice in the matter. Not really. Eva was strong-willed and quite determined where the child was concerned. She would not have presented Zdenek with the decision to take in Michal or not. Eva and the child were now a bound deal.

Did her friend need some encouragement in the matter?

"He is a strong lad. He will be a good warrior one day."

Zdenek looked down over the inner bailey. "Yes."

The word was far too quiet. As if Zdenek had reached the end of his ability to speak on the matter.

She offered a change of subject. But perhaps one they did not truly want to broach either. But she wished to know what information he might have. "What of the Hussites?"

He set his hands on the battlement, leaning over as if he studied the preparations with intent.

There was that silence again. Was it because he knew nothing new? Or because he didn't wish to share what he had knowledge of?

At length, he did speak. But it was with rather reluctant words. "There are Taborite offensives. Aggressive moves."

"It is war."

He jerked his regard to her. "General Zizka's tactics were those of defense against the crusades into our lands. These are the result of in-fighting and ideological splintering."

She frowned. In fighting? That was not what they had suffered for. What Pavel had risked his life for. Mayhap even...given his life for.

Pulling back mentally from that thought, she shifted their conversation again. "I know you will keep my family and my people safe."

Zdenek clenched his jaw. Because he felt the weight of the responsibility?

"Aye. And with even my life I will do all I can." He glanced at her without turning.

She let her mouth soften and lift in a small smile. She trusted him. She knew him. And though her heart ached to leave her son, she knew that Zdenek would, in fact, do everything humanly possible to keep them all until she returned with Pavel.

The quiet that passed between them now dissipated the tension around Zdenek. Shouts from below told that they neared the end of their tasks.

"I must go." Her words were choked out. "To see to final things. And say farewell to Jaromir."

Zdenek nodded. "I will rally the guard."

She gave a jerk of her head in assent. Then they both walked below stairs where they parted ways—her to Jaromir's nursery, him to his duties.

And in a matter of minutes, she was mounted and riding out of the castle. She had chosen her trusted steed—though a mare—to lead her on this quest. For she needed a horse she knew and that knew her for the journey and potential battle ahead.

Her eyes were still filled with moisture from her farewell exchange with Jaromir. But she swallowed the fresh tears. She had to show strength and purpose for the men that followed her.

Sir Marek led alongside her to her right, under the guise of leading the camp. The knights and guards knew to heed her orders, but she had to trust Sir Marek to give way to her. She was not naïve. The men would take their cues from him.

Stepan traveled just behind her and to her left as he insisted. She had interrupted his exchange with the healer, Eva's sister. Pressing the memory of the tense and intimate exchange she witnessed out of mind, she did not want to dwell there. For some reason she could not name.

Tomas was farther back where he could be surrounded by guards. As much as she wanted to trust him, in his words, she dared not risk the whole of their contingent by loosening the watch on him or giving him a weapon. Not yet. Perhaps not ever. But the question that lingered in her mind was not for Tomas, but herself. Did she, indeed trust herself?

Determination—heated, like a fire flowing through her veins, overtook her. She would do what she had to, what she must, for her husband.

No matter what.

Pavel awoke to a guard standing over him. How had the man sneaked up? It was discouraging that Pavel had not been sleeping light enough to be able to protect himself. But the sleep he had gained was fitful and worrisome. It should not surprise that once he fell deeper, it was more solid.

Still, the warrior in him was not pleased.

The guard sneered. "It's about time you were awake."

Pavel shifted, with much-pained movements, to a sitting position. "And what might I do for you this day?"

Indeed, he looked to the sun to find that, not only had he slept through someone nearing his person, he had slept into the day. Perhaps he wasn't even fit for battle any longer.

The man curled his lip in an uglier snarl. "Lord Ulrich sees value in keeping you alive. I disagree, whelp."

Pavel just stared. Perhaps this loose-tongued mercenary might reveal more than he should.

"Make no mistake…" The man jerked Pavel to his feet.

More pain flared through him from injuries incurred at the hands of these men…and bones he was certain were fractured.

"Ulrich will not let you live to see another fortnight. But he thinks he needs you for the time being."

Pavel bit his lip to keep from blasting the man with a response. As much as he wished to push back and rail against his fate, none of this was news to him. So, it was best to remain quiet and let the man sink himself.

"Do you hear me?" The man shook Pavel, pushing him forward.

Pavel stumbled.

Another jab from the guard saw Pavel lose his balance and fall.

He twisted to land on his right side, which had not sustained as much damage. Still, the impact was jarring…and shot pain through his being. Clamping teeth together, he fought the urge to cry out.

The mercenary leaned over him. "Ah yes. You may think you are being strong, but I know you are a weakling."

Why was the man baiting him? Did he truly want to see Pavel's wrath? Not that a bound man with wounds such as his—and surrounded by the enemy—could hope for anything to come from a short confrontation. He would not turn loose of his reasoning.

"If you care so little, I will tell you of my hope that Ulrich gives us the same freedoms with your wife as we've had with you."

Pavel ground his teeth. How dare this man threaten to do unspeakable things to his Karin!

The man's snarl became a menacing smile. Did Pavel's features betray his ire? They must.

Leaning closer, perhaps to enjoy his verbal spar's effect on Pavel, the man said in a low voice. "Mayhap you are willing to...share?"

Pavel no longer cared about potential retaliation. He gathered all his strength and thrust his legs out and up toward what he believed to be the man's midsection.

A satisfying thud placed the man partly on him, but grasping for the area he had left vulnerable. The grunts and shouts of pain brought Pavel a small measure of satisfaction.

One he knew he would not regret, even as other guards rushed over to punish him.

Kicks and rough hands assaulted him. It did not matter one bit.

"Hold!" The voice cut through the mob of guards, silencing them.

There was only one man who could do such. And, while Pavel could not hear well due to the pounding of blood in his ears...and something else...perhaps an injury to one side, he knew full well who it was.

Two guards jerked Pavel up only to find that he could not stand on his own. They ground out curses but held him firmly between them.

Pavel tasted blood and had the urge to spit it out. But lacked the strength to do so.

He was pleased to see that the first mercenary still huddled on the ground, his hands covering his ballocks.

"What goes here?" Ulrich demanded.

"He..." the first mercenary managed to press out, "He kicked me in me pintle!"

"Aye," Ulrich ground out. "You probably deserved it."

The mercenary's eyes widened. Mayhap there would be more punishment coming his way for creating a situation in which the prisoner could injure him.

Pavel did not wish otherwise. He wanted the man to suffer.

Ulrich walked to him. "I expected some trouble from you."

Pavel glared at him, but one of his eyes would not open all the way.

"But I also thought for better restraint from a fine warrior such as you are told to be."

Pavel narrowed his gaze as much as he could. Then he spit the blood in his mouth at his captor.

It splattered Ulrich's chest. The man's face reddened.

Ulrich calmly reached out a hand for a cloth and wiped at the blood. "We shall consider that but a beginning of how your blood will be spilt."

Pavel kept his features steady. Again, this was no surprise.

"You may outlive your usefulness, after all. You are only valuable as long as Bohemia remains in the hands of my enemies. But..." He paused.

Why? Had he said too much? He hadn't truly revealed anything.

"However," he started again. "With the death of Zizka, Bohemia's true future is possible."

Pavel bit the inside of his cheek to keep from showing any emotion.

"Yes. You might think you are not an open book. But I know you, Pavel Krejik. I know your Achilles heel."

Did he refer to the spy in the Krejik castle? To the risk to Karin and Jaromir? Pavel refused to jump for the bait. But his eyes mayhap told all.

"'Tis time we moved out." Ulrich turned away from Pavel.

"What are we to do with him, my lord?" one of the men called after Ulrich's retreating figure.

"If he can't stand, strap him to the back of a mule."

Not that there was truly any other way Ulrich could humiliate Pavel. Not any that mattered.

For his heart was wounded. Shredded. And perhaps forever now beyond repair. Time would tell. And he was doubly alone for God had abandoned him...in this greatest hour of need. It was not just his suffering that prompted this conclusion. But that God would have him so impotent to help Karin and Jaromir. That was the core of it. How could God allow evil to befall his family—his beloved Karin and innocent Jaromir? It wasn't right or just.

And Pavel could not see past it.

CHAPTER 21
ANICKA & LUKAS

Anicka was thrust into consciousness with the rapid movement of the horse beneath her. What necessitated that?

It took her a minute to remember why she sat so awkwardly upon the animal and whose arms surrounded her.

She shifted, trying to gain herself a better situation upon the front of the saddle.

Arms tightened on either side of her.

"Be still," Lukas hissed. "But hold tightly."

Immediately, she obeyed, sliding her arms around his midsection and gripping. Still, her mind wandered. Where was he taking her? And why couldn't she resist him?

She pulled all her sense of patience and duty from deep down and tried to keep her body still. But it was difficult. She was frightened...by the jostling and by her husband.

The urge to twist and see what may be the problem was great. Dare she defy Lukas and do so? Dare she not?

She peered over his shoulder to see two men on horseback

following. Biting her lip, she was a little too late to halt the screech that came unbidden to her throat.

Lukas growled.

Because he was upset with her? Or because of these men that pursued?

Where was the rest of the guard? Had they been abandoned and left to fend for themselves? And were these mere brigands that pursued them? They did not appear so. Even at their rapid pace, she saw that the men were well dressed. Perhaps not nobility. But fine guards.

She clung to her husband, all too aware of the firmness of his frame and torso as his muscles moved to direct their horse's flight.

He ducked over her as he veered left.

A branch swooshed over his back.

What was this?

"Lukas!" Her voice sounded tortured even to her ears.

He muttered something that she couldn't discern.

It was only a matter of time, if experience held true, before a panic would overtake her. So great was her fear in the moment.

Clutching his shirt, there warred within her a need to know what went and a desire to let him take charge. As he clearly was. But shouldn't she know?

He shot out a breath. "We will not outrun them."

It was said with some level of resigned dismay. What would happen to them should they be overtaken?

"Lukas," she fairly seethed. Not for anger, but for fear.

"Quiet," he commanded in a hushed, but harsh tone.

He maneuvered the horse left and right. Did he truly hope to evade the men?

Tearing of brush behind warned that they drew closer, only momentarily delayed by Lukas's sharp turn.

Lukas pulled the horse to the side.

Even the little contact she had with the horse's flesh revealed a sheen of sweat upon the overtaxed animal.

They could not push it any harder. It may already be too late.

That thought saddened her, but her concern for her and Lukas's safety overshadowed it. What were they to do? Who would want them captured or killed that they would send these men?

Lukas set her upright then dropped down from the horse. But as he lifted his arms for her, a massive dark horse crashed through the underbrush, aiming for them, the rider's sword drawn.

Would he run Lukas through with one move?

Anicka screamed as Lukas grabbed her and pulled her to the ground.

Her voice was drowned out by the rearing up and neighing of their horse. Had it been injured?

The villain and horse continued several feet.

Lukas jerked her to her feet and tugged her onward, deeper into the forest.

This was madness. How could he possibly hope for them to come out of this alive if they struggled on foot while their would-be captor maintained his horse?

Still, she grabbed for her skirts and allowed her husband to half drag her through the thick of the trees. She sent up a quick prayer for their protection.

Her heart raced—from exertion and fear, but also from some strange excitement. Wasn't this the kind of rescue she had envisioned for the characters she created? The daring hero seeking to save the damsel who was in need of assistance?

Still, she pressed such young girl fantasies to the side. This was no story, no conjuring of her imagination. This was real. And the risk was not a wasted paper, but their lives.

Lukas halted, looking back.

No longer could she hear the clomping of horse hooves. Were they safe? Had they evaded the menacing figure?

"Lukas," she said, quite breathless.

He held up his hand, his gaze on her discerning and worried. Perhaps no one else would see it, but she knew him well.

There was a good amount of concern in his eyes.

A rustling in the leaves nearby had him crouching, pulling her down with him.

She knelt but maintained her readiness to run. Would they have to? She was quite winded, and her side hurt from the spent effort. But if she must, she would.

He caught her gaze again, then said, "If I give the signal, you run. In that direction." He pointed farther east. Or what she thought was east. Curse these clouds overcasting the sun!

She nodded as if she understood. Whereas she did not.

"Don't stop until you reach the castle walls."

She widened her gaze. "What of you?" Her hand was shaky even as she gripped his arms tighter.

"Do as I say," came his harsh reply. "Do not stop for *anything* until you reach the walls."

How would she leave him to his fate, should it come to that?

"Promise me," he insisted. His piercing eyes delving into hers.

She nodded quickly, not certain she could.

Another crunch in the earth brought her attention around.

Then all was quiet…eerily quiet. She couldn't catch her breath. Her desire to beseech him for her own comfort tugged at her. But she mustn't. His thoughts were on survival. Plain and simple.

He turned his head, perhaps looking for any sign of impending attack. His blonde curls plastered to the top of his head. But his stance was more ready than she'd expected of a warrior long from practice.

Yet he was.

He shifted his focus back to her and reached for her hand.

But as they started, a war cry tore from the throat of a man leaping from among thick shrubbery.

Lukas stood, with sword in hand, and pressed her behind himself in one motion. "Run, Anicka!"

Metal clashed as the attacker's sword came down on Lukas's, with which he blocked the blow.

"Go! And do not look back!" His words were grunted as he utilized his firm footing and shoved at the man.

Then the swords scraped each other in a way that jarred her teeth.

Clamping them shut, she turned to flee.

The battle now behind her, she did her best to keep true to the direction Lukas had pointed her in.

What would she do if he were killed? She halted, looking over her shoulder.

The warriors were no longer visible, but the sound of their battle echoed in the trees.

And for that moment, when she was caught in her indecisive hesitation, the forest closed in around her. She whirled toward another sound. But it was a hawk swooping down upon its prey.

Then, as she recentered on her mission—the castle walls—she realized she'd lost place of which way that was.

How could it be? She wasn't daft. And she wasn't helpless...or didn't truly want to be. In all the time she had dreamed up stories, it never entailed a damsel that was completely useless.

She couldn't let Lukas down. She had to find the castle and rally for help.

Moving in the direction she was almost certain was the one she had been on, she stumbled upon something as she struggled to keep her gaze forward. So great was her pull to return and help Lukas in any way she could.

As she worked to right herself, she tripped over a branch or root... something...and the earth rushed toward her.

The wind knocked out of her, the moment it took to catch her breath extended.

But she made it to her feet once more, though her knee was weakened. Had she injured it?

It mattered not, she had to get to safety. Not only for her, but also for Lukas.

One more look back, she turned as she moved.

And hit something solid. For a second, she was dazed by the impact. Had she struck a tree?

Then the heated breath of a man pressed reality back.

Looking up, she found herself staring at the other man who had pursued them. She opened her mouth only to have a hand clamp over her lips and muffle her scream.

Lukas stared at the fallen figure of the man he had put down. The fight had been fraught with worry over his ability to rise to the occasion. And for Anicka. But he had taken care of the immediate threat. Though he was dismayed to see the colors of the guard's garb.

Very much dismayed.

Though he had been in a battle for his own life, he could not rejoice in taking another's.

Still...

A scream pierced the air before it was muffled.

Anicka!

He scrambled in the direction she had gone, the direction of the scream. Was that the other man that had pursued? The one that Lukas had lost sight of?

As he ran, he discovered he was more exerted than he should be for a trained knight. It was enough to drag at his confidence. But he couldn't permit that. Not when Anicka needed him.

He rushed through, coming upon a scene that drew his blood to boiling.

The other guard had one arm wrapped around Anicka to hold her to himself. And the other sealed her lips shut.

Enraged by the assault upon his wife, he let out a cry and launched himself forward.

The guard seemed surprised at the attack. He jerked Anicka to the side as Lukas charged into the spot they had just vacated.

"Do not make this worse," the man's deep voice grated.

"No," Lukas fought to keep his breathing steady. "You need to release my wife before I must take action upon your person."

"Your wife?" The man looked confused.

"Yes." Lukas lifted his weapon a little higher. "If you harm her, I promise you...I will not cease to work revenge upon you until there is no more breath in my body."

Anicka's eyes upon him widened. Had he scared her with his claim? The reality of a man accused of murder making such a statement fell upon him. A man who had just put down another in battle.

But he knew it was so. If Anicka were injured...in any way...he would use every last piece of life to see that this man's life was forfeit.

Anicka hissed out a breath through her nostrils and shut her eyes tightly as she attempted to jerk away from the man.

It was only then Lukas realized the arm that held her captive had a dagger, aimed at her midsection.

Flames lit Lukas's belly. He would never be able to contain such ire. Nor would he ever attempt to.

"Release her," he bit out.

"But I don't understand," the man managed. He did seem rather confused.

Lukas couldn't make sense of it in the haze of anger that overshadowed his mind.

"Put down your blade and I will release her." The man's response was a surprise. What could he mean to gain with that? Would he take advantage of Lukas's weapon being sheathed to take Anicka's life?

"I cannot." Lukas had to do what he could to preserve all lives here.

Still, as Anicka opened her eyes, there was something there that brought an ache in his chest—her pain. At his declaration?

Did she think he spoke thusly because he did not care for her?

He couldn't worry with that now. He had to do what he could

here. "If you will put your dagger down and let her go, I will not harm you."

The man appeared caught in great turmoil. "Lower your sword. I will put my dagger away. Then we can speak on her release."

The guard continued to hold her body against his. Though it was not menacing. But as if she were the only thing keeping him alive. Perhaps, in fact, that was the case.

The man held up his dagger and, opening his hand, let it fall.

Lukas nodded. He pointed his blade toward the ground.

Then the man removed his hand from Anicka's mouth and propelled her toward Lukas.

He caught his wife as she started to stumble. That had been the miscreant's prime opportunity to make his getaway.

Not that Lukas cared. He had Anicka. She was safe.

But when he looked up, the man still stood in front of him.

Why? He'd missed his chance.

Lukas held Anicka close but gripped his sword firmly. "What do you want?"

"Want?" the man sputtered. "Don't you understand?" The supposed attacker gripped his red tunic. "I—"

A shush cut through the moment and then an arrow protruded from the man's heart.

He fell to his knees, confusion filling his eyes.

Lukas would have rushed to assist him, but he instead pressed Anicka's tear-streaked face to his shoulder. She needn't see this.

"Lukas," she murmured, her voice tortured.

He held her more tightly as he tugged them behind a tree. What if the archer targeted them next?

After some moments, it seemed less likely they would become victims of the same bow.

Still, he retreated from the place, bringing Anicka with him.

They came to a shaded spot, surrounded by trees. They would be safe here. He turned his attention to Anicka, rubbing a hand down her hair and tried his best to soothe her.

He wanted to. But his rage still blinded him.

"Did he...injure you?"

She pulled back, rubbing a hand along her abdomen. "I don't think so." But her hand shook.

And he saw then. There was a red stain upon the side of her dress. He reached for it.

She pushed his hand back. "It is nothing."

He clenched his jaw. "I daresay it is."

She held his hand.

He marveled at the strength there even as she gripped his hand as if it were a lifeline. Straightening, he met her wide-eyed gaze.

The brown of her eyes wavered and moisture pooled there. "I was so scared," she finally pressed out.

"I know," he pushed out between sucked in breaths. "I know."

He needed to meet the soft of her with tenderness. Even now, he risked putting her off with the force of his ire. How could he treat her with the gentleness she needed?

Then he put to mind the way he had always held her hand or admired her beauty. With a quiet reverence.

Even now, she was beautiful—though tears stained her dirt-marred features that had contorted. Even with hair that had long since torn free of its bindings. She was beautiful because she leaned into him. She needed him. Without reservation. Without judgment.

He set a hand to the side of her face, wiping at her tears with a thumb. "I am here," he breathed. "And I'm not going anywhere."

She fell into him, clinging to the front of his tunic.

He held her, securely and surely, while she fell apart.

The information he held would wait for now. For how could he tell her that the men that attacked them had been from Zamek Kopec, their future home?

CHAPTER 22

PATRICIE & STEPAN

Stepan pressed his horse along behind Karin's. He dared not rush her. But he longed for a quicker pace. Such was the struggle with being led by a lady. And he considered the source of that thought. Was it for concern over Karin? Or was it borne of his farewell with Patricie merely a couple of hours before leaving?

The words they had exchanged would be long with him—torturing his memories and tugging at his heart.

"Stepan?" Patricie called to him in his mind.

He had, against his better judgment, let himself be drawn to her side. He'd been intent that he would stay away. That if she wanted to speak with him, she must seek him out.

In the end, that had not been the case.

Even so, it stung to see surprise light her features when he entered the chamber set for her and her sister, who had been speaking softly to the young child when Stepan was granted permission to open the door.

"Who did you expect?" The words shot out of him before he

could stop them. Was he truly concerned about who she might have wanted to enter the room? Or was he just injured himself?

"N-no one else. I just..." She looked at her sister, who held her hands out toward the small child in Patricie's arms. Patricie released him into Lady Eva's care. "I...expected that you would be preparing to leave, my lord."

He frowned. She need not maintain such pretenses. Or did her sister not know that he and Patricie had...what? Had an understanding?

Did they?

They had at one time. But his concerns over how he would provide for a family with his father disowning him. Then news of Pavel...

It had not been the time.

"You need not title me so formally." He almost uttered her Christian name, but he dared not. Especially in front of her sister who may be offended at his familiarity.

"Might you..." Patricie shifted her focus to her sister once more.

Lady Eva nodded. "I think I should look in on the baroness. She may require assistance." The lady gave her sister a hard look before leaving the room, jostling the child on her way out, and spearing Stepan with a glare as she passed.

Then perhaps she knew that he had not made his words true upon his and Patricie's arrival to the Hussite camp after being held captive by his father. He would certainly never be a favorite of hers.

Lady Eva left the door open, likely thinking of her sister's virtue. That insulted him. He and Patricie had been in much more compromising situations, and he had not trespassed. Except the shared kisses...

He pushed those out of mind. There were things he needed to say...about his parting and about the way he had left things previously.

Looking to the ground, he stepped forward. "Patricie, I...regret the way things are." He peered up at her. "Between us."

She watched him, her eyes glistening. Had he truly pained her so?

That sliced through him. How could he have neglected what his actions would do to her?

She sniffed and glanced toward the wall. Then pierced him with another look. "Do you still love her?"

"What?" He didn't understand. Love who? Did she think he had left because he loved someone else? Who? Then he realized...he had shared about his betrothal and feelings for Karin.

"I..." He wished to naysay the very thought. But the truth would be best. Always. "I do not."

"Then..." Her lip quivered. She paused and seemed to gather her strength. "Why did you run from me...for *her* sake?"

Stepan took another step toward her, wanting to reach for her. "Is that what you think?"

She drew her arms to her sides as if fearful that he would do just that. "Shouldn't I?"

He let his gaze hold hers. There was, in fact, pain in her regard. "I came as a duty to Lord Krejik. I owe him much. How could I not do everything in my power to see him returned whole?"

She nodded, slowly, lifting a hand to press a cloth to her nose. How much was she holding back from him?

"You must know...how I feel about you. How I feel *for* you. Only you."

She bit at her lower lip. Did she want to keep her emotions in? He was grateful for that. For he might well lose all resolve were she to spill them.

"I thought I knew. But then..." She looked to the floor.

He rushed forward. "You do know. I do care. Don't let your fears tell you otherwise."

Reaching for her hand, he felt her trembling. He clasped both of his hands around hers and drew her fingers to his lips, pressing a kiss to her knuckles.

"Don't belittle what we have been through together. The things we said, the words we shared. The..."

She lifted an eyebrow. "The what?"

"The things we shared that proved how I feel."

Her gaze softened, the tension around her eyes melting.

Footfalls in the corridor should have made him pull back. But he wished he could kick the door closed and pull her to himself. Though...

"My apologies," a voice that did not belong to Lady Eva said into the room.

Patricie's eyes widened and Stepan turned to find Sir Antonin in the doorway.

"Is all well, Lady Patricie?"

Lady? Who did this knight think he was? Did he misunderstand Patricie's station?

Then he realized. Sir Antonin titled her with a warmth that Stepan could not ignore. Nor did he wish to. He started to turn, dropping Patricie's hand.

Patricie gripped Stepan's hand and spoke quickly. "Sir Antonin, what can I assist you with?"

"I..." The knight looked between her and Stepan. His features betraying his confusion and concern. "I but came to speak with you."

"The lady is otherwise engaged," Stepan challenged him. But as long as Patricie grasped his hand so, he would not dishonor her by pushing her away.

Patricie stepped forward, moving between the men as she should not. "I will find you after the rescue party has left, Sir Antonin."

Was this one of the men staying behind with Zdenek? What would he need to speak with Patricie about? Would the man step into a place he was not welcome while Stepan was away?

Stepan wanted to pull her back behind himself. Just in case this came to blows.

But Patricie stood her ground, intent on the opposite. Perhaps she wished to keep peace in this place.

"Aye," Sir Antonin said as he kept his gaze on Stepan, but then nodded in Patricie's direction. Then he looked at her. "You are well?"

Well? Did this man think Patricie was in any way at risk of harm with him? Of all the presumptuous...but Stepan would do the same in Sir Antonin's shoes. Even did he not care for the lady. Though as he watched Sir Antonin's gaze on Patricie, he had reason to believe this was not simply platonic concern.

"I thank you, Sir knight, I am quite well," Patricie assured the man. But why did she have to look so kindly upon him? It heated the fire in Stepan's gut. Unpleasantly so.

The interloper stood in the door for several more seconds, just staring at Patricie.

Just when Stepan shifted to challenge the man, Sir Antonin tore his gaze away, sent a warning look toward Stepan, and then excused himself.

As the sound of the man's boots hitting the ground faded, Stepan turned to Patricie, his jaw clenched. Indeed, all of him felt ready to launch into an attack.

Patricie's eyes glistened. For him? Or for Sir Antonin?

He couldn't let himself be in this position. He would not be hurt again. "I see." He pulled back.

"No!" Patricie grabbed for his arm, pulling him farther into the room.

He turned to face her. His heart closed to anything more.

"Don't do this," she said as her gaze searched his. Her words were barely more than a whisper. "I don't want us to part this way."

He swallowed. He didn't want this to be cinched in his memory either. "I just..." He let out a long exhale.

"But don't." She filled in the gap. "Don't. Let us part well and trusting that there is more for us beyond this."

Her words tugged at his heart. A tug that should not happen had he succeeded in closing it off. But as he settled his gaze on her and allowed himself to rest in the hope that she might speak true, he leaned toward her. Still, he paused just short of her lips, not wanting to force his affection on her. Especially if she did not feel for him as he did her.

Yet as he paused, she lifted herself on toes and pressed first her mouth, then her body to his. She wrapped arms around his shoulders, still tense from the earlier exchange.

He allowed his muscles to relax as he tasted her lips. And reveled in what she offered for this moment—an assurance of her feelings for him. Dare he crack the door of his heart and trust that he could follow through on his offer of marriage? For not even he knew if he was brave enough. But he longed to be. If there was a God in heaven, he prayed that he would be.

Patricie watched from the top of the wall as the figures on horseback faded into the distance. She touched her lips, remembering the feeling of Stepan's mouth on hers. That rush of excitement and the heat that flushed through her. It had been warm and comforting... and so reassuring. But were they in a better place? Had his assurance been sincere? More...would he be able to fulfill the things that were promised in that action?

"They will be well." The voice belonged to her sister, who stood beside her, Michal in her arms.

Patricie nodded. But there was no way Eva knew that any more than she did. There was little truth to any expectation of safety for the group.

Michal's mutterings and attempts at speech became the background, replacing the thudding of horse's hooves. That, too, was reality.

"How is your husband?" She turned to her sister.

Eva's gaze flitted to Patricie before settling on Michal once more. "He is well. Better than expected."

"That is good. Mayhap I will speak with the healer about his—"

"That is not necessary."

Eva's interruption surprised Patricie. What was that about? Eva's tone softened as she said, "I mean only to tell you that he has much to attend to in the baroness's stead."

Patricie nodded. "It is fortunate he has the dowager baroness to assist."

There was a pause. What troubled Eva?

But then she spoke. "True. But I would prefer he be able to rest."

"I understand. Perhaps I can help with that?"

Eva shook her head. "'Tis best you leave it be."

Again, that bothered. Did Eva not trust Patricie? What was this?

"Let us return. There may be preparations for the noon meal to be made." Eva spun toward the stairs.

"Sister..." Patricie entreated.

Eva halted but looked over her shoulder. "Yes?"

"What is it that offends you so?" Patricie could not let this thing live between them. Especially unspoken and unknown.

Eva took an exaggerated breath and let it out. "I'd prefer not to speak of it."

Patricie wet her suddenly dry lips. That, she could not abide. "I'd prefer that you do. For I cannot mend what I am unaware is broken."

Eva shifted to facing Patricie once more. "It is Lord Dvorak."

Something rose in Patricie. Something defensive? Or uncertain? "What about him?" Her words were tighter than she'd intended.

"Let us not quarrel. We will speak of it when you are in a better mood."

"I am in a fine disposition right now," Patricie argued. "Let us speak of it now. What do you have against Stepan?" Too late, she realized she used his Christian name.

Eva lifted an eyebrow as she sighed. "I do not think he is right to play at your emotions."

Patricie drew in a breath, prepared to launch into a defense.

But Eva held up a hand. Not an easy thing to do with a squirming youngster. "Do not be so. I am simply worried."

Patricie counted five breaths, slow and steady. "What worries you, dear sister?"

Eva gave her a pointed look, but continued, "He promised you would wed, but has...postponed the nuptials. That does not bode well. Then, when you have another prospect, he makes his ardor apparent, ensnaring your favor."

"Another prospect? What are you saying?" But Patricie could guess. She wasn't blind to what went in Sir Antonin's actions. The man did, indeed, find her before they departed.

He spoke kindly to her, assuring she was well once more. Then he spoke words of farewell and told that he would seek her out when he returned.

She should have discouraged his attentions, but perhaps deep down, she did worry about Stepan's intentions to actually marry her.

"Sir Antonin is a fine man." Eva's words cut into Patricie's thoughts. "His intentions are true."

Patricie straightened her shoulders, unwilling to give up on Stepan. "So are Lord Dvorak's," she shot back.

Eva chewed at her lip. "Are they? Did he speak more of it?"

Patricie looked after where the last view of the men had been. "He did not."

"Then perhaps you are free to consider...other options." Eva's voice was kind, but firm.

Patricie clenched her teeth together. She did not wish to have this discussion further. Or for her sister to voice her own fears of Stepan's intentions...or lack thereof. It wasn't right. Not when there were other things Eva should be concentrating on.

"How did Lord Ambrose feel about taking on a son not of his body?"

One glimpse in Eva's direction told that Patricie's barb had hit the mark.

Eva's eyes widened and her mouth fell open. But she was silent for several moments.

It was unfair. And Patricie knew that well. Yet she could not take the words back, nor did she truly wish to.

"He..." Eva swallowed and looked at Michal who slapped at her face with his chubby hands. "It will take some adjustment."

Patricie bit at the inside of her mouth to keep from speaking further. There were questions she had that demanded answers. Though she wasn't certain it was her due.

A figure topped the stairs behind Eva, drawing Patricie's attention. It was a maidservant, approaching with hesitation.

"Patricie of Hradek Kralove?" the girl asked.

"I am here," Patricie turned fully toward the younger woman. "What have you need of me?"

"Is it true you are a healer?"

"Yes," Patricie said as she stepped around her sister. She wanted to give a quick apology for her words, but it was not appropriate to do so in front of the servant. Nor was she certain she was ready.

"There is someone in the village that has fallen ill. The village healer has not been found. You are needed."

Patricie nodded, girding herself internally for what she might find. She let the veneer of the physician fall over her. No longer was she Eva's sister...her skills were needed. And she would answer that summons.

Perhaps more readily than usual. For the tension that had spread between her and Eva was heated with much emotion. But that would have to be a later problem.

"Take me there," she commanded the maidservant.

Without looking back at her sister, she trudged forward. For that was the only place time took anyone. No taking her words back, even should she want to. Forward. Ever forward.

CHAPTER 23
KARIN & PAVEL

Pavel couldn't see beyond the back of the mule he had been strapped to. He'd been slung over the animal's back, his arms and legs bound and tied. Indeed, not only was the view backward blocked, neither could he see much past its hair-packed neck. The coarseness of the mule chafed in places, but he was thankful he was secure upon it. Even if his position was a bit...odd.

Pavel had certainly exaggerated his weakness before. That could only help him. For now, he would continue to feign greater injury than what he had incurred. Not that it was far from what he pretended. His legs might, in fact, be incapacitated. If the pain that raked over him was any indication, they may very well be broken.

Still, he could not risk trying them. For there were too many eyes. Someone would note the truth were he able to bear weight upon them. So, the playacting it was.

The company continued to move forward despite the darkening of the sky. Would they journey into the night? Perhaps they were closing in on their destination. Did Ulrich have somewhere he intended to stop for the night? Or...might they be near his stronghold?

A fight rose within him. He could not let them get him within the walls of the castle. Any hope of escape would be eliminated. His chances of getting to Karin and Jaromir would slim to virtually nothing.

The passage that spoke of nothing being impossible with God rang in his head. But he pushed it to the side. He wasn't ready to speak with God yet. Or acknowledge the possibility that He did care to even see Pavel's plight, much less help.

Indeed, he was quite angry.

"What do you think?" One of the mercenaries nearby grunted. Had another guard come closer?

"How does he fare?"

There was a pause. "I think he breathes. Maybe even listens."

"As if that will matter," the other man scoffed. "Dead men cannot betray what they have heard, can they?"

"That's true. Do you think Lord Ulrich intends to..."

"Most certainly. And he's daft if he thinks otherwise. Once Ulrich is done with him, he'll have long outlived his usefulness. I wish 'twere already done. Then we could move on to the next job."

"Aye. But I have taken a position at Lord Ulrich's castle. I will not be moving on."

"That madman? I wouldn't trust him. He has a...temper."

"'Tis true. But every day that goes by, the more it seems he is no longer on the losing side of this war for Bohemia."

"Truly?"

"Since Zizka's death, the Orphans and Taborites are restless, leaderless, hopeless."

"Perhaps it will heat the flames of unrest between them. Without that one-eyed warlord, they'll be easier to pick off...one by one."

"You are wrong," the mercenary-turned-guard muttered.

"What about?" the first man's tone darkened.

"Zizka had lost *both* eyes."

The pair laughed. It was a menacing, gruff thing. Nearly enough to give Pavel reason to strike out.

How dare they speak so about the great general who, against all odds, had led the misfit band of Hussite farmers and peasants with naught but farming implements to victory. It never mattered that they faced a large, well-trained army with fine weaponry. It never mattered that everything was against them. General Zizka had been a clever strategist and a more than capable tactical leader.

But he was gone.

Leaving broken Czech lands and people in the wake of his death.

Again, Pavel wondered how a good God could allow it after working miracles through the small army. Now the brethren were fractured, splintered, and hopelessly lost.

Would God give them another leader?

Something shifted about the way the mule moved.

"There," the first guard said, breaking into the silence that Pavel hadn't realized befell them. "See the turret over that tree line?"

The other man must have nodded.

"That is Ulrich's castle."

"Doesn't the Botic River cut through the land somewhere around here?" the first man muttered.

"Aye. There is a bridge."

"I should hope so." The first man's graveled response did not sound enthused that this would be his new home. "Somewhat dark, is it not?"

The second man laughed. "As if it should be anything but."

Pavel risked discovery by opening his eyes slightly. Indeed, what he could discern beyond the mule's rough mane was not much. But there were splices of visibility as the animal moved its head and neck. The outline of the castle was all he glimpsed. And even that only for a moment. While it was only partly visible above the tree line, the sinking sun behind it provided a silhouette. It did create a dark and rather foreboding first glimpse.

Again, Pavel's thoughts wandered to his fate. What would Ulrich do with him? Why keep him alive for now? Why not just kill him with the rest of the men? Did he have some purpose in keeping Pavel? He must. And it could not be good.

But what of Karin? His nose stung with the onslaught of emotion. Did someone with malicious intent stalk his home? Mayhap have taken it under his control? What would become of his wife? She had endured so much these last years. She was fair and, while not completely helpless, she needed his strength. And he had promised before God to protect her.

Perhaps that was why God had abandoned him. He could not keep his word, so would it be that God did not intend to watch over him?

He resisted being pulled further into that belief. But it gnawed at him all the same.

The mule turned and Pavel noted that the animal clomped upon stone now, no longer soft thuds on the earth. Were they upon the bridge the mercenary had mentioned? Were they soon to be in the stronghold? What could he do? Could he overtake his guards by surprise? Utilize the mule to escape? That would be folly. Mules were meant for labor and sure-footedness. It was not a warhorse. Nor would it outrun one.

So, he could do nothing more as they moved ever forward.

Even as they shifted and slowed, there was the wood of the drawbridge under the animals hooves.

It was to be soon—the passing of his last hope of escape.

Where was God? Why would he not provide an opportunity for Pavel? Even the smallest chance and Pavel would risk his life to take it. But there was nothing.

As the iron gate fell closed behind him, Pavel swallowed back any fear of what was to come. God was, in fact, his *only* hope now.

Karin was thankful for Sir Marek. He was a wise, capable leader. She would have pushed the company further, but he called for them to stop more frequently. Was it for her benefit? She found she didn't care. For she needed the pause. She was not used to being in the saddle for such extended times.

Perhaps it was for the benefit of the horses—to water and rest them, but it was more likely on her behalf.

The men grumbled but did so briefly and lowly. Out of respect for Sir Marek? Or out of fear of him?

He led well. But he did not tolerate any amount of disrespect toward Karin or himself. Indeed, he shot a harsh look toward the few men that made huffing sounds.

They quickly quieted.

"The horses need respite. As do we," Sir Marek announced. "There is no need to push them harder."

Karin looked away from the group. Though she recognized her need for pausing more often, she couldn't bear the men's scoffing faces. They already sacrificed so much for her family. Regularly. She dared not find fault in this minor infraction.

She turned to find Stepan to the side of her horse, offering to assist her to the ground.

Mayhap she had more pride than she should, for she ignored his presence and dismounted while avoiding his hand. It was done awkwardly, and she nearly found herself a heap on the ground, but she managed...barely.

As she came to her balance, Sir Marek approached. There was a glint of something sympathetic in his gaze. But it was gone too quickly for her to be sure.

"Lady Karin, I would suggest we plan to camp here for the night. There is a place near the stream that would be well suited for our tents."

She frowned. Was this, too, for her benefit? She could go on...she was certain. But the ache in her hips told otherwise. Indeed, Sir Marek was a good leader.

Though the longer they tarried the more likely her husband

would be abused...more. She wanted to get to him and feel his arms about her and know that he was safe.

As if reading her thoughts, Sir Marek interjected, "There is not much daylight left for us to find another place to stop. Nothing can be gained by continuing."

Sucking in a breath and letting it out, she nodded.

She scanned the group and her gaze landed on Sir Tomas. The men guarding him assisted him to the ground as his hands were bound. They led him toward the stream. In order to get there, they would pass closer to where she was. She couldn't deny the pull of her heart toward him. What, in fact, had happened to him in those intervening years? How was one to reject old feelings for someone that were no longer appropriate?

Karin cared for him. But how much? At one time, her heart was more fully turned to him as she anticipated their future betrothal. However, that was not to be. She was Pavel's wife. And she did not regret that one bit.

So, she turned from him. Though, she found Sir Marek still stood nearby, watching her.

His frown spoke volumes. He didn't trust her with Sir Tomas. Should he not?

"Come, my lady, let us refresh you at the stream." Sir Marek took her elbow gently and shifted her toward the water source.

She allowed it.

But as they moved in that direction, she noted that some of the guards and knights had pulled out their swords.

She jerked to a halt. "Is there danger?"

Sir Marek shook his head. "No, my lady. There is not cause for concern. The men will practice at arms with each other in the time we have. Skills must be honed with some of the younger men and others must keep their keen edge."

She nodded, letting him lead her once again. But she looked to him after a few steps. "Perhaps I might seek to learn alongside them?"

Sir Marek fairly stumbled but smoothed his pace quickly. He coughed. "Why, my lady? We are capable to protect you."

It was she who stopped then. "But am I not one of this company? Should I not be trained with the sword to fight with my men?"

Sir Marek met her gaze with eyes that did not show surprise, but rather intention.

The men nearby snickered and then sputtered.

Sir Marek's hard gaze did not move from her, still the men moved away out of respect for their privacy and stopped their sputtering.

"Lady Karin." Sir Marek addressed her as if he spoke with a child. "There is no cause. And I fear my lord baron would not approve."

She jerked free of him. "Am I not your mistress? The lord baron is not here to command you, but I am in his stead. I care not for his concern, but for his rescue. And I will not be found a liability for these men." Her voice was firmer than she'd expected but impassioned as she deeply was.

Sir Marek looked to the ground as if considering her words. Or did he gather his wits about him to scold her again?

"I will insist upon it."

"Mayhap..." Sir Marek met her gaze again. "I might train you on the bow and arrow. That will make good use of your strengths, allow you to fight with us, and keep you far from danger."

She frowned.

"Besides, the swords are heavy. You are not practiced with their weight. It would be difficult for you to maneuver with them."

"Do we not have any smaller blades? Or lighter swords? Perhaps among the squires for their own training?"

Sir Marek's lips tightened. "A shorter blade would put you in greater danger, not less."

"I don't care." Something rose within her—a desire to have her will obeyed. No matter the personal cost later on. Was she not the true leader of the contingency?

"This is madness," Stepan said, coming up from her right side. "We do not wish to risk you in this mission."

Of all the... She spun on Stepan as he approached, straining Sir Marek's grip. "I did not ask you. Nor do I seek your approval."

He frowned, his gaze intense.

Sir Marek muttered, then spoke. "That may be, my lady. But I will not command any of my men to train you. I daresay, you will not find one you can convince otherwise."

"This is a command," she seethed. "Not a request."

He waved a hand. "In this, you may insist all you would like, but I will not dishonor my lord baron this way. Find someone if you can that will." His gaze wandered over the men that had paused to listen.

Their grim-set faces did not waver. Indeed, they had heard the exchange. And those in the camp that had not, soon would know all.

There was little hope for her, then.

A strong voice called from somewhere off to the side. "*I* will train you."

She knew who it was before the men parted to reveal Sir Tomas standing tall. Karin permitted a small smile for him before she turned to Sir Marek.

The man was, again, not surprised. Did he think this was a ploy by Tomas to be unbound? To have time with her such that he might work ill upon her?

And more...was he right?

CHAPTER 24
ANICKA & LUKAS

Anicka had relished the minutes she had Lukas to herself. Even amidst such challenge. There had not been much in the way of conversation. His anger ran too deep. But she appreciated how he had held back the worst of it for her benefit. Would he ever feel safe to share the whole of it with her? No matter how difficult?

For now, however, they neared the walls of Zamek Kopec. There would be safety there for them. Perhaps they would be met with ire equaled to Lukas's at the attack. Mayhap they would reunite with those that had been set upon—and they would be whole and well.

That was much to hope for.

Lukas drew her closer.

She came willingly, wanting to press all the more into his strength.

"Anicka," he clipped.

It was not a favorite uttering of her name. Certainly not from his lips. But she wanted to understand that it was time to put aside fairy tales and romance, for the real of it. He was angry.

She offered her gaze, and the full attention he commanded of her.

He examined her features as if looking for something. What was it? Compliance? That, he would have.

"Yes, my lord?"

He frowned at that.

Why? Wasn't that what every good wife should say?

Either way, he seemed to push whatever it was to the side. "I want you to stay near me."

She nodded, uncertain of how to parse that.

"No matter what happens, stay near and listen to any instructions I give."

What could he mean? He spoke as if they approached danger rather than sanctuary. It didn't make sense.

"Promise," he rasped. Was that due to the force of his need for her agreement? Or due to something she wanted to name more moving?

Put those things to the side, she told herself. This was not the place or the time for girlish fantasies.

"Aye." The word held less weight than she'd intended. But the blue of his eyes had caught her.

Was that concern deep within? Concern for her wellbeing? Or something more...intimate? Dare she hope?

He released her arm but retained a hold of her hand while his other lingered over the hilt of his sword. It made no sense. It was as if he prepared for a fight.

Taking a deep breath, he expelled it and led her past the tree line and into the open.

There, the walls of the castle rose to the sky beyond a deep ditch that lay between them and the fortified estate. The dark and gray of the sky nearly matched the stones. But they would soon be out of the open and by the hearth. She chose not to worry with the coming rain.

Rumbling in the distance bespoke that the earth would receive its refreshment soon. Yet, Lukas moved without haste.

Someone in the watchtower gave the hue and cry. Then the battlements were flooded with guards with weapons at the ready.

Lukas's grip tightened to the point of pain, but Anicka bit back any sound. The scene seemed rather tense.

The men atop the outer wall clustered and shouted indiscernible directions. But what was evident was that they readied the archers, who drew back their bow strings niched with arrows.

"Do not!" Lukas shouted with a voice that was impossibly loud. Even as he spoke, he pulled Anicka squarely behind him and unsheathed his sword as if that would protect them from flying arrows. He would put himself in such a position? For her? Her heart fluttered.

Not now! This was the wrong moment to relish such a flight of fancy.

The men paused but did not lower their weapons.

"I am Baron Lukas Vitek...your lord," he called. How was he able to keep any trepidation or fear from his voice? Did he not feel those things?

For her part, she longed to drop to the ground and make herself as small a target as possible—or better, run for the forest again. But she would not dishonor Lukas's attempt to protect her so. She would trust.

"Lord Vitek?" a voice called from the wall.

"Yes! I demand you bring me and my lady wife into the safety of the walls."

There was a pause and more scurrying.

"Lower the drawbridge and open the portcullis," Lukas commanded in a firm voice. There was a boldness to his affect that surprised her, defying his earlier concern.

Were they or were they not in danger?

Another flurry of activity atop the wall was set in motion. However, the archers did not relax their stance.

That was odd indeed. Lukas had declared his identity. What went here?

After some moments in which Lukas's grip did not ease and Anicka's hand began to ache, the drawbridge lowered.

Lukas's hold on her remained firm, but no longer painful. And he kept his sword at the ready as he took tentative steps to lead her to the lowering bridge.

Soon enough, they were over the older wooden structure and through the gate.

They were greeted by more guards, led by a man who stood but a few inches shorter than Lukas, but had more bulk about himself. "My lord baron," he greeted them. "I feared for your safety. There were reports of brigands in the region."

Lukas did not say anything but dragged her forward as he advanced on the man. Then he released his grip on his sword's hilt and swung a solid punch to the man's jaw.

Lukas would have relished the moment the knight fell over, but he was far too angry. The heated sensation pulsed through him, tensing his muscles and setting him on edge. This man had not only tried to end his life, but the guards would have no doubt snuffed out the bright flame of Anicka.

That, Lukas could not abide. And he would not.

Sir Warren looked up, his eyes filled with fury. But there was no confusion about them. Yes, he knew.

Anicka's hand trembled in his.

Should he release her? But he would not risk that others within the walls were untrustworthy.

"You attempted to steal all that is mine." Lukas's voice was harsh, and he intended every bit of it.

"I...that is a lie!" Sir Warren rose.

His men did not come around him as Lukas feared they would.

There was, indeed, uncertainty about them. Because they didn't know? Or because they weighed who to follow.

It would not take much for them to finish off Lukas and Anicka. But Lukas prayed that the men were—as was the knight in the forest —unaware of Sir Warren's plot.

"Do not think that I shall heed your pleas," Lukas ground out. "You are relieved of your station. We shall see what will become of you. If I have a say in the matter, it will not be well." There was a voice within that whispered for mercy of some sort. But Lukas was far too angry to give it credence.

"W-why?" Sir Warren dared to keep up the pretense.

Further evidence he did not wish his men to know what Sir Warren had intended.

"You sent those men to attack us. To bring a permanent end to the rival of me to your position."

With firm-set jaw, Sir Warren's face reddened. From anger? He dared not put forth any manner of defense.

Lukas would not have it. "You'd best hold your tongue. For anything you say may only further incriminate you."

Tearing his gaze from Sir Warren for a moment, Lukas scanned the cluster of guards about them. None reached for their sword. Were they all truly surprised? That bore investigation but portended well for retaking charge of the castle.

In that moment, however, Sir Warren lashed out, shoving Lukas to the ground.

He loosened his grip on Anicka as he fell, but a thud and her cry told that at the very least, she had fallen as well. Though he could not concern himself with her in this moment.

For he found a dagger appeared in Sir Warren's hand that thrust toward Lukas.

He caught the man's forearm before the fatal blow could be struck, but just barely. Grappling for the weapon, Lukas pulled from the well of anger that had filled him. It gave him strength.

Though, it was for naught. For the weight of Sir Warren over him was relieved soon enough.

Lukas looked about.

The guards that had been idle and confused had leapt into action. They now held Sir Warren firmly between them.

There were other guards that stood, hands on sword hilts, as if they readied to do battle with those that would pin down Sir Warren. Perhaps they weighed the situation at hand. Dare they assert any allegiance to Sir Warren now?

Lukas sat upright. "Take him to the dungeon."

The guards holding the squirming man nodded.

Again, others looked to Sir Warren as if awaiting instruction.

"You will be sorry," Sir Warren said. "You have no right to take what is mine!"

The man's raging continued as the men half dragged him away.

Lukas met the gazes of the few that had seemed torn between their new lord and the man who had but held his place for a time. He would watch them, but he was ready to forgive the temporary pull between authority.

A groan to the side reminded him that Anicka had fallen as well.

He turned to her, but another knight already knelt by her side.

Lukas rushed forward, pushing through to her other side.

Anicka's eyes were open. When her gaze settled on Lukas, she moaned again. "Is all well?"

"Yes. Sir Warren has been taken to the dungeon. We shall settle the rest, but we must get you a healer." He put hands to her head, searching for a wound from the fall.

The other knight reached to help her sit.

As she sat up, her face paled, and she set the back of her hand to her mouth. Was she going to be ill?

Lukas positioned himself such that he might support her weight with his body.

But she leaned forward.

"Are you unwell, my lady?" he said, his tone gentled from that of just minutes ago. He glanced about at the gathering crowd of guards. "Give the lady some space. And you," Lukas said, pointing at one of the nearby knights, "go for the healer."

"I beg your pardon, Lord Vitek, but the healer passed this time last year."

Lukas frowned, his heart sinking. "Send someone to the next village."

Anicka set a hand to his arm. "Truly, I am well. I just need a minute."

Turning his focus back to her, he threw another demand in the knight's direction. "Go."

Anicka turned to look at him better. "I may need assistance to stand." Her voice was low as if she, too, did not wish to show weakness.

He was grateful for her sensibilities, but wholly concerned that she was, in fact, not well. "You must lie still. What if you have a head injury?"

She offered a weak smile. "Trust me, lord husband, I am well enough. Twill only be bruises, as much to my pride as my body."

He allowed the levity, though he did not feel it. But, as she insisted, he reached around her and helped her to her feet.

To her credit, she did not waver, but held firm to her stance.

"I will escort my lady wife to the solar. And you," he said to the knight nearby who had assisted with Anicka, "ready men to ride out for my escort. We were attacked beyond the forest."

The men did not seem as surprised as he would have expected. But then, they were dull witted if they could not piece together what they were unaware of.

A cry came from the watchtower.

The knight closest to Lukas said, "Perhaps, my lord, that is news. Shall I go?"

Lukas wished to find out the news for himself, but he was beholden to help Anicka to her rest. Torn, he waivered for a moment.

But his duty was first to his wife. "Aye. And report to me as soon as you can."

When he looked back to Anicka, she had an odd expression about her features. Had she noticed the minute he nearly left her for the safety of the castle? Or did she wonder why he chose her? That was difficult to discern, but he muttered soft words and then led her toward the donjon.

Would he ever be split in two like this?

CHAPTER 25

PATRICIE & STEPAN

Patricie ran the back of her hand along her brow. Another would fall to the plague. And all her efforts were for naught. Nothing she did made any difference. The best she could offer was to keep those afflicted comfortable.

She leaned over yet another victim of the ailment. He finally rested. But for how long? The swelling under his arms and to the sides of his neck had risen. In her experience, death would soon follow.

"Are those...the black swellings?" The priest beside her paused. He had insisted on coming to pray over the sick.

She nodded, a slow, tired movement. "Yes. He won't be with us long."

The priest clung to his rosary and shuddered as he murmured a prayer for protection. "Is it for certain the black death?"

"I fear it is."

Father Boursek drew back slightly. "Will you not release the poison?"

The man referred to lancing the lumps. "I have not found or

heard that that will help the patient in the least. It will only bring discomfort in his final hours."

"Perhaps then there should be bloodletting?"

The man was insufferable.

She shook her head. "That, too, has not proven effective. I prefer to let the patient rest as much as possible."

Father Boursek stared at her, wide eyed. "So, you will do nothing?"

"As I said, I will make him as comfortable as possible and apply poultices. That is the best I can offer. But we'd best tighten our quarantine."

The priest did not seem ready to agree with her. Clearly, he thought her incompetent. What did that matter? He hadn't already struggled through watching many fall to the sickness. Father Boursek would simply pray over the patients and walk away, considering his job done.

This time, however, there was an air of foreboding about him.

Patricie rose with her bowl of water, carrying it to the side. She should refresh her supplies and the water.

For several moments, she worked at that. The patient's wife stared on from nearby.

"I am sorry. I wish there were more I could do."

The woman shook her head. "Twas bound to happen. I only regret it would be my Martin."

Patricie frowned and dipped out garlic, rue, and sage into her bowl. "Ill befalls the righteous and the unrighteous, as the Holy Writ says."

"'Tis of the unrighteous sort."

Did the woman speak ill of her husband?

"For that devil child brought this on us."

Patricie's brow furrowed. "Devil child?"

The woman permitted but a glance in Patricie's direction. "Father Boursek tells that devil child is in the castle. And he has brought this plague upon us."

Patricie's heart stopped. Did they speak of Michal? Did these folks truly believe that the child carried some manner of evil about him? "You cannot mean that. The plague afflicts without discernment. It has simply come upon a traveler no doubt."

Martin's wife fixed her gaze on Patricie then. "Have you seen the mark upon the child?"

Patricie squared her shoulders. "Aye. I have."

"Is it not...of the ungodly sort?"

"Absolutely not! It is only a mark painted on him at birth. Surely by God's hand."

"To mark him as evil." The woman concluded, turning back to the priest, whose voice over her husband rose.

Patricie let out a breath. She wanted to argue more but found herself out of sorts.

"That is what Father Boursek tells. And I believe him."

Patricie simply shook her head and turned her attention to the mixture. She would have to speak with the priest about spreading such falsehoods. Though she doubted her words of reason would be well-received. The man was rather determined when it came to his beliefs.

"That witch child should be destroyed," the woman murmured.

Patricie halted, jerking her head in the woman's direction. "You can't mean that."

"Aye, I do. For the sake of my Martin. And for the rest of the village." There was a glassy look about the woman's eyes. Moisture gathered there.

A muffled shout came from the far side of the small house.

Patricie spun around as Sir Antonin burst within, seeking the source of the trouble. She rushed toward the man that had shouted. To her horror, she saw a dagger in the priest's hand. Was he trying to kill the man?

"What are you doing?" she said, setting herself between the now injured and sick Martin and Father Boursek.

The priest narrowed his gaze. "I do what must be done."

Sir Antonin must have taken in the scene well enough for he relieved the priest of his weapon.

She turned toward her patient to find that Father Boursek had crudely lanced the swollen places upon his neck. But there was much blood. Too much. Had he cut a vital blood source?

Patricie grabbed for a cloth, unsure where it was from and pressed it to the wound. And she felt for Martin's breathing. It was shallow. Moreso than it should be. "You've killed him!"

The priest was stoic. "It was only my intention to help him." Why was the man not more remorseful?

Sir Antonin gripped the holy man's arm. "Let me take you outside."

"He was doomed anyway," Father Boursek said. It was a mournful sound. "We all are."

Patricie spared him a hard look as she fought to staunch the bleeding. "Get out!"

When Sir Antonin grabbed at the priest's arm, the man flinched as if hurt. Did the knight grab him tightly? But Sir Antonin jerked back as if surprised.

Dread filled Patricie. The priest had been with her for several visits.

She directed Sir Antonin to hold the cloth to Martin's neck.

He complied, their hands sliding together for a moment.

She wouldn't have considered it another second, but for the way Sir Antonin's gaze sought hers. Her face heated. Still, she must see to the priest.

Standing, she stepped toward him. "Let me examine you."

The priest shook his head. Was his resolve so firm?

"I insist." She prayed he would yield, for she could not force him, and Sir Antonin needed to apply pressure to Martin's wound.

"My lady..." Sir Antonin called.

She whirled toward him.

"The bleeding eases!" The knight lifted his hand for a moment. Indeed, the rush had calmed.

Another wave of dread passed over her as she crouched once more.

"Does he not improve?" Sir Antonin's jaw was set.

"No." She set a hand to his chest. "He has passed beyond all human aid."

Sir Antonin shook his head as if disbelieving.

She looked at him. "He is in God's hands now."

Martin's wife let out a wail.

Patricie rose as she twisted around. "I'm so sorry."

The woman caught the edge of the table for support.

"I wish I could have done more."

The woman quaked and set teary eyes to Patricie's. "That devil child will be the end of us all!"

Patricie turned toward the priest.

But he was gone.

"Sir Antonin," Patricie shouted. "Father Boursek is gone!"

"What?" He stood, leaving the soiled linens where they lay.

"Where did Father Boursek go?" Patricie asked the distraught widow.

The woman dipped her head as she shook it.

Patricie wagered such was true. Even if she did know, she probably wouldn't tell them.

"Why is that our concern where he has gone?" Sir Antonin stepped closer, their arms were barely separated by an inch.

She turned on him. "Don't you see? He has the plague. We cannot let him roam freely."

Sir Antonin's eyes widened.

"We have to contain this as best we can. He must be found." She strode for the door and stepped out into the rain.

The sun had dimmed from the clouds, and the rain obscured what might have been visible.

If Father Boursek did not wish to be found, there was little hope they could do so. But every risk that he would spread the Great Death.

Stepan watched closely as Sir Tomas was released of his bonds and began the instruction of Lady Karin. When Karin demanded the man be given a weapon, it gave Stepan pause. Would she be so reckless? To be close to an armed prisoner...a man who may be in league with the enemy?

Regardless, she insisted upon it. And Stepan was not the only man that stood watching. Though the others scoffed at her somewhat clumsy efforts, Stepan was concerned. Why would she insist upon learning the weapon? Did she truly intend to engage in close battle?

In truth, she struggled with the heft of the sword. More and more as she fatigued.

But he watched, torn about joining in the effort to properly train her as much as possible in this short time, and holding back that she may lose hope in the idea.

Her irritation grew. She wiped perspiration and fumbled more and more with the sword.

Indeed, Sir Tomas held back his impatience well. He clamped his mouth when she had a fit of frustration. His ability—or his care for her—became more evident as the moments passed. Should Stepan remain in the background? Did he care about Karin's determination? Or worry more that the two would keep close? Perhaps, if he held back, they would become so put out with each other that it would create greater distance.

But as Stepan watched Karin try again and again to no avail, though Sir Tomas was truly patient with her, giving her chance after chance, Stepan could bear her scrunched features and grunts of worry no more.

He stepped forward as he called a man at arms to his side.

"Bring a bow and arrow," he commanded.

The man quirked an eyebrow but moved off to obey.

"Lady Karin," Stepan said, drawing her and Sir Tomas's attention. "I think it is time we put that to the side."

A bow and arrow appeared as if from nowhere, thrust into his hands.

"Mayhap you try your hand at this?" Stepan offered. "I am ready to teach you as well."

Tomas's gaze darkened.

Stepan cared not. Perhaps even relished the opportunity to bring the man down a bit.

Karin lifted her chin. "I will not be consigned to the side."

Stepan blew out a breath. He should have anticipated that. "I would not suggest such. But the sword is not a weapon that can be mastered easily."

"No more so than the bow, I wager," she shot back.

"Indeed," Stepan admitted.

"Pay him no heed." Tomas urged her to lift her sword once more.

She struggled to do so, grimacing as she tried.

"I would suggest the crossbow, but that is heavier than that sword."

She lifted the sword with a grunt. "Are you implying that I cannot manage it?" She swung at Sir Tomas.

"Aye." It was not in Stepan's nature to appease and placate. He would not disguise the truth.

Her eyes widened as she turned back to him. Was she surprised by his frankness? She should not be. Of all involved, she knew he would be straightforward.

"I will not speak in fairytales to you." He thrust a hand in Tomas's direction. "The broadsword will not work."

She frowned. "I will not work the bow and arrow from the back."

Stepan motioned for the man at arms. "Give me your sidearm."

The man gave Stepan a quizzical look.

Stepan pressed out a hand. "Now."

The man surrendered the short sword.

"We should try with something lighter."

Tomas's jaw clenched. "That has much shorter reach. She will be run through before she has a chance to engage her enemy."

"She is lighter on her feet than a typical warrior. She can learn to maneuver quicker to avoid a blade and slip in closer."

Tomas remained stoic, frowning.

"Besides," he said as he neared Karin, "she cannot lift this blade. What use is it to her if she cannot wield the weapon for more than a handful of minutes?"

"She will gain more strength in her arms," Tomas argued.

"In a matter of days?" Stepan lifted one eyebrow. "That does not seem likely. To think so is folly."

Tomas clenched his jaw, clearly not pleased with the turn of events.

"Are you uncomfortable with the short sword?" Stepan baited the man.

Karin took the sidearm that Stepan offered, testing its lighter weight. Hope shone from her eyes.

"I am not." Tomas's answer was short. "I daresay I could best you."

"Oh?" Stepan met Sir Tomas's gaze, unwavering. "Shall we put it to the test?"

Karin's gaze flung between the men as if uncertain what occurred between them.

"It would be my pleasure to school you, sir."

Realization dawned on Karin's face. "No!"

Stepan stepped forward, unfazed by Karin's protest.

Sir Tomas did not seem dissuaded either. He threw the wooden training sword to the side and reached out. "Bring me a baselard."

Stepan paced in an arc before Tomas. "Lady Karin, you must step away."

"No," she fairly shouted as one of the knights removed his sidearm as if to pass it to Tomas. "I will not have it!"

Stepan ignored her and set his focus on Tomas. "I think I'll enjoy this...lesson."

Though they both knew it was more than that—it was a challenge, an opportunity.

"Step aside, Lady Karin," Stepan insisted.

She shoved her way in front of Tomas. "No. I will not allow this."

Tomas gazed at Karin with an admiration that made Stepan nauseated. It was not proper for someone to look at another man's wife in such a way.

Stepan swung the blade to test its reach.

"Stand down, Sir Stepan." Karin firmed her stance. "That is an order."

Stepan paused for a moment. Then glared at Tomas. He was fortunate that Karin did not permit this. For Stepan was not certain he could hold back from visiting real injury upon the man.

"Stepan!" Karin's voice was sharp.

Tomas jerked back as Karin addressed Stepan by his Christian name.

Stepan held out the short sword, blade down, for the man at arms.

The stocky man took back his blade.

Karin visibly relaxed.

But Tomas's gaze bore into Stepan.

And Stepan knew...this was not over. They would find an opportunity. He just had to bide his time...and be watchful.

KARIN & PAVEL

Karin retired from yet another day filled with travel and searching for clues...and training. She was weary. Worn to the bone. Her fingers ached from the weight of even the lighter sidearm and the force of clashing with other weapons as they worked to gain her skills.

This night she was grateful for her lady in waiting that came with them. She had hated to bring the frail woman but having someone assist her out of the armor she had acquired and her more simple dress was a Godsend this eve.

How she longed for a hot bath. That would be heaven in this place and time. But the best the maidservant could offer was a basin of clean water. It would have to do.

Karin relished it as she splashed cool liquid upon her heated features. Though her arms ached almost too much to lift them to do so.

Her gaze flitted to the bed that had been prepared for her. And she longed to simply lay herself down and surrender to sleep. But it would no doubt be a fitful sleep...full of bad dreams of what may be happening to Pavel. Such images visited her frequently in sleep, preventing true rest from claiming her.

Could she bear to see his face contorted in pain or frozen in death as she had these past several nights? But she could not resist sleep any more than she could stop her breathing. Not on this night.

In her chemise, and with the maidservant moving about her tented space, Karin opened her mouth to tell the woman to find her own rest that Karin may have respite to stretch out upon the bed.

But she was cut off by the sound of her guard outside.

"My lady, I must speak with you," the man called.

She glanced down at her chemise. The ability to care if he saw her dressed thusly had long since faded. But for his sake and for her husband, she would not.

"One moment," she said as her lady in waiting grabbed her plain, simple robe.

In a few moments, she was decent enough for the man to enter.

"Come in," she said, as her maidservant stepped to the side.

She was surprised when it was not the stout guard that entered, but Sir Marek.

"What is amiss?" Karin's thoughts spiraled in many directions. What could cause Sir Marek himself to seek her out at this hour? Her heart clenched. What if it were word of Pavel?

He frowned. "There is sickness in the camp."

She let out a shuddering breath. That could not be the worst of it. For he would have tended to the matter on his own.

"Yes?" Her breathing remained ragged.

"It is bad, my lady. And it has started to spread. Many of my men are capable of tending wounds and a great number of ailments, but for this...we need a healer."

As she sought his gaze, she found an apology in his eyes. And so, it should be. She hated to delay their mission even a few hours when they would stop for rest. But this...could be days.

"Is there a village nearby?" She thought of those towns they had passed near. The ravages of the war had taken their toll on these places in ways she had not known. The children ran about in mere rags for clothing. And the people had great need of food and other provisions.

He shook his head. "There is a stronghold—Zamek Kopec. I understand the lady that now resides there has knowledge of healing."

How did she know that name? Zamek Kopec? Whatever the information was, it wasn't rising to the surface. "Do I know this place?"

"It is held by the Vitek family. I believe the wayward son is now residing there."

Vitek? That was Lukas's family. "Would that be Lord *Lukas* Vitek?"

"I cannot be certain, but I believe so." Sir Marek lifted an eyebrow. "You know him?"

And how. Images of the night he attempted to take her life flashed in her memory. The dagger, Lukas's pleading, the regret in his eyes, the comfort of Stepan's arms...all of it.

"Lady Karin?" Sir Marek's voice brought her back from her musings.

"Yes," she murmured. "I know him."

"Is it not safe to journey there?"

She set her features. "There is nothing to fear there." Or so she hoped. "Certainly not if that is our best option."

"It is." Sir Marek's face darkened. "But only if you are sure." There was a question in his eyes. As if he wanted to know more.

But dare she speak of it? She could not. Her hand sought the outline of the small dagger she carried upon her person. It was there, strapped beneath her robe. The hard surface gifted her a sense of security. Regardless of what she may fear, she must look after the camp. And what was best for her men. This was it.

Firming her stance, she lifted her chin in hopes to display more confidence than she could muster.

"Then we shall go."

CHAPTER 27
TOMAS

Tomas tried to find rest. The day had been long and filled with much work on his body. But sleep eluded him. Every time he closed his eyes, he saw Karin, her eyes bright as her gaze found his. Perspiration only made her seem to glow…an ethereal creature in the wood. Then her nearness as they clashed in training.

How he had wanted to breathe her in. To reach out and…

But Sir Stepan had continued to be a thorn in his side. He was ever present, ever watchful, ever on guard. Ready to pounce if anything seemed amiss.

As if he could read Tomas's thoughts. Read his intentions.

It was enough to keep the man from discerning his true motives, but all the more—and increasingly so—difficult to keep him from seeing into Tomas's heart. And what secret lay there. Hidden. Buried. Begging for release.

Could he keep from Sir Stepan what he found impossible to keep from himself?

He loved Karin every bit as much as he ever did. Perhaps more.

CHAPTER 28
ANICKA & LUKAS

Lukas moved toward the Great Hall. He had wearied himself with sword practice. His skills had proved far too weak when he'd fought off the castle knight in the forest. And he refused to find himself...and Anicka...at anyone's mercy again. Not when he could prevent it.

Thank the Lord Almighty their escort had arrived yestereve. Many had been lost, but most had fared well, beating back those sent by Sir Warren. He prayed that would be the end of it.

As Lukas shifted his body, he felt in his arms how vigorously he had been about it in the training yard today. Not only that, he tired from being on alert constantly. What if there were knights and guards at Zamek Kopec who remained loyal to Sir Warren? That left him ever on his guard. And rather reluctant to let Anicka out of sight. Yet the situation demanded he be at swordplay today. So, he trusted his new wife into the care of the lady's maid that would now be her lady in waiting.

He entered the Hall to find it prepared for the evening meal. Had Anicka so quickly assumed her duties? Or did the steward's wife continue to direct the castle folk as she had in the absence of the ruling lord and lady?

As the knights with him trickled in, Anicka rushed into the large room. She spun immediately and went back from whence she came. Was she upset? Had something happened?

He moved in that direction, his longer steps carrying him toward the kitchens with haste.

So much so that he nearly ran her over as she re-entered the room.

"My lord," she said, almost breathless.

From the surprise of him being in the doorway? Or from something else?

He opened his mouth to ask after her wellbeing, but she cut into the pause.

"Please, take your place at table. The meal is ready for you and your men."

He arched an eyebrow. Truly? It seemed she had taken her place at the stronghold quite well. A warmth filled his chest. Was that...pride? In her? For he certainly was surprised—and yet pleased.

Dipping his head, he hid a slight smile before turning and moving toward the high table. He took his seat at the center of the table and indicated that Anicka should sit beside him.

Was that a blush about her face?

She said something to a passing maidservant and then turned toward him.

He couldn't help but notice that she had bathed and put on fresh garments. But they fit oddly. The dress stretched taught across her chest and hung more loosely about her midsection. Were the elements borrowed?

Of course they were. Her trunks and contained garments had been with the carriage. And those things had not yet been recovered. It was one more reminder of his duty to those men and the nursemaid.

Where had she found the dress? It mattered not. She was lovely as she moved toward the dais.

He stepped to the edge to offer her a hand and guide her to her seat.

Movement at the edge of the dining hall drew his attention for a moment. It was only the servants bearing platters of food and pitchers of wine.

Redirecting his attention to his lady wife, he offered her a smile.

Her face colored again as she allowed a polite smile before looking down...perhaps to ensure she made the step up properly.

Drawing her closer for a moment, he said for her ears alone, "You are lovely this eve."

Again, her features darkened in color. "I thank you, my lord."

He breathed in the scent of her—that light floral scent caused his pulse to pick up a bit. But he schooled his body. He would not insist on his husbandly rights until she was ready. Of that, he was determined. No matter how the urge to claim her as his own thrummed through him.

Shifting his focus to his own steps, he turned and led her to the center of the table.

His men filled in around them as the platters were set about the table and goblets were filled.

Relaxing into his oversized chair, he wanted to lean into it more, but his stomach's churning insisted that he attend to that first. Especially as the realization struck him that his men waited to eat until he started. As was only appropriate.

No sooner had he lifted a piece of roasted pork toward his lips than a loud slam of the door sounded, echoing in the large room.

He set the bite back down and trained his gaze in the direction of the entryway.

It was a knight who entered, somewhat hurriedly. "There is a small contingency moving this way, my lord."

He rose. "I will meet them."

Anicka then stood as well. "Shall I go with you, my lord?"

He met her gaze. Though loathed to leave her, he knew he must trust that nothing would befall her here. He would not take her into a possibly greater risk as an unknown band of men coming their way.

Lifting a hand to her upper arm, he cupped her elbow. "Remain here."

Her lips parted, perhaps to protest, but he shook his head and she resealed them.

Then, in a more hushed tone, he said, "I will not place you in harm's way."

Her gaze softened and she moved her mouth. Perhaps to speak against his plan, perhaps to speak to his words. He did not know.

But he would not delay.

Squeezing her elbow gently, he released her and turned opposite to gather his men.

Still...he would not look back.

In a few moments, he was in the saddle with a few men he had come to trust, and moving their horses toward the portcullis.

As they approached the iron gate, the coming group became more visible.

He did not recognize the figures. Except one. Make that two.

But it couldn't be.

Flaming red-blonde hair that had filled his disturbed sleep flashed behind one of the riders at the lead. But it couldn't be.

Then he spotted an old friend.

But his gaze turned to the rider at the head again. She was not supposed to be here. He could not face her...not now, perhaps not ever.

Yet come closer, she did. It was inevitable.

He would have to face the woman he had tried to kill—the Lady Karin Krejikova.

Anicka stood in the inner bailey. Rain poured down upon her, but she refused her maidservant's pleas that she return to the donjon. Her husband may need her. And she would not give up her vigil.

Indeed, she thought she could discern figures approaching upon horseback. She would discover soon enough who had come to trespass upon them. Would it bring more fighting?

The very memory of the attack upon them as they approached the stronghold caused her heart to beat harder. First, for the fear that filled her, then for the moments of her husband's strong arms about her, carrying her, protecting her, holding her. She could not have written a rescue better herself. Yet it was real. And it had happened to her.

The men slowed their horses as they neared the portcullis.

They were more difficult to see through the sheets of rain. But that could not be helped.

As the knights and guards entered the inner bailey, her eyes were drawn to Lukas. His features were set and taut. Something bothered him. Greatly.

The moment he spotted her was obvious as her gaze was trained on his face. A shift in his expression told that he was surprised, then pleased, then concerned.

He urged his horse forward, coming close to her before dismounting. "My lady, you should not be out here in this mess."

Was it her imaginings, or was there more to his concern?

"I wished to greet you and our guests. And..." She swallowed, loathed to expose her true feelings. But she could not stop the words. "...I worried."

Something softened about the edges of the lines in his face. And his hands on her arms tightened as if he prepared to draw her to himself.

Her eyes slid closed as she waited for the warmth that would come from being against him once more.

But his hold eased. "My lady?"

She snapped her eyes open to see his wide-eyed expression. Had she misjudged? Then she must look the perfect fool. She dipped her head so he wouldn't see her face color as heat crept up her neck. Yet she remembered their guests and lifted her chin. "Who has come?"

He grimaced. "Those seeking shelter...and a healer."

Her eyebrows shot up. "Are there wounded among them?"

"Sickness." His reply was short as he looked over his shoulder at the contingency that entered and dismounted. There was someone his gaze was drawn to.

She tried to look around him, but it was difficult.

At last, he shifted and she followed the line of his eyes. There was a woman among the warriors. And she, too, was fit for battle with ill-fitting armor. Her red hair was dark—perhaps due to the rain.

Who was she? And why was she dressed as if she belonged with these men going into battle?

It was no matter. She strode toward them with a man in tow.

"As I said, I apologize for the unannounced visit. But if you could send for your village healer...that would be most prudent." The woman's gaze drifted between Lukas and Anicka.

He cleared his throat, seeking out someone. Perhaps a man at arms to summon the healer. As they had not been in the region long enough.

A young man came closer to grab for Lukas's horse's reins.

Lukas called in his direction. "We have need of a healer."

The man, not much more than a lad, startled at his lord's address to him. "My lord?"

"A healer. Had the healer an apprentice?" Lukas's voice betrayed his exasperation. Did he worry that everyone would question his leadership?

"My lord," the lanky man said as he bowed his head. "The healer died last winter."

"Yes. I understand that. Is there no one to take his place?"

"He was a hermit of sorts. And did not pass on his knowledge to anyone."

Lukas muttered something indiscernible.

Anicka put a hand to his forearm and looked to the strikingly beautiful woman. "I will tend the sick."

Lukas jerked around, surprise filling his face.

"I have training in healing. Bring him into the Great Hall and I will see him."

Lukas opened his mouth as if he would protest, but he quieted. And nodded. "So be it." He turned to the armored lady. "Do so."

The redhaired beauty's hand drifted near her waist, but there was no weapon there. Anicka examined the woman's face. Did she conceal a dagger? For what purpose?

Anicka looked to Lukas. Should she tell him? Might the woman wish to work ill upon someone within the walls?

The woman shifted her focus to the man at her side and she spoke low to him.

"Lukas," Anicka tugged on his arm and drew nearer his side. "She conceals a—"

"I know." He jerked his regard to her as if to quiet her. "I know." His eyes trailed the lines of Anicka's face. It was a tender gaze traveling her features. She hated to break the spell of the moment.

"Do you not fear that she may...think to use it?"

He grimaced. "I do not. It is for her own protection."

Anicka furrowed her brow. "Her protection? From whom?"

"From me." The harshly spoken words were pressed out before he turned and moved off, shouting commands.

Feeling someone's eyes upon her, Anicka looked about. And found the red-haired woman glaring at her.

Upon being discovered, the woman blushed and turned away.

What had she to reasonably fear from Lukas? It seemed more than simple protection that a woman must be concerned with. And Lukas certainly seemed to know what it was about. She would inquire further later. Would he tell her?

Grabbing drenched skirts, Anicka moved toward the donjon. Now that she did not have the warmth radiating from Lukas's body, she was chilled. Such was her due for her choice to wait in the rain.

As she entered the Great Hall, men were already carrying two knights in and setting them upon blankets that had been prepared by a maidservant.

Anicka shook her head, hoping to release as much of the rain from her hair as possible. Still, tendrils fell over her face. It was no use.

She moved to the men, kneeling beside the first one.

He burned with fever.

She instructed the knight that had set him down, "I need to inspect him. Can you remove his armor?

The man nodded and instructed the guard behind him to do the same for the other poor soul.

She stood and instructed her maidservant, also drenched head to toe, to go for her herbs and to ask the cook to boil some water.

As Anicka turned toward the men once more, she caught sight of red-blonde hair. The woman that seemed to be in charge of this group had entered the Hall and moved in her direction, the same older knight trailing her.

Anicka had no desire to speak with her. She was...concerned about the looks between the woman and Lukas. There was something more. Something deeper there.

But the woman crossed the Hall faster than Anicka would have expected and drew up alongside the lady of the castle.

"I am Baroness Karin Krejikova."

A baroness? And a married woman? Did that assuage Anicka's worry about something unspoken between this woman and Lukas? Not one bit.

"I must tend to your man."

Lady Karin caught her arm. "I thank you. For your efforts. Whatever you can do, it is appreciated."

There was a kindness in the woman's bright green eyes that seemed to almost glow in the light of the nearby fire.

Anicka nodded. "Of course." There was only a moment of lingering before she shifted her focus again.

The man now lay in tunic and chausses. Even those were damp but had been somewhat protected by the armor.

She ran a knowledgeable gaze over him, seeking out signs that would be a cause for greater concern.

The baroness was still behind her.

"When did the men take ill?" Anicka asked, shifting into more of a no-nonsense air.

It was not Lady Karin that answered, but the knight with her. "Early yesterday for Sir Sedlak, and Sir Pekar became unwell this afternoon."

Anicka nodded without looking up. The man did not so much as look up while she examined him. Though the knight beside him groaned as if pained.

As she ran a hand over his face, she felt a swelling at his neck.

Her heart stopped.

Jerking the collar of his tunic down, she saw the black spots.

It couldn't be!

She whirled toward the baroness and the man with her. "Did you stop in any villages these last days?"

Lady Karin turned to the man at her side as she answered. "We passed near a village, perhaps through one. We only left Krejik lands some four days ago."

Anicka closed her eyes. Had they spread the sickness anywhere? She stood and closed the distance between herself and the lady. "You must send a man back to the villages you passed near or through."

"Why?" The woman's fine features were strained by her concerned expression. "What is wrong?" But even as she said it, her eyes widened, telling that she suspected the truth.

Anicka swallowed her own fear. "Your man...he has the Plague."

CHAPTER 29
KARIN & PAVEL

Karin watched the Lady Anicka as she moved down the corridor. The woman escorted Karin to her chamber for the evening. But Karin was deep in thought. The Death Plague? Could it be? Had they indeed picked it up in a village? It didn't seem likely. They had only passed near a couple of small towns. Could the soldier have interacted with the townsfolk in any meaningful way? Enough to be struck with the sickness?

Blowing out a breath, Karin settled that there was no way to know. What was important was that they take measures to keep the rest of the men sound.

Lady Anicka paused and looked at Karin. "Do you require anything?" Concern...and something else...shown bright in the woman's soulful eyes.

"I am only worried after Sir Sedlak...and the rest of my men."

Anicka's mouth tightened and she looked down but didn't pick up her step again.

"He will die, won't he?"

The lady nodded. "Soon."

Karin's heart ached for the guard who she hadn't known well.

But he was one of Pavel's men...one of hers now. And his loss would hurt even more for that. "And Sir Pekar? Is there anything that can be done for him?"

Anicka looked at Karin but gave a slight shake of her head. "I'm so sorry, Baroness. I can make him comfortable. Try a poultice. But there is not much hope."

Karin frowned. She had known that. Yet the woman's words struck her as if an arrow had pierced her flesh.

"We will have to limit any interaction with them. And seek out those who were in close contact."

Karin nodded.

Lady Anicka's voice was soft as she held up a hand. "We are nearly to the chambers."

Karin gave her a nod that she hoped was encouragement to continue. It must have been, for Lady Anicka stepped forward.

Indeed, it was but a few paces before the lady opened a door and led the way within.

The chambers were larger than Karin expected. And seemed comfortable with a bed meant for two and a fine chair by the fire that had already been started. Did the lady give her the solar? But Karin saw no sign of a desk or area to receive.

"I hope this will suit."

"Aye, it is a fine room." Karin offered the lady a smile.

"I shall have water sent up for a bath if you please." Lady Anicka looked to a tub basin that Karin had not noticed before.

A bath did sound wonderful. But should Karin indulge in such luxuries while her men were camped outside the walls? It felt wrong.

She opened her mouth to refuse but thought better of it. This was a hospitality gift that Lady Anicka was offering. Dare she turn it down?

"That will be well. I thank you." Karin glanced toward the window and the hills beyond. But, closer, her men's tents were set up. Perhaps it was best to keep them as far from the ailing guards as possible.

"Sir Marek will have the room to that side." Lady Anicka indicated the eastward wall to her right.

Karin dipped her head. That put her at ease.

She paused then. "What of Sir Dvorak and Sir Tomas?"

Lady Anicka's eyebrows creased.

"The prisoner and his watcher."

"They are still within the camp."

Karin inhaled sharply. Would Stepan take this opportunity—in her and Sir Marek's absence—to battle out his frustrations with Tomas? She prayed not.

"If you have no other immediate need, I will leave you now to have the water prepared." Lady Anicka passed by her.

Karin met her gaze. "Thank you...Baroness Vitekova."

Lady Anicka dipped her head and moved toward the door. But she paused just short of it. And turned. "Is it true what I have heard whispered? That you worked to transcribe the Holy Writ?" The woman's eyes widened as if hopeful.

Karin let a moment fill the space as she contemplated her answer. There was little reason to hold back the truth. "Yes."

The lady's eyes became wider. "That is so honorable," she breathed out.

That was not the reaction Karin expected. Her work to transcribe the Writ was a crime in the church. She could be excommunicated... or worse...should it be confirmed that she did so.

But this was a different Bohemia than it had been years ago...so many years ago.

That reminded Karin that the Czech lands had been in such turmoil these last weeks. The wars had been bad enough...but the kingdom once united under General Zizkas' banners, now splintered faster than the enemy could regroup. She had heard of Prince Kory-but's arrival and attempt to bring unity. But, while half the leaders saw hope, others feared a crown more than a sword at this point. Would there ever be peace?

Lady Anicka stood quietly, fidgeting with the fabric at her waist. Did something bother her?

"Lady Anicka?" Karin hoped it wasn't that she had trusted someone with the truth that would betray her. What did it really matter though?

"I..." The woman's voice was impossibly quiet. "...have some writings myself."

Karin arched her brow. "Oh?" A small smile took over her lips. Did the woman do the same work? Might they combine their efforts?

Lady Anicka watched Karin as if weighing her own words with care. Then, at last, she spoke. "They are stories. Of fantastical things and knights and damsels and things."

Karin widened her smile. She stepped forward and took Anicka's hands. If not to connect in some way, to keep her from worrying her seams at her waist. "That is wonderful. Such a gift."

The lady looked to the side. "You think so?"

"Of course! That is a piece of God's creativity in you." Karin angled her head as she sought the lady's gaze.

There was a small smile as Lady Anicka's regard lifted to Karin's face. "I...thank you for such high praise."

Karin squeezed her hands. "It is the truth."

A measure of peace fell over the woman. It was as if a bit of joy blanketed her.

In that moment, however, Karin felt not only a sense of camaraderie with Lukas's wife, but also an awareness of how her body ached. And she wanted for the warm water to soak even more.

As if reading her mind, Anicka released Karin's hands. "I'd best ensure that the water is being prepared. I will leave you." She bowed her head briefly and moved toward the door again.

She placed a hand upon the latch and again halted. Yet it was several heartbeats before she turned once more. What now?

The lady seemed even more reluctant to broach whatever held her mind captive and kept her planted in the room.

"Is there something else?" Karin tried to keep her fatigue from entering her voice but failed.

Though Lady Anicka did not seem to notice. Another few beats, and she spoke without looking directly at Karin. "I sense that you knew my husband before this day."

Karin nodded, taking in a long, weary breath. What did the lady know? "I did. We became acquainted just before the Hussite Wars."

The woman's eyes widened. "Before his imprisonment?" The last word was all but whispered as if shame overshadowed her statement.

"Aye."

Karin could sense Lady Anicka's war between asking further and letting it be. Yet, at length, she continued. "Pardon my intrusion, Lady Karin. But were you...well acquainted with Baron Vitek?"

What was she asking? Did she think that Karin had somehow been...involved with Lukas? The truth must be known. By all. Lady Anicka deserved to know.

"Not in that way." Karin waved her hand as if to dismiss the very idea.

Lady Anicka seemed to breathe easier.

Yet Karin could not let it lay as it was. "I...am the woman he attempted to murder."

Pavel tugged against his chains for the millionth time. There was no give there. These men may have evil intentions, but they weren't as dimwitted as he had hoped. Nor did they seem to have any mercy for him.

Again, Pavel struggled with God's choices where he was concerned.

But then, Pavel bore some of the responsibility for his situation. He had left Karin and Jaromir vulnerable. He had struck out to come to Zizka's aid...a man who was now dead. Though...

The next question tore at Pavel almost as much as Karin and Jaromir's safety.

Would Zizka be dead if Pavel had been able to come to his side?

That bothered. More than that, his heart ached for the loss of the great General. For he had been faithful to his calling—both from his countrymen and from the Lord. And God had showered favor upon Zizka's efforts.

But now, all was lost. Wasn't it? Zizka was gone. God's favor had left. There was nothing to put stock in—either for himself or for the Hussites.

He sank down to the floor. What was the use in fighting?

His chains clanged as he shifted to lean on the wall. He longed to pull his knees up and lean on them, but his legs were still sore and healing from abuse dealt upon them.

A soft voice called out in a nearby cell.

Who was that? Pavel had believed himself alone down here.

He strained to hear more.

Indeed, it was a voice, soft. Yet it was a man's voice.

"...be with me Lord. Yea though I walk through the valley of the shadow of death..."

Was he only reciting Scripture? Or praying?

How could anyone in this forsaken place think to beseech God?

How could they not?

The question taunted him. But he shoved it to the side as he struggled to the corner of the cell closest to the voice.

"Thou art with me, Father. Help me be strong. Help me find peace. Help me..."

Praying, then.

Pavel wasn't certain why, but he listened, though he grimaced.

Fool man.

There was no God here.

He moved to distance himself.

Then the man called out. "Are you awake?"

Dare he answer? The man was clearly aware that he was in here.

"Aye," Pavel rasped, unable to keep his anger from his voice.

"Are you well?"

What kind of a question was that?

Pavel blew out a breath, then drew another in slowly, weighing his words. "I am not."

"Father in heaven, help this man—"

"I'd rather you not do that." The gruffness of Pavel's voice surprised even him.

"Sir, as I cannot render you aid, I must call on the only One who can."

Pavel pushed out a grunt. "He has made his choice. That is why we are here."

All was quiet. Maybe he had put the man off so much he would not respond.

But Pavel thought better of alienating the man who may be his only assistance in any attempt to escape. And may well be a source of information. "I apologize. You are well?" he called in the direction of the man's cell though he could not see him in the darkness.

"As well as I can be." The man's honesty was refreshing. At least he wasn't completely deluded. "As the Lord's great mercy—"

"Don't," Pavel growled. Why was he being so antagonistic? He rubbed hands over his worn and bruised face, not caring if it pained him.

The man quieted again.

"Who are you?" Pavel called, against his better judgment.

"I am a priest. Father Lesak."

"Priest? What put you in this dungeon?" How ungodly could Ulrich be to imprison a priest? Had he no fear of God in him?

"I...was a priest in the chapel of this very castle. I angered Lord Ulrich."

Imagine that—a holy man angering an evil overlord.

There was no room for Pavel to be angered about this man's unjust imprisonment. Too much emotion had been spent on too many things.

"What is your name, sir knight?"

"I am Pavel Krejik." The words were out of his mouth before he could stop them.

"Krejik? I know this name." The man's words were not a question.

"My lands extend near Tabor. Perhaps you have heard of my family."

"Yes." The man made that one word sound cryptic in its slow delivery.

It gave Pavel reason to pause. But only for a moment. For what did it matter? They were a lost cause.

"Mayhap we will seek the Lord together?" Father Lesak's request was almost timid.

"I will not, Father. As much as I respect you and your place in this world. I will not."

Silence.

"Then I will ask Him to be near to you."

Pavel wanted to scoff but held back. He would not deny the Lord and His rule. Only His care after the lowly situation Pavel found himself in...of his own doing. He could accept that much.

"Do as you will," he said low.

The man shifted not as far away as Pavel would have thought for the softness of his words. And then the man was praying...aloud.

Pavel laid his head in his hands. Would he ever escape his guilt? For he was to blame for not only his most dire situation, but the danger his wife and child were in. Not to mention his people. And the thing he typically sought for strength and solace—his faith— was now hopelessly lost to him.

Heat built in his stomach and filled him once more.

So be it.

CHAPTER 30

ANICKA & LUKAS

Anicka took a step back from Karin. Her breath pulsed, but it seemed as if she couldn't get enough air. It wasn't possible. That had surely been an exaggerated charge. Anicka knew Lukas...perhaps better than anyone. Or had known him. Could he have changed so much that such darkness was within him?

"You..." Anicka's head swirled.

Karin was beside her in the next moment. "Lady Anicka? Are you well?"

Anicka pressed a hand to her forehead. Was she? How much could she fight this news? Fight the mounting evidence?

"Perhaps you should sit."

"Aye." Anicka allowed herself to be led to the chair by the fire.

Karin crouched nearby. "Shall I send for someone?"

Anicka shook her head as she worked to even her breathing.

"At least let me send for your lady's maid." Karin stood.

Anicka grabbed her arm. "Do not."

Karin's features contorted into a strange expression. "I am sorry to have brought such disturbing tidings. I thought you knew."

Anicka was coming more to herself. "Aye. There is some I know. Some I do not."

Karin settled in the other chair, a frown now marring her perfect features. "Still, I should not have presumed to—"

"I should know."

Karin nodded without another word.

"Will you...tell me?"

Karin rubbed her lips together as if in thought. Indeed, the look of her eyes deepened. Would she tell all?

"I want to know the whole of it." Did she though? Would it shatter every bit of peace she had found with Lukas?

Likely.

Still, she had to know all.

Karin let out a long breath.

"I believe I deserve to know." Anicka's voice was steadier.

Karin nodded.

"There is a chateau...in Hradek Kralove. One that the royal family uses for hunting forays. My father's friend, Viscount Dvorak, invited me and him to visit for a season."

Karin paused as if she weighed something. But she soon continued.

"Lord Dvorak's son and his friends, including my future husband, came for a holiday. Lord Vitek was among them. We all enjoyed each other's company, but something evil lurked at that place."

Karin shuddered as if even the memory caught her still.

"The Viscount's wife decided that I was a threat to her station. For whatever reason. There was a...history...of young ladies finding unfortunate ends at the chateau. For whatever reason, I became her next target. She had some damaging information on Lukas and sought his assistance in snuffing out my life. The blackmail was enough to enlist him."

Anicka noticed that her hands shook. She clasped them in her lap and attended to Karin's story. Though she wasn't certain she wanted to hear the rest, she would.

"One evening, the Viscountess embraced a moment of vulnerability for myself and sent Lukas to do the deed."

Bile rose in Anicka's throat. All the heat drained from her face.

Karin set a hand on Anicka's forearm. "Mayhap you do not need to hear more."

Anicka swallowed. "I said I would hear the whole of it. And I will." She prayed that her tone was more confident than she felt.

Karin gave a small nod. "He had a dagger. But, in the end, I believe his conscience got the better of him. He had the chance, but he did not perform the deed. I firmly believe that God would not let him go to that place in which he would be capable of such. But that is how he found himself imprisoned."

Anicka heard every word, but her picture of Lukas in her mind began to crack and splinter. And it tore at her heart.

"There is not much else to tell. I had not laid eyes on Lukas again until this day."

Anicka nodded. "This is...much to take in."

"Surely you were told he had been accused of—"

"Yes." The word came out sharply.

Karin pulled back slightly. Had Anicka's tone been too harsh?

She could not help it. There was much to consider. And much fear...in her being. How could she reconcile what she knew of Lukas —as a kind, considerate, caring friend—with the monster he must have become to be a party to something like this?

One thing became clear—she could not linger here. No more. Looking into Karin's understanding, sympathetic face and bearing the weight of her concern. It would not be tolerated. It couldn't.

Anicka stood so suddenly she wavered between light headedness and a determination to remain steady.

"Let me get you some water, my lady."

"No." Anicka's tone was abrupt. She had to get out of here. That was all she would entertain in this moment. "I must take my leave." She moved toward the door.

"My lady," Karin rose. "Anicka."

The use of her name without formality gave her pause. She turned.

"I believe there is much good in your husband. I also believe he struggles."

Anicka chewed her lower lip. "I have long since needed to take my leave. I will send for that bath."

Karin did not step forward. Did not move. "Aye."

Anicka reached for the door's latch.

"But know this..." Karin called out, halting Anicka's progress. "I will answer any questions you have with honesty and care."

The woman's kindness and graciousness in the face of what they all faced became too much.

Anicka offered a curt nod and, opening the door, stepped out of the room as quickly as humanly possible.

Then she was in the corridor. She leaned against the nearby wall and tried to steady her breathing.

Voices filtered down from the side stairway to the tower. She wished at first to dismiss them, but something drew her to listen.

"Quiet! This place is not safe to speak of such things."

"But I am not certain there is cause to—"

"I said silence! I can see you are concerned enough to run and hide behind your mother's skirts, but that is not to be. You must finish what we have started."

Silence from the second voice.

"Do you hear me?" It was the first tone again. Harsher.

"Yes." The second voice finally responded.

Then there were steps coming down the stairway.

What would happen should they find her in the corridor? Would these men decide she may have heard too much?

She brushed down the passageway for her chambers. Then, slipping into the room, she listened at the door while the footfalls moved down the hall and then as if they parted ways at the second set of stairs.

A sigh escaped as she relaxed, grateful to finally be alone.

"Something amiss?"

She spun to find Lukas staring at her.

CHAPTER 31
PATRICIE & STEPAN

Patricie sighed over yet one more victim of the plague—Father Boursek. He had not been able to fight the sickness long. But he had been difficult to find. She prayed he had not interacted with many people along the way. Not that it would stop the spread of the Black Death. It was everywhere. Except in the castle. Eva, Zdenek, Michal, and the working servants in the castle had all been quarantined. For safety, both she and her helper—Sir Antonin—took residence just within the walls of the castle in rooms separate from the others and from each other.

Even now, he set a hand to her shoulder. "You did all you could."

She nodded. She knew this was true, but it didn't stop the knife of guilt from stabbing her deeper with each person lost to her.

He crouched beside her. "You know it's true. And..." He paused before continuing, "Even if you don't, everyone else does."

That was some comfort.

"Even Father Boursek."

A laugh sputtered from her lips before she could stop it. The man's final hours had been spent railing against the injustice of it all.

He had cursed her, the Lord, as well as Jan Hus and his followers too many times to count.

"Patricie..."

She turned as it surprised that Sir Antonin would eschew her title.

"I know it." His gaze softened and his eyes took in the whole of her face, resting longer than necessary on her lips.

As much as she wanted to lean into the comfort he offered, she dared not. Her loyalty was to Stepan. Her heart belonged to him. So, she turned as if she had not noticed and set the thin blanket over Father Boursek's head. Yet one more.

Sir Antonin cleared his throat. "Will you speak with Lord Ambroz?"

It was a moment before her head cleared enough to understand his meaning. When the priest had called out a pox on Michal and the whole of Zdenek's house, it had injured her. But she had also assured Sir Antonin that she would speak with her sister and brother-in-law about what the villagers were saying and believing about the illness following Michal...whom the people called 'the devil's child.'

She pushed out a long breath. Did she have the strength for such a conversation? Did she have the clear mindedness?

Sir Antonin stood and tugged at Patricie's arm as if to help her rise.

She allowed him to assist her to her feet, but she wavered, her head feeling light at the rapid change in position.

Sir Antonin gripped her shoulders. "You are not sleeping well."

It was not a question.

"How can I?" she challenged as she pushed him off as she did not wish to do in that moment. "There are too many to tend to. And their lives weigh on my heart and mind, preventing rest."

Again, his gaze fell on her but this time focused on her eyes. It was as if he could see through the façade of her features and into her soul. He leaned toward her. "I..."

She drew in a breath. He had paused. But dare she let him speak further?

"We must get you to your rooms."

"But Father Boursek..." She looked back to the man's body.

Sir Antonin took her arm and drew her toward the door. "Let the others tend his body. You need rest."

She let out a sigh. "After we seek an audience with Lord and Lady Ambroz."

Sir Antonin halted. What for? Did he wish to protect them from the Black Death or make her find rest as soon as possible?

She felt it in her body...the fatigue. It was true she needed solid sleep. And the only way she would find it was to relinquish the burden of the forthcoming conversation. And only one way to do that.

"I promise I will take my leave as soon as I speak with my kin." She met his gaze and wished she had not. The care in his eyes nearly drew her to lean toward him. But she held firm.

Sir Antonin was kind for certain. And gentle as he resumed their pace out into the corridor. True, he had stayed by her side through much these last days. He had been faithful and protective and everything a man should be.

That did not mean she had to pretend all she had with Stepan did not exist. Or that his considerate nature was not more appealing than Stepan's passionate impulsiveness.

She shook her head to clear it. This was not the time, and she was in no condition to assess her emotions on any matter. Yes, she needed rest.

They traversed the hall and moved toward the Great Hall. How would they protect others from the plague? It seemed they were not likely to have it as they had no signs of it. But that didn't mean they could not carry or spread it.

She put a hand to Sir Antonin's arm.

He paused.

"We must remain as far away as possible. Let us insist upon meeting in the Great Hall rather than the solar."

He nodded and called out to a servant passing near the kitchens. "You there!"

The younger man stopped and looked in their direction. "Sir?"

"We seek an audience with Lord Ambroz and his lady wife."

The boy's eyes widened.

"Go," Sir Antonin demanded in a sharper voice than was perhaps necessary.

Patricie looked to the floor. Did he respond harshly because he wanted to get her to her room quickly? If so, she hated to be responsible for the young man's discomfort.

But the footfalls pattering away from them told that the servant had taken haste in his errand.

"Are you certain you can do this?" Sir Antonin said.

She glanced up to see his attention on her. "Aye."

He turned her toward himself. "I am capable of sharing what—"

"It should be me." She cut into his words. Then said more gently, "It should come from me."

The look in his eyes deepened. He reached a hand toward her face as if to cup her cheek. Should she permit such familiarity?

Still, she did not stop him.

He seemed to think better of his movement and shifted his hand to tuck hair behind her ear.

It had been impossible to keep it tied back.

But the gesture seemed so...intimate. It was something only Stepan did for her. And it was his face she saw before her.

In that, she was safe to lean into him.

He responded, wrapping hands about her upper arms, then sliding to her back.

She murmured something she wasn't even certain of and laid her head on his chest.

Then solid arms encircled her. Soft lips pressed to her forehead. "Patricie, I..."

Yet it was not Stepan's voice...nor his arms or lips.

She wanted to jerk back, but she was so tired. And so at peace in this embrace.

The sound of boots upon the stairs stirred her swimming thoughts back to reality.

She pulled free, looking up to find Sir Antonin's face before her. Furrowing her brow and narrowing her eyes for a better view, she wondered at how she could have permitted such closeness. Did she... feel something for Sir Antonin?

He was slower to release her, but he did as he turned to face those coming into the Great Hall.

Zdenek reached the base of the steps first. His gaze hardened as if he had seen...and not approved.

Patricie swallowed hard and put another pace between her and Sir Antonin. What must her brother-in-law think?

Eva was just behind Zdenek, carrying little Michal, his mark shining in the open for all to see...and fear.

Patricie jerked her head side to side to see if anyone watched. The servants that had milled about had vanished. Because of Michal coming? Or because of Patricie and the risk of the Black Death?

It mattered not.

Only it did.

Two others followed Zdenek and Eva. They were dressed in the finery of nobility but did not seem familiar.

Patricie opened her mouth, intent that she would ask who they were.

But Zdenek spoke into the moment first. "Our friends, Lord Radek Miklas and his wife, Lady Hana, are here as well."

"There is something of great..." What was the word? "...sensitivity...that I need to share with you, Lord Ambroz." She was all too aware of Sir Antonin shifting beside her as Zdenek's gaze bore into him.

Patricie stepped forward, but not too close, and stepped to the side in an effort to block Sir Antonin.

"There is nothing we need to hide from our friends." Zdenek looked at those with him.

"I appreciate that, my friend," Lord Miklas responded. "But I would prefer to see Lady Hana settled. She has not...fared well on the journey."

"Oh, perhaps Patricie could tend her?" Eva said, looking toward her sister with shining eyes and pride.

Patricie hated to disrespect her in any way. But she must. "I fear I have been tending too much to those who are ailing from the plague. It may be best I keep my distance."

Eva startled. "But, I—"

"It is nothing that a little rest cannot cure." Hana looked between them. "I assure you..." She touched Eva's arm. "I will let you know if I need the healer's attention."

Was the woman fearful? Or just being kind? Or perhaps truthful? Indeed, many women did not fare well on long travel.

Patricie dipped her head. "I thank you. And I would be happy to tend you if you have a great need for me." As the words escaped, she wanted to pull them back in. It would be best if Lady Hana did not have need of her. Not until this plague ended.

Lord Miklas led his wife up the stairs.

As they disappeared from view, Zdenek stepped forward.

Patricie held up a hand to stop him. "It may be best for you to keep your distance."

He frowned but complied. "What do you have need of?" His words were genuine. He cared for her as family and appreciated her sacrifice to see to the sick in the demesne.

"It is...a matter of great concern."

"Oh?" Eva stepped to be alongside where her husband stood. "What is it?" Worry threaded her words.

"It is something the villagers are saying." Patricie chose her words carefully.

"What could that possibly mean? Their words cannot have any

bearing on us." Eva laughed. But her words were shaky. As if nerves influenced her speech.

Patricie's heart ached for her sister.

"It seems there is a rumor…a belief…" Patricie again hunted for the right way to present it to both ease their reception of it and deliver truth.

Sir Antonin came alongside her. "They believe Michal has brought this sickness."

Patricie shot a hard look at him. Why would he say it so harshly? Did he not trust her ability to deliver the information?

Michal took that moment to make a cooing, gurgling sound. It broke the stillness.

"That's preposterous!" Eva declared. "Why would anyone think such a thing?"

She had truly blinded herself to this situation. How could she have done it so completely? Did she not understand the strength of superstition among the peasants and servants?

"Regardless, it is true." Sir Antonin's voice was strong.

"I cannot abide such talk," Zdenek said, though his firmness seemed forced, put on. He stepped closer to Eva and put an arm about her.

"It is not just that," Patricie muttered.

"They call him the devil's child." Sir Antonin again stepped in where he should not. Was this some strange way of protecting Patricie? Taking the burden from her? It was wrongly placed and ill-timed.

"What?" Eva fairly screeched.

That made Michal flustered. He grabbed for her face, pinching the skin at her jawline.

She took his hand and pulled it free. "He is a darling. Anyone can see that. And how could anyone truly think that a child can bring about something like this?"

Zdenek's face took on a strange look. Almost haunted.

"Eva," Patricie said, trying to appeal to her sister. "There is talk of an uprising."

Now Zdenek's face hardened. He was charged with the safety of these people. Could he put down an uprising that may cost lives?

"Perhaps," he said carefully. "We could try to cover the mark. Maybe if the servants and villagers don't see it, they will forget all this nonsense."

Eva bristled. "I will *not* hide any part of him as if I am shamed by him!"

"You will not?" Sir Antonin's shoulders stiffened. "There is widespread unrest and shortages of goods. The people were struggling to survive—before this plague. They tire of the war and what it has cost them. They do not have the patience for this. Do you not see that they believe the child is to blame for their hardships and loss?"

Patricie set a hand on his forearm in an attempt to calm him.

He did not push her hand away, but he did not back down.

Zdenek's eyes widened. But he did not chastise Sir Antonin as was his due. "Is this true?" He looked at Patricie.

She nodded. "I'm afraid it is. All of it."

"You would side with them?" Eva glared at her. "With the people who would say such things...such nonsense about my son?"

Patricie fought to keep her cool. "You know that I don't. I do not believe what they are saying. I do not agree with such thoughts. But I cannot deny the reality of the situation either."

Eva seethed.

Zdenek put an arm about Eva's shoulders as if he feared he needed to hold her in place.

"You would speak to your sister this way?" Sir Antonin's voice became louder. "She labors night and day to tend the sick in this demesne while you sit in the comfort of the castle walls."

"Careful." Zdenek warned. "This is my wife."

Patricie saw that while he defended Eva, he did not disagree with Patricie's assessment.

"We will strengthen our defenses," he said finally.

"What if the attack comes from within the walls?" Sir Antonin challenged.

"Those here are loyal to us," Eva shot back without looking away from Michal as she rubbed a hand down his back.

"Where do you think the rumors started?" Sir Antonin bit at her.

She looked to him with eyes widened to the size of saucers.

As Patricie looked around the room, she saw that it became clear to all...this was only the beginning of their troubles.

Stepan groused as he stared across the campsite. He had been offered a fine room in the castle, but he would rather be here with the men. Or, more specifically, here where he might keep an eye on Sir Tomas. Not that he was pleased to leave Karin in the castle with Lukas about. But he was assured that Sir Marek posted a guard outside Karin's room and he would be in the chamber beside hers.

That was some comfort. But not much.

Shouldn't he be thankful for the respite? For the chance to pause?

As much as he was eager to find Pavel and redeem himself by aiding in the man's rescue, it was a good thing to rest. With Karin's training, he had not stopped much even when the movement of the camp paused.

Even now, he rubbed a hand across the tension knots in his shoulder muscles. How long could a body sustain being on guard and on alert? He might just push those limits.

Still, Stepan could not escape the sense that they shouldn't have come here. If he had known Lukas was the lord of this castle, he would not have allowed Sir Marek to come to this place. Regardless of the state of the sick men.

He'd not had the opportunity to interact directly with Lukas, and for that he was thankful. Such forthcoming exchange would not be pleasant. It took but a look at Lukas's face to remember that fateful night. When he'd come upon the man hovering over Karin's form, a dagger in his hand and ready to strike.

It didn't make it any better that Lukas was connected to Stepan's mother's plotting. The ache from his mother's betrayal and crimes still pressed deep in his heart. And so, Lukas was an enemy. For his complicit actions if nothing else. If not for that, would his mother have stepped so far into such evil? Had she no one to aid her, would she have been left to simply think on her wicked desires?

Stepan jerked his regard toward Tomas as the man shifted. There seemed to be a lot of enemies, Stepan mused. But he had always been a more contrary type of personality. Rough around the edges. He knew this. So, what surprised was not the number of enemies he'd made, but that someone as gentle and kind as Patricie had seen through that to capture his heart...and give hers to him.

Tomas stilled again.

Stepan closed his eyes and conjured an image of his beloved's face. She was soft where he was abrasive, skilled where he was impulsive...truly his other half. And though he came to her an enemy, she saw him.

Perhaps he might do the same for Lukas. The man had been imprisoned for some years due to his crime. And he had been enlisted by Stepan's mother's scheming. He had sworn that night that he did not want to hurt Karin. Indeed, he had not...though he'd had the opportunity. His conscience had held him back apparently.

Had not Stepan himself attempted to kill Karin? That thought was unwelcomed. It had been in a moment of anger...when so much weighed on him. And when his father had held great power over him. It, too, was not truly who Stepan was.

Pavel had seen fit to give Stepan room to be redeemed. Mayhap... no...

But there may be reason to let Lukas prove himself worthy of friendship once more. But Tomas...that was another story.

Something whispered in Stepan's mind, telling him that he had been forgiven much. And had, then, the capacity and call to forgive.

Shaking his head, he rejected the notion.

It was true he had been forgiven, but he could not accept that. He had to atone for his actions. And he would. He would do whatever he must to see Pavel freed and returned to Karin. Then...and only then could he allow himself to embrace a future with a good woman.

Tomas shifted again. Did he seek a more comfortable position?

"I don't know how I am to sleep with you glaring at me." The man's words surprised.

"I but do my duty to the lady and to this camp, traitor." Stepan's voice was gruff.

Tomas sighed loudly. Enough that the guard watching him looked in that direction. To assure himself that Tomas remained bound and still?

Stepan rose to a sitting position. "You must get used to others watching you sleep. For it will be your due for the rest of your years."

"Aye." Tomas spoke with a quiet assent. Did he, then, agree that he should be imprisoned for his treachery to the Czech people? "I only wish to assist Karin."

"*Lady* Karin is well cared for...as you see." Stepan indicated the men about them.

"That is what I fear. A knife in my back as I sleep."

Stepan considered that. It wasn't likely, but he understood the concern. "Surely you know that I am watching your every move."

"Aye."

"You should know, then, that no harm will come to you as you sleep. No one here will be the cause of such a cowardly injury upon you. Even should someone intend such. I watch your movements and watch over you."

Tomas met Stepan's gaze, a question in them, as if he considered the veracity of Stepan's words.

"You have my word, now gain your rest." Stepan hardened the look he settled on Tomas. This was but a small reassurance. Didn't Tomas understand that Stepan would not let anyone slip a knife between his ribs in sleep because if anyone were to lift a blade to Tomas it would be Stepan? And it would be in an honorable fight.

Tomas closed his eyes and did not so much as stir again for the several moments that followed. His breathing deepened.

Stepan shifted to lean against a tree. He would keep his word—to Tomas and to himself. The man would never know freedom again.

Of that, Stepan was determined.

CHAPTER 32

ANICKA & LUKAS

A nicka stammered and jerked back only to hit the door. "Lukas!"

His brow furrowed. "Is something amiss?"

She hunted for the right words. They weren't coming. "I just… didn't expect to see you in my chambers."

"Did you not just escort the Lady Karin to the solar?"

"Y-yes…" And her thoughts caught up with her. If Lady Karin was in the solar, Lukas would need a place to bed down. Did he intend to share her room with her? "I just didn't think…" How could she end that sentence?

"I see." His expression spoke of his skepticism. And concern. "That is not all." He stepped toward her.

She wanted to move away, but the door was solidly at her back. "N-no…I did not know you would be back so soon."

"It is late. I wanted to change out of the drenched garments before we resume the evening meal.

"Of course." Reality slammed again. She was needed in the kitchens to ensure the food was warmed. And she had promised warm water to the Lady Karin.

She spun about, grabbing for the door latch.

"Where are you going?" Lukas's voice accused.

She pulled open the door. "I need to tend to the meal and secure water for the baroness's bath."

He shut the door, his extended hand so close to her face. "Not until we speak."

"But the Lady Karin is expecting—"

Tugging Anicka further into the room, he leaned outside and called to a passing servant. "The baroness requires heated water for a bath. See to it."

The servant must have agreed and set out to obey, for Lukas closed the door and stood between Anicka and her escape into avoidance.

"Now tell me; what is wrong? You're shaking." His voice was softer, but his eyes had narrowed. What did he think? Did he suspect Karin had told her about their past?

"N-nothing." Anicka backed into the room, turning and adjusting something on the side table.

"I would know what troubles you." His voice became iron-like. And the sound told that he drew near again.

She all but dropped the small object and moved away, toward the window. Was she ready to have this conversation? Everything in her fought it. How would he react? She didn't wish to bring any more tension between them.

"I would know, Anicka." His voice was hard now.

She fidgeted with the fabric at the waistline of her dress.

"What did Lady Karin tell you?"

So, he had guessed there was something there. How could she avoid it now?

"She shared about the...events that led to your imprisonment." Anicka closed her eyes. How could she look at him?

"I see."

"But..." Anicka grasped for any sign of hope. "I know you...you are not the kind of man to visit violence on another."

"Yet I am." His words were clipped.

She spun. "No!" The word was out before she could stop it. She only then noted that he had stepped closer and was only a few paces away. Pressing away, she found her back to the wall. Dare she slip away from him again? Would that only prove that she feared him now? Did she?

"But I...I know you."

He closed the distance, caging her with his hands on either side of her head. "Do you?"

"Yes," she challenged with greater vehemence than she'd expected. "None of that matters to me."

"Why should it not?"

"I don't care about that...any of it. Because I..." She let her words trail. There was space to admit what was in her heart, but she feared jumping off that precipice and owning it.

"You...what?" he demanded. His face was so close to hers. And though his voice was forceful, it had quieted.

"I..." It was now or never. "I care about you." Her face heated and she looked down at the way she had made her heart vulnerable. "And I..." Tears welled. She wanted more than anything to reverse the clock. To not know what she knew. To not be having this conversation.

"What?" His words were soft. With a finger and thumb, he tipped her chin upward, forcing her to look at him. The storm in his eyes had calmed. And there was something else there...something she couldn't quite discern.

She bit at her lip.

His gaze dropped to her mouth. The heat between them threatened to burn her alive. But she didn't care about that either.

He was so close...his body nearly pressed against hers. And she ached to feel him do so. To feel the contours of his frame holding her, loving her.

Something like hot liquid pooled in her center. And it spread. She wanted...more. What exactly, she wasn't sure. But a desperation overcame her. It was almost impossible to hold back from setting her hands to his chest, tugging him to her, giving him what he sought in her lips.

Yet she didn't want to force her affection on him. Did he even want her? It had seemed so at times...in their adolescence and since their wedding. But he always held back. Why?

She searched his features. His emotions—anger and hurt among them—were raw and real on his face. It nearly broke her heart. Would he ever see her? Care for her? For her heart ached terribly for his touch that was just beyond her skin.

Unable to look at him lest she give away more of herself, she closed her eyes and let out a breath, hoping it would cleanse her being. It only made her feel more fraught with the need to be seen.

"I just..."

"Look at me."

It was not a request.

She pressed her lips together. Perhaps that would stop their want. But she lifted her gaze to his.

There was the same raw energy there. And a need of his own.

His mouth crashed down on hers. He pressed her to the wall, the whole of his body against hers.

She let out a whimpering sound as she dipped her head back, answering the fervor of his hunger with her own. Though her hands were not as strong as his, she gripped his tunic for all she had.

His hands moved too, diving into her hair, loosening pins and braids.

As the kiss continued, he gentled his touch on her. Though the hunger remained.

She gave herself over to it. He may not feel as she did, but she wanted this, wanted to answer his need with her own. Even if only for tonight.

He pulled away and breathed heavily. "I won't push, Anicka. Not if you aren't ready."

She opened moisture-pooled eyes and caught his gaze. What she saw drove her all the more. She did want this. So much.

Rising on her toes, she reached her arms around his shoulders, pulling his mouth back to her swollen lips.

He obliged as if he hadn't eaten in days.

Her desire echoed years of want, even if his did not. She couldn't ask that of him. Her heart was content in this moment for this joining. For this expression of love.

And all was well.

Lukas lay beside Anicka, pressing a kiss to her brow and running tentative fingers through her hair. She smiled up at him. But he fought with the feeling that he had taken advantage of the situation.

Anicka had come to him and given herself freely...or had she? Could a wife refuse her husband's affection? Had he been too blinded by his own needs to sense a resistance in her?

He let his hand drop.

"What is it?" Her face contorted in concern.

"Nothing," he rasped.

She reached for him, laying a hand on the side of his face. "Don't do that." Fear reflected in her eyes. Perhaps he dared not broach the subject. It would be horrid if she were made to feel used.

The situation couldn't be further from the truth. Though he had tried to distance himself from his feelings, his ardor had grown since reconnecting with her. She deserved better than a criminal. But he couldn't deny his great desire for her.

Was it...more than that? He couldn't say. He had always felt strongly where she was concerned. And that had only increased since their wedding. No matter how much he tried to push it to the side.

He propped himself on his elbow. "Was it...painful?"

She ran a hand over his mess of curls. "A bit."

He frowned. He hadn't wanted that to be her experience. But he understood that it could be for women.

"But it was...also good." Her features reddened as she admitted it.

He wasn't certain how to respond. But as her hand slid back to his face, he pressed a kiss to her palm.

This wouldn't do. Not with what lay between them. He couldn't lose his senses, lose *himself* in her.

He cleared his throat. "What...did Lady Karin say?"

Her features fell at his question. Did he bring the mood down? But he had to know.

"That you were part of an attack on her. That you entered her room when she was asleep and tried to stab her."

He nodded slowly.

She bit at her lip. That lip again. It entranced him.

"That may be what you did. But it's not who you are." Her voice was adamant. So much so he looked at her.

Those deep brown eyes welled once more. Her belief in him, in his goodness, was so...warming. He wanted to kiss her again. But he held back.

He fell onto his back to keep from giving over to the impulse.

She leaned up on her arm, pressing to his side. "I know it, Lukas."

He looked up into her face, now shaded. "I wish I could believe that as much as you do."

With all his strength, he tore himself away and sat on the edge of the bed, his back to her. Where had his tunic gone? Spotting it at the foot of the bed, he reached for it and pulled it on.

"I'm not afraid of you."

That gave him pause. He turned to look over his shoulder at her.

"I never have been. And I never could be."

Could he risk his heart? He wanted to. But there was too much within him that she didn't deserve. Perhaps, her goodness would save him...would heal the dark within him.

He stood and tugged on his chausses. "It is...regrettable. But I must tend to my men. And see that our guests have been fed.

Anicka's eyes widened. "Our guests!" Her hand flew to her mouth. "What they must think!"

He leaned down, a lightness in his heart from her innocence. "They will consider that the lord and lady are spending a quiet evening."

"Do you think they...know we were...?"

He stifled a laugh at her horror. It would not be a welcomed reaction. "Perhaps. What if they do?"

She fell back on the bed, pulling the covers up to her neck.

He settled back on the bed. "It is well. We are wed. What wrong is there in others knowing we have been together?"

Turning her head, she faced him. "I suppose you are right."

His leg rubbed against something abrasive. Was there something caught in the mattress? He bent over to look.

There were papers sticking out from under the mattress.

"What is this?" He reached for them, worried about the secrets that may yet lay in Zamek Kopec. Secrets that may mean ill for him and for Anicka.

She shot upright. "No!"

He tugged the parchment free and looked at the writing.

"Don't read that," she insisted, grabbing for the papers.

He stood, pulling them from her reach. Did she hide something from him? But as he looked at the top paper, it was the scribbles of an accounting. A maiden who needed rescuing. How had she come by it? "What is this?"

Anicka's face was covered by her hands.

Leaning over, he tugged her hands down. "Anicka?"

She groaned. "Do not be angry."

His heart hammered. Did she have something to hide? Another man in her life perhaps? That made his heart squeeze painfully. He knew he shouldn't risk his heart where she was concerned. There was too much at stake.

"It is...nothing," she said at last.

"It is *not* nothing." He glared at her, willing her to be truthful, but fearing that she would be.

She swallowed. "I...write stories."

"What?" Had he heard her correctly?

"I create tales. Fiction. Fantasies."

Reality dawned and coalesced in his mind. These were works of her imagination. But he paused. If that were true, why was she hiding them? Why was she afeared of him finding them?

"Please..." She looked at him, her eyes wide and pleading. "Don't be angry."

Why would he be angry? Unless there was more to this.

He folded them and tucked them into his things. "We will talk more on this...later. I have to tend to our guests and my men."

She deflated into a seated position on the bed. "Yes, my lord."

After all that had happened in these last moments, this was how they would part? With formalities and seemingly forced submission?

Maybe it was naught but her paying of the marital debt.

It was all Lukas could do to make his feet carry him out of the room and into the hall.

CHAPTER 33

PATRICIE & STEPAN

Stepan shuffled into the Great Hall. A servant had summoned him in the night. The very long night, fraught with his watch over Tomas. There was no one else in the camp he could trust to look after Tomas. No one but Sir Marek, who kept watch over Karin's safety.

But Stepan hadn't a choice when the guard came and collected him. Karin had need of his presence, he was told. And, as he could not trust Tomas's manipulative ways with the other soldiers, Stepan had insisted he be brought along.

That may create a greater risk for escape, but perhaps not.

Either way, he and Tomas moved toward those clustered in the Great Hall.

Karin and Lukas's wife were the only two women present. And both had dressed already. It was but the wee hours of the day, before dawn yet, but they had come all the same.

Lukas and Sir Marek stood about as well.

Sir Marek nodded toward Stepan in greeting. A strange look passed over his features as his gaze landed on Tomas, but it did not linger. For certain, he would not have expected the rogue to be with

305

Stepan. That mattered not, Stepan had made his decision on the matter.

Karin offered a slight smile to Stepan before her jaw dropped at the sight of Tomas as well. She had clearly not anticipated him either. Her posture did not recover as Sir Marek's had. She remained fixed on him.

In fact, Sir Tomas's steps altered as her gaze rested on him.

Stepan did not like it. Not one bit.

"What goes?" He brushed into the moment, preferring to get this over with.

Lukas looked to the strange man as well. "I mean no disrespect," he said as his gaze wandered to the bindings about Tomas's wrists. "But this is a rather...sensitive matter."

"Sir Tomas may stay," Karin asserted, whirling toward Lukas.

"My lady," Sir Marek muttered low. "Are you certain?" Then he seemed to remember his place and stood straighter. "I can take this prisoner to the dungeon."

"No," Karin snapped. Then she bowed her head. When she lifted her chin again, her voice had softened drastically. "I mean...I am well with him staying."

Sir Marek leaned closer and said something too quietly for Stepan to distinguish.

Stepan stole a glance at Sir Tomas. The way the man looked at Karin was much more akin to a lovesick young man than a man of war...especially one that peered at someone else's wife.

Stepping between the line of sight between the two, Stepan shot the man a harsh look. Not that Tomas seemed to care.

Lukas squared his shoulders. Was he not comfortable with Stepan's presence? Should he not be? After all it was Lukas that had trespassed during their last encounter that night of the attempt on Karin's life.

Then Lukas spoke. "We have received a message...from Krejik lands."

Karin's regard fell to him. Her eyes were...sad. There was no denying it.

Stepan's heart picked up its pace. Patricie? Had something happened in their absence? Something Zdenek couldn't withstand? Or perhaps that Sir Antonin had taken liberties with Patricie?

An ire rose in Stepan that he didn't want to suppress, nor did he wish to give them full rein. So, he pushed them down enough to even his breathing. "What has happened?"

"A messenger told that the Black Death is in the castle and upon the surrounding lands."

The plague?

Stepan's heart skipped a beat. Patricie was at risk. And, as the most competent—if not only—healer in the area she would no doubt be in the center of it. Risking more. And no one would be capable of stopping her. Not even her sister. That is if Eva wasn't too wrapped up in Michal to take notice.

"What can be done?" he pressed out.

There was a pause as those present exchanged looks.

Sir Marek cleared his throat. "It may be best if you return to Krejik lands to assist in any way needed. Especially providing strength to the defenses during this vulnerable time." Sir Marek seemed rather uneasy.

"You would take a number of our soldiers with you." Karin's voice wavered. Because she was sacrificing some of the men needed to free Pavel?

Dare Stepan leave Karin open to Sir Tomas's advances? For Stepan needed to protect his friend's home, but also his wife. And see to it that Pavel could be rescued.

But Patricie may need him...

His heart rent within him—remain loyal to his friend, the one he had wronged, or rush to his beloved's side?

"I say that this will not be necessary," Lukas offered. "I can take some of my men and assist."

"But you would leave your own stronghold lacking." Karin worried where Stepan believed she should not.

"My lady wife and man will stay here in my stead."

"No," Lady Anicka asserted, her eyes shining in the flickering flame. "I will aid. The healer may need my assistance."

Lukas's jaw muscles clenched. And Stepan understood. She had been at risk already with the interactions with the soldiers. Did he care so for this woman that he would prefer she not further risk herself with the plague?

Still, Lukas's willingness to sacrifice his own lands for Karin's felt...right. As if he sought redemption as well.

"What of the soldiers that ail here?" Stepan couldn't believe he alone brought up the obvious. "Do they not deserve your care?"

Lady Anicka met his gaze. Her eyes were captivating in the tenderness about them. "They have passed. Both."

Stepan tried to disguise the sharp inhale that gave him needed air. He had heard tales of the Black Death but had not seen it. Nor had he realized it would take so quickly and viciously. His heart squeezed for Patricie again. And he nearly denounced the cause for Pavel's rescue.

When he glanced at Lukas, he found his former friend's eyes on him. But there was quiet reassurance there. As if Lukas wished him to trust that he would defend and protect not only Lady Anicka, but all there—including Patricie—with his very life.

And Stepan believed him.

Stepan swallowed.

"It is decided then," Karin said into the silence. "Stepan, Sir Marek, and I shall lead the men onward toward Ulrich's lands while you assist with whatever is needed upon Krejik lands."

Lukas nodded.

But Stepan did not miss that Sir Tomas's eyes widened. And he dropped his jaw as if he wished to speak. Yet he noted Stepan's gaze on him and he clamped his mouth shut.

Were they walking into a trap? Very well...so be it.

Loud slaps upon a hard surface jerked Patricie from a fitful sleep. Struggling, she dragged herself from the darkness of unconsciousness though her rest had been fraught with trouble. Images. Worry. Still, it had been heavy.

A voice boomed just beyond the door, which she could now identify as the source of the banging.

"Do you know the hour, my lord?" It was Sir Antonin, his voice edged with frustration, though he worked to restrain it. "The healer is likely at rest."

If only.

"It is my wife. She needs care." The voice was that of the Lord Miklas. He had mentioned yesterday that his wife was unwell from the travel. Had something more happened? Had she contracted the plague?

Patricie rose and wrapped a thin robe about herself. Then realized she had gone to bed completely dressed. How tired she had been! Still, she did not make an effort to remove the robe. Again, fatigue dragged at her senses.

Sir Antonin continued to try and dissuade the man. "Mayhap you can seek her out in the morning. The lady needs her sleep."

"Can you not understand? I fear my wife ails quite seriously."

Patricie made it to the door and pressed on it.

Both men turned in her direction once the door swung wide. Was it just her, or did their gazes widen. She must be a sight—disheveled and still rather fatigued. No doubt the clinging sleep was evident in her face and affect.

She gripped the edges of the robe and tried to pull it closed...only to remember that she was still dressed. Though a glance downward told that her appearance was in sore need of attention. It mattered not. If someone needed her skills, she would answer.

Lord Miklas was the first to shake his head. "My wife. She is worse." He struggled to get even those words out, so great was the emotion welling behind them.

Patricie nodded. "Take me to her."

Sir Antonin stepped in Patricie's way, reaching to touch her arm. "Are you certain that would be prudent? You must rest. There are many depending on you. But they cannot come between you and your own wellbeing."

As much as his care moved her, she shook off his hand. "There will be time to sleep...later."

She stepped around him, though his features belied a renewed attempt to protest.

"Lead on, Lord Miklas."

The man's features eased ever so slightly, but not completely. If she had to guess, his great worry was due to a deep regard for Lady Hana.

As she, then Sir Antonin, trailed behind the nobleman, she wondered after Stepan. Did he care so deeply for her? Would he be so shaken and concerned if she were to become unwell?

Such was the stuff of nonsense. Not for a sensible woman to worry after. Stepan did care. He had professed his love for her. And his farewell had assured her of his feelings. She must cling to that.

They arrived at one of the rooms above stairs. Patricie recognized it as the chamber she had occupied before the Black Death visited them. Just beyond the doorway, further down the corridor, was the nursery kept by Michal and Jaromir and their nursemaid. No sound came from the room. If only she might sleep so...ignorant of the trials of life.

Returning her focus to Lord Miklas, he set a hand to the latch. Then, before opening the door, thought better of it and turned back to look at Sir Antonin. "I beseech you, sir, to wait out here."

Sir Antonin set his gaze on Patricie, as if assuring himself she would be well with that. Did he think these kindly people would mean her ill?

She nodded, then shifted her attention to Lord Miklas again.

He pushed the heavy door open.

The room was lit with a fire in the hearth and candles set upon a stand near the bed.

Lady Hana sat up. "Radek, I told you I would be fine."

Patricie stepped within.

"You are not fine," Lord Miklas argued. "Will you not let the healer examine you?"

Lady Hana's gaze moved between him and Patricie before settling on the healer. "I do apologize for bothering you at this hour. My husband, as you can see, is a worrier. And quite insistent."

He strode forward, stopping short of the bed. Almost as if he wished to sit on the edge of the bed but held back for propriety's sake. "I have a right to be concerned for my wife."

Patricie sighed. As endearing as it was, she didn't have the time to wade through these pleasantries. "What seems to be the trouble?"

Lady Hana shot her husband a harsh look even as she reached for his hand. Then turned to Patricie. "I have had a few nosebleeds."

"A few?" Lord Miklas huffed. "They have come nearly every night."

Lady Hana pushed out a breath. "As I said, a few nosebleeds. Including tonight."

Patricie took in the scene and noted discarded bloodied linens to her side. Nosebleeds in and of themselves were not a cause for concern. They happened. Especially as dry as the air had been. She opened her mouth to say as much.

"She also has been kicking me at night...supposedly in her sleep."

"Every night?" Patricie pondered out loud.

"Yes. Vigorously." Lord Miklas frowned.

"Are you certain I am not doing so intentionally?" The lady but attempted to lighten the mood.

But when he glanced at her, her features softened into a smile.

Again, Patricie wished to push their banter aside. Perhaps that desire was more due to her fatigue. "This is a new thing? The kicking?"

"Yes." Lord Miklas's arm muscles clenched and moved as he squeezed his wife's hand.

Patricie needed to speak with the lady. While Lord Miklas offered solid observations, his recounting was colored by his concern. "I must...ask you to step outside, Lord Miklas."

He jerked his regard to Patricie. "Outside? As in, leave my wife?"

"She will be safe with me." Patricie couldn't believe she had to mention such. "But I must examine her properly. And it would be unseemly for you to be here."

His face reddened...possibly he came to understand her meaning.

Looking back to Lady Hana, he leaned in and pressed a kiss to her forehead. "I'll be just in the corridor."

Lady Hana looked up at him. "I'll be fine."

He set a hand to the side of her face, rubbing a thumb in a caress. Just as Patricie prepared to insist he leave, he pulled back and walked to the door. Pausing there, he glanced back at them.

"Go," Lady Hana insisted. "I'll be right here."

Without anything further, he stepped into the corridor.

Only then did the lady lean back heavily against her pillows. Had she been feigning strength for her husband's sake?

Again, it tugged at Patricie's heart. But this was not the time.

"So, you have started kicking in the night. And nosebleeds..."

Lady Hana nodded, but her eyelids slid closed. She looked as exhausted as Patricie felt. "And I can't seem to recover from travel these days."

Patricie sat on the edge of the bed and felt of the lady's forehead and cheeks. Normal. No fever. "In what way?"

"I am tired. So tired. All the time." She opened her eyes and met Patricie's gaze.

Patricie nodded as she continued her examination, prodding and poking in places.

"Oof!" Lady Hana cried out as Patricie pressed on her abdomen.

"Does that hurt?"

Lady Hana nodded.

"Sharp pain?" Patricie wanted to prod further but did not wish to injure the woman.

"More of a dull ache. Perhaps more of a tenderness. And my... chest is tender too." Lady Hana looked down, avoiding Patricie's direct gaze.

Kicking, bloody noses, as well as tender breasts and abdomen.

"My lady, have you been sick at your stomach?"

Lady Hana blushed. "Mostly when traveling. I don't recall struggling with it so."

"Only when you travel?"

The lady shook her head slowly. "It becomes more pronounced."

Patricie considered that.

"Please," Lady Hana beseeched her as she gripped Patricie's hand. "You must tell me. Do I have the plague?" The woman's eyes widened more than Patricie thought possible.

Patricie flipped her hands to hold the lady's. "When was your last menses?"

Lady Hana seemed to weigh the question. "I...do not have regular menses. Nearly every month, but not every one. It has been three months."

Patricie struggled to hold back a smile. This would not be terrible news at all.

But Lady Hana's face lifted as if she guessed what Patricie would say.

"I believe, my lady, that you are with child." Patricie allowed a smile to cross her features.

Lady Hana's widened gaze did not ease. "But the kicking...the bleeding...are you certain?"

"Those are less common signs of a babe taking residence. But they can be."

Only then did Lady Hana's face reflect the joy of such news. She set her hand over broadly smiling lips. "Can it be?"

Patricie nodded. "I can think of no other ailment that would present this way. And the pieces fit."

The lady's eyes glistened, and she moved her hands to splay over her abdomen.

Rising from the bedside, Patricie said, "I will let Lord Miklas in. Would you prefer I tell him?"

Lady Hana followed Patricie's movements with her eyes. "I... would like to tell him. But can you stay and answer any questions he has?"

"That would be best for the midwife. But I will remain if you would so choose."

Lady Hana nodded.

Patricie shuffled to the door and opened it.

Lord Miklas stood to one side, moving as if he had paced. "Is she well? May I come in?"

"Yes." Patricie offered a small smile. "Go to her. I will be within in a few moments."

She closed the door behind Lord Miklas and leaned back against it, closing her eyes and imagining the delivery of the news. How the nobleman would burst with relief and pride. And how he would adore his wife all the more.

"You need to return to your bed." Sir Antonin's voice was soft yet insistent. He reached for her hand.

Dare she allow these interactions to continue? She found such warmth in them, but what would Stepan think? Her passionate, impulsive Stepan?

Tugging to free her hand, she attempted to stand upright, off the door.

But Sir Antonin did not drop her hand.

She jerked her head to look at him.

"Is the lady the next victim?"

Patricie allowed a smile to retake her features. "No. It is good news."

"Ah." Sir Antonin looked at the door as if he could see beyond. Then it occurred to him...and he emitted a more emphatic "Ah!"

Patricie nodded. "Is it not wonderful?" A wave of fatigue swept over her. Because she was suddenly awakened out of such heavy sleep? Or was it the weight of all that had transpired these last several days?

Sir Antonin came up beside her. "You are not well. I will take you back to your bed." His voice was gruff and determined. "You have given the lord and lady enough of your time."

She glanced at the door but could not deny how her legs barely held her. So, she permitted Sir Antonin to lead her down the corridor. Her feet felt so far away...and but shuffling along.

Sir Antonin grunted. "You have pushed too hard."

"No..." she argued. But she knew he was right. And leaned even more into him.

He lifted her off her feet. "Let me ease your burden."

She wrapped her arms about his shoulders. The thought occurred to her that he would have to take her into her bedchambers...alone. They would be alone there. But there was little she could do to protest as unconsciousness claimed her.

CHAPTER 34
KARIN & PAVEL

Pavel listened to the gentle snoring of the holy man. The priest had been a comfort. More than Pavel cared to admit... even to himself.

For how could God allow this—first Ulrich took Pavel's father's life and now he would take Pavel from his mother and his family? It was true that God's goodness was an all-encompassing part of who He is. But that didn't mean bad wouldn't happen. It didn't mean that Pavel's father's death wasn't bad and evil. And that God either allowed it or caused it to be so. Pavel wasn't sure...and he didn't wish to pull at that thread. Not even in the state of his dwindling faith. There was still a seed of trust in Him, though the light of it burned so dimly such became harder and more difficult to see.

The man nearby stirred.

Pavel stilled. He didn't want Father Lesak to realize he did not sleep.

The priest shifted and groaned. These conditions were difficult for even the warrior in him...how much more would it be for a man who had led a simple, comfortable life all his days?

Then there was mumbling coming from the nearby cell. What did he say? Pavel strained to hear.

"...and lead us not into temptation..."

Why must he do such? He was praying. At least he beseeched the Lord on his own behalf.

"...and strengthen Pavel. Expand the borders of his tent...and his faith. May he find the hope he once clung to."

God's teeth! Why must the man pray for him? For him?

"Save your words, priest." Pavel muttered.

The man quieted. For a moment. "What vexes you? That you know He hears? Or that you fear I pray in vain?"

Pavel wanted to growl at the man. But the truth was that his faith was not so far gone that he doubted God's ear was turned to the righteous. "As you well know, I am but angry that He hears...and yet denies me hope of goodness."

That shut the man's lips. A long stretch of quiet followed in which Pavel became certain the man had fallen asleep.

It became so still that Pavel caught a few words that the guards spoke to one another. These snatches were all the happenings of the outside world that he could garner.

"...come now, this war is no longer righteous."

"Indeed."

"With the infighting and exhaustion, these Hussite scum are ripe for the taking...and we are minding a whelp!"

Is that what they thought? That Pavel was so helpless? Had he not fought them hard and strong? Or was it simply that he had given up?

While there was some basis to it, he had told himself he but saved his strength and bided his time. But was their assessment the truth?

"Do not listen to their venom." The priest's words covered anything further from the guards.

It riled Pavel anew to be cut off from any new information, but he heeded the moment and tuned his heart to the man's words...as much as he could. "Do you not?"

"No. The Holy Writ tells us that God will bring good from all, for those He has called according to His will."

"Perhaps," Pavel said with a gentled voice, "He has not called me, then."

"You cannot think that. You believe in Him and give credence to His word. That is not the situation of an unrighteous man."

"Doesn't the Writ also say that even the demons believe...and tremble, giving credence—as you say—to His words?"

The man was quiet again.

Sleep tugged at Pavel. Mayhap he should give in. For he didn't know when Ulrich's purposes for him would wear out and he would be brought to a noose, a knife, an end of some sort.

Fighting once more, he found strength in the fact that Karin and Jaromir needed him to be strong.

"What of your son?" Father Lesak's words were firm, but almost too soft to take in. "What would you have him believe?"

Should Karin and Jaromir come out unscathed—as he fervently prayed they would—what would he wish his son to know of his father? And of his faith? How would he prefer his son move forward in his own knowledge of Christ?

The priest had not held back. And the question had hit the mark quite well.

"Why must you pepper me with such questions? Don't you know I am a dead man?"

"That...is precisely why I persist. For your soul."

The man cared too much. Beyond his duty certainly. Why would he not leave Pavel alone...to sit in his misery?

But Pavel knew...the priest could not switch his heart for others. He was a true man of God...one that sought to lead others to the Father. How long would it take for him to give up on Pavel as God had?

This was not a place of hope. It was where hope went to die.

Yet the thought of this evil snuffing out the holy man's light was harder for Pavel's heart than anything these men had done to his body. Or could.

Was Pavel's care for another indicative that the seed of faith still germinated in good soil within Pavel? Had it simply faced a fire of testing? More...would the tender shoot thrive again?

Karin moved among the guards making preparations for the ride back to Krejik lands, where they had just come from. But there was a need. And Karin was relieved that Anicka and Lukas would risk their own place here to meet it. Lukas had been rather insistent when he placed one of his men in charge of Zamek Kopec. What more went there? He'd been almost reluctant to leave. But, in the end, he'd agreed it was best.

As Karin moved through the thick of things, a hand gripped at her shoulder. She whirled toward the figure off to that side.

Anicka stood, her gaze wide and rather timid.

"Lady Anicka?" Karin firmed her lips. What might the woman wish to tell her?

The lady gripped her hands together at her waist. So much that her knuckles began to pale. "I...thank you for telling me what you did. Lukas...Lord Vitek and I have come to an understanding about the matter."

Had they? What kind of understanding? While curiosity shot through Karin, she dared not intrude further. But as she looked toward the woman opposite her again, Lady Anicka seemed to wait upon a response.

"That is good." Karin offered a small smile. It was the most she could give in these circumstances.

Lady Anicka appeared to be at a loss. Was that all she had wished to say?

"If you are worried, I will share freely what has happened at Lord Vitek's hand, I assure you, I am the picture of discretion."

Lady Anicka arched a brow.

"Indeed." Karin allowed a brief smile again. "Here, I will share one of my secrets. I have spent the last several months transcribing the Holy Writ into Czech."

The lady's eyes widened all the more.

"Is it not only right that the people have access to the Words of God?"

"I suppose...but you must have been frightened."

"Yes. But it was my calling." Karin watched for any further reaction.

Lady Anicka seemed to consider what Karin had said. And suddenly, Karin wished she had not felt so free to share. She did not truly know this woman. "If you will excuse me, I must attend to—"

The lady grabbed at Karin's forearm, drawing her attention. And the woman tugged slightly. "Might we...speak privately?"

Again, the tear between wanting to know and fearing such would trespass on intimate matters filled her.

"Please?" Lady Anicka indeed looked desperate. "It will only be a moment."

Karin set her features in place and nodded.

Lady Anicka led her farther off to the side, but still in viewing of the rush of those gathering supplies and provisions.

Karin watched the lady as she seemed to war within herself about what to say. Clenching her teeth to keep from saying something that might offend, Karin weighed how much time she had for this sort of thing. But Lady Anicka's struggle pulled at her.

"You know my husband. Better than some."

"I don't know that I would say that. I kept company with him for a short time one summer many years ago. And..." She swallowed the words she almost said.

"And prison can change a man," Lady Anicka said the words she had almost uttered.

Karin paused and took in a slow breath. "Yes."

"I know." Lady Anicka looked off for a moment.

Again, Karin felt for her pain, but didn't know what she could do to aid the lady.

Then Lady Anicka glanced down. "He is much changed from the boy I knew."

Karin nodded. "I imagine so." What had she done? Had she caused a rift between husband and wife in revealing the truth?

Lady Anicka met Karin's gaze once more. Then seemed to decide something and spoke with a firmer tone than she'd expected. "I have long poured my frustrations and hopes into stories."

The last word was said more quietly as she scanned about them. Did she fear someone might overhear? What she spoke of was not a crime.

"Perhaps that is good that you—"

"My mother warned me over and again that such was not becoming of a lady. That I had best put my efforts into more domestic practices."

Karin frowned, beginning to see the lady's pain for what it was.

"If ever she found writings, she would throw them in the fire." That last brought with it a shadow of real grief over the lady.

Karin reached for Lady Anicka's clasped hands. "That must have been difficult."

Lady Anicka's eyes glistened as she nodded, but the tears did not fall. "And...my lord husband just yestereve found some of the papers."

Karin remembered when Pavel had discovered her own work with the Holy Scriptures—his alarm and fear for her safety. Was that the case here? That couldn't be it. Again, the work Lady Anicka described was not a crime.

"I am not certain what he will say."

Was that it? Karin opened her mouth to speak.

"Everything between us is so...tense. And strained. I don't wish to make that worse."

One look at the moisture now escaping Lady Anicka's eyes told that she was in earnest. She must really love Lukas.

Karin took her hands. "I wish to encourage you to be true to yourself. Let Lord Vitek care for who you are. Not for who you think you should be. *That* is the makings of a lifetime of happiness."

Lady Anicka wiped at the few tears that fell as she gazed at Karin with a rather uncertain look. Her regard shifted to something over Karin's shoulder.

Karin squeezed her hands. "Trust me."

The wide brown eyes rested on Karin again. And, after a moment, Lady Anicka nodded.

"I wondered where you had wandered. Did I not warn you to stay by my side?" Lukas's voice came from behind Karin.

She looked over her shoulder to see a shocked Lukas. Why would he worry about Anicka wandering off? Was something amiss? Was Lukas lording over her?

Karin paused. *No. I will not let what has been color my view of what is.*

"Forgive me," he said quickly. "I did not mean to intrude."

Karin nodded slightly and turned so that husband and wife might face each other.

Lady Anicka had shriveled somewhat, her shoulders slumped and her affect fallen.

Karin pressed her hands again before releasing them. But as she moved to walk off, an inward tug. And she looked to Lukas.

His gaze would not hold hers. He glanced down.

"Lord Vitek," she said before she really thought about her words.

He coughed. "Baroness?"

"I hope you know that you are forgiven in whole."

His eyebrows arched. "Excuse me?"

She steadied herself. "I hold no ill will against you. No longer are you bound by a debt you owe me for something God has pardoned you for."

Without waiting for a response, she spun and walked off, saying a quick prayer for Lady Anicka and Lukas. That they would truly find love and happiness. And that Lukas would no longer find shame in who he was. But that he would know freedom in Christ.

She moved straight toward her horse, mounted quickly, and rode for the campsite where her men awaited their lady and her instructions. And she didn't look back.

CHAPTER 35

PATRICIE & STEPAN

Stepan continued his vigil over Sir Tomas as he fought a wave of fatigue. Perhaps staying awake throughout the night was taking its toll. Mayhap there would be a few hours yet until they departed. Would it be a better use of his time to rest?

He adjusted his position to a more comfortable situation. No need to keep himself alert any longer. Glancing at Tomas, he noted that the man still appeared to sleep. And Stepan hated him for it.

The camp around him was inactive yet as well. But for two men off to his left, in the direction the prisoner lay. Were they the guards who had been charged with this watch?

Quieting his own mind, he strained to hear what they discussed.

"...I tire of all the in-fighting," a gruff voice said.

The other replied quickly. "I am weary of fighting altogether."

"Everyone is. Did you take note of the state of the villages we passed through? Children in rags that barely covered them, burned chapels, impoverished and hungry people... Can they sustain more war?"

"It's not about faith anymore—if ever it truly were—it's about power and revenge."

327

Was that true? Stepan wondered at their words. Had it come down to that—a power struggle? At one time, he had admired the faith undergirding and spurring on everything the Hussites were about. Was that no longer true?

"There are radicals who are calling for another march on Prague. Did they not learn from the last bloodbath?"

The first man sputtered. "Better that than sitting on our hands while Sigismund sharpens another crusade!"

The conversation came to an abrupt halt. So much so that Stepan peered through slitted eyes.

There was movement in the camp. The soldiers stirred about, awakening each other. Was something amiss?

Mumbles of "Sir Marek calls for attention" and "the Lady Karin is among us" sounded around them. Karin? Sir Marek? That couldn't be so. They would have seen those off to Castle Krejik then settled in for some rest themselves.

Surely so, however, he caught a glimpse of the red-blonde hair as Karin bisected the campsite.

Many gasped around him.

And he soon saw why. She no longer wore the adornment of a lady but had donned armor.

Men rallied to their feet despite the hour.

Karin's posture commanded their entire focus...and devotion.

How well Stepan knew it. She had held his heart for a time. But this was different. She had a confidence he had not known before. What brought that on?

It mattered little. For an image of his softer, but equally stubborn Patricie came to mind. She had more gentleness about her edges. Even as she bore just as much grit. That was what he needed. Not the sharpened edges of Karin's ire.

The men scrambled to find their footing and placement as Karin and Sir Marek passed, moving to the edge of camp, leaving the soldiers and knights to follow in their wake.

At last, Karin paused near Sir Tomas. The lines about her eyes eased when she met the man's gaze.

Though she quickly straightened and moved off.

Once they reached some manner of pre-determined place, she and Sir Marek turned.

Sir Marek spoke. "We have our orders, men. We have our mission. And we will ready this camp to move within the hour."

Within the hour? Stepan was glad he was not responsible for any of that.

"Some have departed, headed back to Krejik lands."

There was a grumble of murmurs among the men. Much of what Stepan overheard was the same echoed...how would they march on Ulrich's camp without the full force they began with?

Sir Marek raised a hand as if to silence the men.

The restlessness did not ease.

"I know," Karin called.

A hush fell among those present. It wasn't right for the lady to address them. Though anyone who believed Sir Marek did not deliver her orders was daft, still...this was not done.

Karin's jaw firmed as she waited.

When all was still, she stepped forward, shaking free of Sir Marek's restraining grasp on her arm.

"I know what I am asking of you. Each of you." She scanned the men before her. It seemed as if she made eye contact with each, though that wasn't possible.

Stepan wanted to steal a glance at those about him, but he was completely captivated by her brazenness. And she was that...perhaps too bold.

"I will not force anyone to come. Any who wishes may journey back to Krejik lands and find a place in the castle defenses."

Not a word could be heard.

Was she mad? Would she release all the men who found her so? Who would help them? How would Pavel be saved?

"My husband trusted his men. Trusted you." Her voice broke on the words, but then she paused, and collected herself. When she continued, her tone was even once more. "And I trust you. Our scouts have told that Ulrich's men are no longer camped by the river."

Had they moved out of Bohemia? Was Pavel in the grips of Sigismund? Or worse...unreachable? Is that why she released any who would not risk all for her?

"They are now securely in Ulrich's stronghold. And are setting up their defenses."

Then this mission was suicide.

Stepan glanced at Sir Tomas, whose features were set...and grim.

"But I will not rest until my husband is returned to us...whole."

If he were even still alive, Stepan mused. How could she think otherwise? How could she ask such of these men—to follow her into the lion's den on the slim hope that their baron still lived, much less could possibly be rescued.

Many would die...if not all.

Sir Marek held out his blade and knelt before Karin as if offering it to her. "You will have my sword. Wherever this may lead."

A cry went up from somewhere in the group. The slip of metal against metal filled Stepan's senses as others unsheathed their swords and followed suit. And a wave of movement came over the group as men took a knee before her.

He noted a twinge in Karin's features, before an invisible mask fell over them.

All quieted as the men waited to see what she would do.

She jerked her smaller sword out of its place at her side and raised it in the air. "Then we ride!"

Patricie struggled to wake. The pull of the darkness was strong. And the fall back would be so wonderful. No sickness, no despair, no danger, no war...

But she rose toward the light regardless. Was there something tugging her in that direction? Something indeed. Her concern. Her love for her sister. For her brother-in-law... And the hurting people that desperately needed her skills.

Her eyes fluttered open, and she took in the room, awash with sunlight that came from an open curtain.

And a figure silhouetted by the brightness.

Someone watched her.

She jerked upright. That was a mistake. Her head ached and her vision swam.

The urge to lie back down and close her eyes was overpowering. What would happen to her if she did? Would this person visit harm upon her?

Pressing her fingers to her forehead, she let out a breath, hoping that steadying herself might calm the swirl of her perception.

"Who is there?" She ventured. Setting her hand behind herself to push her body to the edge of the bed, she swung her legs around. If she had to run, could she escape unscathed?

The figure shifted and—his?—head tipped up toward her. "Pardon?"

She pushed off the bed and wavered slightly.

The man crossed the room and worked to steady her in a moment. Or was he trying to take hold of her and prevent her from eloping?

"Let me go!" She pushed against a muscled chest.

"Patricie," the man's voice cut through her struggles. "Be still."

She paused her struggling for a moment. There was reason to think. To plan.

"Who are you?" Patricie stood more firmly on still shaking knees.

"You don't remember?" The voice was more...familiar...now. Was that...?

"Sir Antonin?" It couldn't be. Why would he trespass on her privacy? It was unseemly.

"Yes." He loosened his grip, but not his hold on her.

His hands and arms were not comforting as she would have expected. They hemmed her in, providing a solid and secure place.

"I...can't remember." She shoved the heel of her hand to her forehead. "Did you...bring me here?" Scanning the room once more, she found that it was, indeed, her chambers.

"Yes. You passed out, you were so exhausted."

Trying once more to create space between their bodies for propriety's sake, she leaned away.

He allowed it.

"And you stayed? Watched me sleep?"

He looked down briefly. "I only wanted to ensure you rested undisturbed."

Could he not have done that by keeping vigil outside her room?

"I see." She stepped away from him, pushing at his hands.

He did not release her fast enough.

"I am well now, thank you." She continued to pull back.

He loosened his hold. "Are you certain?"

"Yes." She drew the fabric of the robe she still wore closer as if covering herself could erase his presumptuous overstep. "W-where is my sister?"

He moved toward the window but remained a couple arms' lengths away from her. "She is with the small children—Michal and the baron's son, Jaromir."

Patricie sucked in another breath. "I must speak with her."

"I shall send someone for her." He walked toward the door.

"It is important. Would you...?" She pondered how best to encourage him to leave. If others discovered he was in her room... while she slept...it would not be acceptable.

"Yes?" He took a step closer.

She backed away as casually as possible. "Would you fetch her?"

He gave her a strange look. But much of his face was shadowed by beams of light, making it difficult to truly discern his intent. "It is not safe."

That was curious. "I am well enough to ready myself alone." Lord

Almighty, he didn't mean that he would remain while she...disrobed, did he?

"Have you neglected to remember? We have worked with many plague victims. I dare not trespass on the children."

There was something...deeper...in his gaze. Something unyielding. What was she to do?

A knock sounded on the door.

Patricie's eyes widened as she glanced from the door to Sir Antonin.

"A moment, please!" she called out.

The voice that called from the other side of the door was one of the maidservants. "The cook...she ails. And Lord Ambroz asks that ye tend her."

"I will attend her." Even as she said it, she searched for a way to dismiss the girl that Sir Antonin would be able to slip out unnoticed. Even if he must go out the window. "Please let Lord Ambroz know that I will be detained but for a few moments.

There was silence...for longer than she cared for. Then the girl spoke clearly. "Aye, I will sit with her until ye are able to come."

As soon as the sounds of the servant's footfalls quieted, Patricie set a stern look on Sir Antonin. "Go. Now."

He nodded. "I will be just outside."

She wanted to argue, but she counted herself fortunate that he would be out of the room. Dare she insist he seek an occupation for his time? Still, all she said was, "Thank you."

His steps were slow...painfully slow...as he moved to the door. Did he wish to be discovered here? To what end?

He paused just as he should have pulled the latch. "Do not worry, Lady. I will be waiting." He smiled and offered a brief nod.

Then he was outside, and the door closed behind him. And she was anything but comforted by his words. Only then did she consider how...present...he had been these last days. Ever at her side. She had believed it was a part of his aid to her. Out of a kindness, a consideration. Yet now... She couldn't shake the feeling that something more went here.

She dressed in a hurry, partly fearful he might open the door while she was naught in anything but her chemise. Soon enough, she tied the last set of laces on her right side.

Clad in a simple dress, she finished tying her single braid as she stepped to the door. And then into the corridor.

Sure enough, Sir Antonin stood just beyond the door. He turned as she opened the door. A small smile lit his features. "So glad to see you are more refreshed."

She flushed from the rush of dressing. But perhaps it appeared as just a healthy glow. She hoped.

"I must tend to the cook." She indicated the corridor to the right. "I am well enough if you have other duties to attend to."

The lines about his eyes seemed to strain. Was there something more behind his gaze?

"I am at your command, Lady."

She thought quickly but saw no other way to dismiss him. "I would prefer to tend to this patient on my own."

He jerked back and a frown replaced the tight line that was his mouth. "I only wish to assist—"

"I understand. And I do not wish to be ungrateful. Surely, Lord Ambroz could better use your skill."

An odd smile tugged at the side of his lips. "Not while the people present such a hostile front to the child."

He had her there. Indeed, there had been moments he'd been forced to brandish his sword in a threatening manner to keep the villagers from taking action.

"Very well." She turned and moved in the direction of the kitchens. There would certainly be a way to slip free of his vigil...

A hand clamped around her mouth and she was jerked to the side. Then dragged down steps leading into a storage cellar.

She scratched at his hand, fighting in futility to drag in a breath that she may release a scream.

What was this? What did the man intend to do to her?

CHAPTER 36
ANICKA & LUKAS

Anicka looked at her husband's profile. It was difficult to see him so concerned and not be able to reach out to him. Everything in her begged for her to touch the stubble of his unshaven jaw. And to soothe him with a kiss to his furrowed brow.

Yet more than the fact they rode separately prevented her—there were the angry words spoken the previous evening. Words that felt odd to have followed such intimacy.

Odd...and wrong.

But those moments in his arms...

She shook her head. It didn't matter. None of it. Not with the strangeness between them. Was he so vexed about her writing?

Turning her head, she watched him again. There was no other way to say it...she loved him. Could she give up her writing for his sake? She would try.

That thought tore at her heart. But her mother once told her there was a cost to everything. Perhaps that was true even of love.

"Do you intend to stare at me the whole of the ride?" Lukas's voice was gruff and startling.

Her face heated and she jerked her regard to her horse's mane. "No."

Then he watched her. She felt his gaze on her face. Dare she meet it?

He muttered under his breath. "I did not mean to be so harsh."

She peered to the side, noting that he still gazed at her. Then she inclined her head in a brief nod.

He shifted his focus forward.

The moment of connection was over too suddenly. And she was deprived of him too quickly.

"Lukas?" The word came out as more of a plea than she'd intended.

He steered his horse closer to hers. "Yes?" His voice gentled.

She swallowed. What to say? How to broach the subject? Mayhap it was not necessary. She needed to quiet her concern and let it be.

"What is it?" His eyes shone a level of concern when he turned to her, with the blue stormy and his brow slightly furrowed.

She took in a breath and looked about them to ensure no one was near enough. "Will you not speak of it?"

"Speak of it?" He appeared truly worried now. "Do you refer to things best kept to the privacy of a man and wife's chambers?"

Again, a flush of heat overcame her. He believed she referred to their intimacy.

"Anicka?" The word was insistent and harsher than she'd have liked.

It gave her pause to wince.

Dare she offer him the topic of her writing in this setting? Perhaps his words spoke wisdom to that account. What could she put before him then?

And she remembered. "I heard something."

"What?" His voice was lowered.

Yes, this was safer. "In the corridor last eve. I overheard two men talking."

Silence fell between them. Did he consider her words? Or whether to be concerned with them. "What did they say?"

Again, it was her turn to burn with embarrassment. This had been an ill-timed idea. "I didn't hear much. But one man did say. That is, I heard something that concerned me."

"What was it?" Lukas's voice pressed.

She became all the more flustered whenever someone spoke to her in that tone. "It is just that...what I meant to say..."

"Just tell me." He shot out as his gaze hardened.

She closed her eyes and swallowed against the rising trepidation within her. "I heard very little. But one of the men did say 'we have to finish what we started.'"

The furrow in Lukas's brow deepened. "Finish what they started? What else?"

A thickness built in her chest. Indeed, she should not have gone down this path. So much for avoiding trouble. "After that, they moved down the stairs and I thought I should hide."

He nodded slowly. "I see."

Yes, she should have kept her thoughts to herself. But the deepened lines of his features betrayed that he was not quick to dismiss the information. Did he weigh it against the fact that it was she who claimed to hear it? Many did not regard a woman's reporting to be wholly factual. But she knew what she had heard...and was careful to not say any more than that. Yet would he trust her words?

At last, he nodded. "Thank you."

That was all? He would not speak further on it?

Without glancing in her direction again, he urged his horse to speed up.

She hunched her shoulders and fairly deflated, barely remaining upright. He didn't believe her. Nor did he wish to ride alongside her any longer. Because she had stared at him?

Frowning, she attempted to right herself in the saddle. She was used to being dismissed. Had been by her mother and father her whole life. Why should Lukas be any different?

Lukas prepared himself for a coming confrontation as his cluster of knights and others drew nearer the castle. An urgency beat within his chest. When Anicka had told him about the overheard conversation, he'd wanted to dismiss it. Yet something nagged at him. She had always been quite observant and very reliable. He could not, in good conscience, think that there was nothing more to it.

But was that conversation in reference to his lordship of Zamek Kopec? Perhaps something went with an attempt to usurp his authority? Or it mayhap it was that men in Karin's camp worked against the leaders? Her men had been at the stronghold...moving freely within the safety of the walls.

Either was possible. But which was likely? More...if something were problematic in Karin's camp...shouldn't she and Sir Marek be made aware? Didn't he owe her that duty? An obligation to warn her?

He wanted to turn and look upon his wife, for she grounded him. Always had. Would she have been in Hradek Kralove with him at the time he became vulnerable to the Viscountess's schemes, perhaps he would have been able to resist. That was an interesting thought. One he dared not dwell on. For his life could have looked rather different. Would he be married to Anicka now? Or would his family have sought a better situation for him?

There was reason, then, to be thankful. For Anicka was home.

A call came from the top of the walls as the archers readied themselves. Soon thereafter, a group of knights rode to meet Lukas's contingency.

It was a short matter to explain his identity and his purpose. They were then escorted within the walls and brought to the sitting lord of the castle.

As he'd expected, Zdenek came into the great hall, but so did Radek. That surprised. Yet when was the last time he'd seen one and not the other?

Zdenek's features betrayed the war that must rage in his mind. Did he wonder whether to trust Lukas and welcome him? Their history was not the foundation upon which trust existed. Did the man know before this moment that Lukas had been released and since married?

Lukas inclined his head forward and tipped into a slight bow. "Lord Ambroz, Lord Miklas, it is an honor to stand with you again."

The faces of his once friends appeared uncertain as to how they should proceed.

"What can I do for you, Lukas?" Zdenek finally said, dispensing with any formalities. He was always the one to forego such. The expected familiarity proved refreshing.

Lukas waved a hand in Anicka's direction. "I would introduce my wife, Lady Anicka Vitekova."

Zdenek and Radek both nodded in a polite, expected greeting. But no welcomes were extended. Did they deem him nothing more than a traitor and criminal? Perhaps they simply wanted him out of their company and their sight.

This would be more painful than he'd thought.

"My lady wife is skilled in the art of healing. We were made aware of your...situation...and came to aid in your cause."

If Zdenek was surprised, it did not show in the whole of his features...except in the lines about his eyes. They tightened slightly. "What do you know of our need for assistance? Or that we are even in such a need?"

"Baroness Karin Krejikova passed the night at Zamek Kopec, which is now under my purview. It was there that the messenger found her...and requested aid. We are her answer."

Zdenek and Radek looked at each other, passing curious glances between them. Did they weigh how much to believe him? Were there actual ideas, or words passed in their minds as if they could read each other's expression so well?

Lukas stepped forward to speak again, but Anicka passed him to his left side and spoke before he could stop her.

"Please, Lord Ambrose. My husband speaks true. I am trained well and ready to help. We only wish to bring relief and assistance... at great risk to our own people."

Zdenek's eyebrows lifted before he schooled them.

Lukas reached out and touched Anicka's elbow. He prayed she would not give away the trouble they had experienced at Zamek Kopec with his father's power-hungry reagent. But she held her tongue.

Therein lay their hope of getting out of this with their dignity intact.

Just as Lukas prepared himself to give in and take their leave—regardless of what his former friends may need—Zdenek's affect fell. A crack in the hardened exterior.

"We thank you."

The muscles in Radek's jaw tightened and his fingers twitched as if he wished to reach to his friend.

It was no matter. Zdenek would welcome them. He was certain of it.

"We shall see you to a chamber. Then our healer will speak with you."

A woman rushed into the Great Hall. Her eyes were wide, and her movements jerked. She was frantic. Seeing the group gathered, she hesitated before stepping forward.

"My lady, what is it?" Zdenek stepped off the dais and moved to her.

It was then Lukas recognized her—the woman who had captured Zdenek's fancy at the chateau's ball. Could it be that she was now his wife? Lukas watched the scene unfold.

Zdenek attempted to scoot her toward the corridor. Perhaps seeking a more private conversation.

"She's gone," the woman cried as tears flowed easily down her cheeks. By the look of her red-rimmed and puffy eyes, they were not the first to fall.

Zdenek paused his shuffling movements and gazed at her more intently. "Who? Who is gone?"

But his tone betrayed that he knew very well whom she spoke of. "My sister."

Zdenek's face paled, but the way he held himself together for his wife was admirable. "Mayhap she is gone to the village?"

The woman shook her head quickly. "No one has seen her since early this morning. I have asked. I have sent people to the village. She is gone."

Zdenek frowned as he clenched his jaw and glanced at Radek.

"We will search her out. She must be about. What of Sir Antonin?"

"He is gone too."

Lukas would not speak such, but it sounded that the lady's sister and the knight had absconded together. Dreadful business.

The woman gripped Zdenek's outstretched arms. "I am afraid. What if some great ill has befallen them?"

He drew her to his chest. "All will be well. We will find her." There was a darkness behind his gaze that surprised Lukas. He'd never seen Zdenek appear so...serious. Mayhap years of war had scarred the man deeper than the cut that was still healing above his eyebrow.

Zdenek's intense gaze landed on Lukas.

The urge to shield Anicka was nearly overwhelming.

Then Zdenek turned to a nearby servant. "Show Lord and Lady Vitek to the chambers in the upper corridor."

The man nodded and moved toward Lukas and Anicka.

But Zdenek continued, shifting his focus to his wife. "I will find her."

How could he make such a promise? Still, something about the way they looked upon each other...the way the woman fell into his embrace...there was a trust there that stirred an ache within Lukas. Would he and Anicka ever have such?

As the manservant neared, Lukas turned to Anicka. "Go with him. I will aid in whatever way I can."

He felt Zdenek's piercing green eyes on him again. But they softened.

Lukas nodded at him. "My men will settle just beyond the walls to the forested side. But you have my sword."

The hair on his arms strained. And those on the back of his neck. He turned to find Anicka watching him as well.

He furrowed his brow. Would she disrespect him in front of these men?

"I..." She glanced at the gazes upon her. "I would speak briefly with you, my lord."

He gripped her arm and tugged her to the back of the hall, far enough that no one would overhear.

"What is it?" he hissed. Why would she make him seem weak when he was trying to make a show of strength?

She bit at her lower lip and looked down toward the rushes. "I...it is nothing."

The hardened edges of his chest eased. This was Anicka. He drew in a breath, knowing he still had to make a strong stand in front of the men.

He leaned closer. "Tell me."

"I...worry, my lord, about the way these men received you. The way they look upon you. Are you certain we can trust them?"

She was worried about him? That touched a piece of his heart and filled the space with warmth.

"It is nothing to be concerned about." His words came out tighter than he'd expected.

Her wide-eyed gaze lifted to his face. "What if...something has happened to put Lady Karin in danger? It seems as if there is no safety in the world anymore."

He grimaced. Indeed, he worried the same thing. "We can discuss it after I fulfill my word to help with this search."

She swallowed. "Thank you."

He had been ready to turn away. But her words caught him. "What for?"

Her eyes delved into his. "For lending me your ear."

The urge to glance at Zdenek and Radek to see if they watched him was almost overwhelming. Yet he could not tear himself from her features.

"Always," he breathed out.

She looked down. Did she consider something else? Or did she prepare for him to depart?

He opened his mouth to confirm that he would ride out soon to the village and speak with her when he returned.

"And thank you for not tearing up my words."

That gripped him. Her words?

"My writings." The words were barely above a whisper.

Understanding flushed through him. Why would he tear up her writings? Why would she think he would?

But she passed him and walked after the manservant to the stairs.

He wanted to call out after her. But the words caught in his throat.

Indeed, he was every bit the coward his former friends believed him to be. Not in body, but in heart.

CHAPTER 37
KARIN & PAVEL

Karin was tired but dug deep to find the reserves she had depleted. Then she grasped for the rage that burned within and pushed on. Sir Marek tried to draw alongside her. And she knew...he would beseech her to stop. But they neared Ulrich's stronghold. She would not be the weak member of the contingency, the one that made them linger when they could get there quicker. Pavel's life may depend on it.

How long had he been in Ulrich's clutches? What did the man intend for her husband? Would Pavel share his father's fate? She couldn't even think on that. Not now. And her heart tugged for Krejik lands. For she had left a piece of herself there with Jaromir. Her son.

Shoving him, too, from her mind, she would not be dissuaded from her mission. Not by her heart. Not by her body. And not by any of the men that questioned her.

Sir Marek urged his horse forward. To the point that Karin could not outrun him.

"My lady!" he called. Would he yell so loud the other men would overhear?

She did not wish for that to happen. So, with great reluctance in her spirit, she turned to him and slowed her horse.

Sir Marek's features were hard set. "My lady, I beseech you." His breaths were rapid, but not as much so as hers. Had she pushed herself past the point of wisdom?

"If you will not consider yourself, think of your men. Think of the animals."

She paused in her determination. He spoke truth. Her horse heaved. It had given much more than she should have asked of it.

Reining in, she signaled to the men that they would stop.

As they slowed further, she turned to Sir Marek. "For a half hour."

His eyes widened and he drew closer. "The horses need more rest than that. Permit that they be watered and refreshed. We cannot go into battle with wearied animals."

He was right again. And she hated it.

"For an hour only."

He grimaced. "I must ask for the night. Not only do we need more respite for the horses, but the men should have such an opportunity as well. And you..."

She jerked her regard to him as he trailed off. Yes, it was best he not continue that statement.

"The men will greatly benefit. As well, it may behoove us to plan our approach. Fully rested."

She considered his words. Again, it was maddening that he was right. It caused her to question her ability to lead appropriately. But she pressed that back. And gave a curt nod.

Sir Marek jerked his head in agreement and moved off toward the others. As usual, he would pass along the necessary instructions for the men to halt and make camp.

Why did she feel a failure? Because she had not anticipated the needs of the many? Or because she could not force them to press on?

She turned her horse and found her gaze drawn to Tomas.

His kind expression offered some solace. Heat crawled up her neck at the memories of how often she had found comfort in that face over her adolescent years. She jerked her gaze away. It had not been possible. And now it was too late.

Stepan shifted his horse to move between them.

It chafed...more because he was right to do so than anything else. Karin must not forget herself. Not now. Not ever again.

Karin once more shifted her attention forward. She urged her horse to follow the men angling their horses into the tree line across the meadow. As she neared, the trickling of a stream told that Sir Marek had chosen his moment well. They, and their animals, would find refreshment here.

Once within the shade of the oaks, she dropped off her faithful steed and led the horse to the stream. Not only did the horse replenish itself, but Karin dropped to her knees and took in some of the cool liquid. Then splashed some on her face. It served to awaken her weary senses but did not take her mind off Sir Tomas.

What had happened with him? How could he have disappeared from her life? He clearly had not been slain as believed. Then why did he not return to her?

She shook her head. It didn't matter. Pavel was her husband. And she was grateful for that. He was, in truth, her match in every way.

Standing, she grabbed for her horse's bit. But another hand intercepted it.

She spun to find Sir Marek looking down at her.

"Allow me, my lady. You have earned a reprieve."

She wanted to argue that he had pressed himself to the edge as well, but that wasn't true. He did not look nearly as worn as she felt. So, she nodded.

"I thank you."

"Return to camp. Find your rest."

She set a hand to his forearm and offered him the best smile she could. It was likely a feeble attempt. But it was what she could give.

As her shorter strides carried her toward the camp being built, she wondered at the men moving about her. They would have set up her tent first. How could she properly express her appreciation without seeming weak?

Typically, her tent was pitched a short distance from the men. But Sir Marek posted a knight to guard her overnight. Whether she approved or not.

She spotted the tent being erected, but her focus was drawn to a scuffle in the camp.

A voice rose. Stepan's.

No.

She ran—as much as she could—in the direction of the mass of bodies. Men worked to drag Stepan away from Tomas. It was a task indeed to push through to the center of the melee. But she managed.

"What goes here?" she demanded. Her voice lacked the strength she would have preferred to exhibit.

Stepan glared at Tomas, tight-lipped and seething.

"Is anyone going to answer me?" She speared the two with her gaze before scanning the cluster of men about. "Will no one speak?"

She shifted her gaze back to Stepan and Tomas. "Is there not enough to dwell on? Enough tension without the two of you going at each other?"

Neither eased their stance.

She waited.

Nothing.

The men about the area showed fatigue around their eyes. This was the last thing they wanted to manage either.

"Take Sir Tomas to the stream," she commanded, finding something within to give it force.

A couple of men led Tomas off. But his gaze moved to her face. There was a pleading there—something she'd best not heed.

So, she turned to Stepan.

Once Tomas and his guards were beyond hearing, she walked to Stepan, still restrained by a pair of knights.

"Tell me." A fury had ignited in her. Who did Stepan think he was?

He glared at her. "You forget yourself, Lady Karin."

She jerked back. Then firmed her stance. "I daresay it is you who has forgotten yourself."

Their eyes clashed. Would he yield to her authority in the matter? Or was he too heated to relent?

"Might there be need to see you bound as well?" Her threat was not idle.

His eyes darkened. "No, my lady."

She jerked her head in the direction of the knights that held Stepan's arms.

They released him and he pulled free as well. A show of strength that was for naught.

She stepped closer, staring him down. "I *will* have you bound. Know that. This mission is too important to risk your temper going unchecked."

His mouth tightened again. It appeared he considered visiting harm upon her. It wouldn't be the first time. Perhaps he should be kept under guard.

Soon enough, he eased. "I understand."

She nodded. Then turned toward her tent.

"But you do not know him. Not as you believe."

She whirled around, her face heating. How dare he insinuate such in front of her men!

His gaze pierced her. "He is not the same man you knew."

She bit her lip to keep it in check. Perhaps she might allow that this was the case. And that Stepan was not the same man either. Was it possible *he* was the hero of this tale and Tomas the villain?

Exhaling a long breath, she turned away. Only time would tell who she could trust between them.

Pavel awoke to the sound of his own labored breathing. Indeed, everything ached, pained by every limb and joint. The whole of his body cried out for respite. Perhaps it would be best if he just gave up.

But his mind turned to his wife and son. They needed him to get through this. They needed him to rescue them from Ulrich's schemes. Though in that moment, it was Pavel who longed for—no, needed—the comfort of his wife's arms. How could he have ever left her? For what cause would be so great as to sacrifice even a moment of life with her? Did he even believe in the efforts of the Hussites anymore? Hus was gone. Their great General, Zizka, likewise, had departed this world. And left those that remained fighting a losing battle.

For what? Why did they even resist Sigismund? Were the lives lost, the lives ruined, the bloodshed...was it worth it?

Pavel rolled as carefully and painfully slowly as he could. The priest nearby would have words of solace for him. Words of clarity. And purpose. Pavel both loathed and longed for them.

But as he shifted, he found that there was light beyond his closed lids.

Peering out through battered eyes, the light of a torch stung them anew.

It was only a moment before Pavel realized that someone stood over him.

He jerked backward, using his feet to propel him toward the wall. How had he been so deep in sleep that he'd allowed the fiend to sneak up on him?

Pavel's vision cleared as he peered through the darkness.

Ulrich.

And a pair of his guards.

Pavel looked up at the unimaginable height of the man standing in the center of the cell. Would Ulrich now accomplish what he meant for his enemy? The boorish man laughed, a maniacal sound. It set Pavel's teeth on edge.

Words climbed Pavel's throat. But he kept his lips sealed. He would neither urge nor dissuade this madman from what he intended.

"A fine knight you must have made." Ulrich's thick voice grated. "It was not difficult to sneak up on you, Sir Pavel." The last words were spoken as a curse.

"Why have you come?" Pavel croaked out. "Can you not leave me be and let me die?"

Ulrich leaned down until his face drew closer to Pavel's.

The desire to flinch and back away was an instinct, but Pavel would not give in to it. He stood his ground, as it were. His back was to the damp stone wall already.

"You think it is enough for me to simply kill you?"

Pavel narrowed his gaze and nearly grunted at the pain near his left eye.

"I want you to watch your wife and child suffer. I want you to beg for mercy."

"What have I done to draw such ire from you?"

Ulrich leaned away. "It is what you represent. Everything you stand for, Hussite."

Pavel frowned.

"I could not strike out at Zizka as I wished. But that won't keep me from visiting every bit of pain upon you that I wished for him."

It still didn't make sense. If Ulrich wanted to use Pavel as a bargaining chip, why bother with this?

Ulrich leaned in again. "For every blow I wished to visit upon your father."

Pavel's eyes widened. And anger burned in the pit of his stomach.

"He took everything from me. All that would have been mine."

What was the man speaking of? Pavel's father had not known Ulrich...or had he?

Pavel spat in the man's face before he could consider the wisdom of such. "That is what I think of your threats."

The guard to Ulrich's right side brandished his sword and moved forward.

Ulrich stood up, wiping his forearm across his face as he held out an arm to stop the man. "It is no matter."

The man paused and took a step back but did not re-sheath his weapon.

Pavel's anger made him feel powerful. Gave him a brazenness he had not known was possible.

"In fact..." Ulrich grinned. "I have a gift for you."

He rose and nodded to the other man, who handed something off to Ulrich.

Making a show of examining whatever it was, Ulrich ran a finger over the item in his grasp.

"I never had a son," Ulrich said, his voice sounding as if he were anywhere but here. As if the man barely held his sanity. "Perhaps if your father had not stolen..." The far-off gaze landed on Pavel.

Had the man truly taken leave of his senses?

Ulrich clasped the item in a fist. "Ancient history."

Pavel didn't dare speak. He could scarcely breathe. Had his mother somehow gotten caught between his father and...no, it couldn't be. It was unimaginable.

"The line of Krejik must end here," Urich said as he flung the item toward Pavel.

He had the thought he should duck, but he couldn't make himself move. The air was tense with regret and an anger that might well consume him as well.

But he looked down at the item which had landed on his chest, sliding a bit to one side. It was a delicate cloth of linen and lace. Such as one that Karin would carry. Was it hers?

Yet it was the other item that had been nestled within that disturbed him most—a lock of dark blond hair.

Jaromir's.

The emotions that swirled within Pavel sought release, fighting with his body to draw him to his feet and attack the man. Indeed, the father and husband of him struck out, regardless of his wounds.

But his shackles held true, jerking him back just short of Ulrich's face.

The man looked at him with an almost sorrowful expression. It could never have been. Never.

He lashed out with his hands, but they, too would not reach his captor.

Ulrich watched Pavel's struggle, the flame of the torch flickering in his gaze.

Then the man looked down and stepped back. "The next time I come to you. It will be in your last moments." The words were flat, no affect about them.

He left Pavel then.

As the door to the dungeon clanked shut in the distance, Pavel sank to his knees, feeling every ache sharply. But he pressed the fist that held his son's hair to his face. Karin's scent was still on the cloth. It was faint, but discernable.

Pavel cried out, railing against his plight.

Then he dropped to the cold floor...and wept.

CHAPTER 38

ANICKA & LUKAS

Lukas pressed onward on his assigned mission. While he believed it unwise to push into the darkness, he knew he must. As much as he had loathed leaving Anicka in the vulnerable state of their joining, he had to answer the call. Zdenek, Radek, and he had decided it was Lukas who should go. He had traveled for a couple of days now, riding hard, seeking the camp. He had to warn Karin. And he would.

Still, Anicka's face haunted him. Their parting had been sweet but hurried.

"I have to go." He had been strong, holding his features taut so as not to betray his concern or his weakness reflected in her eyes.

Those eyes had turned glassy. And he'd prayed the tears wouldn't come. How would he manage to leave her in such a state?

"There is more at stake here. I must go. It could save the entire contingency...and Lady Karin."

She had nodded. "I understand."

The desire to reach out to her became overwhelming. He set his hands on her arms and gave them a gentle rub. "I will return. And we will finish what we started."

Her regard had jerked to him.

He'd leaned in and pressed a kiss to her temple. Meaning to stop there, he pulled back, but only slightly. The scent of flowers and the powerful draw of her made it impossible to tear himself away.

Her breath caught, shattering the last of his resolve.

His mouth found hers. The kiss was everything they should be and should have—tender but needing. With a promise of more to come—a promise he intended to keep, so help him God.

Would the Lord Almighty be with a man like him? A man whose weakness and mistakes had nearly seen a life cut short? There was not space in him to broach such a thought. Best leave it at a cool distance between himself and God.

Turning his full attention to the present, he spotted campfire lights ahead, dim as they were. The light pierced the darkness still.

He was almost to the camp. He prayed he wasn't too late.

It was only a matter of moments before a guard intercepted him.

"Are you friend or foe?" the man asked, weapon at the ready.

Lukas raised his free hand, keeping both far from his sword hilt. "Friend. I have a message for the Lady Karin."

"In the middling of the night?"

"It is imperative that I speak with her immediately."

The man's brow furrowed. "We will let Sir Marek decide."

Could he trust Sir Marek? If he couldn't, then perhaps all was lost. For he likely had the loyalty of the men. Even beyond what Karin had garnered.

He nodded. Then followed the guard as they walked their horses toward the cluster of makeshift shelters and tents.

The quiet was chased away by the rousing of men upon seeing a stranger in the camp. Lukas ignored the looks shot his way. This was not about how the knights and guards received him, but how much Karin believed him.

It struck him then. Zdenek was right, he should have allowed Radek to go in his stead. Yet his desire to prove himself worthy bade him step into Radek's reluctance to leave his wife, who struggled with the sickness of pregnancy.

That only proved advantageous for Lukas...or so he thought.

By the time they approached the lead knight's tent, Sir Marek stood outside, waiting.

Lukas saw no need to waste time or mince words. But he needed to be leery of who could hear. "Sir Marek, I must speak with the Lady Karin."

The older knight offered a slightly raised eyebrow. "I will not wake the baroness for a late-night chat."

Lukas glanced about. There were several guards gathering—more ears than he cared for. He took a step toward Sir Marek. "I beseech you, sir knight, to hear me out. And not with an audience."

The man's gaze bore into Lukas, his eyes hard and unrelenting. Did he suspect Lukas of wishing foul upon him...or Karin?

"I tell you, I mean only to warn the lady of something foul afoot. Perhaps enough so to set the safety of this camp on the edge of a thin blade. From which there can be no return."

The men about him did not move, but there was the altering of their breathing. Yet they looked to Sir Marek to command them.

Sir Marek's jaw clenched. When he released it, he muttered gruffly, "Walk with me." Then he stepped into the dark without another word. The men surrounding them did not follow.

Dare Lukas? Was this merely a chance for Sir Marek to see to the end of him with finality? And then he fully appreciated the situation the knight was in. Lukas would be risking his own wellbeing.

He firmed his stance and then trudged after the older man. If one must be the first to trust, it would be him.

Sir Marek awaited him just beyond the camp. He watched Lukas approaching without any sign of reassurance.

Nothing told Lukas he had made the right choice...until he paused just short of Sir Marek.

"This way." He slipped farther into the thick of night.

It was only a few more paces before Lukas noted the dimness of flame flickering just ahead.

A pair of guards became more alert as they neared, their swords at the ready.

"All is well," Sir Marek said. "We must rouse the baroness."

"But..." one of the men countered.

A sharp glance from Sir Marek silenced him.

"Of course," he said, sheathing his sword.

The other guard followed suit, and both stood aside to let Sir Marek pass. And they both glared at Lukas. If looks could pierce him, these would.

Sir Marek halted just beyond the tent flap. "My lady," he spoke in a loud voice directed into the tent, the cloth of which somewhat muffled the call.

"Sir Marek?" came the reply of Karin's distinct voice. Her unique lilt and inflection had haunted many of his nights as he had lain in that dungeon. Each intonation stabbing at him with regret.

"Yes, my lady. Word has come...from Krejik lands."

The flap was swept aside as she pressed out of her shelter, her braid askew as she pulled a robe closed at her front. When her gaze landed on Lukas, her eyes widened. "My son...?"

"Is well, Lady Karin. It is rather for *your* sakes that I have come."

Her delicate brow furrowed. Worry etched lines into her features that she was far too young to have mar her. She looked at Sir Marek before glancing to Lukas again. "Our sakes?"

"Yes." Lukas looked to the two guards. Were they to be trusted?

"I rely on only my best men to watch over the lady." Sir Marek's hard gaze was on him again, speaking as if he could read Lukas's mind.

Lukas jerked his head in a nod before directing his attention back to the bright green eyes that were lit by flickering flames being brought back to life.

"Go on," she urged. And he knew she would believe what he said.

That was a greater relief than he realized. For she must. Or else, all would be lost.

"There is danger... here, in this camp. An agent of the ruthless madman you pursue."

Karin set her jaw. "You must be assured of this fact to have come all this way. And to see me wakened in the night."

He nodded. "Yes. The healer upon your lands has vanished. As well...one of your knights."

Karin frowned. "That is unfortunate. But that does not speak to subterfuge in my camp."

What brought such a resistance? Lukas remembered that Stepan had suspected her of having softer consideration for Sir Tomas. Did she think to defend him? Or did she just doubt Lukas's concern?

"There is reason to believe that the knight is at fault for kidnapping the healer."

She crossed her arms. To better keep her robe closed? Or as another line of defense? "While I appreciate your errand. Logic speaks that someone creating problems on Krejik lands *since* my departure could not have absconded from there and be in this camp at the same time."

He nodded. "Yes. But upon searching his rooms, we found this." Lukas produced a rolled parchment. Urging it into her hands, Lukas watched as she read it.

The lines about her face darkened further.

He had read the lines penned by Ulrich of Rosenberg. They detailed the knight's mission, that the young Jaromir was his intended target.

"Who is this knight? Why would he, then, take the healer?"

Lukas broke his line of sight on her to glance at the elder knight beside her. As if he feared the man would betray that he'd held knowledge of the situation. "Perhaps," he said absently, "She discovered something she shouldn't have."

"Lukas..." Her teeth were clenched. She had to know. "Who?"

He directed his focus to her. And could not tear his gaze away from eyes that were no longer gleaming from the fire in the camp, but from a fire within.

Swallowing, Lukas pushed out through his own disgust the name that he had borne with him these long hours in the saddle. "Sir Antonin."

Anicka slid an arm about the slender shoulders of Lady Eva. The woman had been inconsolable since her sister's disappearance and the subsequent discovery of the knight's treachery. To know that the healer was at the mercy of that man...it burned Anicka, though she'd not had the opportunity to know Patricie.

Lady Hana approached from Anicka's right side. The hesitant lady had a cloth drenched with cool water that she had retrieved from the basin near the bed. Although...she looked as if she could use some comfort as well. A maidservant had mentioned just the evening prior that Lady Hana dealt with a severe sickness from being with child.

With her limited training in healing, Anicka had known it could be so. But she had yet to see a woman so pale and washed of life as she noted in this lady this eve.

"It will be all right," Anicka soothed, directing her attention back to the distraught Lady Eva. But did she speak more to herself than to the others? For she had been loathed to part with Lukas. Yet she knew he must do what he did. He had some rabid need to redeem himself. It would always tear them apart if she didn't let him satisfy it. Why couldn't he let her love him and approve of him herself?

"How can you say that?" Lady Eva rolled from her sitting position on the edge of the mattress to lie on her side, curled into herself. "You cannot know that she is well even now."

Anicka let out a breath, trying to tamp down her frustration with herself. She had let her own feelings muddle her words. "I understand that. But we must have faith. We must believe that all is not lost."

A moan pressed out of Eva as Lady Hana set the damp cloth to the woman's forehead. "There, now. Let this bring some comfort."

Though Lady Hana quickly gripped her hand across her midsection as her other hand flew to her lips. Was she going to be ill?

Anicka was torn again...but in a very different way. Should she stay with the teary-eyed Lady Eva? Or urge Lady Hana to seek her own rest, ensuring that she obeyed?

As if sensing her thoughts, Lady Hana raised her hand from her stomach. "I am quite all right. I just need to sit for a moment."

Anicka doubted that would cure all. "Perhaps you should retire to your chambers? Take a rest yourself?"

Lady Eva glanced up from her position on the bed. "What is this? You are unwell?"

It warmed Anicka's heart to see the woman set her mourning aside to aid another. It spoke well of the lady.

"I thank you," Lady Hana said, her voice timid as if she were unsure herself. "But I would prefer to remain at your side." Blue eyes landed on the dark ones that belonged to Lady Eva.

The lady wiped a hand across her red-rimmed eyes and sat up. Then rose and crossed the room before Anicka could react.

"Please." Lady Eva appeared stricken almost more than before. "I will not have you tire yourself. Nor risk your child."

Lady Hana let her fingers drop from her mouth, which cut a small smile. "I say, all *is* well."

Taking her hand, Lady Eva's features tensed. "Do not neglect this gift you have been given."

What was this? Lady Eva's expression said as much as if she had not the pleasure of such a gift. But what of Michal? Or had something occurred that prevented the lady from conceiving again? Some trial in the birthing?

Lady Hana's eyes were sad as she looked back at her friend. "I do not. And will not. Though it was unexpected, and though it wearies my body, I know it is indeed a gift."

"One that not all women are given." Lady Eva added. But it was unnecessary. For the deep sorrow in her gaze told all now.

As if Anicka could summon someone with her very thoughts, knocking vibrated the door to the chamber.

"One moment," Lady Eva called.

Did she really think to entertain anyone in this state?

But she moved to the basin, splashed water on her face, and wiped it away with a remaining towel.

Anicka hated to see her so pulled. "You don't need to—"

Lady Eva shot her a look that silenced her. "I have duties to perform in the baroness's stead."

"Do you not think the dowager baroness can—"

Again, she was cut off.

"It is my duty. And I will have it." Lady Eva dismissed Anicka perhaps a bit too easily as she strode across the room and tugged open the door.

A nursemaid held a crying Michal. Had the lady somehow known it was her son?

Without a word, Lady Eva reached for him.

Short, cherub arms grasped for her as she pulled him into her embrace. "There, there. What is the matter?"

The nursemaid's face seemed rather strained. "He has been nigh' inconsolable for the last hour."

Lady Eva shot her a stern look but spoke with a kind gentleness. "It is all right. You could have brought him sooner."

"What with your sister and all, I..." The woman paled. "My apologies, my lady. I did not mean to—"

Lady Eva waved her off while setting Michal a little away from her such that she could look into his face. "What is the matter, little sir?"

"I don't think he likes being cooped up."

Lady Eva nodded and stroked the child's tears away tenderly. "I wish he did not have to be confined."

"I say, he and the baron's son have been fast friends, but they miss the courtyard."

That set Anicka to wondering. Why had they been thusly constrained? Because of the plague? That made sense. No need risking the small ones.

"Mayhap I shall take him for a quick stroll."

There, that would make it better. Anicka nodded along. "I will come along...with your permission, of course."

Lady Eva pressed a kiss to the child's forehead as her gaze darted toward Anicka. Did she suspect Anicka only wished to fulfill an obligation to stay at her side? It was not the case. Anicka needed the company as much as Lady Eva did.

"I should like some sunlight as well."

"My lady," the nursemaid interjected. "Do you think that's wise?"

Lady Eva turned a stern look on the servant.

"That is, perhaps I should fetch his hood?"

And Anicka put the pieces together. The child's mark. Had the villagers been unkind? People could be terribly superstitious about such things.

"That will not be necessary." Lady Eva's words were as hard and strained as Anicka could have ever thought possible.

The servant backed away, ducking her head.

Lady Eva's gaze remained on the servant for some moments. Anicka feared she might say something harsher. The way her mouth pinched spoke of how upset she was.

"You are excused." Lady Eva turned to Anicka. "If you would like, I shall have you join me." Then she looked to Lady Hana. "I would prefer you find what rest is to be had."

Lady Hana did not argue but nodded her thanks and quit the room.

But as Anicka watched Lady Hana step beyond the door, she noted that the maidservant still stood in the way.

"Is there anything else?" Lady Eva said, her words abrupt.

"I..." The woman's eyes peered upward. "No, my lady. I shall be about when you are ready for me to collect him."

Lady Eva nodded and moved passed the servant.

Anicka reluctantly followed, wishing she could somehow soothe the situation between the two. But she knew it was not her place. She simply offered the woman an encouraging smile and followed Lady Eva.

And, while she sought solace in a stroll about the courtyard, she feared that was not what she was to find.

CHAPTER 39
PATRICIE & STEPAN

Patricie stared across the small campfire at the man she had come to loathe. The popping of the fire and dancing flame highlighted his turmoil.

Good. He should feel conflicted.

He had yet to talk with her. Nothing more than cursory demands.

Why had he taken her? What was his purpose? Where was he taking her?

At first, she had feared he but wanted to carry her far enough away such that he could work evil upon her. But that had not been the case. They had been alone for a couple of days now, with no one to stop him from any design he had on her.

There must be a reason.

Sir Antonin had been someone she trusted. Someone she had even...admired. How could she have been so wrong?

"Are you hungry?" he muttered. Again, only words that were absolutely necessary.

"For a reason," she challenged, lifting her chin in an attempt to banish all fear within her. And, though her belly ached for sustenance, her heart needed answers more.

He frowned and looked at the ground.

The urge to run filled her. But she had been down that road already. His strength and speed far outdid hers. Such action would be moot soon enough.

She pushed out a breath and opted for a different approach. Gentling her voice, she tried again. "Please. I just want to know why."

At that, his gaze lifted and met hers. Briefly. Then he looked to the fire and tended it.

"Sir Antonin..." she pled. His name slipping out far more easily than she liked.

That gave him pause. He set down the stick that he'd been using to poke at the base of the flames and rubbed a sleeve across his forehead. Then he closed his eyes. "Please do not ask that of me."

A part of her wanted to let it go. That was the piece of her that had cared about him. And it needed to be quashed.

"I need to know," she pressed. For the first time, she had hope he might speak to her.

Tension stretched the muscles about his mouth.

"I beg you." So close.

Then he seemed to shutter his face, hiding his emotion. When he opened his eyes again, there was iron behind his gaze.

But she couldn't let it go. "Tell me with whom your loyalty truly lies."

He grimaced and threw the stick.

"Not that I can believe anything," she scoffed. "You pledged your fidelity to Baron Krejik and yet here you are, stealing into the night with a hostage."

That had him riled. "It is for the best."

Her eyebrows rose. "The best? Lying, kidnapping, and who knows what else?"

He shook his head and looked to the ground again. "I don't expect you to understand."

Heat rose in her. "You of all people should know I am capable of understanding a great many things." Not only had he seen her knowledge of herbs and medicinals, but they had also conversed freely about a variety of topics.

"You live unscathed by this war," he accused.

She was taken aback. Indeed, it caused her to jerk away. "What can you mean?"

He shook his head.

"No. Tell me what my weak, female mind cannot possibly comprehend."

He glared at her; the depths of his ire became evident. As did his pain. "You live on the outskirts of this bloodbath. You haven't seen what I've seen. What I've been through."

She narrowed her gaze. "So you say. But I once served in the midst of General Zizka's camp. I have seen much."

His eyes widened slightly.

"Yes," she snapped. "I have seen much. Sacrificed much." How dare he presume she was uninjured by the war?

"Still," he said with clenched jaw and hard words, "You cannot possibly know my pain."

She softened again, moved by the flash of regret in his eyes. "Then tell me. Make me understand." She tried to tamp down her eagerness. For she was finally getting answers.

"I once fought on the side of...well, what we were told was 'right'."

What was that supposed to mean? But she kept her thoughts shut up for the moment, hoping he would speak further.

"I was a loyal Hussite. As was my brother." He looked down again, his head falling as well as his shoulders. Therein was the source of his pain.

"What of your brother?" she urged quietly. And hated that her heart tugged toward an ache for him.

Sir Antonin ran a hand over his face. Did he think to erase all signs of his pain so easily?

"My brother fell in the Battle of Usti."

She jerked away. Not at the words she had known would come, but from the mixture of hurt and steel coming through his gaze that he set on her.

"He gave his life for a cause that he wasn't sure he believed in." Then Sir Antonin looked to the side. "Because of me."

She bit at her lip to keep from responding. She wasn't altogether certain what she would have said.

"I was the one who believed. He had doubts. Yet he paid the ultimate price in a fight that will never end. In a war that is not altogether just. For it demands the blood of many Czechs."

She frowned, finding it more difficult to not feel for his pain.

"That is why I found Ulrich's offer appealing. He is the answer. The way to bring an end to this madness."

"Ulrich?" The name slipped past her lips before she could stop it. Though she had suspected Sir Antonin worked with a Royalist noble, she had not imagined this.

Sir Antonin's nostrils flared. "I would do *anything* to see the Hussites brought to heel." Emotion cracked his voice. But he sealed his lips and fought with the battle surely raging within him.

Trying to remember Sir Antonin's actions rather than the depth of his grief, she cleared her mind. "But this cannot be the way. How did I challenge you? What have I done to warrant kidnapping me?"

He looked to the side, and she knew...it had been an impulsive choice. Did he seek to win her to his side? That didn't seem right. He'd have had more luck with that would he have not taken her.

"As if you don't realize," he sputtered.

What could he mean?

"I didn't want to. If you'd have kept your suppositions to yourself... If you hadn't figured me out..."

Figured him out? True, that last morning she had suspected him of crossing a line, but not this one.

All of that was moot, however. It was past. What did her future hold?

"Then...what do you intend for me?" Her statement was devoid of emotion.

"I will let Ulrich decide." His voice was not as firm as it had been. Indeed, he must have doubts.

For she was certain no good outcome would be forthcoming for her from Ulrich.

She watched Sir Antonin shut down as surely as if he'd said as much. He would not speak further this eve. Her work was thus...she must convince him to let her go. Or escape. For certain, her life depended on it.

Stepan bit back a growl as he shifted on his bedroll. He had been trying to sleep...to no avail...for some hours. How many exactly was anyone's guess. The night was thick and unyielding of what peace it might offer but did not. There was naught but the distant sound of the stream and the lapping of flames in a distant fire.

It was no use.

Thrusting the thin blanket to the side, he shoved to a sitting position. He rubbed a hand over his eyes as if that would clear all errant thoughts. It did not.

Yet as he stilled, he heard the low hiss of voices nearby.

Careful to move slowly lest he generate more noise, he turned in the direction of where Sir Tomas was kept. He needed no excuse for why his thoughts went there first. It was only to everyone's benefit that he make his bed near the place where the prisoner was held. Stepan had settled a few yards away, hopefully that now concealed his state of wakefulness.

For when he peered about, he found that not only was Sir Tomas not asleep, rather he was engaged in conversation with the guard that kept watch.

Stepan saw red. And fury burned in his gut.

It was all he could do to maintain his position and breathe. That was wisest. That was best. How else was he to determine what was afoot?

His blood thundered so loud in his ears it made that impossible.

Still, he watched as the two men conversed for several moments.

Then they halted and the guard jerked back.

Stepan heard, as well, what had given them pause. Others moved in the camp further in...toward Karin's tent.

The thudding of footfalls betrayed that whoever walked through the thick of the trees made no effort to disguise their movement. Tearing his gaze from Sir Tomas and the turncoat, he homed his senses on the movement. There were multiple footfalls moving in the dark. Had other knights stirred as well?

A torch led the way for a man—who appeared to be Sir Marek— and a few others. One of the men looked a little more familiar than he should. Inexplicably, it was Lukas. His steps were hesitant, and his shoulders hunched as if weary. Who wasn't? It was late into the middling of night after a number of sleepless hours.

Stepan drew in a much-needed cleansing breath and released it. He would not be ill-tempered. He would not.

Or else he would.

He rose bit by bit...and, grabbing his sword, he then moved in a wide arc around the path they took.

While he had not forgotten the Tomas problem, he wasn't about to be left out of whatever his old friend brought. Why wasn't he still upon Krejik lands? Had something gone awry? Had something happened to those there? Did Lukas bear ill tidings of loss?

Stilling his racing heart, he pushed Patricie to the edges of his awareness. It would be impossible to free his thoughts completely of her—something he had yet to do since their first meeting.

Sir Marek slowed, coming to a halt near Karin's tent.

Stepan, too, stopped and crouched a few feet away, shielded by the night.

Karin appeared soon after, and there was an exchange between the three.

The urge to draw nearer to hear better tugged at Stepan. He inched forward, but only just. That's when Lukas revealed his purpose and produced a document. What was this?

Stepan moved ever closer.

"Who is this knight?" Karin's voice became louder than perhaps was prudent.

The friend-turned-enemy glanced at Sir Marek. But Karin would not be put off.

"Lukas...who?" she insisted. Her voice was like iron.

Lukas paused before he produced the name. "Sir Antonin."

Stepan gasped before he clenched his teeth tightly. The cur! There had been more than a bit of unease within Stepan about Antonin. He'd told himself it was naught but a desire to protect Patricie and stake his claim on her. In that, he resisted treating her as property that she was not.

Now to know that his instincts had been right, and he'd ignored them? It turned his anger inward, leaving a foul taste in his mouth.

What was being done about Sir Antonin? Did Patricie know of his betrayal?

Suddenly, there was a blade pressed against Stepan's back.

Without making any big movements, his hand, already at his side, closed around the hilt of his own sword.

"I wouldn't dare," the man seethed.

"Ah...so courageous, are we?" Stepan muttered. "Brave enough to strike down a man from behind?"

"Silence! It is you who trespass."

Stepan took a chance and turned. "Indeed, I do not."

In the distant flickering light, he could make out nothing more than the vague outlines of the man.

The pressure of the blade eased but slightly.

Stepan sprung from his position, bringing his sword around, slicing through the air to relieve the threat altogether.

Surprisingly, the man held on to the blade that Stepan knocked sideways.

Then they were facing off, but in the dark. And neither seemed to know the other's identity. Though this was a decided disadvantage to risk himself first, he could not delay himself longer.

"I am Sir Stepan Dvorak, protector of the Lady Karin."

The man stepped back. "Sir Stepan. My apologies. I thought you were an interloper."

Stepan could make out the man's sword arm lowering.

"Aye. As it would seem." Stepan dropped his own weapon. "And who may I congratulate for sneaking upon my distraction?"

"Naught but an elder knight, too alert and too ready for a real rest."

The man's voice sounded strangely wearied. Did he not sleep either? Or had Stepan's movements disrupted his slumber?

"My apologies." Stepan's words were more sincere than he'd have thought. "It was not my intention to wake others. "Quite the opposite."

"It is no matter." The gruffness of his voice came out somewhat resentful.

"I encourage you to find your rest." Stepan sheathed his sword but kept his hand near his dagger. One could never be too careful.

"There will be no rest for me."

That was a strange thing.

"I remember the first marches on Tabor. We thought ourselves righteous then...as do we now. And yet...look what we've become—fighting against each other while the empire watches and waits."

There was more going on here with this man than first imagined. He was not just weary from lack of sleep, but from lack of peace.

And Stepan knew that way all too well. How close had he perched on the wall, nearly falling into madness when he pursued his former friends in battle? It was by the grace of God Almighty that he was sane to this day. If he even were that.

"Still, sir knight, I would that you find some respite. For who knows what tomorrow might portend?"

The man made a small movement that Stepan believed was a

nod, before he stepped away. But Stepan wasn't so thoughtless to believe that the man truly walked away. He would be watched.

When he turned around, the threat neutralized, he found that Karin, Lukas, and Sir Marek were no longer where they had been.

How could he have let himself lose track of them?

Scanning the area, he discovered that men gathered near the center of camp. Guards and knights had roused en masse. What went?

He pushed through the underbrush and into the clearing along with countless others.

Karin stood in the center with Sir Marek. Where had Lukas gone? Did it matter?

"There has been news," Karin said, her voice carrying though she didn't shout. "And we must move up our plans."

Stepan held his breath for what he feared was coming but knew must be.

"We will march on the enemy before daybreak."

Shifting of bodies off to the left distracted Stepan. Did someone shove their way forward? He pressed in to cut whoever it was off.

Sir Marek must have seen the same thing because he stepped in front of Karin, unsheathing his blade.

Soon after, Sir Tomas, still with bound hands, rammed his way into the open space in front of Karin.

Sir Marek lifted his sword and called for the man to stay back.

"I only wish to help." Sir Tomas sounded pained.

Would they believe that act?

Karin set a hand to Sir Marek's arm and urged him to draw back.

The older knight resisted but obeyed.

"What is it?" Karin asked, her features drawn and tight. Did she war with emotions she didn't want to show?

That stoked the fire of Stepan's anger once more. And he shoved through some of the men but struggled to get to Karin.

"I will go in and retrieve the baron."

Karin's face paled and her eyes widened. Did she believe this craziness?

"No," Stepan shouted. At last, the way cleared for him as several men stepped to the side.

But Karin would not look in his direction.

"Do...not...listen to that snake," Stepan seethed.

"Snake, am I?" Tomas challenged. "Who of us has tried to strike down the lady?"

Stepan's face warmed...his ire fueling the heat that drew perspiration. "And who conspired with his guard to take advantage of any weakness you could find?

"No," Karin's authoritative voice broke through. "This is not the time."

Stepan bit back further response.

Sir Tomas set his gaze on Karin. "I came to warn you, at great risk to myself. Why would I do that if not to see your husband freed?"

Stepan wanted to point out that he may be wriggling into Karin's good graces in an attempt to take most advantage of Pavel's absence...or death. But he held his tongue. That, after all, would not be a welcomed interjection.

"Karin," Sir Tomas started.

Stepan had just about reached the limit on his fury. But Sir Tomas eschewing her title once more and addressing her so informally pushed it farther.

"You know me. No one knows me as you do. And so, I beg you... this one last time, trust in that. Trust *me*."

The agitation among the men in camp was widespread.

But Karin's eyes were caught on Sir Tomas.

And Stepan knew...she was going to agree.

CHAPTER 40
ANICKA & LUKAS

Anicka had expected they might keep to the castle gardens or courtyard. Certainly not traversing the outer bailey. But Lady Eva continued their stroll with Michal far closer to the village—and the plague—than she'd have liked.

She had started to speak to that very matter a couple of times, but the memory of the lady's reaction to the nursemaid forced Anicka to keep her thoughts to herself.

"Is it not the most glorious of days?" Lady Eva stretched out her arms and leaned back to allow the sun to warm her face.

Michal toddled just in front of her.

The lady was careful not to avert her gaze for too long.

They passed a couple of villagers bringing their empty carts from the direction of the castle. Had they delivered their foodstuffs? Either way, they veered widely in an arc away from the two ladies and the child. The looks they threw were not reassuring.

In fact, Lady Eva had wandered far too close to the village. They could see a few of the houses from their position in the dip of slight valley.

Between the looks the villagers had given them and the foreboding tone of the nursemaid's warnings, Anicka decided it was time. "Should we not make our way back?"

Lady Eva turned to her, eyes dark and wide. "Whyever? Are you not enjoying the fresh air? We've been cooped up for so long."

"I am, I assure you. But I am only concerned about the sickness in the village. It seems children fare far poorer with most ailments."

Lady Eva scowled. "I would never risk Michal's wellbeing. We will turn back soon enough. Besides, as you see, the townsfolk will not draw near."

Was the lady baiting the people? Taunting them? Forcing Michal's presence on the people who, with their superstitions, believed him to be the cause of all the evil that had befallen them?

It wasn't wise.

A slight tremor went through Anicka at that thought. "What of your lord husband? Does he know we are so near the village?" It was, after all, he who had warned the castle folk to do their best to keep from the small town.

At that, Lady Eva pursed her lips but did not look in Anicka's direction.

Michal became interested in something near his feet. He stopped to watch.

Sure enough, a frog jumped away from him.

He followed.

Not wanting to end up chasing the toddler, Anicka rallied her courage and scooped him up. She could fairly feel Lady Eva's glare burning into her.

"My, my little sir, what have you found?"

Though the boy wiggled and pushed to be free, she held tight and shifted that he might be able to watch the frog.

"See how it goes about, looking for bugs to eat?"

He looked at Anicka with his big amber eyes and then back in the direction of the frog, attempting once more to escape Anicka's arms.

"Do you know, I once knew a frog named Ocko. He was a very

adventurous frog." She lilted her voice up and down in a rhythm to catch Michal's attention.

It worked. He stilled his movements and gave her a quick look.

She was thankful for the part of her that could weave stories from anything. Even Lady Eva's features had smoothed.

"Ocko loved to jump and see new things. One day, he wandered far from his family's home near the little pond."

"O-to." Michal shouted his attempt at the name.

"Yes." She swayed the boy slightly as she subtly turned back toward the castle. "And you have wandered far from your home too. You are very brave."

"Bahv," he tried again.

She nodded. "Yes, you are brave. And so was Ocko. But as the day became night, Ocko missed his mother and father and brothers and sisters."

Now the boy was mesmerized by Anicka—her story or her tone, she wasn't certain which. Still, they were moving in the direction of the castle, so she felt more at ease.

"Ocko wanted to go home, but he was so very tired from his day of hopping...and he didn't remember the way to the little pond." She frowned.

The boy reached a finger toward her lips.

She smiled and kissed the tip of his small digit. "Ocko was very sad."

Lady Eva muttered something behind her. Perhaps the woman was frustrated with Anicka's game. Yet Anicka persisted. It was best.

"And it became darker. Then a large bird landed near where Ocko sat on a rock. Ocko was afraid. Would the great bird eat him? He wanted to cry."

"Oko," Michal's pronunciation was improving.

"Yes. And the bird asked Ocko what was the matter. Ocko decided to be brave and said he was far from home and missed his mama.

"The great bird thought for a moment. Then he offered to take

Ocko home to the little pond. But Ocko had to trust that the bird would do as he said and not eat Ocko."

Michal's eyebrows arched as Anicka's tone became more serious.

"So Ocko jumped to—"

Something hard struck the back of Anicka's shoulder and thrust her forward.

Lady Eva screamed as she ducked beside Anicka.

Pain shot through Anicka. She wanted to test out the area, but her mind thought more of Michal and the need to keep him safe.

"Stay down," Lady Eva said as she crawled to Anicka. Then the woman's hands and body covered Michal and part of Anicka.

Michal wailed. Did he sense the fear rippling through Anicka?

The whoosh and thud of more objects flew overhead.

Anicka peered up and saw a rock the size of a fist land nearby. Was someone throwing rocks at them?

They continued to come, a few pelting Anicka on the hip and leg. She also heard Lady Eva grunt and cry out as she must have been struck as well.

"Protect my baby," Lady Eva pled, her voice nearly hoarse.

Anicka tightened her hold on Michal. Would it be better for them to run for the castle? They would be better seen, but it was surely more difficult to hit a moving target.

Though as quickly as it started, the onslaught stopped.

Anicka's breaths came in heaves and Michal's cries were insistent.

But Lady Eva had quieted.

"Let us make for the castle," Anicka said, trying to rise, but Lady Eva's body prevented her from doing so. "My lady, I think our chance is now."

But there was no response.

Anicka wriggled herself and Michal from under the lady, shifting sideways as she rose to her knees.

Lady Eva slid off her and landed on the ground. Which is where she continued to lie.

"Lady Eva?" Anicka called, sparing a hand to shake her shoulder.

Michal pushed and fought against Anicka.

She dared not let him go. Glancing about, she could see no signs of those who had attacked them. Or anyone else. Their surroundings were oddly...and eerily...still.

"Lady Eva?" Anicka scooted closer, not an easy task while holding a squirming youngster.

The lady lay on her side, leaning facedown.

It did not prevent Anicka from noticing that blood seeped from a wound on her head. Had she been struck thusly?

Fear gripped Anicka. Her grip on Michal and on her courage threatened to slip. But she held both.

Looking in the direction of the castle, farther than it should be, she needed a plan.

Could she leave the lady here? How else might she get Michal to safety and seek out help?

There was no other choice.

Clamping her right arm around Michal's waist and securing him to her side, she used her other arm to turn the lady face up. Her left shoulder screamed in pain as she moved it, but she had to push through it to ensure the woman breathed.

Sensing warm breath exhaling from the lady's nostrils, Anicka thanked the Lord for that mercy. Then she ripped a piece of her own hem and pressed it to the wound on Lady Eva's head. There was nothing more she could do for her companion, nor for the other wounds she had sustained.

It took even more effort for Anicka to gain her feet with an increasingly pained shoulder on one side and holding tight to the wailing child on the other.

But she did, emitting her own cries as searing heat tore through her shoulder.

She loosened her hold on Michal but urged him close with a gentler motion. Pressing a kiss to his forehead, she spoke in a soothing tone. "I know, I know. You're all right. We'll be all right. I just need to get to your father."

The boy's cries eased just slightly, and he now clung to Anicka.

She sent a silent apology to God and a prayer as she regretted having to leave the lady unprotected but having no other choice.

As she stepped toward the castle, she found that her right leg had been injured as well. Putting weight on it was difficult. Yet she couldn't give in to that. Michal and Lady Eva needed her to be strong.

She advanced, half dragging her right leg along, but progress it was. Arduously slow, but steady.

Shushing Michal as she went, she could not help the way she had to grit her teeth against groans as she went.

How long she continued like that, she didn't know. But she soon arrived at the gate. The guards spotted her coming and rushed to assist.

They came to either side of her, but upon a better look, they stepped back. Was that from fear of the boy? How crazed were these people?

"Please," Anicka said, pressing her misgivings to the side. "The Lady Eva and I were set upon. Near the village. She is badly wounded. We need to send help!"

One of the guards motioned for the other to rush ahead. He then took to the side of Anicka opposite the boy.

How could the villagers hate this small child so much they would attack him and two women? Did their ignorance and vileness know no bounds?

Soon enough, the nursemaid appeared from somewhere and took Michal. Now that he was safe, Anicka leaned heavily on the guard that escorted her. She hoped he was taking her somewhere soft and comfortable...a place she might rest, close her eyes, and be at peace.

If only she could...but she needed to help Lady Eva.

Lord Ambroz rushed to her. "My lady, what has happened?"

"I...Lady Eva...she...needs...help..." It became increasingly difficult to keep her eyes open. They were so heavy.

The guard that now half carried her, eased her onto a cushioned surface.

Lord Ambroz shouted orders in the opposite direction before his voice became closer and clearer. "We'll find her."

Anicka prayed that they would. And that she would be well.

That was all before the pull to the darkness won.

Lukas was helpless as Karin's gaze locked on Sir Tomas. Was there something between the two? He narrowed his own gaze on them. How was he to intervene? What could he do?

A voice roared from amongst the gathered men. Stepan.

He charged forward, seemingly uncaring about the men caught between himself and Karin.

"Not now," Karin commanded in a sharp tone.

But Stepan continued his forward momentum.

Sir Tomas moved to stand in front of Karin as if Stepan intended harm upon her.

Stepan drew his sword.

Karin broke free from Sir Marek's gentle hold and stepped in front of the coming onslaught, blocking Sir Tomas. "Enough!"

Stepan halted just short of the pair, his breaths coming in heaves. "I will not allow this."

"Who are you to allow me anything?" she challenged. "You follow my orders."

There were audible gasps among the men.

Stepan glared at her but let loose his firm stance, letting the tip of his sword fall to the ground. He looked at Sir Marek.

Lukas peered at the older knight also who shook his head almost imperceptibly.

"My apologies," Stepan finally said.

That brought more shock from among the men.

"But I cannot let you be fooled by this man. By what you may... think of him." Stepan still held his ground.

Sir Tomas stirred but continued to let Karin stand in his defense.

"It is my choice." Karin crossed her arms.

Stepan's eyes darkened. "But it affects all of us...and your husband's future. Would you lead us into a trap and consign your husband to certain death?"

Karin stepped forward and slapped Stepan. "You will not speak to me thusly." Her features were as stone and her eyes as fire.

Lukas realized he was holding his breath. The air was thick with tension. Even Sir Marek shifted next to him.

"You swore your fealty to me," she said, jaw clenched. "Are you a man of honor or not?"

The muscles in Stepan's jaw worked furiously as if he wagered what to say. Many of the men had wide-eyed gazes. What would happen should Stepan choose dishonor and negate his oath? Would the guards and knights be divided between Karin and Stepan? Would a battle break out within the camp?

At last, Stepan let out a short breath. "You still have my sword."

Karin, too, eased in her stance.

"That is why I speak out. My loyalty is with you and the baron. For your best chance of rescue. For your wellbeing. I cannot sit by and let this..." He looked at Sir Tomas with disgust. "...usurper manipulate you."

Karin softened ever so slightly. "I only ask that you trust me...and honor your oath. That is all that is required of you."

Stepan held her gaze for several moments. The war raged again within him. It was plain for anyone to see in his tense stance and nearly bared teeth.

Karin was a statue, the picture of indifference. Though Lukas knew better. With the history here...the reality that these two were once betrothed...it complicated the matter.

Stepan bowed his head. "I will."

A low din of mutters rippled through the men. Had they prepared themselves to turn on one another?

Karin let her arms fall by her side. "Then let us focus our energy on gaining my husband's freedom. And to do that we need to trust each other."

Sir Marek let out a long breath and nodded.

As did Lukas. Disaster was averted...for now.

"I have a plan," Sir Tomas said.

Karin whirled on him. And while Stepan and the men could not see it, Lukas and Sir Marek certainly could...there was a guarded question in her eyes. She did not, then, wholeheartedly believe him.

Stepan bit back his words but scowled at the exchange.

"What is it?" Karin asked, narrowing her gaze.

Sir Tomas held up his bound hands as if to request they be freed.

Karin ignored it. "Tell me."

"There is a secret tunnel that leads into the stronghold. It will get you past the walls and within the donjon."

Now Karin's eyes widened, but her words told of her skepticism. "Where is this tunnel? Why have you not mentioned it before?"

Lukas wondered the same thing. Hadn't Sir Tomas been with them from the beginning of this venture?

Sir Tomas looked over Karin's shoulder in Stepan's direction. "I had my reasons."

Karin waved the comment to the side. "Tell us exactly where it is."

Sir Tomas lifted his hands again. "If I am to trust you, I must be trusted as well."

Lukas balked at his implication. He sought his own freedom. Was this all a ploy for him to be able to sneak out and warn Ulrich?

Karin signaled to Sir Marek, who hesitated but a moment before unsheathing his dagger and slicing through Sir Tomas's bindings.

The knight rubbed his wrists for a moment, then directed his focus back to Karin. "I will show you where the tunnel is...on one condition."

One of Karin's eyebrows arched. "What would that be?"

"That you let me go into the castle first."

The disgruntled knights and guards grumbled. There seemed to be much resistance to the idea.

Indeed, Lukas pondered that it was one thing to trust his information, another to trust his movements.

"I can get to the baron and ready him for your men," Sir Tomas reasoned.

Karin thought, her chest rose and fell as if her breaths came with greater difficulty. "You could also betray us." Her words were quiet. So much so that the men behind her, even Stepan, may not have heard.

"That is true," Sir Tomas said plainly.

The pair looked at each other for a long moment.

"I suppose you will just have to trust me."

Could she? Lukas stared at the pair as the minutes ticked by. Should she? There was much at stake. But as he noted how they gazed at each other, he began to doubt her impartiality. And he began to suspect she would.

CHAPTER 41
TOMAS

Tomas hadn't used the secret passageway for some time. And it seemed that it had, in fact, been many years since anyone had. The ceiling—lower than he'd have liked—was covered in cobwebs and insects. The sides were little more than packed earth. Evidence of the last rain could still be seen, and smelled, in the tunnel. Nodding to the knight that had followed him here, he ducked and went in. The man's uneasy scowl and the light of the torch were left behind...and all was dark.

As he moved through the tunnel, he remembered another time when such dank darkness surrounded him. The night he narrowly escaped Brno with his life, only to be thrown into a cell that smelled and felt of filth.

How his heart had ached for Karin. For the sight of her, the feel of her, the comfort of her arms, and the touch of her lips.

But that was to go unrequited. He'd gone through hell and back to earn Ulrich's trust—a truly hard-fought victory.

What now?

Did he give up the place he had earned with his blood and sweat?

Or give up the chance to bring Karin some happiness and peace in this life?

He had been ready to reveal himself when he'd heard about Karin's marriage. The horrid months of regret that followed rivaled those first days under Ulrich's ire.

All had been lost. Or so he thought.

Then...a chance to help bring this war to an end. While he may not side with Ulrich or understand his purposes, their goal was the same—bring the war sparked by Hus's martyrdom to an end.

So, a thinly strung alliance was made between himself and Ulrich in his mind and heart. Until the baron was captured and Tomas realized who he was to Karin.

So, he had an opportunity to help Karin, to also gain her trust. For noble reasons, he was certain.

But when he had laid eyes on her again, nothing seemed certain any longer.

He reached out a hand. Surely, he neared the end of the tunnel.

Either way, he was done with the memories. He was ready for action.

Pavel fought the hopelessness of waking. There was nothing for him in this dark place...either in his cell or in this world. Ulrich would torture him as long as he'd like...and then kill him in the worst, most public way possible. Could he let himself be used thusly?

He grimaced without opening his eyes. What choice did he have? It wasn't as if he could bring an end to his life here.

"Lord baron," a voice called through the blurriness of despair and the sheen of the netherworld between sleep and wake.

Pavel resisted the pull of the voice. But he found himself helpless in that too. His consciousness came to full alertness.

And pain slammed into him—full and all consuming.

The weight of distress over Karin and Jaromir further clouded his mind. For he was impotent there too. Knowing they were in danger, but unable to help them...it was the worst torture he could imagine. This, Ulrich had planned for as well.

"Baron..." the same voice tugged at him.

And, now that he had come more to himself, he could discern that it was the priest in the nearby cell.

"I'm here, Father." Pavel half groaned as he spoke.

He attempted to sit up. That was a mistake. Sleep had found him as he'd leaned against the back wall of the cell. And now his back and shoulder muscles screamed at him from the awkward position. Not that they could pain him anymore than the injuries done his body.

"I think my time is short," Father Lesak said. There was a sorrow about his tone.

That got Pavel's attention. The man had been such a comfort to him in this place of lost hope. Did the priest mean that his end was near or Pavel's? "What do you mean?"

"That is not important." An urgency had taken over the man. "I wanted you to be prepared."

The blurriness that covered Pavel's mind and the pain that created a muffled situation for him made his thoughts hard to capture. "Prepared?"

"What if my mission is to gird you for this? To assure you that faith is your only lifeline?"

Pavel frowned and leaned back. Not now. "I know you have a firm hold on your belief. But you must see that mine is adrift. I no longer have the ability to weigh anchor."

"It is not so."

Pavel peered in the direction of the voice. He believed he saw a brightness about the man—mayhap nothing more than the paleness of his skin in this place. "It is."

"If that were so, you would have given up long ago. Yet you fight."

"For my wife and child."

"There is more. You think it is futile to resist Ulrich's schemes. Yet, I have heard you taunt him. There is a flame within you...no matter how small."

Pavel considered that. "You are mistaken, Father. It is nothing more than ashes. Shattered beyond repair...naught but dust."

"And what can God do with dust? He can breathe life into it and make it something new."

Pavel turned in the man's direction again. He could almost see the man's gaze. Or at least it seemed he could.

"Where, after all, did all life come from?"

The man had him there. Could it be so? Was it possible for God to take the pieces of himself and resurrect the faith he had once clung to so firmly?

Lord, is it so? Can it be? I struggle to believe. I struggle to see You. But I am willing to be made willing.

"That is all He wants...your willingness."

How did he...?

The door to the dungeon swung open. A figure with a small torch slipped within.

Was this it? Did they come to take Pavel to his death? Or mayhap the priest?

The figure paused at the bottom of the steps and looked about.

"Baron Krejick?" The man's voice was hushed.

"I am here." He would meet his end like a man. Yet when he tried to stand, his body would not obey.

The figure closed the distance to him. Then the clang of metal sounded as he worked a key in the cell lock.

Might Pavel take this last opportunity? There was but one guard. Perhaps he could overcome him...just one last bout of strength.

But the man did not come more than a few feet away before he stopped. "I am Sir Tomas. And I am here to get you out."

Pavel couldn't have heard the man correctly. "You will have to drag me from here, fiend."

The man muttered something. "I have come with your wife, the Lady Karin. Even now your men are about to attack the walls of this stronghold."

"Karin? Here?" It wasn't possible. Didn't Ulrich have her? Unless...it had been an overreach, a lie. Reason overcame him. His Karin was brave but not a warrior. Surely, she could not, would not have risked herself and Jaromir in such a way. Not only that, Sir

Marek would not have allowed it. "This is some trick. My wife could not have come."

The man shuffled closer and held out an arm. Light infusing the space from the small torch caused something in his hand to glint. It was Karin's cross necklace. She never parted with it. Could it be?

He jerked his regard back to the man. "What game do you play?"

"I swear on my life, I speak true."

Dare he trust and risk aiding in his own death display? Or could he hope again?

Saying a silent prayer for strength, he chose hope.

He maneuvered with great effort...and much pain.

"I will help." Sir Tomas unlocked the shackles binding Pavel.

Again, there was a moment he might attempt to overcome the knight. But, again, he chose faith. This may just be God's answer.

Sir Tomas set the torch in a sconce outside the cell and returned to assist Pavel to his feet.

Moments and monumental pains later, Pavel was once again upright. He leaned more heavily than he'd have liked on the man, and they made their way out of the cell.

Then Pavel stopped. "Wait. We must help the priest. His is a death sentence as well."

"Who?" Sir Tomas's face scrunched, clearly confused.

"Father Lesak." Pavel turned toward the holding cell for the priest.

There was no one there. And no sign that anyone had been there in some time.

A disbelief washed over Pavel for a few seconds. Then he felt the comfort of God's presence. And he knew. He'd been entertaining angels unaware.

"We must make haste," Sir Tomas fairly hissed.

"Yes." Pavel took a brief moment to say a prayer of thanks. "Let's."

Karin crouched behind the small hillside and bushes that formed their army's stronghold. She looked over toward the opening of the secret passage...and wished she might be the one to lead the charge. Sir Marek had insisted he go, warning that he would not support her should she decide to go herself. Even so, Karin acknowledged that there was wisdom in that. Should they fail, or worse find that her husband no longer lived, Jaromir would need one of his parents. That was the only thing holding her back.

Sir Marek spoke to the men gathered around him. Lukas and Stepan leaned in as they planned their attack. Something did not sit well with her in that Lukas, the man who had nearly ended her life so many years ago, would be permitted as part of the effort, whereas she would not. And even Stepan...whose blade she had been at the threatened end of at one time.

She pressed down her regret in this. It would serve no one. Least of all her. What was there for her in unforgiveness and jealousy? She must focus all her attention on the rescue.

Shouts from the distance warned that the portion of their contingency that was to lay siege to the castle had been discovered.

Karin breathed a sigh and prayed for their safety.

Their distraction would be necessary to divert all of Ulrich's men to defenses.

Sir Marek turned back to her. "It must be now, my lady."

She nodded. "God speed." Though a large part of her ached that she would have to lay in wait as he went after Pavel. She had prepared for this. Planned for this. Sought this. Only to sit back.

Sir Marek made a signal for the men to follow. He stood and a *whoosh* and *thunk* sounded before he fell back.

A rustle of activity surrounded her such that it took a moment before she realized Sir Marek had been struck by an arrow about his left shoulder.

The men about her jumped into action. Stepan and a couple others broke away and ran into the darkness. In pursuit of the aggressor?

She pushed through to Sir Marek's side.

One of the men already worked to secure his comfort and assess the arrow.

But Sir Marek reached for Karin. "They must go. Now!"

She nodded. "I will lead them."

"No," Sir Marek demanded. He shifted to look at Lukas. "You will take the men forward."

Lukas met her gaze.

Did her features display her mixed emotions? Or had she been able to hide them well enough?

Lukas turned back to Sir Marek. "I will stay at the Lady Karin's side." His gaze met hers again. "You have my fealty."

A rush of surprised relief overwhelmed her. Still, she found the ability to move forward. Nodding to Lukas, she laid a hand to Sir Marek's uninjured shoulder. "We will find victory this day."

He frowned at her but closed his eyes. Was his wound dire? Would he die in the time she was gone?

Shaking her head slightly, she fought it. She couldn't think about that. Not now. She had a job to do. Waving a hand, she stood and pressed on toward the secret entrance.

There was a fear of being struck the same as Sir Marek, but she trusted Stepan to ferret out the archer and mete out justice. Now was the time for her to focus on her mission.

The early signs of dawn touched the eastern horizon as she led the way into the tunnel, which plunged them back into darkness. But she would not fear. Her men and her husband...their lives depended on her.

CHAPTER 43

PATRICIE & STEPAN

Stepan dove into the waning darkness. Where had the villain gone? He'd been on the trail for several minutes. But the lack of light didn't help. Nor did the sounds of battle going on behind him, drowning out the subtle movements of the man he pursued.

He paused to listen, growing more frustrated with himself.

The urge to release the growl that filled his lungs was overwhelming. But he held back...it would not help find his prey.

A crunch off in the distance to his right led him to go that way. He prayed that it was due to the man's movements and not an animal of some sort. There was no way to know. Still, he had to try.

Following the sound, he found himself in a clearing by a stream. Dawn had filtered light through the tree branches, and he now had a full view of what lay ahead with the aid of the rising sun.

That also meant that he would be easily spotted. So, he ducked back behind a trunk as he peered toward the opening. He slammed his fist into the thick bark. As if he wasn't having a difficult enough time tracking the man, the stream would erase both the tracks and any lingering sounds of his escape.

Did the man know he was being chased? He couldn't have found a better way to elude anyone following him.

All the same, Stepan refused to relent. Something in his gut told him that he must. It seemed irrational even to him. He would be more useful at the battlefront. Or with those that sought to sneak in via the tunnel that may or may not be watched...should they believe Sir Tomas.

His thoughts were scattered by a shout.

For sooth, he was too far from the castle to overhear such a cry over the stream.

Scanning the area with the learned eyes of a hunter, he spotted something. Well, perhaps it was something.

Across the stream the hillside sloped upward. But the brush that dotted the base of the smallish rise seemed rather odd.

Another shout. Then, it was cut short.

Did someone call for help?

His pulse raced. The odd drive to capture a scout just became all the more serious.

Holding his breath, he reached out with all his senses.

Movement.

He let out a breath. What was about?

There was a scuffle of sorts beyond that underbrush.

Crossing the stream with slow steps, he made every attempt to make as little noise as possible. He may yet have the element of surprise on his side.

The nearer he drew, the more he suspected something about the area. For the voices, though muffled, and the movements emitted a slight echo.

What was this place?

Perhaps...there was more...mayhap a cave?

Indeed, as he ducked to keep his profile lower, he came around the bulk of the brush to find an opening between the rock. It was much larger than he'd have suspected...especially as he could not discern it until he was right upon it.

Unsheathing his sword, he shuffled toward the opening.

The light of the sun did not penetrate far into the cave. There was a lantern within, yet it only danced a silhouette of a man leaning toward a woman...who may be bound.

"There," the masculine voice seethed. "Are you completely senseless? No one can hear you now."

That voice, it was familiar. But Stepan didn't have time to consider it further.

Grunting and muttering from a higher pitched tone answered.

Stepan prepared to rush in, but the man grabbed the woman and pushed her toward the opening. Pulling back, Stepan maneuvered into the thickest part of the bushes.

Soon enough, the man emerged. Sir Antonin!

But what of the woman? It was as if an anchor dropped in Stepan's stomach.

All the interactions he had witnessed between Sir Antonin and Patricie flashed through his awareness.

And so, as Sir Antonin dragged the woman out into the open, Stepan already surmised it was his beloved. Yet nothing would prepare him for seeing her bound and gagged.

The wave of heat and anger that overtook him threatened his better sense. Taking in a slow breath and letting it out, he prayed.

Lead me not astray.

Then a wave of inner peace swept through him, soothing his ire and leaving a calm that was beyond Stepan in its wake.

Now to right the situation.

Patricie's body had long since tired of the abuse. Her shoulders ached from her pulling at the rope that bound her. As well, her skin was rubbed raw from the rough strands.

But she would not quit fighting Sir Antonin. That could only mean victory to him. And she would not give him that. Never.

The gag he had tied around her head cut into the edges of her mouth, but she still worked to make his life miserable—calling out and sputtering at him. She would be every bit dead weight if it was the last thing she did.

He pulled her out of the cave, and she blinked back from the sudden light.

Then it occurred to her, he might be thusly blinded as well.

She kicked out a leg in the direction she wagered him to be.

Her foot banged into something solid. Painfully so.

She grunted as she lost her balance.

"When will you learn?" His voice was not hard. He but pitied her.

Then she realized, she had struck a nearby stone. Had he been able to move out of the way?

Think, she admonished herself. He was a trained knight. Not likely to be thrown off so easily.

He tugged her to himself and tightened his hold as she nearly fell.

She leaned even more into him, letting all her pain and frustration pour through her. It produced streams of tears down her face and a shuddering of her body.

"Hey," he said, tilting her face upward. "It doesn't have to be this way." There was much care in his voice.

A part of her hated to take advantage of that, but she had few options. She turned away, letting her longing for freedom fuel even more tears.

"Patricie," he said softly. "I'm not the monster you make me out to be."

She allowed his gaze to hold hers.

Then she felt the brush of his hand as he wiped at her tears. He reached for the cloth wrapped about her hair, taking a moment to run fingers through wayward strands.

"Things could be so different," he murmured. "If only I could make you understand..."

His words trailed as he tugged the gag down and pressed his lips to hers, pulling her flush against himself.

She squirmed. Then twisted and rammed her right shoulder into his.

He broke away and took a step back.

She jerked free and ran in the opposite direction, yelling for help and praying that someone…anyone…would hear her.

Sir Antonin let out a frustrated curse. Then he was upon her, knocking her to the ground.

The wind rushed out of her, and she fought for breath.

He released her and stood, but as she turned, she found his blade pointed at her chest. "Scream again, and I will lose any interest in letting you live." His tone had become harsh. He ran the back of his hand over his mouth.

She then noticed blood. Had he bitten his tongue when she'd rammed him? She could only hope. Glaring at him with a defiance she had to dig for, she clenched her jaw.

"Mayhap I shouldn't have let you live this long." The words were eerily quiet. He pulled back his sword.

She knew what would come next. *Dearest Lord!* Out of options, she let her eyes close.

And all mayhem broke loose.

Instead of the point of a sword, there was a rush of wind.

Then a smashing as if one body into another.

She opened her eyes to find Sir Antonin on the ground, grappling with another man. Shifting away, she slinked toward the stream. This may be her chance and she wouldn't waste it. After some distance was created between herself and the men, she worked to raise her upper body. Then she saw.

Stepan.

It was he who had come to her aid.

That wasn't possible! Yet he was here.

The two men got to their feet, and Stepan grabbed for his sword.

But it was for naught.

Sir Antonin looked at her with a wide-eyed expression.

Then she spotted it—his own dagger protruding from his stomach.

Stepan appeared equally shocked.

Sir Antonin sputtered something unintelligible, then fell over and was still.

Patricie closed her eyes, and hot tears fell anew. She couldn't escape that she had once felt for him. Not to the extent he had wanted. And not enough to heal the wounds left within him. Perhaps no one could.

Boots crunched on the rocks, and she opened her eyes to find Stepan closing the distance between them. He fell to his knees and pulled her into his arms.

She let herself cry. "I was so afraid."

He laughed as he ran hands over her hair. "I would never have known." Pulling back, he set hands to either side of her face. "My brave, brave Patricie..."

How she loved him speaking her name. As if she would never tire of it.

"Did he...hurt you?" Stepan seemed to hold back a wave of emotion in that moment. Did he fear such for her virtue? Or for her wellbeing?

Shaking her head, Patricie looked at him.

He moved a hand to brush her cheek. "Thank the Lord."

There was such gratitude in him. And love as he held her gaze.

She leaned forward and pressed her lips to his.

At first, he didn't respond, but then he did, holding her to his chest. His kiss soothed her and stirred something in her at the same time.

But even as a desire for more burned within, she knew this wasn't the time. There was more to be done. More to be said.

As he ended the kiss, he set his forehead to hers. "I would hold you forever, my love. But there is a battle I must join."

She nodded.

He slid his own dagger out and cut her bonds.

She relished the feel of warmth rushing back to her arms.

"Are you strong enough to walk?"

She glanced at Sir Antonin's body before looking back at Stepan. "Yes."

Stepan peered over his shoulder in the direction of her brief gaze.

"I almost feel sorry for him. He believed in what he did. And he acted for good reasons."

"Is not the way to the gates of Hades fraught with the best of intentions?"

She let herself relish the comfort of Stepan's arms for a few moments longer. "I suppose so."

As some moments passed, he released her and helped her to her feet. Only to pause. "There may be more death ahead. I do not want to bring you into the fray only to risk your life again."

She wrapped her arms about him and pulled his head down to kiss him briefly once more. "I shall fight by your side. Come what may."

Mixed emotions passed over his features before he embraced her quickly. "Then let's go."

And so, they ran into the thick of trees and toward the castle only a short distance away with no idea what their decision would bring. Or what may pass in the next hours. They linked hands and braved it.

CHAPTER 44

ANICKA & LUKAS

Lukas followed Karin as close as he dared. There was no way of knowing where the tunnel would come into the castle. And there was only some hope that it wouldn't be watched. Would Sir Tomas have betrayed them—by intention or by torture? It was a risk.

Sounds of movement vibrated in the area above them as the battle waged on within the castle. He sent up a prayer for the men in camp that fought to create the needed distraction. Lukas even silently beseeched the Lord for Stepan's wellbeing.

They certainly neared the end of the tunnel. They had to be close...as the noises about them closed in. Lukas prepared himself to defend Karin should the need arise. It was all he could do to keep himself from maneuvering around her now. However, in his mind, she had well earned the right to lead as she saw fit.

Karin paused in front of him. What happened?

He cleared his throat even as he realized...they had hit a wall. Quite literally. Either the tunnel was a farce, or it had been closed off. Where, then, was Sir Tomas who had gone in before them by several hours?

Karin muttered something as she slid hands along the wall.

Lukas felt a slight breeze from the left. Was it possible the tunnel turned?

Karin must have notice at the same time, for she whispered. "Left." Then, leading the men, she shifted in that direction.

The gap in Lukas's reaction led to a separation between himself and Karin.

Frustrated with himself, he pressed ahead, but a handful of men were now between him and the lady. He could not push past. How could he have let that happen? He had sworn to himself that he would protect Karin...even should it cost him his life. Now here he was, an observer at best should anything befall her at the tunnel's end.

As he considered his willingness to sacrifice himself yet again, thoughts of Anicka flitted across the surface of his mind. Could he leave her a young widow? Would she be destroyed by it? She cared for him, that was certain. She had given all she had to give. And, in his preoccupation with his own redemption, he had set that to the side and treated her as if it mattered less than it did.

The truth was he loved her. Deeply. Always had. And now regretted that he hadn't told her so.

Lukas nearly stumbled into the man in front of him before he became aware that all had stopped again. What now? Was there danger?

But stone scraped against stone and then more movement ahead before a door creaked.

The men in front of him slipped in a forward direction. But little light penetrated through, though by now the dawn was surely upon them. Lukas had to wait a few moments before he stepped from the darkness of the tunnel and into the cellar. Just as Sir Tomas had described. And, true to his word, he had left a lantern for them.

There were no servants moving about. Because they were in a less used place? Or because all were focused on defending against the siege?

Now that there was more space about them, Lukas slipped through until he was at Karin's side again. "My lady?" he whispered. "What is your plan?"

"We make for the dungeons." Her words were simple, plain...and determined.

The group numbered six in all. Perhaps more than should expect to sneak through the castle unnoticed, yet they would do what they could.

One of the men grabbed the lantern and walked with Karin to the narrow stairs leading upward and into what must be the kitchen.

Karin readied her smaller sword and signaled for the man beside her to open the wooden door.

It creaked.

Lukas cringed.

And as Karin rushed forward, a servant girl screamed.

The man behind Karin took initiative to silence the girl with a hand over her mouth.

But the damage was done. That scream certainly would have been heard by others.

Karin hissed at the knight subduing the girl, "You will not harm her."

The man nodded.

"Put her in the cellar...carefully," Karin told him. "No binding."

Karin's instructions were clear in that moment—they were not to harm innocents.

In war, there were no innocents. Just the side one was on...and the enemy.

No one had bothered to relay that to her, however.

The man urged the wide-eyed servant toward the cellar. He did not indicate if he should disagree with his baroness, though he certainly must have misgivings about it.

In that, he did his honor credit.

Lukas came back alongside Karin. "Others would have heard that."

She seemed to consider that. "No one has come."

Just then the sound of rushing steps drew nearer.

Karin's eyes closed. They were done before they'd truly begun.

Lukas pointed at three of the men. "With me."

They drew their swords as if they understood his meaning.

One last look at Karin told that she did not.

Lukas unsheathed his own weapon. "It has been an honor, Baroness. We will lead them away."

Recognition of his intent reflected in her eyes a second too late. For Lukas had already pressed into the corridor, the three knights following.

It didn't take long before the cry and hue was raised. Their presence was further known within the castle. All the more imperative, then, that he lead them away from Karin.

It may be a reckless act...and a final one, but in it, he might find redemption.

Anicka stirred. What had happened? She tried to sit up only to have a hand gently urge her back down.

But the face leaning over hers, though kindly, was not altogether comforting in that she was not known to Anicka.

Who could it be? Where had Anicka ended up?

The happenings outside the castle rushed at her. *Eva!*

Sitting against the gentle pressure, her head swam.

"You've been injured. Please rest."

"But I have to help—"

The woman's features firmed. "Rest back. You'll get all your answers soon enough."

Anicka leaned back on her elbows, not wanting to give in to the advice. But needing the room to stop spinning.

Another set of hands joined the first. These belonged to the dowager baroness.

Just meeting the woman's gaze brought an ease to Anicka's irritation. "Lady Marketa," she started, her voice hoarse. And her mouth impossibly dry.

"Be still," the older woman admonished. "Here."

Before Anicka could utter another word, a cup was passed to Lady Marketa and then pressed to Anicka's lips.

She drank carefully, but not as fully as she wanted. The dowager baroness kept the cup at such an angle to prevent gulping.

After the cup rim was removed, Anicka muttered, "Where is the Lady Eva?"

The older women exchanged a look with each other.

Uneasiness settled in Anicka's stomach, and her heart beat faster. "What is it?"

Lady Marketa sat on the edge of the bed and urged Anicka back to a fully prone position.

Anicka tried to resist, but the older woman was stronger than she seemed.

"All is well," Lady Marketa assured her. "Look." She pointed to the far side of the room.

There was Lady Eva on a cot. She seemed well enough. She even turned slightly toward Anicka, meeting her gaze.

"But she was bleeding...from her head..." Anicka could barely get the words out as memories of seeing the woman lying lifeless in the grass assaulted her.

"She has a wound behind her ear. But she will be all right." The other woman reappeared over Anicka.

Who was she?

Lady Marketa seemed to, yet again, read Anicka's mind. "May I introduce you to Baroness Dominika Ambrozova, Lord Ambroz's mother?"

Anicka watched the other woman. That answered quite a few questions...namely why the woman was vaguely familiar...Lord Ambroz looked much like her. The woman's long limbs and thin face reminded her of him.

Closing her eyes against the pounding in her temples, Anicka fought a wave of nausea.

"You must lie still," Lady Marketa said.

"I don't understand why I am so ill." Anicka couldn't fathom her current state of ache and dizziness.

"You don't understand?" Lady Dominika seemed incredulous. Was something obvious that Anicka wasn't seeing?

The older women looked at one another again.

"Will someone just tell me?" Anicka's tone was borne of irritability.

"You were struck on the back of your head." Lady Marketa's brow furrowed.

"No," Anicka said, shaking her head slightly. Mistake. Big mistake. Her stomach churned and she bit back the taste of bile.

"As said," Lady Marketa spoke with clipped words. "You must be still."

Anicka couldn't seem to hold two thoughts for any length of time.

"You have had quite the shake to your head." Lady Dominika came closer.

Anicka fought to remember her training on the matter. She glanced about and noted that the curtains were drawn, and the room had been darkened. As was appropriate for these situations. And she would wager that these women had been watching over Eva and her through the hours since it happened.

The other thing about the closed window coverings…it didn't allow her to see what time of day it was.

"Have I been…?" Anicka choked on her question. What had happened in the time since she could remember? Sometimes in these cases, there could be wakeful moments that weren't remembered.

"This is the first you've been alert," Lady Dominika said. "It's only been a matter of hours since you returned to the castle. Lord Ambroz went and retrieved Lady Eva soon after. Then you both were tended to."

"But I don't remember your arrival..." Was this confusing? Or was *she* just confused?

"I don't know what to say." Lady Marketa looked to the side. "Baroness Ambrozova came yesterday afternoon. Perhaps you had already left."

The door banged as it was swung open. And Lady Hana stepped in.

"You needn't be here," the dowager baroness scolded. "You should be resting yourself."

"I had to see for myself." Lady Hana glanced at Anicka. "You're awake? Thank the Lord Almighty!"

The rustle of skirts told that the lady moved toward her.

"You cannot imagine how I prayed," Lady Hana took Anicka's hand.

They had not known each other long or well, but the woman's tender kindness brought tears to Anicka's eyes.

Her mother had never been thus with her...only ever wanting her to do better, be better...something. Yet here was this fine lady of rank that genuinely seemed to care.

And it broke Anicka in ways she could not have anticipated.

Lady Hana stroked her hand. "Are you well, my lady?"

Anicka nodded before she realized. Then fought the dizzying stomach upset as hard as she could. After several seconds, things calmed.

Lady Marketa had taken her other hand. "You will be just fine. I promise."

How could Anicka explain it? How could she confess it? Had she never been worthy of this manner of loving attention? The only person who had ever truly seen her was Lukas.

That thought struck her anew and dried her tears. Was it possible that he did love her? In the way she loved him?

A wave of warmth washed over her. And fear came in its wake. Would she ever see him again?

CHAPTER 45
TOMAS

Tomas tugged Pavel out of the darkened crevice they had hidden in. The castle guards and knights busied themselves with cobbling together a defense to the onslaught of Karin's men. He would have smiled to himself. Things were going as planned. He just had to elude capture while half-dragging Pavel to safety.

The baron required more assistance than Tomas had expected. He had truly been brutalized by Ulrich's men. That gave weight to the anchor already in Tomas's gut.

He had sided with these men and fought with them against the Hussites. In as much, he stood by and condoned their actions. Even in this.

But now he was doing what he could to bring things to rights. For Karin and for himself.

The need to resist his inclination to leave Pavel for dead and simply tell Karin he'd been found already deceased left Tomas with a very real war within himself. And his ability to generate such willpower waned.

If he could see Pavel's life snuffed out, that may clear the way for Karin to be Tomas's again.

But at what cost? His sanity? His honor?

How high a price would he be willing to pay?

So, he gathered his courage and forged ahead with the man at his side limping along.

Footfalls sounded in the turn of the corridor ahead.

Tomas pulled Pavel into a carved-out alcove in the corridor and bade him remain quiet.

Was this more of Ulrich's men? Or possibly Karin and her group? If so, his opportunity to give in to the darker piece of him neared its end.

He looked to the man that was battered and likely barely held onto his will to live.

In the darkness, Pavel's muscles tensed. Did he sense Tomas's turn of thoughts?

"I would be of help should you at least give me your side sword," Pavel whispered. It seemed as if he suspected something was amiss in Tomas.

Dare Tomas give him a blade, and in such a chance to defend himself?

Releasing his hold on the man, Tomas reached for his dagger. It may appease Pavel without having to lean too much into trust. The reach of the smaller blade would ensure that Tomas would have a strong upper hand should they come to blows.

He passed Pavel the dagger.

Pavel muttered his thanks but did not reach for Tomas's aid.

The footsteps drew nearer. It was time to choose. Dare he hand over Pavel to save his own skin? Or fight alongside the wounded Pavel against well trained mercenaries?

The small group closed in upon the corridor...they were just around the corner...not so far away.

Tomas peered out from the safety of the inlet. The lighter movements of the group's lead gave proof that it may very well be Karin.

The time was now or never.

He looked over his shoulder at the baron.

Pavel had leaned against the back wall and pulled the dagger against his midsection. He was ready to defend himself. Against Ulrich's men? Or did he now fear Tomas?

"It is well," Tomas said, pressing against the thickness in his throat. "Your lady's men approach."

Then Karin was in the corridor, searching, seeking, moving with more stealth than Tomas would have thought possible for her lack of training.

Tomas stepped into their pathway.

Her eyes widened as she halted. But her gaze lit with recognition soon enough. "Tomas?"

The question under her tone stabbed at him. She didn't just wonder if he was well, but she ached to see her husband alive.

Tomas paused, unable to make himself reveal Pavel's existence.

"Karin?" It was Pavel who showed himself.

Then her focus moved to her husband. The gleam in her eyes was unmistakable. As was the shimmer of tears as she swept past Tomas and rushed into her husband's arms.

Now and forevermore...Tomas would be in the past. And something in him died again.

CHAPTER 46
ANICKA & LUKAS

Anicka settled into her seat by the hearth. The women in the Krejik castle had been so wonderful to her. The sting of realization that it was not how she had ever been treated still stabbed at her.

She looked up from her stitching and watched Eva as she chatted with Zdenek's mother, who held Michal, with a smile on her face that lit the room.

The two had been everything Anicka had wished she could have had with her mother. But it was not to be. And wishing for it wouldn't make it so.

From what Anicka could discern, Zdenek's father had passed on. That was why Lady Dominika had come...to bring the small family back to their new home. Yet Zdenek resisted. He had a job to finish here.

There had been continued unrest in the village...rumors of an uprising, but nothing had come of it. With the castle guards on alert, it likely would not.

Hana's pregnancy sickness had eased somewhat. It was another pang of sorts to watch how Lord Miklas cared for his wife so tenderly.

Could that ever be Lukas? If she were to carry his child, would he love her more?

She directed her gaze back to her lace trim. It was a mess. Indeed, perhaps there had been truth to Mother's insistence that she practice her stitching more.

But the stories called to her, filling her heart until they had to escape. She had never allowed anyone to see them. Certainly not Mother. Now that Lukas knew about it, what would he do? Could she trust him with her words?

She shook her head. That line of thinking was for naught. Things were so tenuous between them...at best.

"What is that you are making?" Lady Hana's voice intruded on Anicka's musings.

"Oh..." Anicka's face heated. "It is a bit of lace." She tried to pull it closer. Maybe they wouldn't notice the errant stitches.

Lady Hana reached for it anyway, snatching it before Anicka could pull it further from her. "Oh my."

Here next would come words of admonition. Of judgment.

"That might make a nice..." Lady Hana's voice stretched out, as if she searched for something kind to say. "Handkerchief." She settled on the word with finality and handed it back.

"I thank you. I am not very skilled...as you see." Anicka tried to duck away. Perhaps she could disguise her reddened face.

"Not at all!" Lady Hana rushed to say. "It is...different. But it is yours."

Those words hit a chord in a melody Anicka's heart had begun to play since coming here. Could it be that simple? Her work was hers... flaws and all. She had no need to hide it.

A cold feeling pierced her between her shoulder blades, spreading through her chest. What was that?

The lace, needle, and thread slipped to the floor as she gripped at the front of her dress. She tugged at the bodice's neckline slightly. Mayhap she only needed more room to breathe.

"Lady Anicka?" The voice seemed far away.

Anicka looked up through tears that blurred her vision.

Lady Hana had put her own stitching to the side and reached for Anicka's hand, tugging it free of her bodice. "Is something amiss?"

Anicka shivered. How could she explain something she didn't understand herself? "I...I don't know."

The tears made their tracks down her face, flowing even more freely.

Lady Eva and Baroness Ambrozova had paused and looked in her direction, concern etched on their features.

Anicka gasped for air. Something was definitely wrong. Her thoughts then flew to Lukas. His face appeared in her mind, lines strained about his eyes and mouth. There was great pain.

Was this what he felt? How was that possible? Had something ill befallen him?

Anicka slid her free hand about her midsection, then wrapped it up around her upper arm, attempting to bring some warmth to the chill that had overtaken her.

The other women continued with their worried words, but she didn't hear them. All she knew was her prayers for Lukas. What would become of him?

Lukas and the three men with him raced through the castle. The enemy guards gave chase...and they were nearly upon them. If they could press just a little more...

Spotting a turn off the main corridor ahead, Lukas pointed and led the men into a chamber. He leaned against the wall and listened. This was their only hope of escape—did such a thing exist—that the enemy would pass by and keep going.

Lukas did a mental mapping of the structure and realized, to his dismay, that the kitchen and the entrance to the hidden tunnel was just beyond this hall and to the right. If the guards were to indeed pass Lukas and his men by, there was great risk they may cut off Karin and the remaining men from their exit. Or, worse, intercept them.

He couldn't allow that.

With a glance in the direction of his men, he jerked his head toward the corridor they had just exited. There was only a moment of confusion before determination set it. And there was more that passed between them...an acknowledgement that this may be their last stand.

Lukas roared and rushed out to find himself amid the enemy. He thrust his sword forth and surprised one of the mercenary knights, who was struck before he could raise his sword to block the swing of Lukas's weapon.

But another of the men reacted faster and his sword's arc made contact with Lukas's shoulder.

Heat seared through him from his shoulder, but he jumped back just in time.

The remaining of Lukas's companions, veered around as they pressed in. Soon, they were blocking the narrow passageway to the right. The one that led to the kitchen.

Lukas side stepped while blocking further swings and stood with his men.

"Hold them here. No matter the cost," Lukas said through gritted teeth.

He could sense the combined assent of the men behind him. And he respected their willingness to put themselves in danger's path for their baron and baroness's safety.

It was admirable.

More than his own stand. For he sought something more...something final...a sacrifice.

The heat of his own blood coming from his left shoulder should concern him, but his sword arm was not wounded. He was able to fight. That was all that mattered now.

What followed was a mass of bodies and the clang of metal as he staggered, blocking blows that he shouldn't have been able to.

One of his compatriots fell to a clever stab from an enemy guard.

Lukas felt the loss of the man as if they were more brothers than strangers. He swung at the mercenary that had just taken a life and locked swords with him.

The man was large. And the force behind his swing great.

Lukas would not be able to hold him. Still, he clenched his teeth and pressed in all the more with sheer willpower. Skill would not save him here. Only grit and determination could see him keep this line.

Another of his companions came to his aid.

Lukas ground out, "Stay the line!" They couldn't risk the remaining two fighters breaching their hold.

The third man cried out as the other remaining enemy guard overwhelmed him with a blow.

Immediately, the press of the larger guard pushed on him even more as the remaining Krejik guard who had tried to assist him turned away to engage Ulrich's other man.

He pushed the dismay of his comrades' falls to the side. They had all known—they were here to delay, not to win. And he prayed they had done their duty. For his ability to hold off this giant of a man would not last.

The press of the man shoved forward as a great force…as if a tide threatened to pull Lukas away. Indeed, if he gave in to the man, his mission would be forfeit.

Suddenly, the large mercenary moved back slightly. What had happened?

Then, he lifted his blade as a bloodied menacing smile met Lukas's gaze. This would be the killing blow. Lukas was as certain as this man seemed to be.

With all that was in him, Lukas moved to raise his own weapon.

And found his strength had been depleted. From the great effort of the battle or the impact of the slice upon his shoulder and ensuing loss of blood, he wasn't certain. But it was his doom all the same.

Lukas closed his eyes, as he whispered a prayer for Pavel's safety and that Anicka would understand. And he took hold of peace, knowing his death would mean their freedom.

The man grunted as his sword began its fatal swing.

Steel flashed, and the man crumpled at Lukas's feet.

Stepan stood in the man's place, chest heaving, blade dripping.

What?

Stepan sucked in a breath and, with taunt features, said, "Next time, leave more than one for me."

CHAPTER 47
KARIN & PAVEL

Pavel embraced his wife, soaking in the warmth of her and the peace that accompanied it. She was whole. She was well. She was here...

He stole one moment more to risk pressing his mouth to hers. There was an ache from his bruised and battered body and face, but it was worth every ounce of pain.

Then he pulled her flush against him again.

Sensing eyes upon him, he couldn't help but peer over her shoulder. The look Sir Tomas wore was difficult to discern, but it reeked of shame.

Had something occurred between the man and Karin?

Pavel pushed the suspicion to the side. It would not help them escape. And they were yet in danger.

Tugging away, he lingered in his wife's gaze on him, setting a hand to the side of her face. There was moisture there. She had risked much, overcome much...to see him rescued.

It was then he noticed that she wore a sort of ill-fitting armor. What, indeed, had she been through to reach this point? What had she endured?

He kissed her again briefly before setting their reunion to the side to focus on what needed to be done to get them out of here.

She wasn't moving away so easily. It became more difficult to shift his attention, but he pressed on.

Sir Tomas had turned his gaze away as well. That was best. "We have to get out of the castle. And quickly."

Pavel wanted to be able to stand on his own, but he leaned heavily on his wife. The wounds he had sustained did not enable him to move of his own accord.

Her brow furrowed as he shifted but did not remove his weight. How could he face her in this weakened state? So, he focused on the men... many of whom he recognized as men of his guard. They, too, had come to his aid at great risk to their safety. And he was grateful for each of them.

The clash of footfalls and swords sounded down the corridor, pushing them into action.

"Let us, then," Pavel said, indicating the opposite direction.

It pained him to run from a fight, but he had little choice...with his wife's wellbeing to contend with as well as his lessened ability to defend her...his options were few.

Limping along and weighing on Karin more than he'd have preferred, they maneuvered their way into the kitchen.

To find Ulrich and several of his men waiting.

Karin jerked to a halt, Pavel nearly stumbling as she did so. She had the urge to reach for him. To steady him. But she resisted. There was more afoot here.

She reached for her smaller sword, drawing it from its scabbard. If Ulrich wanted to take her husband, he would have to get through her and whatever resistance she could muster. As a woman scorned, she knew her odds were better than they would be otherwise.

The whole contingency with them halted.

A face off was coming. She sensed it. And she was ready for it, though Ulrich's men outnumbered her own. Her men were fierce. Beyond that, they had right on their side...and God. She would not discount God's hand in this story.

Ulrich sneered in the stillness of the moment. "Sir Tomas...seems you have chosen your side."

Sir Tomas's heavy breathing and the way he gripped his sword tighter were the only responses.

Then Ulrich turned his gaze on her. "A woman?" He laughed. It was a menacing, evil sound. "I think I will enjoy this." He signaled for his men, and they rushed forward.

The clash of metal rang clear and yet muffled as bodies pressed forward.

Karin defended a few blows here and there but noted that her men surrounded their lady and lord, giving their lives to keep them safe. Dare she leave them and attempt to get her husband to the cellar escape route?

Pavel grunted.

And she knew he regretted his inability to join the fight.

The men had given them a chance...they had to take it.

She maneuvered Pavel toward the cellar door, tears pricking her eyes at the realization that they abandoned the men that had come so far and been so valiant.

A roar escaped from the side.

Ulrich.

He broke free from the combat and rushed at them like a madman.

She raised her sword but knew her strength would not hold.

Pavel's hand covered hers and together, they deflected Ulrich's swing.

The larger man growled and circled them.

Pavel attempted to push her behind himself.

But Karin was not the woman she was before. She would not

back down from this fight—it was as much hers as it was his. And so, she held her ground.

Ulrich came at them again, swinging and charging without relent.

She and Pavel moved as one, meeting his every parry and thrust.

But neither were prepared when Ulrich came at them with his body's full weight, knocking them both over.

She hit the ground on her side, pain snaking up from her hip. But she jerked around to see her husband still a little farther away.

Ulrich stood between them, backing up slightly and coming around, the point of his sword at her chest.

Where was her blade? She noted it to the side moments before Ulrich kicked it away.

She was defenseless then...unable to help herself or Pavel. All would be lost. But she would not slink away. Would not pull back. She would face her end with a strength and peace that went beyond herself.

Glaring at the larger man with the ire of her defiance rushing through her, giving her the ability to do so.

Ulrich smirked. "I only hate that your precious husband will not be able to enjoy this." He raised his arm, bringing his elbow back to give more power to his thrust when he would run her through.

With a cry, he shoved his blade forward.

But someone slipped between them. Steel clanged, and all was still for some seconds.

Then her rescuer fell to the ground. And she saw...it was Tomas!

Ulrich's sword protruded from his side.

The wicked man reached for his weapon, but Tomas held it fast.

There was a rush of movement as the remaining warriors surrounded Ulrich.

Was it truly over?

Not for her. With great pain in every movement, she crawled to Tomas, who gasped and sputtered.

His wound would be fatal. Even now, he was in the last moments of life.

"Tomas..." she muttered as she leaned over him.

"Karin," he said on a breath.

"Don't speak."

He shook his head slightly. "If only...if only...it could have been different."

She bit at her lip, her eyes filling.

He tugged something free of his neck—a pouch hidden beneath his tunic. Pressing it into her hand, his gaze caught hers. "I never... stopped...loving you."

How could she hold firm against those words?

"Tomas..." she whimpered. Hot tears fell.

He fought for breath. But it was pointless to quiet him. She would let him have his last words, no matter how greatly they pained her.

His gaze focused on hers, but there was a vacancy coming over his eyes. "Thank you...Karin...for showing me the way...back to courage...truth...and to...honor."

She held her breath, waiting for one more word, one more movement...something. But there was nothing. Bringing her hands to her face, she sobbed. There had been too much loss. And this had been impossibly hard to live through.

But she had.

She sniffled, drying her tears, and turning to her husband, who stirred.

Looking back to the man she had once loved, she whispered her farewells. Then moved to Pavel, helping him sit up.

He cried out as he did so, the pain of his injuries taking their toll. She embraced him. But he pulled back, setting his gaze on Ulrich.

She glanced over her shoulder. "It's over."

Pavel ground his teeth. "Almost." He moved to stand.

She assisted him.

"I would have a sword," he declared through clenched jaws.

She wanted to protest. He couldn't mean to strike down a defenseless man!

One of the Krejik guards passed him a blade.

He stepped forward, stumbling as he did so. But lifted the sword to point at Ulrich's chest. "You threatened my people. You threatened my family."

Ulrich narrowed his eyes.

"And I will make sure you never do so again."

Ulrich's mouth tightened. "Do what you must." He puffed out his chest as if he sought the blade as much as it longed for his blood.

"Pavel," Karin muttered, gripping his arm with her free hand. "Don't become him."

Pavel's eyes were hardened as stone.

Karin held her breath. Was this not the man she knew him to be? Had he been changed by what he'd endured at Ulrich's hand?

Pavel dropped the sword and hunched over, leaning on his wife. "I will grant you the thing that eludes you."

Ulrich's eyebrows furrowed.

"Mercy."

CHAPTER 48

PATRICIE & STEPAN

Stepan examined Lukas's shoulder. The slice was bad, but not life-threatening as long as they could staunch the blood. Lukas seemed to realize the same thing and tore a piece of his own tunic. He handed the strip to Stepan.

"Do it."

Stepan nodded and wrapped the cloth around his shoulder, covering the deep cut before tying it off securely.

To his credit, Lukas did not do more than suck in a breath.

Stepan had no doubt the wound pained him. But that was all he could offer.

The other Krejik guard had dispensed with his adversary and returned. "We are not out of danger yet."

Lukas nodded.

Stepan wanted to continue his mission, but he wasn't certain what had happened with Pavel and Karin. Had they made it to safety? There had been an exchange of some sort in the direction of the kitchen and the opening in the cellar to the secret tunnel. Dare he lead Lukas that way? He might be risking an already debilitated warrior. But that could have been the other group led by Karin...and they may aid.

"If you can continue," Stepan said, meeting Lukas's gaze briefly, "We should investigate."

Again, Lukas nodded, his breathing still erratic but having slowed considerably.

Stepan jerked his head toward the other guard, and they all picked up their swords and moved as stealthily as possible.

They neared the kitchen to find several fallen men—some with Krejik colors and some that were clearly Ulrich's men.

There, in the midst, stood Karin, Pavel, but a few of the men that they had once had, and a defenseless Ulrich.

Where was Sir Tomas?

Stepan's gaze dropped to the bodies scattered about and found Sir Tomas among them.

He stopped for a long moment to honor the man who had clearly sacrificed for their cause. Or at least he hoped that was the case.

Karin and Pavel looked in their direction.

Pavel's gaze widened as he spotted Stepan. The man leaned on Karin...and his face was battered and bruised. But he was alive...and whole. Yet, Stepan was uncertain what Pavel's regard for him may be. They had parted last on...less than genial terms.

A ghost of a smile teased Pavel's lips as he watched Stepan—and Lukas—stumble through. And Stepan knew...all was well with them.

Stepan noticed a pouch on the ground near Karin's feet. "Did you drop something, Lady Karin?" He indicated the dark colored object.

Karin reached for it. Some manner of sorrow crossed over her features as she held it close to herself. Then, the look was gone, and she stuffed it in her belt—a mystery. Perhaps one best left alone.

"We should get out while we can, my lord," one of the Krejik guards said to Pavel. "What of this...cur?" The man gestured with the dagger he already had pointed at Ulrich's back.

"Let us take him with us." Pavel spoke with firm words. "That way he will not be able to cause any more grief for the Hussite cause."

Ulrich's frown deepened and his mouth parted.

But the poke of the dagger from behind silenced him as it directed him toward the cellar.

Karin led with Pavel, followed by the few surviving of their contingency with Ulrich. Stepan assisted Lukas as needed while they took up the rear of the party.

Moving through the dark tunnel was even more closed in than Stepan remembered. Hadn't he rushed through this space not an hour ago? The slower walk through the blackened space was much more difficult.

One of the men ahead called out and a body was thrust back, knocking Lukas down and pressing Stepan to the dirt wall.

"What goes?" Pavel's voice called from ahead.

"You must continue," Stepan warned. "There is naught for you to do."

The man that had fallen against him stirred beside Stepan's leg.

"Are you well?"

"I think so. But where is Ulrich?"

They were not far from the surface. Stepan could feel the faintest of breezes, but it was there.

Stepan turned in the enclosed space, searching as much as he could for the bulky man.

Lukas called from the right. "There is another tunnel. It branches just here."

Stepan unsheathed his sword and moved in that direction. "Then we give chase."

"No," Karin said, her voice firm and stronger than he'd expected. "He is gone. I will not lose any more men to that man's evil. We rejoin the others together, or not at all."

Stepan halted, searching wildly in the dark that had become tinted with light from the surface up ahead.

"Stepan..." Pavel's voice was the same one that had teased him many times, had given counsel often, and had seen his life spared in this wretched war more than once. "Let him go."

Stepan sucked in a breath then let it out slowly. Only then did he re-sheath his blade. Pavel was right. This was not a time for justice. It was a time to forgive and move on. They had dealt a hard blow to Ulrich's forces—and pride. He would have to retreat, lick his wounds, and decide what to do next.

That should not steal what peace they had won. Not now. Not ever.

"I will follow you, my lord. Lead on."

Patricie held her breath as movement in the bushes told that someone exited the tunnel. She waited behind the guards that held a line there for her own safety. But when Sir Pavel and Lady Karin, then a couple of others, followed by Stepan and Sir Lukas emerged, she let loose of all abandon and ran to her beloved.

"I was so worried."

Stepan did not pull back as the others stared. Rather, he held her and pressed a kiss to the top of her head. How was it that he could have lost his nervousness about displays of affection? He further surprised when he tilted her head back and claimed her lips.

But she didn't mind it...not one bit.

"Ah..." Sir Pavel muttered, then laughed. "I see."

Stepan released Patricie and held her to himself as if he dared not let go.

When she spotted Lukas's bandaged shoulder, it was she who jerked away. "Sir Lukas, you are injured?"

"Aye." He held a hand to his shoulder. "But it will keep. Baron Krejick is in much more dire need."

Sir Pavel had been holding his wife. Patricie only then realized it was more than ardor that kept him to her side. He limped badly and his left arm held to his left side as if protecting some injury there. Not to mention the abrasions and bruises upon his face.

"My lord," Patricie said as she rushed to him. "Let us get you somewhere I can tend you."

He smiled but released a long breath. "I, too, am well enough for now. I would prefer you see to other injuries first."

Patricie frowned.

Lady Karin's eyes lit. "What of Sir Marek?"

Patricie allowed a smile to grace her features. "He is recovering. And rallying the remaining knights and guards to withdraw at your order."

The lady peered at the guards that had been keeping the opening to the tunnel secure. "We pull back now. It is time."

Sir Pavel looked to his wife. "Time?"

She nodded. "Time to go home."

He set his fingers to her jaw. "Whatever you say, my lady."

Patricie turned from the tender moment.

"Then shall we?" Stepan reached for Patricie and led her toward the rest of the company.

Home…

Where was that exactly? For her? For Stepan? Both displaced by the war and changing loyalties.

Only God knew.

She found the strength to trust in that and, as Stepan's hand remained on hers, in the love of a good man.

CHAPTER 49
ANICKA & LUKAS

Anicka settled beside Lady Hana in the Great Hall. The women had all been summoned here for some reason. She wasn't sure why, but there was something within her that feared it meant something ill had befallen the men and the baroness. But she tried to tamp down the rising anxiety. There was no way to know what drew them to this talk until they discovered who would speak with them.

Soon enough, Sir Radek and Lord Ambroz entered. Their faces were grim and set.

Lady Hana reached over and captured one of Anicka's shaking hands. When had they begun trembling? The kind woman leaned over, setting her other hand to her stomach as if to soothe it. Then she whispered. "God is with us. All will be well."

Anicka shot her a look but wasn't at all certain as to the truth of Lady Hana's words. How could she even believe in them? After all, it wasn't her husband that was at risk.

Closing her eyes, Anicka breathed out her growing tension. Such a thought was untoward. And less than gracious. She wished she might absolve herself of her errant thoughts, but Lord Ambroz spoke before Anicka could lift a prayer.

"We have been to the village." Lord Ambroz let his gaze fall on each of the women, but it lingered on her and then came to rest on his wife.

The village? Oh.

Anicka swallowed. Hard. The memory of the attack was fresh and her wounds still healing.

"There will be no need for concern anymore. The town's leaders assured us," he said as he looked to Sir Radek, who nodded, "that those who engaged in the attempt were found and promptly punished."

How could he be certain then? Did the villagers not reveal who had been at fault?

"We are well satisfied that the matter has been taken care of."

Anicka resisted the urge to voice her mind. For it seemed almost dismissive, their tone.

But then the men looked to the door.

A lad—perhaps no more than six and ten years of age—came forward. There was a hesitance to his steps, but he pressed on anyway. He did not look up until he was nearly beside the larger men. Only then did he peer at the women.

"It was my fault," the boy confessed with a roughened voice that wavered.

"Your fault?" This from Lady Eva.

"Whatever drove you to such an...evil thing?" The dowager baroness drew back and set a hand to her chest as she spoke.

"I don't know." The lad's resolve melted in front of them. His face scrunched as if he might cry. Yet, to his credit, he firmed his stance and held back his emotion. "The townsfolk were so angry. So worried. And many were dying."

"Still..." Baroness Ambrozova shuddered. "What would make it seem appropriate to attack a child and two women?"

The young man cringed at that. "There were four of us. We provoked each other."

A sharp inhale drew Anicka's attention to Lady Eva. She rubbed at her arm as if the remnant of the stone's strike pained her even now.

"We didn't truly mean to hurt anyone. We only wanted to scare you into leaving."

Anicka supposed in his young mind that had made some sense. "You say there were four of you. Where are the others?"

Sir Radek cleared his throat. "We only permitted one to appear before you. Josef here volunteered."

Perhaps there was some bravery in that. But Anicka was not ready to relent.

"You could have killed us," she said sharply.

Lady Hana squeezed her hand. Would she deny Anicka the chance for answers?

"I know that." The boy looked to the floor again. "And I'm so sorry."

There was a shaking of his shoulders. And though he would not look up again, Anicka would guess his eyes had filled with his regret.

Lord Ambroz put a hand on the lad's arm. "That is all. The guard at the door will lead you home."

Anicka bit her lip as the boy walked away. Her breathing was ragged. But she knew—her real worry was about Lukas. She need not punish the boy for more than he was responsible for.

"The four are being punished?"

"Yes." Sir Radek's calm, rather quiet timbre somehow filled the space. "To our satisfaction."

That was it, then. Did she trust these men?

At length, she nodded.

Lady Hana's press on her hand let up. "My lord husband," she said as she stood and held out a hand. "Might you escort me to our chambers? I am rather tired."

Then, they would go their separate ways—Lady Hana and Sir Radek to their room, likely Lord Ambroz would see to his wife and Michal as well. And that left Anicka with the older women...widows both. Perhaps widows, all three of them. There was no way to know...

But there was reason to hope. Though her ability to do so waned.

Lord Ambroz lifted a hand toward Lady Eva.

She rose and stepped toward him.

Footfalls clomped on the stones just beyond the Great Hall.

Mayhap it was something of import for Lord Ambroz. They would likely be dismissed...yet again.

Anicka stood and leaned over the dowager baroness. Perhaps the woman would be interested in a turn about the gardens.

But as the guard stopped just short of Lord Ambroz, she froze. There was something odd about the tightness of the man's expression. And she knew...she just knew...it was word from the others.

Lord Ambroz stepped back and conversed with the man.

Then he turned, his gaze landing on Anicka. "They have returned. Lady Karin and those that survived...they are even now being ushered into the outer bailey."

Anicka let out a cry and then set a hand in front of her lips.

Baroness Ambrozova was at her side then, offering comfort and supporting her as she wavered. "You must go! Greet your husband!"

Anicka looked at her through watered eyes. Dare she believe Lukas was among them? Or did she fear the fall from such heights when she would be told he was among those not returning?

Still, she nodded and allowed the baroness to lead her out the doors and to the inner bailey where they were made to wait for the incoming men.

The castle folk made their way outside as well. Their lord and lady were returning. Why should they not be out here to greet them and to celebrate?

Although Lord Ambroz had stated that Lady Karin and the survivors had come. Was that because he had not been informed about the rescue effort's success? Did he not know if the baron survived?

It wasn't long before a ripple of joy and exclamations of welcome came through those around her. And she saw…Lady Karin came, her hair whipping about her in the wind as she brought her steed to a halt. Then, she made merry at seeing her people. Just behind her, staggering a bit as he dismounted and then assisted by his wife, was a man Anicka believed to be Baron Krejik. Certainly, it must be by the reaction of the servants about her.

So, they had indeed completed their mission. Baron Krejick was returned whole.

There should be joy in that for her…that if Lukas gave his life, it was well spent on his purpose.

Yet, that only brought a deep ache to her chest.

Sir Stepan and a young woman who could only be Lady Eva's lost sister, Patricie, appeared next.

By then, the crowd had shifted, and it became more difficult to see over heads as more riders came.

Leaving Baroness Ambrozova in her wake, Anicka stepped forward into the mix of people cheering and moving toward their lord and lady. She had to see. She had to know.

Tears blurred her vision as the pain in her chest spread and throbbed. Had the baron been found only to leave her lost? What, indeed, had been the cost of his return?

A hand found hers in the mass of bodies.

She turned to find the weary and worn face of her husband.

"Lukas," she cried as she flung herself onto his chest.

He wrapped an arm around her, holding her to himself. "I have missed you, wife."

She leaned back, setting her hands to his shoulders. Then she realized his left shoulder was bandaged. Furrowing her brow, she looked at it. "Are you hurt?"

He lifted a hand to capture the side of her face, his thumb

rubbing at the tears that had escaped. "No. Nothing that will not heal."

She watched the movement of emotion across his eyes. Was it possible that he might see her the way she always wanted him to? Did he even now? For the light that shone from within the depths of his gaze told of his own relief and joy at holding her.

Tugging her face gently forward, he met her lips with his own. The kiss was achingly tender...more so than she wanted. She pressed into him, moving her mouth to try and express what she could not say—she loved him, she needed him, she wanted him.

When he released her, he almost appeared dazed. "My lady," he said, his voice husky and almost breathless. "I want to be your husband in truth."

She gasped. What did he mean? They had already consummated their union. Was that what he referred to? Did he want to be her husband in heart as well?

"I love you so very deeply. So very completely. Tell me you feel the same." His eyes pled in that moment.

Her mouth was suddenly dry. Could it be?

"I have always loved you." He set his forehead against hers. "Always."

How could a person hold such happiness inside themselves? For she may well burst from the radiance of her joy.

"Aye, husband," she muttered.

"I don't just want to be your husband...I want to be your companion and your friend. Beautiful, amazingly creative, and kind Anicka, will you let me love you?"

Could it be he saw her...all of her...in the way she had always needed someone to? Could she be so blessed?

"Only if I can love you back, dearest Lukas." She met his gaze and lost herself in him. "For all my years."

His answer was given in the gentlest kiss that had ever existed. And in the way he embraced her, body and heart. At last, she was known in this world...and loved.

Lukas resisted the urge to rub his injured shoulder. The healer had told him again that he must leave it be no matter how it ached or even itched. And she was right—for he currently fought against both. Yet his ability to stay his free hand was, he thought, admirable.

It had only been a week since the injury...he must give it time.

And the couple of days since their return to Krejik lands had been...blissful. He thanked God that he and Anicka were of one accord. And had embarked on a journey to a real marriage after so much separation.

Lukas pushed those thoughts to the side as he stepped into the Great Hall, searching for Stepan.

No such luck there.

He continued to look as he wandered about the donjon and inner bailey...to no avail. Stepan seemed to have disappeared.

As he turned back toward the main doorway, the clunk of sword on wood drew Lukas toward the training yard. Coming over the hill, he spotted Stepan warring against the wooden pell.

He worked different strikes and cuts...perhaps even building up the strength of his swings.

Lukas watched him for several moments, admiring the passion at which Stepan went about even this. He was a man who dedicated himself to everything he did with grit and determination. Even friendship.

Memories of the time before Lukas's arrest pelted him, times when he and the others had known great camaraderie. Would it ever be that way again?

For sooth, Stepan had held great anger for Lukas since the attack on Karin's life. But then, he had saved Lukas's life when it was forfeit. Therein lay hope.

"How long do you intend to stare at my back?" Stepan's voice rang across the yard.

As his back was to Lukas, at first, he believed that Stepan spoke to the men in the fenced-off lists sparring with one another.

But Stepan turned and faced him, a quirk to an eyebrow.

Lukas shook off his trepidation at the ire in Stepan's eyes. "I would speak with you."

Stepan's features contorted. Did he expect something amiss? Or did he just not wish to converse with the man he'd caught in the act of committing a crime? At length, Stepan nodded and, setting his sword back in its scabbard, moved in the direction where Lukas stood.

There was nothing to be done but keep from scratching the blasted stitches as Stepan neared. It was difficult to discern if Stepan carried anger toward him still...or if shared hardship and victory had won him over. That mattered. And it would make all the difference in what Lukas would propose here today.

"What do you have need of?" Stepan's words were curt. No hint of kindness about them. Perhaps that was only because he had been hard at work. Beads of sweat clung to his face and clothes.

"I..." Lukas swallowed. Dare he reveal just how precarious his position was? "I would like to strike a truce."

Stepan glared at him, breaking eye contact only briefly to swipe at his face with a sleeve. "A truce?"

Lukas wanted more of an alliance, but he must approach this delicate subject carefully. "I know you and I haven't been on the best of terms since Hradek Kralove."

Stepan looked to the ground and then shook his head. "That seems but a lifetime ago."

Lukas nodded. "Aye. But it bears understanding."

Stepan peered up at him. "Aye."

"And there is much I must atone for. I might very well spend my life trying to—"

"Or you could let your sacrifice speak for itself." Stepan's statement was delivered plainly.

Lukas swallowed. "Perhaps."

"You didn't just come here to seek my forgiveness. Or did you?"

Lukas watched emotions play across Stepan's features. "No."

Stepan looked out toward the knights-in-training sparring with one another. "Then what do you need of me? I tire of games. Be straight with me."

He was right. There was little place in their current situation to attempt that. "I am to be lord of Zamek Kopec on my father's lands. Until such time as he hands over all the lands to me."

Stepan crossed his arms and stared at him, waiting.

"I...was not received well at the stronghold. In fact, the knight serving as captain there in my stead sent men to attack me and my escort."

Stepan's eyes barely widened. At least that showed he listened.

"I trust your loyalty. And I know you are capable."

Nothing. Stepan wasn't going to make this easier.

"There is a place for you as the new captain of my guard at Zamek Kopec."

Stepan looked at the ground again, shifting his weight to his left leg. Did he consider his options? Lukas knew there were not many. For his father's disowning of him had left him penniless.

"Unless...Pavel has already asked for your fealty." How was this just now occurring to him?

"He has." Stepan's tone was hard. "But I did not accept."

That surprised. Why would Stepan not take hold of such an opportunity?

"There is much history between Pavel and me...both good and difficult. I don't feel ready to bear his trust."

Lukas gave a nod. Perhaps this was a mistake.

"However," Stepan was quick to add. "You and I are so much the same. We think alike. And we understand what it is to need redemption."

Where could he be going with this?

"And so, I feel we are better suited to have each other's backs."

Stepan finished with a look that offered the kind of friendship Lukas thought impossible.

Lukas put out his good arm.

Stepan gripped his forearm and nodded. "You will have my sword."

CHAPTER 50

PATRICIE & STEPAN

Patricie embraced her sister once more. They had not tired of being in each other's company since her return. It was wonderful to be with Eva again.

But there was something of import her sister wanted to speak with her about. Patricie had some idea about it...but was uncertain how to react.

For Baroness Ambrozova had come without her husband. It wasn't long before those returning became aware of Baron Ambroz's passing. That had to mean there was a place for Zdenek and Eva. Mayhap Eva intended to tell her of it.

Eva settled in a chair by the hearth, tugging Patricie down into another, nearby chair. "I cannot contain my happiness. You are well and the plague seems to have left the village. All...has returned to what it was."

Patricie nodded and smiled, squeezing Eva's hands. It had been good to come back to find the people in the village—though mourning the loss of those who had succumbed to the plague— healthy for the most part. While they may not yet fully embrace Michal's presence, they no longer grumbled about it.

Eva's features became more serious. "I will not mince words with you, dearest."

Patricie braced herself for what might be coming. "As I well hope you would not."

"Zdenek will take his place as Baron Ambroz as soon as we are able."

Patricie nodded. It did not surprise, but it brought an ache in her chest and a weight in her midsection.

"I do hope you will come with us." Eva's eyes were bright and earnest. "You will always have a place with me."

Patricie allowed a small smile. Her sister was gracious, but did she wish to live on the charity of her family? Would there be a real place for her—one that found her useful—in their domain?

"It will be like times past, don't you think?" Eva grinned. "We will spend our days caring for the people. Did you ever think we would have such lives?"

Patricie thought about father. He had sent a letter this week full of gratitude for Patricie's work and safe return. As well, he expressed his pride in Michal and Eva's place by Zdenek's side. Then he had bemoaned that his place in Tabor was too much needed for him to be there in person. She was glad that he found himself useful there. She had that same longing in her sprit—to be necessary.

Eva continued her going on about how wonderful their lives would be.

Patricie hated to interject, but she must. "I can't go with you."

Eva's eyes widened. "What do you mean?"

Patricie dropped her gaze to their clasped hands. "I just can't."

"You mean right now. You wish to work out the details with Stepan—if he should wish to make permanent your joining?" There was a spike of bitterness in her sister's tone.

It was true that Stepan had delayed their wedding. As well, there was little indication that he might move forward now. Then again, he was as she...without a place to settle.

"I mean to say that I will not be satisfied in such a situation... living off the good will of my family."

"But..." Eva searched for words. "But you are my sister."

"Exactly. The barony already has a capable healer. I would just be in the way."

"No," Eva protested, pulling at her sister's hands. But her pleas fell silent soon enough. For she knew it was true.

"You have a place there...with Zdenek."

Eva's eyes welled with moisture. "If you don't come with us, where will your place be?"

Patricie hated the truth, but she had to admit it. "I don't know."

Eva dragged in a breath. "There is...something..."

Patricie quirked an eyebrow. Her sister's reluctance to continue was palpable.

"I didn't think it much, as I was certain you would wish to be by my side." The sorrow in that statement deepened Patricie's ache. This was impossibly difficult.

"It is not that I don't want to be with you, dearest. It is simply that I need to be needed. To have a place beyond obligation. Can you understand that?"

Eva dropped her regard but nodded.

Patrice dipped her face, hoping to catch Eva's eyes. "Then all is well?"

Eva looked at her then, a strange expression on her face. "Of course! Always." She leaned forward and embraced Patricie.

As they pulled apart, Eva rubbed at her eyes.

Patricie admired how hard she worked to keep them dry...likely for her sake.

"Lady Anicka...she spoke of the tales she heard of your skill as a healer."

"Oh?" Patricie had had little interaction with the woman. But she liked her already.

Eva bobbed her head. "You are a legend in these lands."

Patricie's cheeks heated. She had felt such a failure these last months. This couldn't be possible.

"She has a desire to train up young women at Zamek Kopec. So that it might improve their prospects. And enhance the surrounding areas."

Where was this going? But Patricie could guess well enough.

"She expressed interest in you joining her effort. I did not mention it before because I thought it was moot as you would want to be with me."

There was no heaviness to the words, but their truth stabbed at Patricie.

"Might you...find that appealing?"

Patricie would have to think on that...should such an offer be forthcoming. But it intrigued.

Still, what would become of her and Stepan? Would he change his mind again? Would there be a place for him there? Should she chance her future on so many uncertainties?

She looked to Eva and shrugged. "I am not certain what my tomorrows hold. Though I thank you for this news. I will have to consider it and wait for such an offer to be forthcoming—if it will be."

Eva pressed Patricie's hands again. "I know that God has great things in store for you. I can feel it. If it is at Zamek Kopec, or Tabor, or Prague...you always find the place you are supposed to be. I will trust in that."

"Thank you. And I appreciate your understanding."

Eva did not wipe the tear that escaped then. "You're my sister... well, that may not be something we could choose. But the bond we share in our hearts...that we get to decide."

Patricie rose as she leaned in to wrap her arms about her sister... and dearest friend. She would have to soak up every moment with her. For she would greatly miss them...and Eva.

Stepan couldn't keep his palms from sweating. It didn't help that Patricie insisted on gripping at his forearm so as he escorted her toward the gardens. So much weighed on this conversation and, from what he could sense, she knew it too. Her breaths were shallow, and he feared she might not be taking enough.

Though when he looked at her, she seemed fine. The pink hue that graced her cheeks was very becoming. How strange, that he had once thought Karin so beautiful. As a fact, she was lovely to look at, but Patricie had his heart. Most assuredly.

"I am worried..." Her words came as if from thin air.

Worried? What had entangled her concern? Him? "What about?"

"There has been such unrest...and internal betrayal, both in this castle and in the reports of the war. Will it ever end?"

Her eyes pled for him to assure her in a way he feared he could not. For there was no easy answer. So, he changed the subject. "Let us not talk of such unsettling things."

She shifted her focus back to the corridor ahead. Had his words been harsh? He'd certainly not meant them to be. How was he to bring the conversation around?

He angled them toward the castle exit into the courtyard.

She paused. "I do not have a mantle. Perhaps we might stay inside?"

The urge to swear under his breath took him by surprise. How had he not thought ahead enough to ask her to grab a mantle? For this had been his plan—to take her into the beautiful gardens.

"It is not so cool today. Perhaps we can manage?" He arched his eyebrows, hoping against hope that she would concede, a part of him feeling quite selfish in it.

But she relented with a nod.

He pushed the oak door open and led her outside. The courtyard was filled with lush plants. Even for this late in summer, with the seasons changing, there was much in bloom.

To his chagrin, he noted that a rather cold breeze whipped about them. He was too eager to be chilled, but she fairly shivered beside him.

"M-mayhap we s-should go b-back ins-side?" she suggested.

No. This was the place. It had to be here and had to be now.

But as he looked at her, he doubted he should push the issue.

So, he nodded and led her back within and to the Great Hall's hearth. "Please, warm yourself."

This was far from the private setting he'd imagined. Anyone could come upon them. And likely would. Even then, servants filtered in and out of the room, preparing for the evening meal.

After she settled in a seat, Patricie patted the area next to her on the bench. "Will you sit with me?"

He smiled but then looked at the flames licking at the air. What was he supposed to say? His thoughts were all a bluster.

"Did you...want to speak with me about something?" Her voice sounded small, hesitant.

He glanced at her. "Yes. I did."

She caught his gaze. And then smiled. "Well?"

Oh yes, he had something to say. He looked about the room and, satisfied that no one would overhear the words he meant just for her, he leaned closer.

"Patricie, I know that you were...disappointed and perhaps confused when I did not move forward with the wedding a month past."

She tore her gaze from his and worried the fabric of her skirt. "Yes." The word was barely audible.

A pang of guilt slammed through him. But he would not let it throw him off. He had a plan here, after all.

"I...am sorry. Even more so that you may have thought it had to do with Lady Karin."

Her lips thinned at his mention of her. "Didn't it?"

"No...well, I mean yes." This wasn't going at all how he'd hoped. He was quick to add, "But not in the way you think."

She was no less flustered by that.

He inhaled deeply and pressed out the air. "I...felt responsible to Karin. And to Pavel. They had need of me."

"I needed you." Her voice was small again.

It tore at his heart. "I know. But it was something I had to do." He paced for a moment. "Pavel spared my life more than once. And Karin...I wrongly accused her and, in my anger, nearly ended her life."

Patricie's eyes welled to hear him speak of it. They had discussed this before, but never so plainly. "But you didn't."

"No. Though I would have. At the time, I thought I was justified in my actions."

She looked at the fire, the dancing of flame and spark lit her brown eyes to amber. "I understand."

He wanted to naysay her, but he was getting way off the path to his intended goal. He had to rein it back in. "When I returned to... assist Karin in her rescue efforts, I did feel responsible. For my actions. For Pavel's safety. For all of it."

She remained quiet but for a sniffle. Were her tears soon to follow? This was going all wrong.

"But you must know," he said as he sat beside her, hoping she might turn toward him.

She did not.

"I found not only a chance at redemption, but a validation of the truth."

Then she turned. "What is that?" She inhaled sharply.

He set his hands to hers in her lap. "I don't love Karin. Mayhap I never truly did."

"What?" Her brow furrowed.

"I have never before felt what I do for you." His words were difficult, but necessary. "I *love* you, Patricie. You have my heart in full."

"I..." Whatever she thought or intended to say trailed off in the workings of shaking lips. Which he wished to claim.

Yet he could not.

Not yet. Not until she understood. Not until he said his piece.

"If you will have me, my love," he said as he tugged her hands upward, "I would have the banns cried tomorrow that we may be wed as soon as possible."

Her mouth parted.

"If you were agreeable, I would be willing to move forward without doing so. We are not under the Pope's thumb any longer. What does it matter?"

She set a hand to the side of his face. "I don't care."

"About the banns or about me?"

She stifled a smile. "The banns." There was a moment of her collecting herself before she continued. "All that matters is that we are together."

He exhaled and rested in her words. She loved him. She wanted him.

"But I worry about where we will live. You may have a plan in place."

"I do." He grew agitated by the possibilities of where this might be going.

She set her other hand to his face, now framing his features with her fingers. "I want you to know that I love you so very much. But I cannot live in a situation where I don't have a purpose. I would die inside a little more each day."

He frowned.

"And, I don't know how I would feel about being here on Krejik lands with Lady Karin. I believe what you say about no longer loving her, but I fear the ghost of that past connection may haunt us."

Did she think he intended to stay here? He had to put her to rights. "Patricie—"

She pressed a finger to his mouth. "Let me speak before I lose my nerve."

He quieted but wished she had not asked it of him.

"I want to marry you, very much. But I cannot ask you to live without being needed either. To be beholden to me or..." She trailed off, tears now making tracks on her face.

"Patricie…"

She shook her head. "I have accepted a place with Lady Anicka. She wishes for me to assist her in training village youths about herbs and healing."

The words hung between them for a moment.

Was it possible that God had been working all things together while he had been making his own plans?

"I just…I don't know how we will live together. And I don't know how I can live apart from you." She dropped her hands to her lap before pressing them to her face.

"Patricie, listen to me." He grabbed her wrists and moved her hands so that he might see her features. "There is no need for this."

Her eyebrows drew together.

He met her gaze. "I am to be captain of the guard at Zamek Kopec."

"What?" Her eyes lit again, burning from a joy within. It brightened her features more than if she had peered too close to a lantern. "When?"

"As soon as I am wed…that is, as long as you will have me."

A whimper emitted from her, lilting up, as she threw her arms around his neck.

He buried his face in her long dark hair. "Say you will, Patricie."

She didn't pull back but drew even closer than he would not have thought possible. "With all my heart!"

He kissed her hair, her neck her jaw, her chin, and, finally, her lips.

Their promise was then sealed between them in a manner that mattered more to them than any ceremony. They were one in purpose, letting their futures intertwine and lead them into the unknown. Which, he did not fear…if she were to be with him. With her as his wife and God as his guide, there would be nothing but light from then on.

CHAPTER 51
KARIN & PAVEL

Pavel stood overlooking the village below. Zdenek and Radek had told him of their talk with the town leaders. Soon, he would be strong enough to visit them himself and clarify what was expected of him and of them. They were his people, but their actions were his responsibility.

He moved along the wall's battlements, nodding to one of the sentries posted there. It did not escape him that the man noted his limp. Would he always carry it? Would it speak of weakness to others?

For him, it told of the trial he had been through...and overcome. It was evidence of God's grace in the midst of it all.

Going down the stairs and into the donjon was more difficult. He had found that he must keep the leg straight when he put weight on it. The healer was unable to determine if that would always be so. Or if he would regain a surer step and less noticeable stiffness about the limb.

Pavel swallowed his pride yet again. This was mercy at work. He was back where he belonged. With his family. There was no need for regret in how God saw fit to make that happen.

Passing the room where Jaromir slept, he peeked past the opened doorway. His strong son toddled about and made a noise that sounded a bit like a roar.

"Oh, a lion are we?" His nursemaid moved about the room, keeping watch, but preparing this and that about the space.

Not wanting to alarm her, Pavel knocked on the door.

She jerked around. "My lord baron! I didn't see you there."

He chuckled and nodded. "As it would seem."

Jaromir's features lit up as his gaze met that of his father.

"And what are you about today, young man?" Pavel motioned for his son to come toward him.

The boy obeyed, moving closer to Pavel's legs.

How he wished to lower himself to his son's eye level. The best he could do was pick up the child that he would be able to meet his father's gaze. That's just what Pavel did, gathering his son to himself.

What would he have done if Jaromir had been lost to him? How could he even imagine his son's life without him too? Indeed, though Karin was quite strong and rather capable, he wanted his son to have the benefit of two parents who loved him and would raise him to be a man.

At the risk of appearing weak, he brought Jaromir to his chest and embraced the small boy.

"Tata?" the boy's innocent voice reached to him.

He pulled back. "Yes?"

Jaromir put his hands on Pavel's face, playing with the skin there. Eventually, his fingers found the scar across his cheek. "Tata ouch?"

He took Jaromir's hand and kissed it. "No. Not anymore." Then Pavel looked in the direction of the nursemaid who made every appearance of not listening in. "I will bring him back soon."

She nodded and made a slight curtsey.

Pavel moved down the corridor to the room he shared with Karin. The days since their return had been strained. There was something between them. And Pavel didn't want to face what it was.

He came to their chamber and sucked in a deep breath. Then turned to Jaromir. "Shall we look in on Mama?"

Jaromir nodded and laid his head on Pavel's shoulder. Perhaps he had collected the child as his naptime neared.

As he swung the door open, he noted Karin sat on the bed, opposite the doorway, her back to him.

The door's creaking must have alerted her to his presence. For she jerked around, tucking something in the folds of her skirt.

His jaw hardened as he noted a coloring of her cheeks. Was she hiding something from him? But was this the right time?

"W-what are you doing here?" She fussed with her skirt. "I mean, I thought you were meeting with Sir Marek."

"I was." He found her receiving of him curious. More so than he ought. It left an ache in his chest. "I am no longer."

A silence fell between them that was neither comfortable nor normal.

"Besides," he said, keeping his voice even. "Jaromir wanted to say hello to his mama." He indicated the boy that was growing heavier by the second. Had he released himself to sleep? Only a moment ago, he had been eager to see his mother.

Karin looked away and wiped at her face.

Yes, there was something here that needed to be addressed. And soon.

Did he have the courage to do it? Dare he not? Could he live without knowing the truth of what may have passed in his absence? Of feelings she may still carry?

"I do think he has fallen asleep." He maneuvered to try to cradle the boy better.

Karin placed a hand on their mattress. "Mayhap he would be well to nap here? Or you could take him back to his room."

Pavel was not about to leave Karin or this moment without some clarity. He stepped forward and settled Jaromir in the middle of the bed.

His back pained him as he leaned over to adjust the boy. When he returned to an upright position, the pain eased somewhat. He supposed he couldn't expect his body to heal as well or as quickly as it once did.

He looked up at Karin as she watched their son at sleep.

"He is perfect."

Was it Pavel's imagination, or did her voice waver?

This was enough. He could bear it no longer. "What is that?"

"What?" Her eyes lifted to meet his gaze. She'd become easier to read over their years together, but now...his concern clouded his ability to do so now.

"What you have in your skirts." His tone was gruffer than he'd intended.

She looked to her lap and, after a few breaths, extracted a familiar pouch. It took only a moment to remember what it was.

"That is the pouch Tomas gave you." It was not a question.

"Yes." Her voice caught. It was unmistakable.

He cleared his throat as he shifted his weight even more from his healing leg. "Have you...opened it?"

Her answer was quick and firm. "No."

He swallowed, unable to control the raging rise of emotion within him. Attempting to keep his words simple and unassuming, he said, "Do you think you will?"

She held it closer to her. "I don't know."

But when she looked at him, her eyes were misting.

He had a choice here—he could rail against her in a justifiable moment of jealousy, or he could trust in what they had built...trust in *her*.

Pavel stepped around to her side of the bed. Then he settled carefully—albeit painfully—beside her, he set a hand to her upper arm. "Do you want to?"

She met his gaze again, her eyes watering even more.

There was more there than he knew about. More behind her sorrow than the loss of a friend. And it jabbed a knife in his heart.

Karin sniffled and, looking back to the pouch, nodded. "I do."

He let his hand fall to her forearm. "Then do." It was the hardest thing he could have said. He wanted to grab the pouch and toss it out the window. But that wasn't what she needed of him.

Regardless of his druthers, she needed him to be strong for her. And he would...even if it killed him inside.

She didn't ask him to leave as he feared, or even turn away from him, as she undid the ties that held the pouch shut. Then she poured out the contents.

It was a single ribbon of a faded blue.

Silence became thick in the room.

She broke it. "He kept it? All this time?"

His throat bobbed with barely contained emotion. "What is it?"

"I gave Tomas this ribbon...years ago. It was to signify our..." She paused and looked at Pavel.

He rubbed a thumb along her arm, tightened his restraint on his hurt, for this was not the time. He needed to know more of her heart in this. "Signify what?"

She seemed to weigh something in her mind. Pavel could practically see her mind churning.

"Our betrothal."

He sealed his lips against words that might well force their way out.

"He...we...were intended."

Pavel nodded. This much he knew already.

"A few days before he was—well, when I thought he was killed —I gifted him this ribbon as a token of my affection." She turned back to the strip of satin and fingered its contours. "Why did he keep it?"

The thickness in Pavel's chest nearly choked his words...and intentions to stay calm. "Because he cared for you. He...loved you."

She nodded.

"Did you love him?" It was perhaps the bravest, most vulnerable thing he had ever asked of anyone.

She glanced at him, a tear falling down her cheek.

He fought the urge to wipe it away. But it had become difficult to breathe.

"I thought I did...once."

Those words ushered in a hope he had nearly forgotten.

"But I was young. And I didn't know." She didn't stop as more tears came.

"Didn't know what?" His words were hoarse. Unavoidably so.

"What love truly was...what it truly is."

He didn't think he could take in air. The space between them seemed as if time stilled. "No?"

She shook her head as a smile played at her lips. "No. Not until I met you."

Somehow his arms came around her and she pressed against him, muttering against his shoulder.

But his pulse thundered in his ears so loud he could only barely make out that she even spoke. This vibrant, brave, warrior of a woman had just shattered all his fear and doubt. And replaced it with a wholeness he didn't know he could feel.

He held her firmly to himself, pressing kisses to her hair. And he knew—no matter what may happen to him in this life, no matter what may come of the wars tearing their lands apart, *this*...this moment, this woman, their family...was the future of Bohemia.

For him, his place in the world was by her side...and that was secure. He was, at long last...home.

The way of the day had been celebration. Karin smiled as the Great Hall filled with her friends and family. For this day had seen Stepan wed his Patricie. The bride had been blushing and beautiful, while Stepan's softer side had peeked out from behind his guarded exterior. All in all, it was a success.

Karin scanned the room and noticed that Zdenek and Eva huddled close, their heads nearly touching as they shared some manner of secret with each other. Michal, on Eva's lap, watched everything around him with wide eyes and a fist in his mouth. Radek and Hana danced with somewhat careful steps, content to join in the merriment. He, too, only had eyes for his wife. Hana's pregnancy had been some of the best news Karin came home to. Anicka laughed while Lukas gazed at her. They had become joined in truth over the last weeks. It had been a joy to watch.

Could it be that these men, almost brothers at one time in their friendship, though scattered in life and across the kingdom of Bohemia, had reunited with even stronger bonds? Those only forged well by hardship and sacrifice? For they had each proved their willingness to fight for each other. Defend each other. Despite where life had taken them. It was a wondrous thing.

Pavel set his hand to the back of her chair even as he leaned to the opposite side to engage Sir Marek in conversation.

Ah, her Pavel.

God had been especially kind to her in bringing her husband back in one piece. Indeed, their marriage, she believed, had only been strengthened by the trials they had faced.

Had she, too, come out stronger?

The movement of celebrants tugged at Karin's heart. What a picture of wholeness, of unity!

She lifted a prayer for such peace and unity in the Czech lands... not by conquest, but by choice. No matter what the future would bring for the Hussites. For God was with them...come what may.

"You are lovely today," Pavel whispered, his warm breath brushing her neck.

She turned toward him and smiled, though the emotions of the moment had overwhelmed her ability to fight tears.

"Are you well?" Pavel's eyebrows lowered and he frowned.

She set a hand to the side of his face. "Yes. Completely."

He didn't seem less confused, but he did appear less concerned as he pressed a kiss to her cheek.

Then he stood, goblet in hand.

Everyone stilled and fell silent.

"This is a day for joy as much as for celebration. My friend has found happiness in marriage. And I couldn't be more excited for the journey ahead of him. Our paths have diverged and converged, but in all, God has worked everything for us. And I do not doubt He will continue to do so. For our people...and for this newly joined couple.

"But this unity does not come easily. It has required commitment, compromise, work. It will continue to demand much from Sir Stepan and his bride. As well, the hard-fought victories of the battles we have faced as a people may hang in the balance. Let us be careful that we are not ruined from evil working its will within us, between us, and among us. That whatever comes, they will—as we will—stand together.

"So, I will lift my cup to a fruitful marriage in heart as well as in body."

There was a ripple of laughter.

"And that there are many years to come. For Sir Stepan and Patricie...and for the Czech lands."

Karin had risen with her own cup and stood beside her husband —in body and in mind—as he wished their friends well.

It was a glorious thing to see—the faces of Stepan, Zdenek, Radek, Lukas, and her Pavel. And the light that had returned to their friendship. God had brought these men back together through much...only with wives and children and somewhat fuller lives.

They added to their numbers...and to their love for one another.

Pavel led the others in a drink to the wellness of the newly wedded couple. Then set an arm around Karin as the music and merriment resumed.

She did not resist as he pulled her closer.

"I never knew my heart could be so full," he muttered. His voice was heavy with emotion.

Setting her hands up to frame his face, she said, "Nor I, husband. But I am excited for what lies ahead for us. God is good...and weaves a rather colorful tapestry of our lives. I know we cannot even imagine what He will do for us. And for our family."

Pavel pressed his lips to hers and once more sealed their own commitment to each other. Though the connection was brief, for propriety's sake, it was meaningful.

God had truly united them as one. And they would let no man put their joining asunder.

For as long as they both should live.

EPILOGUE

I n the years that followed, the Battle of Lipany sealed the fate of the Hussite movement. The Taborites fell and those who remained were scattered. With the last remnants of the Hussite force gone, Sigismund took the long-denied crown of Bohemia. Peace, they called it, but the cost was their brothers...and their dreams.

But Pavel was not there at the battle...he had found greater import in his time at home. With his warrior wife and Jaromir by his side, he affected change starting in his barony and spreading beyond. Sharing the truth of God and His love and goodness no matter what the outcome in life.

They brought five more children into the world, the second of which they named Tomas.

Zdenek took Eva and Michal to live in the castle well-placed on Ambroz lands...along with his mother until her death in the coming years. The castle—and Zdenek and Eva—became a refuge for the orphaned and neglected children in the region. Growing their influence to more than fifteen children.

Michal grew up to become a priest, sharing his adoptive mother's spirit and Zdenek's steadiness.

Radek and Hana took a roundabout way home to assist Lukas in regaining Zamek Kopec and relieving it of the retaliators that had sought to overtake and murder Lukas.

They remained not only neighboring lands, but close in their renewed friendship.

Hana welcomed the first of their four children in the following year.

Radek's two sons followed in his—and his father's—steps as wise, gentle rulers of their domain. His two daughters married well. No grandfather ever doted on their grandchildren as Radek did.

Stepan and Patricie found a home upon Zamek Kopec. Stepan served as the captain of Lukas's guard. As well, Patricie found her place well set in training healers near and far.

Much to his dismay, and despite his efforts, Stepan never saw his father again.

They welcomed three children in the following years.

All girls.

All held Stepan's heart.

After retaking Zamek Kopec and staking his claim as its ruler, Lukas turned his efforts to seeing his wife's mission to educate and train healers from among the village girls made reality.

Lukas and Anicka filled their domain with nine children in the following years and oversaw their lands well.

The villagers spread near and far stories that Anicka told them of her own creation. And her children regaled her as one of the most inventive storytellers that ever lived.

And, for the most part, they all lived happily ever after.

THE END

Thank you, dear reader, for reading along with me! If you enjoyed this story, I would sincerely appreciate if you would submit a review. It would mean so much to me!

AUTHOR'S NOTE

Hello, Readers! Thank you for reading along with me. Pavel and Karin's story has become so dear to me. We have finally reached the conclusion of their story on the page. But the Hussite Wars would continue on for several more years...fifteen in all.

For those not familiar with Czech history, the Hussite Wars were sparked by the martyr of Jan Hus. He opposed some of the practices of the Catholic Church in his day. I generally tell people to think of Marin Luther, but before Martin Luther. In fact, Hus's ideas and writings inspired Luther. Though, Hus himself was inspired by John Wycliff. The Hussite Wars, if I could boil them down, were religious civil wars between the Hussites (followers of Hus's teachings, opposing the Catholic Church in a sense) and the Catholic Church.

Of note, in March of 1430, Joan of Arc wrote a letter to the Hussite factions, beseeching them to renounce their heresy and rejoin the Catholic Church. As it were, the leaders of the movement at that time largely ignored the letter and underlying threat that accompanied it.

In 1999, Pope John Paul II held a three day symposium in Rome dedicated to Hus, in which he (the pope) issued an apology for Hus's "cruel death" and expressed praise for his "moral courage."

And, while this piece of Czech history remains largely unknown in the United States, it is a major event in the Czech Republic's past, and that of Europe. And it is not to be forgotten.

As for the book, all of the characters and their happenings are fictional, except the character of Ulrich of Rosenberg. He was an adversary of General Zizka's. And he went on beyond the (fictional) events of this story to continue to be a thorn in the side of the Hussite movement. As well, General Zizka did lose his remaining eye to an arrow during the Third Anti-Hussite Crusade. And died in the following months due to illness.

Many of you have probably heard of the Black Plague. It made several sweeps through Europe throughout the Middle Ages. This reflects but one, and mild at that.

The stagecoach moved along, bumping and rocking as it went. Trees and other green scenery whisked by the window. Views of mountains and open plains were visible from the seat of the coach, vistas familiar to its occupant. Katherine Matthews was coming home. She returned to Cripple Creek, no longer the scared, unsure teenager who had left to further her education so many years ago with hopes and dreams of a new life in a new place. No, she had matured into a confident young woman who had grown in stature and in beauty. Her hair was no longer the mousy color she always hated, for it had deepened into the same beautiful chestnut brown she had always admired in her mother's appearance. She'd grown out of her awkward teenage features, and was now well regarded among her peers as a rather handsome woman.

Returning to Cripple Creek brought many rather-mixed emotions to the surface. Imagine, one of her first postings would be at the same schoolhouse where she received her educational start. When her mother wrote to her of the interim need, she was glad to help out. What an odd coincidence that the letter would find her, too, in transition. Would this turn into a permanent placement? Did she want it to?

The mountain scenery became more recognizable, and she thought back on her childhood. There were so many happy times here. Unbidden, her mind wandered to the day of the great tragedy that had marred her spirit—the day Ellie Mae died.

Even all these years later, she carried the scar in her heart. The events of that day had left her broken. Why must thoughts of Ellie Mae plague her so? And all the more as her return became imminent? She shivered as the images from her nightmares the previous evening flitted across her mind. They would not stop. These same visions visited her in sleep night after night. All the more frequently these last weeks.

Closing her eyes, the hazy images took form and became memory. It was as if no time had passed. She and Ellie, walking through the schoolyard just as they did every other day . . .

Hooking arms with Ellie Mae, Katherine stepped out of the schoolhouse and into the yard. A rather large group of students gathered off to the right near the old tree. It didn't bother Katherine. She turned her attention toward the path that would lead home.

"What do you think they're up to?" Ellie Mae whispered.

Katherine glanced in that direction and noticed Betsy Callaway at the center, flapping her jaws. Why would anyone listen to anything she said? But they did. The class at large seemed to adore Betsy. It didn't make sense. Clenching her teeth, Katherine grabbed for Ellie Mae's hand. "Whatever it is, we don't want to be involved." She pulled Ellie Mae along as she walked on, trying to pass the gathering.

"I know Miss Matthews couldn't do it," Betsy said loudly.

Katherine froze in her tracks. What had she just said?

The crowd of students parted and glared at Katherine and Ellie Mae.

"Let's keep going," Ellie Mae pleaded, tugging on Katherine's hand.

She should listen to Ellie Mae and not become a part of whatever game Betsy played. But she could not let Betsy get the best of her. What would everyone think of her?

So, she turned to face her accuser. There stood Betsy with Wyatt Sullivan, the most popular boy in school, right beside her. Betsy's blonde pigtails, tied back with perfect pink ribbons, shone in the sun. Her dress was no less perfect, pink with just the right amount of lace and even a slight puff to the sleeves.

"Do what, pray tell?" Katherine shot back. Her heart beat furiously in her chest.

"Go down through the mine shaft." Betsy folded her arms in front of her chest and raised an eyebrow.

Katherine's heart skipped a beat then, but she tried not to show her fear.

Ellie Mae's grip tightened on her hand.

"I assure you, Miss Callaway, it's not that I can't do it. It's simply that I have better things to do than to be traipsing about a mine shaft." She turned to leave and hoped that would be enough to silence Betsy.

"Prove it." Betsy's voice rang out after her.

Katherine's eyes slid closed. Was there any way around this? "I have nothing to prove to you," she called back over her shoulder.

"Fraidycat!" Betsy laughed.

The other students joined in.

Katherine's face burned. A fire had been lit within her. She was not afraid of anything! Releasing Ellie Mae's hand, she then whirled around. "I am not afraid!"

"There's only one way we'll believe that." Betsy's hands moved from her chest to her hips.

There was no way this would be a one-way challenge. "Are you going?" Katherine poked her chin out, putting her own hands on her hips, attempting to puff up her chest as much as she could.

"Of course," Betsy said, though her voice caught.

"Then, let's go." Katherine grabbed after Ellie Mae's hand and headed out in the direction of the old mine shaft. She hoped Ellie Mae didn't feel how her palms had started to sweat. Perspiration covered her whole body. How was she to keep up this façade?

The group of students followed, a din of voices behind. As they neared the cavernous opening, they became quiet as they halted several feet short of the forbidden place.

Wyatt pushed through the crowd once they had stopped. "Now, girls, this is foolishness. Talking about it is one thing, but you're not actually going down there, are you?"

Katherine glanced at the mine opening. It looked dark and ominous. Not what she wanted to see. Then she eyed Betsy. She had everything—the popularity, the most handsome boy in school … But she would not have Katherine's pride, too. "I am."

"Then I am, too." Betsy stared at Katherine, matching her glare through slitted eyes.

"Kath-rine," Ellie whispered, tugging on her hand.

Katherine looked over at her friend. Ellie's eyes begged her not to go. Katherine wondered again at the danger. Her friend had every right to be concerned, she supposed. But it would not last. Betsy would go but a few steps in and give up. Katherine was sure of it. So, she would not be dissuaded.

Wyatt's eyes moved from one girl to the other. A couple of years older than the girls at their thirteen years, he stood a good head taller than Katherine. At last, he threw his hands up in the air. "Then I'm going too."

"And so am I," came Ellie Mae's quiet response.

Katherine leaned toward her friend. "Ellie, you don't have to go." Her eyes held Ellie's. What was she going to do? She couldn't take Ellie into that place. But something had eased in her when Ellie Mae volunteered to go. Was it selfish of her to want her friend to accompany her?

"Yes, I do." Her voice was firm, though her chin quivered. "I'm sticking with you."

A bump in the trail jolted Katherine from her reverie. The scenery outside became blurred. Or was it her? Touching her face, she felt moisture. She wiped at the tears. This would not do! Whatever happened when she returned, Katherine was determined she would face it with as much bravery as she could muster.

To read more, find *Hope in Cripple Creek* on my website:

https://saraturnquist.com/hope-in-cripple-creek/

Buy it HERE

The Lady Bornekova (Book 1)

The red-headed Karin is strong-willed and determined, she tries to keep her true nature a secret to avoid being deemed a traitor by those loyal to the king.

Karin and her father butt heads over her duty to her family and the Czech Crown. However, her heart soon becomes entangled though her father intends to wed her to another.

The turmoil inside Karin deepens and reflects the turmoil of her homeland, on the brink of the Hussite Wars.

The Lady & the Hussites (Book 2)

Karin and Pavel have found their way safely to his parents home, but things are not as well as they seem. There are secrets between them. A wall goes up. And then Pavel is called into battle.

Radek and Zdenek find themselves pulled into the conflict despite their best efforts to remain neutral, while Stepan finds himself ready for bloodshed.

With tensions mounting within their circle and throughout their country, what will become of Pavel and Karin? Can they find their way back to each other?

Acknowledgments

I appreciate everyone who has listened, read, talked, and shared this publishing journey with me. This book is the finale of my first published book some 10 years ago when *The Lady Bornekova* first hit the scene.

And what a wild ride these 10 years have been!

I want to thank Cindy Smith, Kelly Hollman, and Greg Turnquist who read my scenes upon completion faithfully, sit with me when the writing gets difficult, and help with the joys and challenges of plotting. This book...this series...would not be here without you three.

I also am so grateful for my group of writer friends who pray for me and with me every day for my writing and everything involved. So, Mandy Boerma, Tammy Karasek, and Jennifer Chastain...you are seen and loved.

My editor, Julie Sherwood, your eyes on my work have always brought out the best in my characters and narrative. Thank you for your understanding when I create a mess...and your grace and willingness to help make sense of it!

Cora Graphics, I am ever in awe of your talent and graphic artistry. You make my stories shine with your gift.

VerBull Photography, thanks for getting my "good side" :-)

My husband and number one fan, more than any other book, I recognize how much you put up with to make the work come to fruition. You are my partner and my friend...among other things. Thanks for helping my dreams come true more every day.

For my sister, you make me want to be better. For my dad, you make me feel so good to have achieved this dream of writing. For my mom, I will love you forever. And for my kids, you give me every reason to smile.

Last, but certainly not least, my readers, you give me a reason to keep writing.

About the Author

Sara is a coffee lovin', word slinging, Jesus following Christian Historical Romance author whose super power is converting caffeine into novels. She loves those odd little tidbits of history that are stranger than fiction. That's what inspires her. Well, that and a good love story.

But of all the love stories she knows, hers is her favorite. She lives happily with her own Prince Charming and their gaggle of minions. Three to be exact. They sure know how to distract a writer! But, alas, the stories must be written, even if it must happen in the wee hours of the morning.

Sara is an avid reader and enjoys reading and writing clean Historical Romance when she's not traveling.

Please follow along with her journey through her newsletter at: http://saraturnquist.com/list

Happy Reading!

facebook.com/AuthorSaraRTurnquist

instagram.com/sararturnquist

x.com/sararturnquist

youtube.com/@SaraRTurnquist

pinterest.com/sararturnquist

ALSO BY SARA R. TURNQUIST

CONVENIENT RISK SERIES

A Convenient Risk

An Inconvenient Christmas

A Less Convenient Path

A Convenient Escape

An Inconvenient Acquaintance

These Golden Years

A Less Convenient Arrangement

A Convenient Adventure (coming soon)

Ranch Hands Collection (ebook only)

CRIPPLE CREEK SERIES

Hope in Cripple Creek

Christmas in Cripple Creek

Faith in Cripple Creek

Love in Cripple Creek

- Prequels -

Leaving Waverly

Leaving Stoneybrook

RAILWAY ROMANCE SERIES

Laura, The Tycoon's Daughter

ACROSS THE YEARS SERIES

Among the Pages

Between the Lines